SEVENTH PSALM

JONATHAN BRUCE

Outskirts Press, Inc.
Denver, Colorado

ACKNOWLEDGEMENTS

This is a work of fiction. However, the inspiration for this story is drawn from real-life experiences and events. With only two exceptions, any resemblance between real people and the characters in this story is purely coincidental.

We want to thank Gary Alexander, Michelle Beilke, Barbara Burke, Steve Carr, Regina Cassidy, Jon Hunt, Jean Kraus, Dena McClung, Lou Michels, Nancy Morgan, John Richardson, Joe Schumacher and Debbie Stocks for their invaluable critique, insight and friendship. We also offer our profound thanks to our editor, agent and friend, the indefatigable Ora Cummings of the Cummings Literary Agency, Rehovot, Israel. She is a true gem.

Finally, to Colin and Magda: given all that's transpired, "thank you" seems so completely trivial. The world needs more people like you two. (Unfortunately, you must remain anonymous in order for you to do what you do so well.) Nevertheless, call us when (and if) you leave Corfu...Oh, yes...you were right about cooking sherry. Who would have imagined?

J.B.
Washington, DC
November 2007

For Gwen and Mary

Who Dares Wins

PROLOGUE

8 September 2003
Herefordshire, England

The day was uncommonly bright for September in the river country of Herefordshire. A mid-autumn sun glinted off the broad wings of two Royal Air Force C-130 transport planes, as they maneuvered slowly onto their final approach courses toward the British air base at RAF Lyneham. Turning gracefully over the forested, rolling hillsides of southwestern England, the pair seemed to hang motionless against the pale blue sky.

Below, the River Wye meandered slowly through serene autumn pastels before taking speed past picturesque towns and villages such as Hereford, Tintern, and Chepstow, en route to the Severn estuary and the sea beyond.

The pastoral calmness of the English countryside was a stark contrast to the dry, brown scrub of Afghanistan.

Colin Blackford was almost home.

The British Army captain looked out from one of the few portholes on the lead aircraft as it gently descended to the ground and rolled to a stop on Lyneham's tarmac. Blackford's team had just completed a harrowing six-month deployment east of Kabul. The men were exhausted and drained. Their few victories were won at a heavy cost.

As his men deplaned with their dusty and worn equipment, they tiredly climbed into the several lorries sent to greet them for the short ride along the curved two-lane blacktop to their base at Credenhill, the home of the British Army's Special Air Service.

As Blackford and his men rode quietly in the green-sided, open-air trucks, they watched their comrades, elite "special projects" teams, in final training for assignments around the world. As the lorries passed through the gates at Credenhill, Blackford saw a half dozen uniforms he'd come to recognize in Afghanistan. A squad of American Delta Force commandos trotted in silent formation past a combined platoon of German GSG-9 counter-terror operatives and Australians from the First Commando Regiment, as they readied themselves for classified deployments. Multi-national training had taken on a new urgency since the 9-11 attacks on America, and Special Air Service counter terrorism units were needed worldwide. Even at this moment, Blackford knew, SAS "red" and "blue" teams were scattered all over Afghanistan and other classified locations around the world, fully engaged in the covert war against terror.

Gone was the usual cheer and bluster that men freshly home from combat would have enjoyed. Not a word, in fact, was spoken by and between the soldiers as they rode. Their losses had been great, the deaths so unnecessary.

One of Blackford's men silently offered a cigarette to another while, in the distance, small squads of camouflaged soldiers trained, running in time up a steep incline toward a waiting helicopter.

Blackford was exhausted, unshaved and hungry. He had been in combat only three days earlier and after two days in the air, a part of him was grateful to be home. Reaching to the bandage on his forehead, he made a mental note to visit the regimental surgeon who would properly attend to the nearly two-inch cut above his left eye, a shrapnel wound sustained during the firefight that had resulted in the capture of an al Qaeda leader. But beyond his own wounds, Blackford was deeply troubled and enraged at the deaths of seven good men, "Seven of MY team members," he silently reflected. Although proud of his assignment with the Special Air Service, vaunted as the toughest and best prepared counter-terrorist special operations force in the world, Blackford was sick and disillusioned at what he perceived to be the incompetence of the men above him.

The captain sat in the truck, alone with his angry thoughts; both hands on his rifle, his eyes closed. He felt a deep personal responsibility for the deaths of "his" men. The deployment had been his third combat command and he was dismayed that he had failed his team. The losses had, in fact, wounded the entire, close-knit SAS community. Two of the dead, a pair of senior sergeants, had been very popular with the men.

Blackford's team had been assigned to secret search missions in the Afghan mountain country as part of the combined effort to capture fugitive Taliban and al Qaeda leaders. He was keenly aware of the dangers; indeed, the Twenty-Second had suffered more than its share of deaths in the campaign. But this time, the deaths were more personal, for the lost soldiers had been under Blackford's direct command in "D Squadron," and now the impetuous young officer was determined to resolve the reasons for the troopers' deaths with higher command.

The lorry soon jolted to a stop and Blackford's men began the tiring task of lifting duffel bags to the ground and returning weapons to the armory. A squad of new recruits approached the trucks and began the somber, reverent honor of carrying the aluminum caskets to the morgue. Meanwhile, the living spoke few words as they went about their duties. All were exhausted and most wanted little, other than a quiet moment with their families and friends.

But for Blackford, there would be neither the presence of his father, nor the loving arms and warm touch of a woman. His marriage to his ex-wife, the tempestuous Welsh woman, had ended the year before, after his last tour in Afghanistan. "I suppose it was my doing," he'd once admitted to a friend. "She preferred a man who was home every night to warm her bed. Not a bloke who was off in some far-flung, God-forsaken place, fighting for Queen and country." And as for his father, well, Blackford allowed that thought to pass.

Two mornings later, after the Union Jack had furled over the coffins of the dead, the twenty-eight-year-old Blackford gathered himself and walked briskly into the Headquarters of the Twenty-Second Special Air Service Regiment. He'd been summoned to a meeting with his ranking brigadier and he knew the confrontation was likely to be an unpleasant one. As he strode purposefully into the headquarters building, he glanced for more than a moment at the SAS crest and smiled in irony at its famous winged-sword motto, "Who Dares Wins."

Blackford's bearing was imposing, as he stood nearly six foot-three. His smart, tan dress uniform was offset by his green officer's cap, set squarely atop his closely-cropped black hair. Although worn thin from six months in harsh conditions, Blackford's rage would not subside.

"Damn his rank and damn the consequences!" Blackford had sworn to a fellow officer who had counseled restraint the night before. "You should retract your report and temper some of your accusations," the friend had told him.

Undeterred, Blackford waited until just after the soldiers' funerals, then pressed ahead, boldly marching into the Regimental Commander's office and requesting an audience with the Brigadier.

After a brief exchange of pleasantries and a review of the just-completed operation, the Brigadier began to speak. "Blackford, I'll come straight to it. I've read your after-action report; twice, in fact. You seem determined to bull ahead with these complaints of 'bureaucratic incompetence and command irresponsibility.' I take that rather personally, Captain." The general sternly eyed his subordinate, who returned his glare without comment.

"You've claimed 'negligence' on the part of the General Staff and you've openly criticized the failure of military intelligence for exposing your men to an ambush. Is that about it?"

Blackford responded sharply, "Yes, sir!"

Blackford's commander, Brigadier General Arthur Chelmsford-Gray, drew a long breath and slowly surveyed his junior officer without saying a word. Chelmsford-Gray, himself a combat veteran, had been quietly sympathetic to Blackford's complaints. He recognized that fatigue, as much as anything else, had spurred the young officer's intemperate accusations. Changing the tone of the meeting, the Brigadier tried to remind the junior officer that, ultimately, any officer's job was to obey orders without question. But Blackford would not be mollified.

"We're not fighting terrorism, sir...we're Hessians in their damned drug war." The captain's green eyes flashed with anger. "The Taliban is a bloody drug cartel. The other tribes are in the same filthy business. And there are soldiers involved, too. Sir, I have seen what these bastards are all about. Last month, two of them, in uniform, dragged a school master from his classroom and shot him in the head because the man was from a competing clan. They were simply sending a message!"

Blackford continued, "I don't give a damn what MI says, those were more than Pashtun tribesmen loyal to bin Laden. Those were regulars, sir! Well-armed, well-equipped, well-trained…and they were clearly in uniform and fighting alongside the tribal drug lords! We had one of them in hand, but Norwood ordered his release before I could interrogate him."

The Brigadier frowned hard at the accusation. "There has been no report of such forces…."

"Sir!" Blackford responded excitedly. "Exactly…we had no time to interrogate the one wog we'd taken, but I am certain he was, I don't know…light infantry, perhaps Pakistani. But I can't be certain."

"Blackford!" the Brigadier said, raising his voice, again eyeing the junior sternly. "The operation in Helmand Province is perhaps the most complex and dangerous mission we have EVER undertaken. That's the very heart of the Taliban's former empire."

"Yes!" Blackford shot back, "It is the country's

main opium producing area. We're fighting the damned warlords! Sir, they're bloody well playing us one against the other. We're doing their fighting for them! And someone's army is deep in the middle of it."

"Do you have ANY idea what you're saying, Captain?" Chelmsford-Gray answered, "The implications!" Blackford's commander paused, and attempting to change the subject, tried, again, to tactfully subdue the brash young officer's temper. "Reports indicate your personal service and leadership were exemplary, Colin...But you know that men die in our business. Things get confused in battle."

"That's crap, sir!" Blackford retorted, "The bastards in Norwood sit on their posh arses at the Joint Headquarters and fight the damn war over the computer. Sir, I know it wasn't your doing, but our commanders aren't fighting this thing from the front lines, they're sitting in London...nice and cozy!"

"That will be quite enough!" the Brigadier barked in response.

But Blackford refused to yield. "On patrol just ten days ago, we were given horrible intelligence. We had been instructed that the forces against us were al Qaeda, when, in fact, they were the same uniformed regulars sympathetic to the al Qaeda. The prat who provided the intelligence on that operation was damned careless...and it cost me seven men!"

Chelmsford-Gray bristled at the accusation and rose to assert himself over his junior. But Blackford continued his complaint, "Then, of course, we had wounded...the Americans had wounded as well...and my call for the Chinook was not only delayed, it ultimately went ignored! British Army had airlift responsibility for that sector and there was none to be had!"

"Captain...before you say another word..."

But the angry young officer cut Chelmsford-Gray off sharply. "Sir, I was told that the helicopter we called for went ferrying the same damned warlord whose men my squad were fighting! This cannot stand, sir, it simply cannot stand! I've also taken the initiative to notify my local M.P. He'll get to the bottom of this in the Commons!"

The Brigadier stood, stunned. Then, walking directly toward the younger officer, the enraged senior pointed a finger hard into Blackford's chest and shouted, "You've notified a member of Parliament? Have you, by God? That is quite enough! Damn it all!"

Chelmsford-Gray's angry stare bore in on the younger man and, after a brief silence to regain himself, he pronounced, "Blackford, you have overstepped your position! This discussion is concluded and, frankly, I think you shall want some cooling off. Effective immediately, Captain Blackford, you are relieved from your duties with "D" Squadron and you will report to me three days hence at 0730 hours for reassignment. That is all."

The Brigadier pointed to the door and, without saying a word in response, Blackford offered a smart salute, turned, and walked out into the corridor, fully aware he had pressed his attack too far.

Chelmsford-Gray stood at his window for a full fifteen minutes and watched Blackford storm across the parade grounds and back to his unit's command section. The Brigadier then sat for a moment before reaching for his telephone and placing a call to Scotland Yard.

T⊎E PRESENT

10 November
0630 hours
Beit Lid Junction, Northern Israel

Ali al Said peered out through the window of the safe house and quietly rejoiced that he had been selected for Allah's divine work. After all, paradise awaited him on this, his last day on Earth.

A pale red sun rose slowly over the awakening countryside and the cold morning wind carried dust and the odors of diesel fumes and manure from the farm fields nearby. On the highway, lorries, cars, and buses had already begun the morning jostle, as workers hurried toward offices, factories, and shops in Netanya, only a few kilometers distant. The traffic at the busy intersection might have been anywhere in the civilized world.

The slender eighteen-year-old stepped back from the window and seated himself at the bare wooden table, then sipped the strong Turkish tea that Mullah Hotari had just poured for him. He nodded silent thanks to his mentor and returned to his thoughts.

Things had moved quickly in the past three months since that morning at al Said's Islamic school in Ramala. It was then and there that the great fighter, a sheik, had asked the young Palestinian to join in the holy cause. Ali had been chosen; he was special in the eyes of Allah. He would soon be "shaheed;" a martyr.

His schoolmates had been abuzz that day with word that they would meet the Palestinian patriot, Quomuz, whose name was legendary among the young men of the village. The sheik's visit had been quick and clandestine, for there had been a rumor that the dreaded Mossad had sent assassination teams into the West Bank to search for him.

As he sipped his tea, Ali remembered the sheik's oration as though it were yesterday. The angular, middle-aged man with closely cropped black hair had stood before his adolescent disciples and had spoken of the martyred ones, the brave men who had written history in blood. Sheik Quomuz had exhorted the younger men that their blood, too, would free Palestine from the Israeli cur, and that an Islamic state of Palestine would never be established by peaceful surrender or negotiated settlements with the hated Jew.

Quomuz's small hands had swept the air with great passion, mesmerizing his young followers, as he railed with fire against the oppressors who had stolen the land, murdered the innocent, and falsely worn the cloth of the righteous. The sheik's charisma filled the room, but Ali clearly recalled the very words that had touched him most deeply: "You who believe!" the sheik had said, peering into the depths of Ali's soul. "Fear Allah as he should be feared and die not, except in a holy State of Islam! Paradise and glory await those who die in jihad!"

In the very same breath, Khalil Quomuz, the sheik, had implored the presiding Mullah Hotari to find the bravest members of the oldest class, to raise the hands of Islam's truest warriors toward Heaven and to embrace the will of Allah. In the same galvanizing instant, Ali rose to his feet and swore to die for Allah and the cause of Islam and his nation of Palestine. It was at that moment that the youth, captivated by his elder's exhortation, knew that Allah had chosen him above all others for something great; something more wondrous than he would ever know on earth.

The great fighter, Khalil, had rushed to embrace the boy. He placed his hands atop Ali's head, crying "Allahu Ahkbar, God is Great!" The leader then declared to the gathering that anyone who sacrificed himself in Allah's name was assured a place in Heaven, "where the air was sweet and the light was pure and he would be attended well for all time."

Since that fateful day when the sheik's words had stirred him, Ali had harbored no fears about his decision, nor had he any hesitation on this cold, windy morning. The tea tasted good to the boy, as it flowed softly down his throat and warmed his chest against the morning chill. He could feel his heart begin to race with each excited breath he drew.

Neither had the cold deterred an older man, Zahir Fez Abdullah, from his special mission. He had worked quietly through the night in the safe house, with the dexterity of a diamond cutter. He had meticulously laid out the battery, twenty sticks of dynamite, blasting caps, a detonator, and a small coil of insulated copper wire, all the while carefully keeping the nine-volt battery separated from the detonator's terminals. A bundle of nylon strapping, a wooden clothes pin and a roll of electrical tape completed the list of required components. Zahir, the bomb maker, then gathered the pale brown explosive cylinders into four groups of five. He took care to braid the blasting cap wires, marrying them together every three inches with a wrap of black tape.

Zahir had, over the decades of the struggle, built more than a hundred such weapons for his superiors. As he labored, he prayed. "Thanks be to Allah. I thank Him, turn to Him, and ask His forgiveness. I seek refuge in Him from my wicked soul and bad deeds. I declare that there is no God but Allah alone; Mohammed is His servant and prophet."

As he prayed beneath the glare of a single bulb,

the bomb maker cut a piece of rubber from an old bicycle tire and slipped it between the clothespin's jaws, and then held the creation up to his eyes for a close final inspection.

"Bring me the boy," Zahir told the Mullah.

Soon, Ali stood strong and proud, before the older men.

"It fits OK?" asked the bomb-maker. Ali tightened the shoulder straps and adjusted the load slightly. "Yes, sir, it feels fine. It feels right."

Mullah Hotari offered an approving glance at Zahir, noting that the explosive charges were arranged symmetrically along the boy's chest. One cyanide-dipped cluster, encrusted with brass screws, horseshoe nails, and scraps of copper pipe, was taped to the harness on Ali's chest. Zahir then suspended two explosive packets on either side of the boy's bare chest, just beneath his arms. A fourth pack was strapped across his back. All four were wired together in parallel and connected to a small detonator powered by the nine-volt battery. The bare terminal ends of the copper lead wires were each wrapped through the center of a steel split washer. Zahir designed the device so that the two washers were screwed onto the opposing jaws of a spring-loaded clothespin and ensured that when the two washers touched, the electrical circuit would be closed, and the detonator would fire the charge.

To prevent premature detonation, Zahir now double checked that the piece of rubber tire was firmly lodged between the opposing jaws of the clothespin, temporarily preventing a closed circuit. He then attached a short length of nylon cord, which served as a lanyard, to the rubber insulator. Zahir explained to the boy that, once he pulled the lanyard, "Allah's revenge would be immediate and unyielding."

The bodies of Islam's enemies would be many this day.

As the bomb maker busied himself with the final adjustments to Ali's deadly shroud, Hotari pressed the keys on a satellite telephone. It was time to notify the sheik Quomuz, per a previously arranged coded message, that all was proceeding according to plan.

The boy's thoughts then turned briefly to his family. His parents would, undoubtedly, be very proud of his bravery and the manner in which he had sacrificed himself for Palestine. His photograph would be displayed with honor in his family's humble home in the West Bank, as it would be in his father's leather goods shop, where the martyr's father would speak with quiet pride of his eldest son's holy sacrifice. His mother, he knew, would wail tears of anguish, but she too, the son believed, would also cry tears of joy for his selfless and heroic death. The young man's six brothers and sisters would revere his memory for all time until that golden day when he would greet them all in paradise.

Ali was only slightly saddened that he had not been permitted to say farewell to his family. Only the day before, the Mullah Hotari had summoned the youth to a quiet courtyard and had simply announced that the time had come for his special mission. The boy had not been allowed to contact anyone, not even by telephone, as three members of the Mullah's detail had driven Ali to the safe house. There, they had permitted him to make a thirty-minute videotape to be played later for family, friends, and the international media.

Reading the words written by the Mullah, Ali denounced Israel and the United States as whores of Satan. He then cursed the apostate regimes of the Middle East and their non-believing leaders. He decried the imprisonment of Palestine and the murder of its innocents.

Wearing a white silk shroud, Ali then read to the camera what his elders had written: "The young men came to prepare themselves for Jihad, commanded by the majestic Allah's order in the holy Koran." He then smiled into the camera as he explained that he was a righteous warrior in a just cause, and he reaffirmed that he had freely volunteered to perform this final mission, that he was not under duress. He proclaimed that he was proud to bear the title of "shaheed," a living martyr. Ali praised Allah and assured his family and the world that his cause was holy, and he then bowed his head as the video went blank.

The sun rose higher in the dusty sky as Ali gently tucked the lanyard into his waistband and thanked the Mullah for this opportunity to serve the people of the West Bank. Zahir then inserted the nine-volt battery into its socket with a firm snap, kissed Ali on each cheek, and stepped back.

Mullah Hotari grasped the boy's right hand firmly and whispered something in his ear. Ali smiled contently and momentarily raised his eyes heavenward as he zipped up his olive-drab jacket, took his last swallow of strong tea, and stepped out into the crowded street.

Nearby, nineteen-year-old Army private Ye-hudit Shiran zipped her uniform jacket tightly against the wind blowing in from the west. She shivered slightly as she slowly sipped her morning coffee. The young conscript looked around for any familiar members of her paratroop unit, where she had served as a rigger for the past four months. The time had all but expired from her forty-eight hour pass and she was determined to be early for her unit's rendezvous and return to base, lest she miss her bus and suffer a penalty for an unauthorized absence. An earlier punishment of five days restriction to post had made an impression on the errant teenager only two months earlier and she had vowed to earn her way back into the good graces of her sergeant. On this morning, she had arrived at the bus station long before the sun had begun to lift itself from the horizon.

As she wandered among the returning soldiers, the private spied her sergeant and a corporal near the newspaper kiosk. She made her way toward them quickly, hoping that her superiors would notice her prompt return. Checking her watch, the young soldier guessed that the bus was due in less than ten minutes.

The private then quickened her pace, striding past a group of fellow soldiers. She recognized a few faces; among them, there was the regimental medical officer, who lingered near a smaller group of senior officers. Also nearby was her supply sergeant, standing next to an older captain. The private sighed with relief as she passed by, saluting smartly, assuring herself that she needn't worry about being late to post today.

The private reflected on her life and how everything was falling into place so nicely this fine morning. Life was good. She had even remembered to telephone her parents in Ashdod the previous evening to congratulate them on their twenty-fifth wedding anniversary. She had promised to take them out for a nice dinner next time she had home leave. She told them both that she loved them dearly, and she was touched when they told her how proud they were of their only daughter's military service.

She was happy that she could serve her twenty-one months of army duty in the paratroop unit. Although she, like the other women, could not serve in combat, she felt that her assigned duties were important. She took a measure of solace that although she wasn't in the infantry like her father, she, like her older brothers, had been given an opportunity to serve Israel.

Nearby, Ali approached from the east, as he had been instructed. The Mullah Hotari's words were still fresh in his ears, "Better to have the sun to your back. Then you will be nothing more than a silhouette to our enemies. Allah will blind the Jewish dogs to your presence. Allah will shield you and He will be with you." As the words of his handlers repeated in Ali's mind, he reflected carefully on each of his orders, intending fully to succeed. Ali wanted to make his family proud of his efforts to free their homeland from the occupiers. As he had been told, he carefully disciplined himself to keep his hands out of the pockets of his jacket, lest he appear suspicious and invite scrutiny from the Israeli policemen who patrolled this sector.

He wouldn't even need to unzip his jacket to pull the lanyard. His masters had known to cut a slit in the interior wall of each outer pocket so that he could quickly reach the lanyard by simply placing his hand inside either pocket. As he walked toward his enemies, Ali gently slipped his hand into the right-side jacket pocket. He momentarily touched the end of the lanyard and assured himself that it was resting securely in the proper location. He smiled peacefully as he removed his hand and resumed his trek toward the central bus station.

Ali realized that he would never witness another sunrise over his beloved homeland. He stopped and turned and tried to feel the sun's rays playing on his face. He closed his eyes to drink in whatever warmth the morning sun would allow. A new sense of power and purpose swept over him. This was Allah's sun shining over Allah's land. Ali harbored no doubts as he prayed silently a refrain that had been given to him by the Mullah; "Oh ye who believe! Fear Allah and make your utterance straightforward, that He may make your conduct whole and sound and forgive you your sins. He that obeys Allah and His messenger has already attained great victory!" When Ali opened his eyes, he could hear a bus approaching.

Only sixty meters now separated him from the cigarette counter just inside the front entrance to the station. He walked briskly now, eyeing the many Israeli soldiers waiting patiently for their bus. At least seventy-five human targets stood, unknowing, ahead. "And so they shall lie dead," Ali thought. Fifty…forty…now thirty meters from the small, single-story bus station. For Ali there was no turning back. To do so would have meant disgrace and Allah's wrath. Palestine and Ali's family were counting on him. The die was cast and Allah's will was inexorable.

Twenty-five…twenty…now fifteen meters. At no more than ten meters distance, Ali glanced slightly to his left. There was an Israeli private, a young woman, about his age, who glanced at her watch as she walked toward the station's entrance.

At the same instant Private Yehudit Shiran's attention was drawn to the civilian youth with the old military-style field jacket. At only five meters from the entrance, their eyes met and locked for less than a second and the young woman smiled. Then Ali calmly refocused on the canteen just inside the cinder-block walls. His eyes were transfixed and glazed; his mind devoid of any thought, save one: *"God is Great!"*

Ali was completely at peace with himself, as he knew that very soon he would live in paradise with Allah.

A dozen customers stood in line at the cigarette counter. Ali reached the queue just seconds ahead of the young woman, who now stood less than a meter from the Palestinian. Taking a deep and final breath, the youth slid his right hand in the outer jacket pocket, turned, and faced directly toward Private Shiran. He screamed, "Allahu Akbar!" as he pulled the lanyard in one swift and sure snapping motion.

It was over in a terrible millisecond.

10 November
1200 hours
Beit Lid Junction

Director Chaim Aran bit his inner cheek and stared hard into the vacant eyes of the dead woman sprawled legless and tangled on the ground. Aran could only shake his head in sorrow while an ambulance attendant turned the sheet back over the private's face. Aran, head of the Arab Affairs Bureau within the Shabak,[1] took the deaths personally. "Af-

---

[1] Hebrew acronym for Sherut Bitahon Clali – General Security Service

ter all, I am individually responsible for anti-terrorist operations. I might have stopped this!" he pondered.

It had been only a few hours since the explosion. Most of the corpses and the parts of broken bodies and bits of burned flesh had already been removed from amongst the blackened ruins; all that remained of the blast. The lives of sixteen other young men and women, all members of the same elite Israeli paratroop unit, had been ended in a shock-flash of light and fire.

"A horrid shame...a vicious crime!" thought Aran, an experienced intelligence officer, his throat tightening at the irony. The fallen soldiers had been tasked to defend the state of Israel from the same violence that had taken their lives this very day. Aran knew this junction well. Terrorists had murdered here before.

Two uniformed medics lifted a shrouded body away to a nearby van. Aran slowly raised his eyes, heavy with sorrow. He saw several bearded men from the Yeshiva working in the dust and rubble with small knives and paint scrapers, tending to the tedious job of collecting the remains of the dead. Jewish law forbade the burial of anything but the entire body, as Aran knew only too well. He had witnessed the rabbis perform their sad chore many times before.

"Director..." Captain Magda Reisner interrupted. "The television people are here...they want to talk to you."

Aran hesitated, subtly trying to pass the duty of public relations to his female subordinate. Smiling, she gently protested, "Sir, I really think you ought to be the one. This is a crucial time."

Aran didn't need to be reminded of the state of things in Israel at the moment. He turned and walked toward a throng of reporters. He loathed this above all other duties of his office, speaking to the world's press. How desperately he wanted to weep for the dead and their families and for the hundreds who had died at the hands of terrorists in the past year in a score of bombings. His wrath, borne of a lifetime of fighting, had to be steeled away, behind the mask of a cool, dispassionate, professional civil servant. "God forgive me for the lies I tell," Aran thought.

The Director drew a hesitant breath and walked toward the police cordon and the waiting press corps. He winced into the barrage of camera lights, and briefly raised a reflexive arm to shield his eyes from the glare. His agency had taken a beating in the press of late, occasioned by allegations of unusual cruelty in its treatment of Palestinian prisoners.

"Director Aran," an Englishwoman's shrill voice called out, beating the others to the first question, "Regina Quinton, BBC News. Who is responsible and have you any suspects in custody?"

Aran, wanting to upbraid the questioner for her naiveté, pursed his lips and squared himself into the lens.

"We have at this moment only our suspicions as

to who may have committed this attack. Of course, the attack only happened this morning, and as you can see, we are still removing the bodies and other evidence from this place."

"Is it Hamas or the Islamic Jihad, or Fatah, or do you know for sure who may be behind this attack?" was the next question from a Japanese reporter, in stilted English, the semi-official language of international newsmakers and reporters.

"Certainly any of the groups who are opposed to the peace process with the Palestinians." The thought of appearing as an apologist for Hamas made Aran's stomach burn, but the official government policy mandated that he echo a conciliatory tone when talking about Israel's lifelong nemesis. "So we are obliged to assume that this attack is as much against the people of Palestine as it was against our Israeli dead."

Aran motioned to the gaggle of reporters and bade them enter the remnants of the concrete block building that had served as a bus terminal before the blast destroyed one wall and cratered the now-sagging roof.

"We currently believe that at least one bomber died in this attack. He knew there were more than fifty of our soldiers waiting here for a military bus. We think he ran from a car nearby and detonated the bomb near this window where many of the soldiers had been standing."

An older rabbi lowered his head and averted his eyes from the press and shuffled past the Director, clutching a small white plastic bag containing the mangled remnants of a hand.

Just then, an ITN reporter gestured for his camera operator to pan the building's interior, capturing on videotape the background footage for the evening's lead story from Netanya. Two print journalists, one from an Italian newspaper, elbowed their way past portable cassette recorders and cables; each was shouting simultaneous questions to Aran.

"And what of the Syrians...do you suspect they were involved in this attack?" the Italian reporter shouted from only a few feet away.

Aran grimaced, hardly concealing his annoyance at the volume and proximity of the question.

"In the past, we have believed there was strong evidence that any of several nations, uh, states, have financed such operations. The peace process is not well liked...and certainly the current negotiations concerning new Palestinian autonomy are regarded by some in the Muslim world."

(Aran was careful not to use the phrase 'Arab world' for fear of offending the uneasy détente with the Egyptians and the Saudis) as a compromise...."

"But what proof have you?" an American voice interrupted.

"Proof?" Aran's temper was now fully tested, "Proof of what? Proof of murder? Proof of terror? Here is your proof...."

Aran swept his hand toward the unmistakable form of a human corpse outlined in the folds of a soiled white sheet on a nearby litter. "We don't have the luxury of your American courtrooms here, sir!" Aran bore in on his questioner. "This is the same violence that killed innocent people in Tel Aviv only three months ago...Need I categorize every act of treachery that has been brought against our people, simply because we dare speak of peace with an old enemy or attempt to permanently define the boundaries of our ancestral home? I need no more proof that that!" Aran stared sternly at the now-quiet throng of reporters and added sarcastically, "And quite frankly, I cannot imagine that you really need more 'proof' either."

Magda Reisner caught an icy stare from her commander as he brusquely adjourned the interview and stormed out over the rubble of fallen brickwork. Reisner took the lead, calling for assistance from the uniformed police officers assigned to the scene, and ushered the reporters away from the corpses nearby.

An hour later, Aran and Reisner sat in the back of an unmarked armored staff car en route to a briefing with the Prime Minister and select members of the Knesset. Aran was still hot from the encounter with the insipid press, and his silence filled the cramped confines of the car. He raised his left hand to his face to feel unshaven stubble and, letting out a long sigh, turned to Reisner with a grimace. "Do you think Quomuz will be laughing as he watches on television? Does he think me a 'tembel;' a fool?"

"Laughing, sir?" Reisner asked.

"I let them get to me today. I was angry; a luxury a man in my position cannot afford; in these times, especially."

"You were thinking about Ari, no?"

Magda Reisner's question had been, as usual, a perceptive one and Aran nodded in appreciation of his subordinate's insight.

"My son. Yes. Yes, I was. I was, indeed, thinking of Ari. He's only 23, and an engineering student away at the Haifa Technion. He could so easily have been in that bus station this morning. He is a reservist in that unit and it was only because he recently completed his annual training tour that he wasn't there today." Aran paused, considering the gravity of the situation. "But other fathers lost THEIR sons and daughters today and so, I can never forget that...."

Aran's gaze turned outside the speeding car and, as he placed two rugged hands over his tired eyes, his thoughts quickly returned to the elusive and murderous Quomuz.

"Do you think Quomuz was in the country this time?" the elder asked his subordinate.

"No," Reisner answered, almost casually, reaching for some papers in a black leather portfolio. "He's usually in the shadows of these attacks... this was undoubtedly a suicide by one of his true believers. Quomuz has certainly shown a willingness to sacrifice others before, but he's seldom present. No, our latest intelligence says he's still in Syria. But my guess is he's in Iran or even Afghanistan...again. My team just missed him....twice...last year."

The car hit a small bump as Aran surveyed the quiet farmland of Israel passing by his window.

"Of course, Magda, as you well know, the government wants him taken. Quomuz must be captured, as well as the terrorist leaders in Hamas, the Jihad and every other radical group trying to stop this uneasy peace with the Palestinians. There's incredible pressure now to find these men and eliminate them quickly!" Aran looked sternly at his subordinate. "But the Americans are putting conditions on the money. 'No reprisals,' they tell us in Washington. They are insistent that we make peace with the Palestinians and that we must finalize the efforts quickly...." Aran drifted into silent thought.

"The Americans are just now beginning to understand," Magda Reisner said. "The 9-11 attacks awakened them, I dare say."

Aran grunted, shook his head, and resumed his thoughts.

"There is no end to this madness...there never will be, you know. And our American and British friends didn't help the situation in the eighties by financing the Afghan war against our other good friends, the Russians. They spent millions. Then came September 11th. It would surprise some Americans that today's attack may have been financed, at least indirectly, from money the CIA sent years ago to help the Afghans expel the Soviets. The Americans spent so much money, I'm not certain even the CIA or MI-5 in London will ever know how much weaponry found its way to the Mujahedeen or how much of those supplies are now stored in old Hussein's desert somewhere, Damascus, or the Sudan. God himself knows how many guns found their way to the Balkans and Indonesia. Even the U.S. presence in Afghanistan didn't put a dent in the flow of weapons in and out of that part of the world."

Reisner knew from personal experience the weight of things, having served four years' duty in an underground unit of the Shabak, Israel's secret service. She had scoured more than one terrorist hideout, seeking evidence of Quomuz's whereabouts.

Chaim Aran shook his head in slight anguish. "Of course, now that the Soviets are no more, they're selling off their military equipment to anyone with cash. And Saudi oil money buys lots of bombs. God help us if the Hamas buys some MiGs," Aran offered sarcastically.

"And yet despite all that has happened, the Americans are still reluctant to give more aid for our defense..." Reisner said to the older man. "It's the least they can do, since they've inadvertently armed those who are trying to kill us."

Pausing, she recounted to herself the number of enemies who could have caused this most recent devastation. "A many-headed beast, this predator of ours."

Chaim Aran did not answer, but only shook his head and once again began to chew his lower lip as the car sped southward toward Jerusalem.

SEVENTH PSALM

10 November
1600 hours
Damascus, Syria

The setting sun's last rays struggled for life from beyond the peaks of the Anti-Lebanon Mountain Range. Yet, a glimmer of late autumn sunlight flickered along the canals flowing from the Barada River and the rich green oasis on the edge of the Syrian Desert. Beirut, on the Mediterranean, lay one hundred and ten kilometers away to the west.

A diminutive Mustafa Khalil Quomuz was neatly attired in a gray suit and matching overcoat, as he sauntered past the Omayyad Mosque, the grandest building in the old section of the city. A cold evening breeze brushed his angular face and newly cropped beard. Pausing, he reflected that he had not worshipped in some time. In fact, it had been months since he had entered a mosque or fallen to his knees toward Mecca. He had, of late, been preoccupied with orchestrating events abroad ever since things had taken a new and important turn in his native Palestine.

As he walked, Quomuz reached into his suit pocket and checked the batteries on his satellite telephones. With so much at stake, on this day above all others, he wanted reliable communication with his network.

It wasn't all that many years ago, Quomuz believed, that "the dog Arafat" and the Palestinian Authority had nearly negotiated away all that Quomuz

Mö I

and his people had fought and died for over the past quarter century. And what had not been given away, Quomuz believed, was stolen by the Israeli army! How many martyrs had died before that dog sold our blood to the Jew? Quomuz swore to himself, but smiled, knowing that a certain measure of revenge had been exacted in Israel earlier today with the Beit Lid bombing. He knew his benefactors in the new Hamas government would be pleased.

Quomuz checked and re-checked his watch. There were more surprises in store for his enemy and her American ally today. If it were Allah's will, Quomuz believed, more bombs would explode and more unbelievers would die before the sun next rose over the Syrian Desert.

The Palestinian smiled quietly and looked into the city that had been his temporary home for the past two weeks. Although not officially welcome in Syria, Quomuz had, on occasion, found sympathy among those who followed the teachings of the Alawites, a Shiite Muslim sect. Quomuz had been given arms and money by the Alawites, friends not unaccustomed to a controversial role in Syria's political life for the past thirty years. Indeed, Quomuz had sought confidence and secrecy from the Alawites because of their control of the military and their connection with the Ba'ath party in Syria and in the confused and bloody remnants of Hussein's old Iraq as well.

"The enemy of my enemy is my friend," Quomuz had said many times to his Syrian allies, recounting that Syria had become involved in the civil war in neighboring Lebanon more than twenty-five years before. Israel, spurred by the presence of angry Palestinians so close to its Syrian border and an extremely unstable political situation, had then invaded Lebanon. Quomuz recalled how the Israeli invasion thus forced Israel to fight against Syrian air and ground forces, all the while keeping a nervous eye on Palestine.

There was, of course, the historical animosity between Israel and Syria, and Quomuz relished the tension.

But time was growing short, Quomuz reckoned, as he quickened his pace and strode toward his hotel to await word from America.

11 November
1230 hours
CNN Center, Atlanta

Shocking developments in the last hour stretched even CNN's fabled tele-technology. A usually composed Josh Enright struggled with his first report from the scene.

"It was just after noon, Eastern Standard Time," Enright looked unnerved as he spoke, nearly breathless, into the camera. "The first blast rocked the El Al Israel Airlines building on 45th Street in New York City. Officials are only speculating, but they tell CNN that first blast instantly killed more than a hundred pedestrians and motorists in a rain of splintered glass and shattered steel that also wounded three hundred others among the midday crowd walking between Sixth and Seventh Avenues. One FDNY Battalion Chief estimates this to have been an explosive of some type, perhaps containing tons of something like ammonium nitrate. The direction and pattern of the blast energy appears to confirm this."

The anchor had to pause to collect his thoughts, as the video feed took on a surreal quality eerily reminiscent of the infamous terror attacks of September 11th, 2001. Summoning all the composure within him, Enright continued.

"But no sooner had the first police officers, firefighters, and ambulance crews arrived on the bloody scene, than two additional truck bombs exploded in exactly-timed blasts on opposite ends of the block...one near Broadway. The opposing shock waves had a hammer-and-anvil effect on everyone and everything in their path. Rescue personnel, victims, and passersby were whipsawed by terrible pincers of glass, shrapnel, and concussion. As you can see from this unedited video, the blasts from the twin secondary explosions killed and wounded at least three hundred and fifty more, including police and rescue professionals. Let's go now to Washington."

Enright gasped as he completed the last sentence of his hastily-scripted notes, and then silently signaled the floor director to cut to a station break. He desperately needed some fresh air and a cigarette.

As Quomuz had hoped, a mile-long stretch of West 45th looked and smelled of death run rampant. It would be hours before the Mayor's Office could begin to estimate the extent of this most recent carnage. The debris field was not unlike that remaining in September 2001, only a few short years before. As he watched from his hotel suite, Mustafa Khalil Quomuz only smiled, recalling how his own home, as a boy, had been similarly destroyed. "The Americans have no stomach for a prolonged fight! What we cannot do to them militarily, we will do to them politically. For every bomb that explodes," Quomuz predicted, "America takes another step away from Israel!"

Time, therefore, was on his side.

11 November
2330 hours
Gatwick Airport
London

Split-screen videos of the Beit Lid and New York terror bombings dominated the BBC's news coverage, but Colin Blackford was too tired to watch the images on the television display, which seemed to glare in every corridor of the international terminal. Indeed, Blackford had only enough energy to sip tiredly at a cup of lukewarm airport coffee as he shuffled down the busy hallway toward the exit and the Underground for the hour-long commute home. The well-muscled and trim six-footer he'd been in Afghanistan had vanished into a depressed, stoop-shouldered remnant of himself. Pausing at a news kiosk, Blackford slowly scanned the headlines, only to find the same horrible reports from Israel and America. Each of the world's leading media featured the same oversized photographs of fallen buildings, broken glass and mangled bodies.

An extra crew of security personnel from Scotland Yard brushed past Blackford in response to the recent explosions. Gatwick or Heathrow could be next. One never knew in this day and age, he realized full well. Captain Blackford, late of the elite Special Air Service and once well trained in anti-terrorist tactics, angrily cursed himself, "And here I will perish....from boredom." Blackford, officially "on loan" to the London Metropolitan Police as a "liaison officer," yawned and, throwing his empty cup in the waste bin, stepped onto the automatic door pad and out into the cool evening air.

Thus ended an otherwise uneventful evening working the swing shift punishment from Headquarters for Blackford's youthful temper. "Sod," Blackford swore to himself as he disappeared down an escalator toward the waiting Gatwick Express train. "My damned big mouth!"

Back in the terminal, a small crowd of metropolitan policemen gathered in front of the BBC monitor and strained to hear more news over the din of the airport crowd.

"...While it isn't known who will claim responsibility for the bombings, authorities in Washington and Jerusalem are convinced the two are connected and look to one of several radical Islamic factions, perhaps even al Qaeda, as the responsible party. For more on that story, we go to the BBC's Robert Grenville in Jerusalem…."

Blackford made his way onto one of the trains bound for Victoria Station, slumped tiredly into a vacant seat and slouched against the window. Forty minutes later, he would change lines and ride for another thirty minutes to his stop at Finsbury Park, just as he had done nearly every day since he was detailed to airport duty eighteen months ago. He dreaded the ride, because every so often he'd see a young couple very much in love and it hurt him to remember how he'd failed at marriage. His own relationship had not been easy. Despite his physique and ruggedly handsome face, he'd always been uneasy around women.

As the train arrived at Oxford Circus, the car doors whooshed open and a metallic voice advised departing passengers to "mind the gap" and a new gaggle of late-night passengers elbowed their way into the compartment.

Blackford hunched his shoulders and, closing his eyes, replayed the events of the past few years. Perhaps it was the practiced, aloof manner with which he had responded to his wife's tearful pleas. Perhaps it was because he'd been raised by household staff and had never enjoyed the warmth of a mother's embrace or his stern father's approval.

Perhaps it was a combination of both that had led him to his angry rage in the brigadier's office.

"No matter," Blackford sighed, as the train rattled toward its next scheduled stop. "It's all a cock-up now. No woman, no future. I'm well and truly fucked."

12 November
0900 hours
Headquarters, Air Combat Command (ACC)
United States Air Force
Langley AFB, Virginia

The massive video screen flickered to life directly in front of Secretary of Defense Eldon Klein. Seated around the massive glass-topped oaken oval were all the ranking generals and admirals from both the Air Force and the Navy. Two staff officers, both lieutenant colonels, busied themselves distributing sealed folders marked "top secret" in red stencil to each of the senior officers.

Klein looked strangely out of place among the room full of trim, neatly uniformed flag officers and their aides. The Secretary's antiquated glasses and disheveled mop of gray hair gave him the appearance of an Ivy League philosophy professor. However, his professorial, almost timid, appearance belied a razor sharp mind and an unfailing ability to clearly spot the political and strategic value of any information placed before him.

His presence at Air Combat Command this

day was no coincidence. After the latest terror attacks, the President had dispatched Klein to the
Air Force's combat center as his personal messenger.

As a recently published *Newsweek* article had
revealed, Klein was no ordinary political appointee.
His credentials included graduating summa cum
laude from the United States Naval Academy, training as a Naval Flight Officer, and seventy-five
combat missions over North Vietnam forty years
earlier. Following two combat tours, Klein had
earned a master's degree in international relations at
Harvard. Then, after leaving active military service,
Klein attended Columbia Law School, finally joining an influential Beltway law firm with offices
around the world. Working from his firm's Washington, DC office, Klein had specialized in negotiating international commercial agreements, especially
between American business interests and governments in the Middle East.

Although he had long since departed active
military duty, Klein had remained engaged with
military affairs. He had retained his commission in
the Naval Reserve, ultimately retiring with the
grade of captain. While in the reserves, he had
commanded a Naval Intelligence Group. He was
well known among academics as a frequent con-
tributor to a host of national defense journals, and it
was one such effort that got him noticed by the
President. Klein's writings on the moral and legal
justification for the use of nuclear weapons against

international terrorists had earned him an invitation to the President's inner circle.

Klein's thesis was simple. Since international terrorists and their rogue nation supporters did not adhere to the Geneva Conventions or the laws of armed conflict, the nations affected by terrorism should be free to retaliate with all weapons in their arsenals, including nuclear devices. The ensuing firestorm of protest propelled Klein onto the international stage. The intellectual elite and the media had excoriated him publicly, but there were those in high places who quietly admired his principled stance. So, following the mid-term resignation of the previous Defense Secretary, Klein got the nod.

Just as the video screen finished warming up, General Paul Booth, the ACC Commander, surveyed the rich mahogany-paneled room and began to speak. "The CIA tells us these bombings were, most likely, the work of the Islamic Jihad." Klein rubbed his chin as the general continued. "Those digital satellite images were taken three weeks ago," the four-star advised. "Both the CIA and the Defense Intelligence Agency confirm the presence of Islamic Jihad operatives in Syria seventy-two hours prior to the explosions. As of today, our intelligence analysts have completed their survey of the camp at Abu Du'an, in northern Syria. The coordinates are 36° 25' 09" N; 38° 16' 39" E.

It is right along the Euphrates near Lake Assad. Our initial assessments were correct. The Islamic Jihad, Hamas, and some of Bin Laden's hard-core followers, together with a dozen other splinter factions, all trained here. Now these next pictures, uh, slide please, taken on the day of the attacks, show an empty camp. Let's have the next view please."

"By the way, sir," General Booth continued, "the recent pictures came from the SR-71." Eldon Klein chuckled aloud, and then retorted, "Aren't you glad I convinced the President to reactivate one Blackbird for this contingency?"

The four-star let the comment pass. There had been much infighting in the Pentagon over the dismantling of the fabled spy plane program in favor of satellites some years back. Despite its enormous operational costs, the SR-71 Blackbird could fly over any target faster than any other aircraft on earth. Plus, no enemy could ever calculate its overflight, unlike satellites, which were on predictable, known orbits, allowing an enemy to hide personnel and equipment from the space-based cameras. The Blackbird, however, flew high enough that no missile could bring it down and fast enough that no foreign aircraft could intercept it. Hence, its periodic "retirement" from service, occasioned by Congressional concerns over operating costs, was generally short-lived…especially in times of national peril. Its dismantling in the early 1990's had been the source of many hard feelings. Defense Secretary Klein and the Air Force had since been on opposite philosophical sides of the debate.

No matter; for the present urgencies rendered all past disagreements moot.

Eldon Klein nodded and confirmed what everyone else in the room already knew. "Preliminary reports indicate that these New York truck bombs were fairly complex devices. The Bureau of Alcohol, Tobacco, and Firearms has recovered fragments which resembled the 1993 World Trade Center bomb. All three of these bombs look like a mixture of ammonium nitrate fertilizer and diesel fuel packed tightly into fifty-five gallon drums. The drums were probably then arranged in a horseshoe-like formation in the back of the trucks. Electronic time delay detonators controlled the synchronized explosions."

Secretary Klein continued in his trademark monotone. "ATF and FBI technicians have also raised two of the three Vehicle Identification Numbers. It won't be long before ATF will trace the trucks to their source. Smart money says it's the Palestinians, but who really knows? Given the target, El Al, and recent warnings about the peace process, we must conclude this was the work of Hamas or someone franchised by Iran, like al Qaeda. Whoever it was, the President wants them nailed, dead or alive."

"I've got to brief the President late tomorrow after he returns from the Governors' Conference," Klein continued. "General Booth, you get me targets, routes, proposed munitions and an attack plan right away. And damn it; make sure you know where these bastards are. I'll press the National Security Agency for their latest. The President is going to hit 'em and hit 'em hard. Folks, as you know, he's not kidding about this terrorism thing." Pausing a few seconds for dramatic effect, Klein continued, "Remember the President's words, 'Dead or Alive!' The 'talking heads' on network news might roll their eyes, but the President is serious…and so am I."

Standing to indicate that the meeting was over, Klein paused momentarily and slapped the oak conference table with a strong, flat hand, "Twenty-four hours. I want a workable plan in twenty-four hours."

As the meeting adjourned, General Booth turned and spoke to Brigadier General Jack Kilrain, Commander of the 48th Fighter Wing at RAF Lakenheath, England. "Jack, it looks like you have a mission…"

16 November
0900 hours
48th Fighter Wing Headquarters
Royal Air Force Lakenheath, UK

"OK, you guys in the 492nd, let's settle down and take a seat," Jack Kilrain began, "and listen up! This is a full press op. This has been blessed by the Oval Office."

Captain Zach Pollard surveyed the preflight briefing room jammed with a hundred pilots, mission planners and intelligence personnel. Pollard gently elbowed his crewmate, Damian Mercer, one of the few black pilots in the squadron. The pair shared a quizzical glance as Kilrain spoke. "Is this it? Are we going live…?"

At fifty, Jack Kilrain stood just over six feet tall. Slightly gray at the temples, he cut an imposing figure, just as he had thirty years earlier in his Air Force Academy days. Patient eyes and a warm handshake complemented his affable personality and muscular frame. He'd mastered every important job an Air Force pilot could hold, and had fostered confidence in every officer he'd ever commanded. Three thousand hours flight time, including a hundred in combat, plus a Master's in electrical engineering from Purdue, had made him a dead-certain candidate for the general's stars that adorned his gray-green flight suit.

In the early nineties, he was one of the eager young squadron commanders who had flown the missions over Iraq and Kuwait. Now, it was his turn to send young men into battle. But Kilrain, like most who wore the uniform, was no warmonger; Pollard and the others knew that. The general had fought his war in Desert Storm; he'd flown combat and had seen more than his share of death. He'd lost a close friend to a Soviet-built surface-to-air missile over Baghdad. He'd had to write the dreaded letter to that flier's young wife, telling her that her husband wouldn't be coming home.

He'd recalled his own wife's tears just before he deployed to the Gulf. And he remembered his own sadness at missing the birth of his son and never knowing if he'd live long enough to hold the child. Accordingly, Jack Kilrain wasn't one to revel in false glory or one who easily spent young men's lives for meaningless political gain. He was, therefore, no fan of war.

"No one hates war more than a warrior," his pilots had heard him say on more than one occasion.

A murmur rumbled through the high-security briefing room as Kilrain spoke, "OK, guys; keep it down." Several of the hundred-plus pilots, weapons systems operators and mission planners wondered whether this was it - a combat mission to the desert. "The headlines," Kilrain reminded the gathering, "have been terrible. First the September 11th attacks on America. A host of terror bombings around the world and now, the latest blast in Israel. Then the ones in New York."

"Those lousy sons of bitches!" Captain Luis Sanchez interrupted spontaneously from the back of the room with his usual and unmistakable passion.

The general said nothing in response to Sanchez's intrusion. For some reason, the young Puerto Rican could always breach rank protocol with Kilrain, and yet the general never called him down. In fact, Kilrain mused to himself, the young officer was right.

Pollard's thoughts quickly turned to the hastily prepared BBC broadcasts about the al Qaeda and the other group. "What was it, the Hamas or the Jihad something?" he whispered to no one in particular. He recalled the video of the burning American flags and the angry faces shouting rage in the streets. It was the same view shared by all those others who believed Israel to be the hound of Hell and America its satanic leash-holder. "Jesus," Pollard asked himself silently, "Is EVERYONE over there fucking nuts?"

The hundred pairs of eyes had studied the large, detailed maps of Syria that flashed from computerized projectors onto the sterile screens before them. The bright blues and greens from the maps stood in stark contrast to the blackness in the room. Red and yellow computer-generated arrows and figures marked the targets and times. The state-of-the-art graphics reminded the officers of a huge video game.

As Kilrain continued his overview of the mission, "Lew" Sanchez wondered aloud what Jimmy Doolittle would have said about the attack. Brigadier General Kilrain answered his young foil's question; "He'd say 'bomb the bastards.' And that's just what we're going to do!"

The entire room erupted.

Kilrain changed the mood when he began to announce the general attack routes that each of the three flight elements would pursue, as a somber quiet enveloped the room. Only the occasional "whoosh" from the ventilation ducts and the hum of the computers masked the thumping of a hundred hearts. Kilrain turned the briefing over to his Deputy Commander for Operations in the Wing, a lieutenant colonel, named Riordan, who then called for the next set of slides.

"This is a come-as-you are mission, a joint operation with the Navy. As you know, their carriers have been positioned in the Med during the past several months." Riordan instructed, pointing to electronically generated images on the big screens ahead. "We've been tasked because frankly, we're so far away no one will think we're coming! So, rest well fellas, you have lots of flying ahead," Riordan continued. "You see here the current position of the two carrier groups on station. The Joint Chiefs have selected three sets of targets. This is their tasking, and the President wants us to hit these targets hard. All are in northern Syria -- right here along the Euphrates River and near the Turkish frontier."

Riordan then pointed to the illuminated map. "We're hitting an airbase at Jarabulus, as well as some SAM sites and, most importantly, a major terrorist training facility at Abu Du'an. Some are al Qaeda; some are old Republican Guard veterans. There are lots of Jihadists and Hezbollah. It's your basic Club Med for terrorists. They've built up all of this stuff since their cohort, Saddam Hussein, was executed. And there's big pressure from the Israeli government to strike the training compound especially. They are fed up with suicide bombers killing their citizens. The bad guys train the terrorists at places like this, and we've gotta make sure it's taken out. And, of course, the White House won't let Israel do the fighting here. So, we're in the mix."

The colonel paused an extra moment before continuing.

"Our intel believes, but cannot confirm, that most of Saddam's WMD were actually cached in this area, before being trans-shipped elsewhere, but that's another story. I know that's not the politically popular version, but it seems to be logical."

The pilots in the room exchanged glances as Riordan pointed to another briefing slide.

"The Navy," Riordan explained, "precedes our attack. They'll have EA-6Bs with E-2C Hawkeyes in control of the Navy birds. Their F-14s will provide top cover for the Navy jammers, and their F/A-18s will fire anti-radiation missiles. Our own AWACS plane will direct the overall attack, and keep us a safe distance from our Navy brethren. We don't need any friendly fire casualties."

When the next slide appeared, Riordan explained: "We will take out the military side of the Jarabulus airport, its radar installations, and the terrorist training facility. This is where the Hamas and al Qaeda people have headquarters and communications centers. Note, it's just on the Syrian side of the Turk border, but, of course, the Turks don't want any visibility in this. Next slide... Here's the breakdown. The first flight, call sign Swift, with nine aircraft, will target the terrorists. The second flight, with six aircraft, call sign Pogo, gets the airfield. And flight three, call sign Atlas, will be three aircraft--you guys head for the adjacent SAM sites."

General Jack Kilrain interrupted his subordinate. "Gentlemen, we launch with twenty-four. After the first refueling, we pare down to eighteen. Understand? Some of you who launch with us won't get to go all the way. The air tasking order says eighteen planes over the target, so we're taking extra to make sure-- but at some point, six of you are coming back. No bitching either, guys. Go ahead, Al."

As the flight crews turned their attention from the Wing Commander to the next slide, their eyes widened, and, in unison, all leaned forward straining for a view of each attack route. Illuminated on the black screen were three columns. Each column was headed by the name of one of the three targets Kilrain had revealed earlier. Under the first column, second from the top, were the names "Mercer/Pollard: Swift 22."

A murmur grew in the room as flight crews found their names and their targets. A senior pilot, each with special expertise in low-level attack, would lead the raid on each target.

"We're going to a terrorist camp in Syria. Jesus!" Pollard chattered excitedly into his pilot's ear, as did the other aircrews as each pair discovered their respective targets.

"All right, guys, hold it down," Riordan called out.

"Let's take a look at what we're going after. OK. The terrorist complex is eight kilometers west of Abu Du'an, this side of the Euphrates. It's a known terrorist training camp. It was an old French, then British outpost. More recently, it was reconstructed, maintained and staffed with al Qaeda money," Riordan explained.

"The CIA also thinks this place has been a training camp for years...that's where they think the 1985 Achille Lauro hijackers may have been trained. That is, if you young fellows remember your ancient history." The name of the Italian cruise liner, one of many terrorist targets in the past twenty years, still resonated with the senior officers, along with all the other acts of senseless brutality committed in the name of Allah.

Riordan pressed on: "The terrorist complex has complete facilities for teaching underwater demolition and tactics for seizing ships. We have intel from the Israelis that Mustafa Quomuz trains his entire core cadre there. CIA analysts believe that Quomuz's people are presently headed back to the vicinity. We think lots of radical Islamic factions train there...a hundred different splinter sub-groups. Hamas, Jihad, you know. Intel says that even some old ex-KGB advisors are there; former East Germans, Bulgarians, you know--the lot. They're all out of work since the Wall came down and they sell themselves to the highest bidder."

"This next slide reveals the latest recon photos from the Blackbirds. You might want to buy those guys a drink when you see 'em next," Riordan offered with a smile. "This building along the Euphrates, now under construction, is believed to be a maritime academy or a naval training facility. We regard it as a valid military target. Those of you assigned this target will get the latest photo recon and intel so you can plan your radar attack and initial points."

"No iron bombs, fellas; only the smart stuff for this op. Each plane will be armed with eight 500-pound laser-guided munitions. As I'm sure you can imagine, the Pentagon doesn't want to explain collateral damage to *The Times* and the rest of the news media. We're waging a tough P.R. war, so let's not botch it with civilian deaths. We don't need to take out any more baby milk factories." The group let out an instant wave of laughter at the colonel's reference to Saddam Hussein's lame attempts to turn American public opinion during the Desert Storm air war of 1991.

"What about airborne threats, Colonel, you know, their single-seat stuff?" A young officer asked from the middle of the room. "I mean, the Syrians aren't noted for having a great Air Force, right?"

"Not really, Lieutenant," the colonel replied. "But we're entering sovereign Syrian airspace without their permission. If they sense this is a big raid, they'll send up everything they've got. No matter how bad they are, they'll fight extra hard. So don't get cocky! Now, let's take a look at their surface-to-air stuff. Their equipment is mostly old Soviet made, of course, with some modern Chinese stuff thrown in. Intelligence says the airport and the terrorist camp are ringed by radar guided SA-17 mobile SAM launchers; NATO code name 'Grizzly.'

These are the old reliable BUK-M1-2 tracked vehicles. But they have been fitted with the new 9M317 missile; four missiles per mobile launcher. Each is guided by phased array radar--so keep your finger on the chaff button!"

The group let go a nervous laugh. Chaff was nothing more than bundles of aluminum foil cut in long strips. When ejected from an aircraft, the strips float freely in the breeze and play havoc with radar signals from a pursuing radar-guided missile. Enemy radar reflections become skewed when scanning the free-floating metallic strips, and the opposing operators cannot distinguish real aircraft from chaff patterns on their scopes. With a blanket of chaff protection, an attacking aircraft could mask itself from the electronic homing of a deadly missile.

"The 'Grizzly' has a confirmed range of about forty-five kilometers, so they say, but new intel indicates it may be as many as seventy-five, thanks to the upgrades available from our trading partners, the Chinese," Riordan continued.

The mood was somber as everyone listened up; he was describing the very real missile threats that could end the life of a complacent aircrew. "Also look out for the venerable, but still lethal, SA-2 and SA-5 missiles. Those are older but they can give you a headache. The SA-2 'Guideline' still only has a range of about thirty kilometers, but the SA-5 'Gammon' has a confirmed range of about three hundred kilometers. The Navy is going in hot after the radar guidance systems and control centers. The

SA-5s could be a problem when you're out over the desert headed for the water and our base at Incirlik. Kinda like the gift that keeps on giving, huh? Just stay below twenty-five hundred feet on your egress and SA-5 won't be much of a threat. He's not real effective down low!"

Another subdued chuckle from the room; dozens of throats were now drier than they had been just thirty minutes earlier.

Riordan continued. "You guys going for the terrorist training facility, listen up. Look out for the SA-7, code name 'Grail', and SA-14, code name 'Gremlin.' Grails were the first reliable shoulder-fired stingers out of Moscow. They have been in use since 1967, and the current generation has had a serious avionics upgrade. Gremlins came out in 1974 and are considered the second generation of Soviet shoulder-fired SAMs. But just like their predecessor, the Gremlins have been upgraded and they now sport infrared guidance. One can easily fly up your tailpipe and blow your ass to kingdom come. That could ruin your whole freaking day! Do you read me, guys?"

Mercer felt an unusual twitch in his stomach. He quietly reached into his flight suit pocket for a roll of antacids.

After another of his five-second pauses for effect, Riordan pressed on: "We know that the now-destroyed Republican Guards had both systems during the Storm in '91, but we are pretty sure that these terrorist and paramilitary units have them now, too. We just don't know how many they may really have on hand. There's no way the Navy can get them all, because they are so small. And they're portable. We have to assume the terrorist groups are proficient with them. Israeli sources indicate 'Gremlin' has been deployed in Lebanon and in Syria. All I can tell you is to catch the bad guys and hammer them before they can arm and shoot with the little stuff."

"Let's have the next slide, please," Riordan said.

"Right. As you can see, here is the Syrian coast-line. They have radar-guided SAM sites at Al Ladhiqiyah, just south of the Turkish border, down the coast to Tartus. All have state-of-the-art Chinese gear, probably the brand new SA-X-20. Its range is reported to be up to two hundred kilometers. Stay out of this zone," Riordan implored the group. "Your ingress routes have to be tight and low; damn tight! Read me on that? Stay away from the Turkish border. We can't be seen crossing into Syria from Turkey, or back into Turkey on the way out. Syrian radar has been spying on all of our sorties in and out of Turkey--cross over the Turk-Syrian border and you're gonna cause more political trouble than the CINC wants.

And no freelancing, either! Hit your primary or secondary target and get out. Don't go looking for stray things to blow up." Riordan stressed. "Finally, on egress, cross back out over the Med like this slide shows…and only after we're at the designated spot well out over the water can you dip below Syr-ian radar and scoot into Turkey for a landing."

Suddenly, from the back of the room, boomed Kilrain's commanding voice "And, gentlemen, we don't need any heroes! Heroes get people killed."

The Wing Commander's stern warning brought the room to a silent standstill.

Kilrain continued, walking toward the front of the room. "You will be operating under stress, but you are the best-trained military flyers in the world...so we wouldn't ask...no, I wouldn't ask you to do something you hadn't been trained to do and do well. If everybody does what he is supposed to do and nobody tries to be a hero, this thing will work out."

Kilrain let the last few words sink in before taking an empty seat near one of the junior captains in the squadron. A few somber moments later, Riordan asked for the next slide, this one describing the attack against the Syrian airfield, but Pollard didn't hear a word. His mind was already flying at twenty-five hundred feet above the Syrian hard pan.

17 November
1600 hours
RAF Lakenheath

Captain Damian Mercer, aka "Zulu," stared into a dusky-orange evening sun that hung low above the western horizon amidst a thin layer of gray clouds. The day had been cool and wet, typical for England this time of year, and the four kilometers of runway that stretched before him still glistened from a mid-afternoon shower. There would be no more rain today, for a breeze from the south had dusted most of the clouds from the dull November sky. Apart from the business at hand, it had the makings of a pleasant evening.

The nine F-15s operating under the Swift call sign had been divided into three flights of three aircraft each. Swift 21 was commanded by Col. Riordan, who was the flight leader for the first three-ship formation to take to the air. Captain Mercer piloted Swift 22, with Zach Pollard manning the WSO (Weapons Systems Officer) position in the back seat. Swift 23 was the "tail-end Charlie" of the flight. The flight leaders for the other two flights were Swift 24, with 25 and 26 in tow, and Swift 27 leading 28 and 29. After taking off in the more manageable smaller groups, all of the F-15s would combine into a single non-standard formation.

Pollard reached to his shoulder and tugged hard on the straps anchoring him to his ejection seat as Mercer turned the nose of the sixty-five foot long craft onto the run-up area near the end of the runway. As the big jet lumbered along the wide slab of concrete, it handled like an overloaded dump truck, but Mercer aligned it perfectly over the stripe. He set the brake and raised his hands to show that he wasn't moving any of the controls for the benefit of the crew chief and the arming crew, who had followed the flight in a dark blue crew cab Air Force pickup, to do the final exterior preparations. Among other things, the crew removed the locking landing gear pins to enable the gear to be retracted upon breaking ground.

Tension filled the cockpit like a fine mist; it surrounded and bathed both crewmates and smelled of jet fuel and old sweat. In a few minutes, Mercer, Pollard, and fifty tons of winged steel would blast through an English sunset and into the night sky toward Syria.

Mercer's mind darted from the moment at hand to images from the past. His pulse began to quicken and his breathing became short and ragged. He tried to reassure himself that he'd logged 400 missions and more than 1000 hours of flight time in this airplane, in all kinds of weather over all kinds of terrain. Mercer and Pollard had been in some tough spots before, fighting a hundred simulated air battles. But never in all of those flights had a real enemy taken aim and actually tried to kill them. And never, never in all those flights, had either man's gut felt as tight as it did tonight.

Mercer absent-mindedly flexed his fists, while his mind flew alone in a gray haze, racing a course of a thousand thoughts and concentrating on none of them.

Outside the cramped confines of their aircraft, engine noise from the squadron mustered behind them echoed across the American airbase sprawled over the tan and green patchwork farmland of East Anglia. The roar from the twenty-four pairs of jet engines sounded like the cataclysm they were about to create. A thousand freight trains would not have matched the din as each of the thundering dragons emerged from their high-tech, bombproof hardened shelters, lurching, burning, and hissing in procession, a marked contrast to the lush growth of the English countryside in the distance.

A trace of perspiration ran from beneath Mercer's flight helmet. His gloved left hand reached to wipe the trickle away. The ground crew had finished their pre-flight work, giving a thumbs-up signal as they backed away, leaving him to run his before-takeoff checklist. He consciously verified every item, resisting the natural human tendency to point at each instrument but not actually ensure that what he was seeing was correct.

Meanwhile, in the seat behind, Pollard cast his eyes along the neatly set rows of red and white landing lights beaming from both sides of the runway. He, too, noticed that his hands had been working without first consulting his brain. He chuckled a nervous titter and muttered, "Jesus," to no one in particular. He'd been through this drill more times that he'd care to count-without so much as a whisper of doubt in his ability. Pollard knew that only the very best flight crews had been selected for this mission, but he wondered to himself if he would measure up. Pollard wasn't alone in that thought. Forty-seven other men on the airfield were asking themselves the very same question...

Even though the F-15's instruments included a

digital readout of Greenwich Mean Time, Pollard felt a need to check his watch. His right hand scraped back the olive-drab sleeve of his flight suit to study the dial. His eyes wouldn't fix on the hands, even though there was plenty of daylight left in the cloudless sky. His brain either could not, or would not, focus on the simple task of reading time. His eyes blinked; his head shook twice. Only a concerted effort revealed the time.

Thinking of the refueling aircraft that had launched from Aviano and Ramstein a couple hours ago, along with the KC-10s that had been pre-positioned in Turkey, Mercer said, "Thank God for those Guard and Reserve guys in the tankers. They really earn their flight pay."

"Yeah," Pollard acknowledged. He knew it would take at least six mid-air refuelings along the way for the bomber task force to reach Northern Syria, given their flight path. Logistics planning for this mission had been a nightmare. The attack plan involved coordination with the Navy, who would launch a sea-borne carrier assault. Air Force reserve KC-135 and KC-10 tanker units from the States and England were to provide air-to-air in-flight refueling.

In the rear seat, weapons system officer Pollard returned to his own thoughts. His mind again filled with a thousand irrelevant images. At the same moment, he could hear his heart's rushing thud in the earphone of his helmet. He clutched his left thigh and squeezed hard to make himself slow down, but he could feel nothing but numbness. His mouth was as dry as the Syrian desert he was about to visit.

Strapped tight within the beast, the pair waited, and each man's mind raced into the gathering nightfall. Neither officer spoke a word. Gone was the usual banter and bullshit that preceded every other training flight the pair had taken together. Both fliers now busied themselves with the myriad of gadgets in the cockpit around them. Although the flyers didn't need to breathe from the ship's oxygen stores while on the ground, the flight surgeon had suggested the pure oxygen would keep the crews "sharp" before takeoff. Mercer drew a long breath from the oxygen mask that covered his mouth. Breathing from his mask at the end of a green air hose, he could taste his sweat as it dripped from his lips. His eyes scanned the blinking white, amber and green lights from the heads up display.

Riordan's voice over the radio jolted Mercer and Pollard back to the noisy world around them, asking for verification that each pilot was ready. On cue, all three retuned their UHF radios to the tower frequency. They were about to earn their flight pay. Pollard looked back over his shoulder to see their sister ship, Swift 23 neatly abreast.

Speaking for the flight, Riordan checked on: "Swift Two-One." Mercer keyed up: "Two-two." The third chimed in, "Two-three."

"Lakenheath Tower," Riordan called, "Swift Two-One, flight of three, ready for departure."

"Swift Two-One flight, Lakenheath, line up and wait."

"Swift Two-One, line up and wait," acknowledged Riordan. The three F-15s taxied into a perfectly staggered takeoff formation on the runway, designed to ensure the safety of all three even if one or more developed a problem and had to abort.

As Swift Two-Two came to a stop in position on the runway, Mercer and Pollard had a front seat view of the ominous procession of drab-gray, twin-tailed fighters stretched along the taxiway back into the gathering dusk. Each was rolling awkwardly forward as the tower readied the armada for flight.

Due to the clandestine nature of this particular mission, the instrument flight plan had been pre-coordinated and the flight's initial heading and altitude were not broadcast on the radio. Upon receiving permission to release the flight, the tower controller merely said, "Swift Two-One flight, wind one-two-zero at five, cleared for takeoff."

Mercer and Pollard heard Riordan answer, "Swift Two-One flight, cleared for takeoff."

As Riordan fire-walled the throttles, his engines blasted a hot flame back across the tarmac, his F-15 shattering the early evening serenity with a blast of fire, gas and deafening noise as the combined force of sixty thousand pounds of thrust generated by his plane's twin engines accelerated it forward. The after-burner noise from the lead jet had a physical force of its own. Even forty or fifty yards away, the searing hot gas and thrust shook Swift 22 like a bad wind. Mercer had been through at least a thousand takeoffs but none seemed louder than Riordan's.

Aboard Swift 22, Mercer and Pollard saw two fiery red-yellow cones of fire emanating from the rear of Swift 21, now a hundred yards ahead.

"OK, big bird, let's see if your fires are lit tonight," Mercer breathed. His hand braced the throttle and the Pratt and Whitney engines screamed with a white-orange blast of hell's own fire. The aircraft rocked against its brakes; Swift 22 strained to rip away from its earthly bonds.

"Come on!" Mercer urged as he scanned the digital readouts. Every component had to operate perfectly or they'd have to ground-abort and stay home. Those were the rules for this mission. Any defect, no matter how slight, would force a stand-down, and no matter how nervous or scared a flyer might be, he'd rather die than abort this of all missions - and then later have to face those comrades who had flown the attack.

Mercer thought his heart would explode as it raced in sync with the engines behind him. Every readout indicated optimum performance.

"We're go!" Mercer exclaimed, as he released the brakes just 10 seconds behind Riordan.

"Shit hot!" Pollard answered. Their earlier jitters now turned into bravado, their fear lost in the power and excitement of the moment.

As Mercer monitored the various engine instruments even while thundering down the runway, accelerating to takeoff speed, he was amazed at his body's suddenly precise and correct actions. His thinking became quickly focused and sharp, his movements fluid, no longer wooden or robot-like. His adrenaline glands were pumping in overdrive. He felt as though he was detached, watching himself in a movie.

The fighter-bomber accelerated rapidly, the individual panels of pavement sped past faster and faster, and the power of God's hand pressed Mercer and Pollard hard into their seats. The crewmembers strained against the g-forces as Mercer pulled gently on the stick at 160 knots. The F-15 rocketed into the sky, leaving the runway behind and below her, no longer bound by Earth's gravity.

Swift 22 needed all the power she could get, for slung beneath her wings was an unusually heavy rack of bombs: eight GBU-12 five-hundred-pound, laser guided "smart" weapons. With all internal tanks topped off and an auxiliary centerline tank attached to her belly, the plane could hold more than 9,000 pounds of precious fuel. But due to having the maximum load of ordnance, this was an extremely heavy launch, so she took off with less than a full fuel load. The ops plan called for the F-15s to "top off" from the tankers out over the ocean.

Mercer pushed the throttles all the way into afterburner thrust for the mission profile's max power climb. If not for the extra weight and aerodynamic drag of the external stores, the F-15 could have eventually exceeded Mach 2.5.

"Takeoff at 1640 local," Pollard called out.

"1640 local, Roger," Captain Mercer responded, grinning.

As Swift 23 and Swift 22 closed in on Swift 21, the three banked gently to the left and headed for a rendezvous point somewhere over the south coast of England.

Back on the tarmac, the crew of Swift 24 continued the launch sequence as the next three aircraft rumbled into position. At the same time, all over the Lakenheath tarmac, fliers searched their own souls, made a hundred promises to God, and launched into the unforgiving English night.

Mercer's thoughts suddenly darted across the globe to the Navy aircraft carriers on station in the Eastern Med. There, two squadrons of EA-6B Prowlers would soon be going through the same preflight ritual. Those planes carried special electronic jamming gear instead of bullets or bombs. Each Navy jammer carried as many as ten high-powered transmitters, each capable of frustrating an enemy radar installation from as far off as one hundred sixty kilometers. Once the attack began, Mercer knew, the jammers would operate near the Lakenheath bombers and transmit false radar signals to the Syrians to confuse their antiquated Soviet-built air defenses.

Much earlier, at the American air bases Germany and Italy, the fuel-heavy tankers and their crewmen had launched. It would take some doing, everyone understood, to get this multitude of men and their machines to the right places at the precise

times. Hoping all the Air Force tankers would rendezvous on schedule in a black sky, Pollard wished
to himself, "God, I hope we find them," referring to
the game-plan that called for the bombers and tankers to meet up over the star-lit ocean without the
benefit of free-air radio communication for in-flight
refuelings. "Can't let the bad guys in the 'fishing
boats' know we're up to something," one pilot had
mused, referring to the still-intact elaborate radio
detection equipment in the arsenals of nations yet
unfriendly to the United States.

Once out over the Mediterranean, radio silence
would be maintained, at least until the force appeared near their targets.

As soon as the twenty-four F-15s had established themselves in a loose formation, Mercer adjusted the controls to enable him to fly a little less
hands-on. Next, he set the radio to a pre-assigned
tactical channel so they could monitor all in-flight
communications. "We're tactical from here on out,"
Mercer said, indicating that for the remainder of the
flight, he and Pollard--just like the other pilots on
the mission--would use their call signs instead of
their given names for any emergency radio communication. Any broadcast reference to a pilot's real
name could provide valuable information to enemy
forces. Thus, each crewmember had a call sign or
tactical name he used in flight. Usually, the names
were given by squadron mates at the beginning of a
flier's career and generally stuck for life. Even on
the ground, pilots called each other by the tactical

names. It was all part of life in the fraternity of fly-ers.

But not tonight. After the armada had cleared English airspace and begun its flight south, strict radio silence would be observed, unless an emergency dictated otherwise.

"Gimme a time hack," 'Zulu' Mercer called into his oxygen mask.

"I make it 1642 hours local. We're over Bury St. Edmunds; climb to 20-thousand and come right to 230 degrees."

"Roger," Mercer replied.

The flight of twenty-four F-15 "E" models had soon joined up in a thirty-mile long procession, streaming south, southeast toward the easternmost tip of England, just off Dover.

Several hours later, Brigadier General Jack Kilrain walked nervously forward, toward the cockpit of the lead KC-10 Extender tanker. The co-pilot gently controlled the huge craft with the practiced skill of a seasoned aviator. "We're already five minutes behind," Kilrain complained. "It's not your fault, Major," Kilrain half-barked to the pilot. "But I'll be damned if I know why that sergeant chose today of all days to be late for launch. He and I are going to have words when we come back..." The tanker pilot, a reservist, smiled and shook his head as Kilrain patted him on the shoulder. Both men had been in the Air Force long enough to know that no matter how hard one trained or how intensely one planned, some knucklehead could always botch the works by a momentary mental lapse.

"We're OK, sir, we're level at 29,000 feet," the major responded. "All the Eagles from Lakenheath are away. I'm cutting back a little on the airspeed to compensate. We'll make the rendezvous point on time. Radar has a fix on your guys, sir."

"Any word on the Navy boys?" Kilrain asked.

"Yes sir, a coded message just came in. The Prowlers are on the flight decks, fueled and ready."

Kilrain's eyes scanned the instrument panel of the huge plane. Everything appeared normal as he glanced at his watch and thought to himself, "1805. Good."

Kilrain turned and made his way from the flight deck to the rear of the giant jet. He took a deep breath and looked around its insides. He had spent his flying career crammed into single-seat fighters. More than once he had wished he was a few inches shorter when he found himself squeezed by the cockpits of the F-4 Phantoms and F-16 Falcons he had flown. No, this airplane was entirely different. It could carry more than two hundred thousand pounds of jet fuel for the gas-hungry fighters it escorted. The plane, the military variant of the civilian DC-10 so commonly seen at major airports, was "...damn near longer than the Wright Brother's first flight," Kilrain allowed his mind to wander.

"A job with Delta would be a hell of a lot safer..." the general rued. Tonight, Kilrain, a veteran of several dozen combat sorties in the Gulf War, had operational command over all the F-15s and tankers speeding through the night sky toward Syria.

Less than ten minutes later, as the armada crossed

landfall and headed out over the dark Channel, a voice called from the flight deck of the KC-10 flying command post. "General Kilrain! A coded transmission from the Lakenheath ships is coming in."

"Horses at the gate; all starters!" crackled flight leader Riordan's voice over the secure radio that shifted frequencies so that no one outside the task force could intercept or jam communications.

"Place your bets," came Kilrain's predetermined, coded response which indicated that each of the flight leaders was to check in with the aircraft under his command to determine which planes would make the journey and which would turn back.

In turn, the three F-15 element leaders made radio contact with the pilots under each leader's command.

"Zulu and Buster. Check saddles." Per instructions, Mercer and Pollard quickly reviewed the status of their aircraft, paying particular attention to engine temperature, terrain-following radar and attack radars. Mercer's reply came a quick moment later, "Saddles tight!" indicating that all his tactical and operational systems were working to perfection. And so it went throughout the flight, each crew checking and responding.

Swift 29 reported a hot wheel well, that portion in the body of the plane where the landing gear was stored during flight. Swift 26 reported loss of primary hydraulics; it had switched to its backup system. Pogo 36 was experiencing low oil pressure in number two engine. Those three aircraft would have to turn back. Riordan reported in coded message to Kilrain aboard the lead tanker that all his ships were ready to go, save three. The general issued instructions to the element leaders to dispatch all faulty aircraft and return them to the Lakenheath airfield. Twenty-one starters remained at the gate with saddles tight; Kilrain would still sideline three others before the attack began.

With that task complete, the remaining twenty-one F-15s regrouped in flights of three and joined with either a KC-10 or KC-135 tanker. One plane formed on each wing of the tanker and one plane settled itself under and behind the tanker's belly.

As the task force headed south and along the French coast, the planes reached a cruising speed of four hundred fifty knots at an altitude of five thousand feet. Each of the tankers, and its three-ship complement, settled in about a mile distant from the next contingent. To the French radar operators below and to the east, each tight formation of aircraft and their mother tanker ship appeared as one plane. The fighters had long since deactivated their transponders, making it harder for ground-based radars to see them. Not that the French posed any threat, but there was never a substitute for professionalism. And a pro always flew a tight formation, Mercer reminded himself.

"Fair weather friends, indeed," Mercer concluded, as he gazed down toward the darkening French coastline.

JONATHAN BRUCE

17 November
1930 hours
Off the Iberian Peninsula

After two hours of flying tight on the tanker's right wing, Mercer looked back to his crewmate and smiled, "My hand's getting tired. I'm not used to flying formation for this long." Pollard returned with a smile and chided the pilot, "That's what you get all that big pilot bonus pay for." Mercer, who had been tracking his ship's fuel consumption, then noted, "We gotta refuel. And in the dark with no radio, this is gonna be fun."

"I'll hit the lights," Pollard responded. A flip of a switch activated the red-rotating beacon on the middle of the Strike Eagle's fuselage. Mercer then gave the stick a gentle nudge down and to the right; then he throttled the engine back just enough to allow him to slip underneath and behind the tanker's tail. The flashing red light told the tanker that Swift 22 was getting thirsty. As Mercer guided his craft into its standard pre-contact position, the refueling boom operator, a staff sergeant perched in the belly of the KC-10, responded with a flash of green and red lights. Mercer then knew it was safe to inch his way toward the larger, speeding craft in order to get close enough for the boomer to reach him with the fuel line.

Mercer's hand actions were like those of a concert pianist. His eyes never wavered from the boom operator's red and green signal lights. His hand movements were slight, subtle and sure. Each twitch of the stick maneuvered the speeding jet yards...feet...inches closer to potential disaster. A sudden wrong move could hurtle the smaller craft into the larger, fuel-laden supplier or its extended fuel boom. Yet Mercer's practiced hands made gentle and easy motions as the F-15, now slowed down to just over two hundred fifty knots, inched closer to the tanker's lower tail section.

Above in the tanker, the boom operator flicked a signal switch: Green light--come closer; red light--back off.

"Green...green...red, slow down...green, come on," Mercer counted aloud.

Soon, he had closed to within fifty feet, then forty, then thirty...the boomer and pilot, tanker and jet, flying together in a carefully synchronized aerial ballet.

Then, looking above his head, Damian Mercer saw solid red light from beneath the belly of the KC-10 tanker. The fuel operator now sat directly above the Strike Eagle. Through his picture window, the boomer could see the dimly lit, helmeted faces of Mercer and Pollard in the ebony night.

The boomer then toggled the long, winged refueling tube and lowered it from beneath the tanker. As it swung down, another lever ordered the boom to expand and stretch toward the hungry jet below. Faint lights illuminated the refueling receptacle on the F-15--and with deft control, the operator guided the shaft into the opening. "Contact light," the boomer noted through his interphone. "Engage transfer now..." he called, as precious gallons of jet fuel began to fill Mercer's aircraft below.

Zach Pollard, sitting in the rear navigator's seat, allowed his mind to wander. Things had happened so fast in the past two days.

Swift 22 hit an unexpected pocket of clear air turbulence and Pollard raised his glance to the back of Damian Mercer's helmet. But the pilot had already compensated for the jolt with slight back pressure on the stick.

"Hey, Zach!" Mercer called back over his shoulder to Pollard.

The pilot smiled and called into his microphone, "You still with me? Refueling's done. Take this bitch, will ya? My hand's tired."

Pollard nodded, and then focused his thoughts on the task at hand as the F-15 slipped away from the tanker above and into the star-sprayed blackness.

18 November
0100 hours
Terrorist training compound – Abu Du'an, Syria

A single searchlight swept the grounds of the paramilitary training center, then out over the black waters of the Euphrates River. The beam skimmed the roofs of the two rows of single-story cinder-block barracks, and then across an open field and toward the two-story building where a large pool for underwater training was housed. There, terrorist frogmen learned the art of underwater demolition and attacks against ships, oil platforms and bridges. The beacon then turned toward the near foreground, illuminating a mess hall for trainees and instructors.

Not far to one side of the compound the light shone on one of the barracks rooms where Mustafa Khalil Quomuz sat reviewing new photographs of the international airport in Frankfurt, Germany. The commercial air terminal shared a common runway with the once-sprawling American Rhein-Mein air base, now no more than a cursory presence, thanks to the Pentagon's downsizing. "An opportunity, a wonderful target it would have been. Perhaps, we should have…but there are now other attractive opportunities within Europe." He smiled to himself and raised his eyes as he peered through a cloud of cigarette smoke at the bare walls of the spartan room. Only pictures of his current benefactors, Osama bin Laden and Syria's Assad, broke the monotony of the gray cinder blocks around him.

Reveille would sound with the dawn, just five hours hence. Even at this late hour, the murmurs of a half-dozen Arabic dialects quietly whispered through the dormitory buildings, as the warriors stirred in their cots and latrines while others sought refuge in sleep following another hard day of training. Some of the men were simply too tired or too excited to sleep. A few bare neon tubes flickered and hummed, illuminating the passageways to the squad bays with a weak, orange-yellowish haze. Outside in the compound, rusting loud speakers

quietly played a nasheed; a song of Islamic devotion. Quomuz himself had allowed the rhythmic
chants, calling them "halal," or permissible as
ordained by the mullahs.

The next morning, boots would be laced tight,
desert camouflage uniforms buttoned, and caps fitted tightly on dust-covered brows. With fifty men
bunking in each squad bay, and two squad bays per
cinder-block building, the four dormitory buildings
housed nearly two hundred trainees. A fifth structure, two hundred meters distant, housed the training cadre; the instructors who oversaw the men's
training. Yet another barracks housed the cooks,
medical technicians, and administrative support
staff. Over two hundred and fifty men, and a handful of women, lived within the fence that surrounded the age-worn encampment.

Abu Du'an had begun its life eighty years ago
as a remote communications station and supply depot for the British convoys that patrolled the region
just after the First World War. Back then it was
hardly more than a dusty and forsaken crossroads
with several stone huts and three-score Army tents.
Slowly the British Army had strung telegraph wires,
built wooden structures, and improved the roads.

By the time of the Second World War, Abu
Du'an boasted a field hospital, a small airstrip, and
nearly sixty permanent buildings. Abandoned by the
British at the time of Syrian independence, the base
surrendered to the ravages of neglect, the brutal
elements and scavenging nomads. When radical

groups like al Qaeda took an interest in the site nearly twenty years ago, nothing remained but the concrete foundations originally laid down by British engineers over eighty years earlier.

With money from Iraq and Libya, Abu Du'an sprang back to life as a pan-Islamic training facility, albeit officially disavowed by the host Syrian government. The underwater training facility, constructed by Soviet engineers along the banks of the Euphrates, was the jewel in the crown. More than one maritime terrorist expedition had been planned and practiced here. Not far from the four main dormitories, four separate small arms ranges ringed the perimeter, with one facing in each direction away from the camp. Recruits were schooled in the proper use and care of the venerable AK-47 assault rifle, rocket-propelled grenades, bazookas, and shoulder-fired anti-aircraft missiles. Quomuz had insisted that hand-to-hand combat, bayonet tactics, and sniper training were also included in the harsh curriculum.

Of particular interest to the cadre was demolition and explosives training, with emphasis on design and construction of improvised explosive devices. No recruit was considered ready for "graduation" until he had designed, constructed, and detonated an IED capable of destroying a two-ton truck. Results from the struggle against the infidels in Baghdad had proven the worth of the improvised weapons and Quomuz himself had overseen the instruction of the teaching cadre. Other explosives instruction included the manufacture of suicide vests, as well as placement of booby traps and land mines. "There is no weapon," Quomuz constantly reminded his charges, "that Allah disfavors, if it will kill infidels."

At forty-three, Quomuz was a revered figure in the jihad, a friend to the al Qaeda organization and every other group dedicated to the destruction of Israel. Yet he hardly looked the part of killer, terrorist or murderer. Rather, his small frame, closely cropped black hair, beard and brush mustache suggested a clerk or shopkeeper. Multilingual, he'd played many roles on every continent with al Qaeda and the Fatah Revolutionary Council and the Islamic Jihad, off and on, for the past twenty years. In that time, he'd altered his appearance as many times as he could; one year affecting longer hair and a small goatee, the next, a full beard and a shoulder length mane.

In late 2001, he had barely escaped the American dragnet in Afghanistan's Tora Bora Mountains, fleeing overland into Pakistan, where he found safety with clandestine cells funded by al Qaeda.

Doubtless, the CIA and the Israeli intelligence agencies had pictures of the man. But no two of them would ever look the same. That would offer some sense of security, Quomuz reasoned. Of the hundred senior officers in the cause, only Mustafa Khalil Quomuz and a handful of others now enjoyed the complete, personal trust of the bin Laden inner circle, for Quomuz had shown a willingness to obey bin Laden when other Palestinians would not.

Not only had Quomuz personally directed or taken part in more than fifty of the organization's terrorist attacks, he had been the triggerman in a score of assassinations of certain disloyal Palestinian officials. He had only narrowly missed killing Arafat in the late nineties.

Many in the West, the Israeli Shabak included, believed that Quomuz and bin Laden and their organizations were not so much Islamic rights armies as they were "for hire" death squads, willing to sell their services to the highest bidder. More than once, Quomuz had pledged allegiance in the field to Libya, Syria, and the Taliban...even al Qaeda. Loyalties in this part of the world were as unstable as the shifting desert sands. Mustafa Quomuz however, had proven himself able to maintain alliances among a variety of interests, tribes and armies. He was the perfect "master" for this training brigade.

Quomuz smiled to himself, as he turned off the light in search of a few hours' sleep. The day had gone well. He recounted the members of the training brigade in his mind. The terrorist smiled contentedly, recalling the day's exercises: new recruits running the length of the obstacle course and threading themselves through the barbed wire entanglements. He had personally designed the course, and it was based on photographs he'd taken of the defensive perimeters of certain farming communes in the north of Israel. "Realism, my brothers," he thought silently. "Realism is training, and training is realism. We will defeat the Jew by training like the Jew."

The terrorist reminded himself of the dozen female volunteers in the ranks. Although he personally considered women inferior to men, he was nevertheless an opportunist. "These women will serve my purposes, someday," he chuckled. Four of these female recruits had lived for several years in Western Europe; two in Belgium, one in France, and one in the U.K. They brought with them detailed knowledge of Continental customs, traditions, and lifestyles. Such information would prove invaluable when it came time to attack the public transit systems and other infrastructure of the Western puppet masters who were in bed with the whore of Zion. Quomuz believed that in the West, women were not immediately suspected as terrorists, and hence, they could penetrate deeper inside targeted areas before being challenged.

As he relaxed and pulled his camouflage jacket close around his shoulders, he mentally surveyed the camp from west to east and north to south. He was pleased with what he recalled. The pace and intensity of training had been increased. The depth and breadth of the explosives instruction had increased, as well as the variety of the high explosives being used.

The quality and number of recruits had expanded also. His facility now boasted copious numbers of volunteers from all the mainstream Muslim countries of the Middle East and North Africa. But increasing numbers of disaffected brothers had been appearing in recent months. There were new arrivals from Surinam, Belize, Jamaica, and Mexico. Half a dozen men had journeyed all the way from Cebu City, Philippines. Another dozen were in from Indonesia, while one even hailed from Nagoya, Japan. But the biggest surprise was the number of trainees who held European citizenship. Fully three score naturalized Europeans were in the camp at that moment.

Quomuz smirked at the irony.

As he drifted toward sleep, he yawned and considered that it had been a very good day indeed. His al Qaeda masters were pleased with his work here. He would have no trouble sleeping contentedly tonight.

Surely the coming day would offer even more opportunities to instill the warrior spirit in the hearts of his trainees. With Allah on his side, Quomuz felt invulnerable.

In the next building, Petra Voss slept soundly. She had exhausted herself that day teaching young Palestinians the art of high explosive demolition. Although her students, young Arab men in their late teens and early twenties, clearly resented the presence of a woman, her willingness to share much-needed information allowed them to overlook their religious and cultural bias. Voss was an enigma to her Arab partners. Her petite form, short red-blonde hair and almost child-like features belied her true identity: a cold, humorless, and distant killer.

Voss was superbly conditioned; even the men in her company could not match her stamina under the searing middle-eastern sun. Yet, dressed in desert fatigues, she still exuded a raw, powerful, almost animal sexuality.

But Petra Voss had time for no man, save one. Neither the Arab men nor the other European operatives assigned to the facility drew her attention. A child of the radical Bader-Meinhof sect, she, like her mother before her, was consumed by her devotion to radical socialist ideals and a passionate hatred of the capitalistic West.

She was the prototypical socialist warrior: an androgynous true believer, clever, daring, and ruthless.

Her credentials were impeccable in the minds of those who commanded the Jihad Revolutionary Council. She'd exploded a dozen bombs as a member of the Antiimperialistische Zelle in Germany in the mid-nineties. There, she helped plan and execute a series of attacks, including a lethal assault on the top-secret GSG-9 counter-terrorism organization. She had proven her worth to the Fatah organization in the 1995 bombing of the Cafe de Sol in Rome, which had killed a score of British and American tourists. She had passed, quite unnoticed, through the streets of Rome for days before the bombing and had facilitated the delivery of the explosives and detonators to Quomuz himself, just as she had promised.

The terrorist command had a year ago insisted that the German woman remain as part of the school cadre. Despite the fact that she was a "Western" woman, even the most fervent zealot was happy to use her services and acquire her deadly skills. Most recently, the commuter train attacks in Madrid had been, in great part, orchestrated by the petite killer.

Three days before, Voss had mustered her thirty young charges near the south rifle range. The lesson was an intense introduction to the AK-47. But before anyone had been allowed to fire a single round, they had spent two hours field-stripping, cleaning and reassembling their weapons. Only after each Kalashnikov passed her personal inspection, was its "owner" allowed to fire on the two hundred meter range. Voss was meticulous, intense and unyielding in her instruction.

A partnership, of sorts, began on the Madrid mission between the German woman and Quomuz. Before the attack, there had been several nights spent together in a safe house. Despite their cultural differences, their common mission and backgrounds as terror operatives made for a compelling, if not perverse, relationship which resulted in moments of passion and violent, almost physically abusive, sexual encounters.

Quomuz marveled at her sexual stamina, and he was obsessed and enthralled by her violent orgasms occasioned by his brutality toward her. Despite the intensity of their physical relationship, no romance had ever grown between them. Their's was by day a cold, calculating professional partnership. By night, they had developed an almost animal ritual, borne of the violence and pain that was the essence of the other's soul. There would be no future for the pair beyond the mission at hand. Neither wanted, nor sought, any semblance of love. Both encased their cold hearts in hatred.

Quomuz's taste for sex with a non-Arab woman posed a compromise with his Islamic up-bringing. So, too, did his fondness for certain wines and brandy. He rationalized his sins of the flesh as a forgivable frailty, for Allah was sure to smile on him as a warrior who had already sacrificed family and relations for the service of the Almighty. When the time came, Quomuz knew that Voss could easily be sacrificed for the greater cause of Islam. The fact that he had shared her wild intimacy would matter little. As long as she proved useful, professionally and personally, Petra Voss would remain an asset to Quomuz and the struggle. Indeed, when male members of the Jihad had proven inept, Voss had displayed the nerve and a fanatic willingness to fight when others would not. She was neither a Muslim, nor an Arab, nor a man. But she had served Quomuz and his cause well. To Quomuz, however, the German woman would never live in paradise.

She was, therefore, expendable.

18 November
0125 hours
Over the Mediterranean

Following the latest aerial refueling, Zach Pollard noted aloud, "Two hours to go." Mercer didn't respond, as he busied himself reviewing the in-flight checklist affixed to his left leg. Swift 22 had been the last F-15 to top off.

As the boomer in the tanker above retracted and elevated the winged fuel nozzle, Mercer lowered the craft's slender nose below the horizon and gathered extra knots of speed. As soon as he was sure he had safely cleared the underbelly of the KC-10, he pressed gently on the right rudder and nudged the joystick slowly to the right, avoiding sudden movements so close to the tanker's belly. When the maneuver was complete, the sleek-looking F-15 was now fully abreast of the giant tanker. Looking at the cockpit of the larger ship, he could make out the faint glow of the craft's instruments reflecting off the windscreen. Below his own ship's left wing now lay Sicily and the lights of several villages flickered in the blackness below. Mercer held the plane in a tight turn to the right until he came about, facing almost due south. Ahead in the darkness by about three kilometers were Swift 27 and 28.

Zach Pollard buried his face in the black radar visor, his eyes following the green tracings of the radar return from the semicircular sweep of the transmitter. "I've got contact..." Pollard called out to the pilot. "Stoves and 28...pick it up a few knots and we'll be right on them," Pollard said in a businesslike tone, as Mercer tapped the big jet's throttles.

As Mercer and Pollard began to speed away into the moonless sky toward their three-ship strike team, they looked to the north and saw the navigation lights from the fleet of tankers reforming after their just-completed refueling evolutions.

Back aboard Kilo One, Jack Kilrain checked and rechecked his watch. Kilrain and his tanker gaggle would hold at the heel of the Italian boot, before turning east toward the island of Crete and then toward the target in Syria, and with luck, an eventual safe landing in Turkey.

The mission was on schedule, more or less. Earlier in the flight, Kilrain's own KC-10 command tanker had been late receiving fuel from one of the smaller KC-135 tankers. The delay had put the general and his flight of three following F-15s nearly fifteen minutes behind the rest of the task force. But Kilrain had made a command decision that lesser men might have avoided. Faced with the prospect of being fifteen minutes late to the target, Kilrain ordered the command tanker and the Eagles behind him to stray from the prearranged flight path over international airspace. "But sir, that'll take us over Sicily. We don't have clearance to fly in their airspace," the tanker pilot reminded the general.

"I'm not going to risk this mission or the lives of thirty-six crewmen over some damn lines on a map. If I'm wrong, I'm wrong. It's my butt, my responsibility. Besides, that's why we hire Air Force lawyers, to get our asses out of jams like this."

The major laughed aloud, knowing full well that the general was right. "Just hope some of our friends in the media or Congress don't get too excited about those lines on the map, sir."

"It's not Congress I'm worried about," Kilrain observed. "It's the Italian government. Italy is supposedly on our side in this war on terror, but they're not real gung-ho. Their leadership will cut and run for cover if the world's media portray them as aiding and abetting this attack."

The tanker's co-pilot interrupted the geopolitical conversation. "Sir, Swift 22, 27 and 28 are clear. En route to target; saddles tight."

"Good," Kilrain spoke softly as he looked out into the blackness. By his watch, the attacks would begin promptly as planned. Theoretically, a lay down attack such as this was choreographed like a ballet. Such a tactic called for the bombers to attack in flights of two or three ships, with one flight following another at intervals of only a few seconds, and sometimes from different directions. This technique, perfected by the Air Force in Desert Storm, concentrated maximum destructive firepower on a target, while minimizing the enemy's opportunities to lock on their defensive missile capabilities.

Ideally, all the actors in this drama would find their marks. Atlas flight would strike first. The next up was to be Swift flight, timed so that the last plane over the terrorist training ground would drop its bomb just as the first plane over the airport would drop its weapons. The timing had to be perfect in order to confuse the Syrian air defense system. Kilrain knew his Air Force attackers would be right on time. But even with the airborne traffic cops aboard an AWACS plane orbiting over the Med, only God knew if the Navy would be on time and on target coming from their carriers further out to sea.

Now the time was at hand to cut some players from the team roster. Kilrain abhorred this particular decision, for he knew it would devastate certain members of the squadron who had trained so hard for their first taste of combat. But orders were orders, and personal feelings were irrelevant. The aging warrior believed in one maxim for military success; group integrity must be paramount, and individual concerns were of only secondary importance.

Kilrain sent the following coded message to Riordan. "Scratch Atlas 14, Pogo 38, and Swift 25." Minutes later, the three unhappy aircrews were directed to divert to Turkey. True to their professionalism, no one verbalized their disappointment over the air. There would be plenty of opportunities to vent back at the Lakenheath Officer's Club.

Riordan sent a brief encrypted reply message to Kilrain which displayed on one of the many communications computers aboard the KC-10. "Three starters scratched; returning to stables. Eighteen starters at the gate, saddles tight." Kilrain exhaled, wiped his brow, and reached for his sixth cup of coffee.

Now it was all up to the younger warriors, Kilrain knew, for he could only watch from the safe confines of the distant tanker, as the newest generation of officers flew into battle. The General pondered, silently, hoping their training had been enough to see these men home safely.

18 November
0330 hours
Over Northern Syria

Captain Damian Mercer prepared to dive deep into the blackness and begin his attack run along the desert floor. The Syrian coast was well behind him and, oddly, no radar had acquired him or his wingmen. He thought momentarily of his wife, and then drew a deep breath from his oxygen mask.

This was it.

Less than fifteen kilometers away, Atlas 11 had begun its bombing run over the radar emitters near the airport. Air raid sirens had begun to wail their sickening warble a full minute before the first attacker arrived. All over northern Syria, the air defense network was suddenly on full alert, as AAA tracers filled the night sky. Atlas 13 was the next ship to make its run into a veil of hot-jacketed steel.

The first tones from the air raid siren perched atop Quomuz's barracks had surprised the Palestinian. With reflex action, he reached for the AK-47 assault rifle that lay near his cot and, almost without thinking, he jumped for the light.

Nearby, Petra Voss awoke in an almost serene state. Hearing the siren, she smiled sardonically and reached beneath her pillow for the loaded Glock handgun that was her constant companion. She relished the thought of a fight.

"Descending through one thousand feet; Tally Ho!" Mercer shouted, his heart racing, as he guided the hurtling aircraft below the enemy radar sweeps.

The jet accelerated to over six hundred nautical miles per hour in a sharp attack profile as Mercer pointed the craft's long, slender nose toward the target. Both men's stomachs began to float as the craft sliced into a negative-g dive, quickly leveling off at eight hundred feet over sand and scrub below. Highlighted against the blue-black horizon ahead, Pollard and Mercer could see the compound's perimeter lights shining in the distance. "Jesus," Pollard exclaimed. "They've left the lights on for us!"

As the big jet's wings stabilized parallel to the ground, Mercer called, "George has the airplane." Pollard reached for the knobs just below the terrain-following radar scope located squarely in the center of the cockpit console. It was almost 0335 hours when the jet's nose pitched slightly upward then returned to level flight as the LANTIRN terrain-avoidance system activated. Pollard shot a quick glance to his instrument panel and saw the image echoes from the big radar dish in the craft's nose as it swept back and forth, reading the topography ahead. The on-board computers registered the radar return and ordered the craft to fly higher or lower -- as needed -- to avoid any obstacle and still hold minimum altitude.

Experience told him the system worked perfectly. Nevertheless, Zach Pollard's throat felt as if he'd swallowed a brick.

Both men had flown hundreds of practice missions using the automatic terrain-following system, but neither had ever fully trusted the computer to not fly them into the ground. Tonight, though, was not a night for doubts. Even so, both carefully eyed the radar return, hands at the ready to fly the plane manually if need be. The bottom green line on the radar screen indicated the irregular terrain ahead; the top indicated their flight path. If all was working as designed, the top line would be a mirror image of the bottom, and the two would never intersect.

"Shit, I hope this thing's working tonight..." Mercer wished aloud. Pollard said nothing, but silently prayed the same.

Pollard, the navigator, who doubled as weapons officer, had little time to worry about the autopilot. It was time to concentrate on the bombing run he'd be making in less than a minute. Sitting behind Mercer, Pollard buried his face into the attack radar display. His face fit snugly into the hood that surrounded the radar screen and blocked out any other light that might interfere with his vision. His eyes quickly focused on the sweep, which resembled a quick metronome, counting rapidly left and right. In the radar's far-reaching arc, fuzzy outlines of buildings, towers and landscape appeared. Pollard's trained eyes deciphered the grainy images in search of his preordained targets.

"There!" Pollard shouted to his pilot. "Contact...initial offset point. Come left ten degrees and hold."

Damian Mercer grabbed the stick and in doing so, deactivated the autopilot. He looked up momentarily to see, in the distance ahead, Mike Richter banking hard to the left. Swift 27 had begun its attack run on the terrorist training compound. Two-seven's primary target was the indoor swimming facility believed to be the site for underwater demolition training.

At the same instant that Richter began his bomb run, overhead and far behind the Air Force bombers, the Navy EA-6B Prowlers switched on their high-power jamming equipment, which, in turn, confused the enemy surface-to-air missile batteries by blanking out their radar screens. All over the region Syrian missile crews nervously checked and rechecked their computer screens as radar beams swept the sky looking for the onrushing marauders. Syrian defense radar impulses below soon bathed Mercer and Pollard-- and just as quickly, a red light began to flash on Pollard's electronic countermeasures indicator, just below the terrain-following radar scope.

"They're manually painting us, trying to lock onto us..." Mercer called out, but Zach Pollard was deeply intent on finding his first aiming point in the attack run. Mercer's left hand instinctively reached for the chaff button in case a missile fixed on Swift 22's radar signature.

Just as planned, the jammers had confused the Syrian radar network. But when the enemy defenses began to emit radar signals, the Navy Hornets were waiting to pounce with radar-seeking missiles, hitting the radar sites as quickly as a mongoose strikes a cobra. For if the Syrian radar could lock onto an American raider, a Soviet-built Surface-to-Air SA-3 missile could then track and kill the interloping warplane.

A mile off his left wing, Mercer glimpsed four streaks of red light blazing through the air toward the hills. "Navy FA-18s going for the net with anti-rad missiles," Mercer called out.

A millisecond later two, three.... four brilliant flashes of yellow light illuminated the desert as the Navy's radar-seeking missiles sped to the ground with deadly accuracy. Mercer was startled by the intensity of the blast.

"Fuck! Hit! They got 'em! They fuckin' got 'em!" Mercer shouted wildly.

Another blaze of red light seemed to shoot past Mercer's window. "Jesus!" Mercer exclaimed, "What the hell...." But before he could complete the question, another of the Navy's anti-radar missiles found its intended target. A blinding flash marked the point of detonation where the air exploded with a million shards of steel, rock and glass. Just as suddenly, the radar warning light on Swift 22's console went dark, evidence that the Navy had silenced the battery of anti-aircraft radar.

But Mercer's warning system didn't remain black for long. Suddenly, lights flashed red again, indicating that a second SAM site was searching for a radar lock. At the same time, a series of beeps rang through Mercer's headset, an audible warning that the Syrian SAM battery was trying to find a new target. "I'm heading down," Mercer shouted.

"We gotta get below that radar. To hell with the rules of engagement! I'm not getting killed for some dumb-fuck rule."

Mercer squeezed the control stick and angled the nose of the speeding craft toward the earth. Pollard, whose face had been buried in the attack radar hood yelled back, "Shit, bring it up...I'm too low...can't get a fix on the target." At the same instant, an automatic warning tone echoed through both men's headsets, indicating the low flight auto-warning system was alert to the new altitude. Two new trails of fire sped toward an unseen point in the dimness below, as the Navy jets found another SAM site and had fired to silence its radar, thus protecting the Air Force fighters.

"Holy Jesus!" Mercer swore to himself, as a bright orange ball exploded five kilometers distant. That blast was followed by a larger, secondary explosion that could be heard in their cockpit--even above the roar of the twin engines working so furiously behind.

"Come left ten degrees...and hold at three hundred feet," Pollard called. As the pilot followed Pollard's navigation order, he could still see the twin flames shooting from the engines of Swift 27, a half-mile away. Mercer felt reassured that he wasn't alone in the air.

"All right, we're up again," the pilot called to Zach Pollard. "Got the laser on?" Pollard didn't answer, but checked the left side of the cockpit console to confirm that the laser guidance unit was operational and ready to guide their "smart" bombs to the target below.

Meanwhile, several kilometers to the east, Atlas 12 dropped the last of its smart weapons on a Syrian missile battery and then turned north toward the empty desert to begin the trip home.

Aboard the command tanker, General Jack Kilrain listened intently to Atlas flight reporting in as the speeding craft headed for the safety of Turkish airspace.

"Atlas 12. Feet dry," the pilot called. "Feet dry and....GOD DAMN! Somebody's hit, somebody's hit...." On instinct, General Kilrain instantly toggled the tactical mike and ordered Atlas 12 to maintain silence.

Aboard Swift 22, Mercer and Pollard heard none of it. Both men tightly focused on the bombing run before them. Hearts raced and sweat streamed from every pore--eyes and ears focused more keenly than ever--men and machine were in perfect harmony.

"I've got the training center, there's the barracks. I've got it, I've got it. We're six nauticals out..." Pollard yelled into his mask, as he intently surveyed his targeting radar. Mercer glanced at the airspeed indicator. His ship was streaking toward its target at just under a mile every five seconds.

Lining up his primary target in the crosshairs of the laser attack module, Pollard called out, "Okay, release in thirty...counting, counting..."

Only a hundred yards beneath their wings, a gun battery opened fire at the hurtling jet. In their headphones, Mercer and Pollard again heard the sickening "beep, beep, beep" warning that enemy radar was again trying to acquire.

"Chaff and flares...pumping chaff!" Mercer yelled, breathing hard. Then he hurriedly called to his crewmate, "You ready?"

"I've got it," the bombardier replied, as he found a clear view of the compound rushing toward him through the Pave Tack infrared-laser cameras.

"Laser on..."

As Swift 22 began its attack run, ahead by a mile, Captain Coleman in Swift 28 pushed his throttles into full afterburner and pulled hard into the sky to dodge the antiaircraft fire from below. Coleman and his crewmate were slammed back hard into their seats by the force of the five-G climb.

On the ground below, the air filled with explosive thunder as the guided American bombs crashed into their targets. Quomuz screamed a hundred confused orders to his men in the compound, who shot wildly into the air with their assault rifles. Hot phosphorous tracer fire and steel laced the sky as the defenders fired at deafening jet sounds above them.

In a corner of the compound, a crew of four pumped away at the unseen invaders with a Chinese-built ZSU anti-aircraft gun. As Swift 27 sped away, their bombs tracked toward the laser-designated target, the two-story training building less than a hundred yards from where Quomuz and his men furiously blasted away.

In the same instant, a wave of superheated air washed over the men below, then a deafening roar from the mighty jet's engines was followed by a blast, and another, and another as the ground shook furiously and chunks of brick and steel flew indiscriminately through the air. Quomuz was momentarily blinded by the flash, but saw the silhouette of Petra Voss, running from her barracks toward a sandbag shelter a few feet away. The flashes were instantly followed by a massive concussion that lifted the Palestinian off his feet and slammed him into the ground twenty meters distant. Nearby, the building that had been his barracks was now a pile of smoldering rubble.

Swift 27's aim had been textbook perfect.

The shock waves from Coleman's bombs had barely subsided when Zach Pollard took careful aim and then cried, "Pickle! Bombs Away!"

Mercer yanked back hard on the control stick and, with his right thumb, pressed the bomb release button atop the stick, and jettisoned the rack of eight 500-hundred pound bombs. The jet rocked as two tons of high explosives fell away.... Mercer kicked the right rudder hard, cranking the craft into a sharp turn as the force of five times normal gravity crushed against each pilot's chest.

Mercer could see new streaks of tracer fire racing toward his ship, and he jerked even harder on the stick, increasing the g-load by half again. Below, three former Russian KGB officers and their Palestinian comrades fired away at the American fighter-bombers, in a futile gesture of defense.

Out of breath, and heart racing wildly, Mercer yelled, "You got the laser on that thing?"

"Laser on, it's a go!"

The Pave Tack pod in the F-15's belly shot a beam

of invisible light toward the enemy compound. Inside the cockpit, Pollard tracked the flight of the falling bombs as they sped toward their target. As long as the weapons officer kept the laser crosshairs on target, the "smart" bombs would know where to fly.

"Tracking; it's tracking!" Pollard yelled, monitoring the bombs' flight path.

Swift 22's eight bombs found their mark in rapid staccato. It was as if hell itself was raining fire on the compound. The combined force of two tons of high explosives hit with a heart-shattering crash: debris filled the air, bodies and body parts splayed everywhere, as the ground shook violently. In the shelter near her disintegrating barracks, Petra Voss covered her head with her arms and screamed her rage and hatred and fear into the plywood floor. The blasts from the first bomb attack had blown a young Palestinian into the shelter and on top of Voss. The blood from his armless corpse now gushed into her hair and eyes as the second string of bombs hit the earth with a crack and a blast that shattered the East German woman's eardrums. Her own blood trickled from her ears, nose, and eyes and mixed with that of the dead man atop her.

"Jesus H. Christ!" Pollard screamed, as he watched the bombs slam into the targets. "Shit! We hit 'em; we hit 'em hard!" Pollard screamed. His brain was awash in a sea of adrenaline, his heart speeding faster than the turbines behind him. "Let's get the fuck outta here!"

Mercer's eyes found the airspeed indicator and, focusing quickly on the readout, he urged more speed from the jet. In what seemed like only a moment, Mercer coaxed the plane to level flight and headed west toward the relative safety of the tanker task force circling out over the Med. The rapidly retreating scene revealed fireballs on the ground as stored munitions ignited in spectacular flares of red, white and orange. Luckily, Syrian air defense radars were now silenced all across the region. In his headset, Mercer heard the crew of Swift 24, two nautical miles behind, chattering wildly about the smoke from the blast. He heard the pilot call out "feet dry," the coded signal that the last of the attack flight had made it safely away from the target and was headed for the Mediterranean.

A short mile ahead, inside Swift 22, Damian Mercer glanced up to the north to see the twin red-orange fires from Richter's engines bright against a deep, black sky.

As quickly as it had begun, the attack was over. Aboard the command ship out over the dark waters, Jack Kilrain kept count.

"Swift 21, 22 and 27...good, they're back. Pogo flight's all checked in and coming back from the airport attack...Atlas 11, good; 12, good; 13...One-Three?

Kilrain walked toward the bank of communication operators in the mid-section of the tanker. He looked around at the men's faces, then he checked the scopes and computer screens, asking, "Anybody hear from One-Three? Atlas 13?"

No one aboard the tanker could answer.

18 November
0745 hours
Incirlik Air Base, Turkey

The first rays of the pale, eastern sun greeted Swift flight as it vectored above the tranquil Turkish hardpan. As the flight line crept into view, a tired and emotionless Damian Mercer toggled his mike and asked for landing conditions. Still about thirty kilometers out, Mercer strained to listen to landing instructions from the tower below.

"Swift 22. Landing runway two-niner. Winds 220 at ten. Cleared to land."

"Runway two-niner. Two-two zero at ten. Swift 22 landing." Mercer repeated; he smiled at hearing a female controller's voice.

"OK, stud," Mercer said to himself. "No time for errors now."

"Maintaining altitude…holding at 250 knots steady…turn downwind and reduce speed."

The *Eagle* slowed to just over 220 knots as Mercer called, "Drop gear."

"OK, now, watch the angle of attack; check the flaps," Mercer said to himself, running through his mental checklist.

"Tower, Swift 22 turning final."

The pavement rose to meet the descending craft and pilot Mercer applied a gentle back-pressure on the stick to flare the ship onto a cushion of air. He reduced power, and the craft gently touched solid ground for the first time in more than fifteen hours.

Meanwhile, in the hangar area, the men of Pogo flight were already winding down their engines and preparing to dismount their ships. Tired pilots, their muscles aching in their clammy-wet flight suits, made final equipment checks as the ground crew chiefs connected the land-communication wires and landing gear safety pins on the jets. Elsewhere, the pilots and crew from Atlas flight were already filing into the intelligence briefing vault for the mandatory post-flight debriefing. Fatigue, tension and uncertainty were clearly visible on their faces.

"Did anyone see anything of One-Three?" several squadron members asked each other in the gathering group. The missing pilot, Luis Sanchez, was a squadron favorite. His back-seater, a "newbie" from Texas named Paul Barker, had barely introduced himself to the other pilots before the mission had begun.

"No, we were three ships ahead. I saw a lot of flak and a couple of explosions, but nothing in mid-air," one pilot answered.

"We were over the target just ahead of them," another offered, his eyes watering from fatigue and the growing sense that good friends had died that day. "And when we got out over the river, I looked back and saw a big yellow and red flash, but I didn't know if it was a late bomb or one that hung up and didn't release or what."

"Yeah," the first pilot continued, "there were a lot of audible SAM warnings about then. I guess the Navy didn't get all of them. Maybe an SA-2 hit 'em or something." Several in the group shot angry glances at the speaker who had dared suggest the unthinkable.

Another in the squadron asked, "Did anyone spot chutes, or maybe hear a Mayday?"

Lieutenant Colonel Riordan quickly interrupted. "No one knows for sure, fellas. But we're reporting them as missing in action…. Look, they could have landed at an alternate site; they could have had radio trouble. I have no idea, and neither do you. Hell, if they're down, I don't know if they took a SAM up the tailpipe, ground fire or they flew into the ground by themselves. Their LANTIRN pod might have gone haywire on the egress, who knows? It's just too early to speculate. But we'll pass along any news we get to you as soon as possible. We still have some tankers inbound. We'll see if they have anything."

Those in the debriefing room sat silently. Lt Col Riordan then introduced the debriefing team from Intel/Ops. Those people, in turn, broke the flight crews into small teams to record every detail of the completed missions that their tired brains could remember. After ninety grueling minutes of intense questioning, the sessions ended. There was little else to say and nothing more to do than wait.

Outside the confines of the debriefing building, the mid-morning hues were ablaze, a colorful duel between earth and sky. Earlier, the dawn had broken like any other morning, but none of the tired aviators thought they would ever take another sunrise for granted. The airborne warriors had taken and passed the test of live combat; having survived, none of their lives would be the same again. Every day from this moment forward would be treasured.

Twenty minutes after landing, Jack Kilrain gathered his pilots around him.

"Guys," Kilrain began. "You flew a hell of a mission. I'm damn proud of you and you should be of yourselves." Kilrain averted his eyes momentarily.

"It looks like we lost Atlas 13. No other offsite landings by anyone. The Navy confirms a midair hit on an F-15. No word on crew egress. We just don't know...but it doesn't look good."

As he surveyed his combat-weary men, the general knew only too well that more good men like Luis Sanchez would die in battle. Kilrain could, for the moment, only concentrate on the living. He ordered the squadron to their makeshift dorm rooms for a meal, hot shower and crew rest.

"Next situation briefing at 1930 hours. That's all."

Riordan dismissed the group as Kilrain plopped down in an empty chair, slowly rubbing his head.

There was always a price for freedom, Kilrain knew. "Why," he asked himself, "did the best and brightest young men have to be the ones sacrificed?" The same questions he'd first asked during the Gulf War echoed in Kilrain's tired brain. He closed his eyes and breathed deeply. Who else would pay for the maniacal actions of these terrorists? Kilrain knew there would be more deaths before it was all over.

JONATHAN BRUCE

18 November
0900 hours
Terrorist Training Compound
Abu Du'an, Syria

The sun was well into the sky over the shattered remains of the terrorist complex. After removing the mangled remains of a faithful follower, a pair of dirty hands uncovered a shock of blood-matted blonde hair.

"This one's alive," a medical orderly shouted in Arabic to a nearby stretcher-bearer.

Petra Voss hung limp in her rescuer's arms as the ambulance team brushed the blood, sand and dirt from her nose and mouth. One man poured water over her face in an attempt to revive her. She would not regain consciousness for another three days.

Quomuz hadn't been able to think in the hours since the attack. Although his religion forbade the use of tobacco, he had grown accustomed to its taste. Quomuz slouched against the remains of the barracks and found a broken cigarette in his shirt pocket. He had no matches so he held the limp paper in his lips as he picked the dirt from an oozing wound on his right leg. Broken glass or metal, he guessed, in a state of semi-shock. His breathing was shallow and quick. His head hurt and a small rivulet of blood had dried on his neck, evidence of the punctured eardrum he'd suffered from the force of the blasts. An empty AK-47 lay in the dust beside him.

The hardened terrorist had never been so shaken in his entire life.

His eyes lifted and spotted a sandaled foot hanging limply from a broken leg beneath a mountain of cinder block rubble. Small fires still burned around what was left of the compound. In what had been the mess hall several yards distant, an ambulance crew covered the bodies of two men with a canvas tarp. Syrian soldiers now picked their way through the rubble and began to carry the dead away on canvas stretchers. Near the camp command post, a German dressed in a western-style business suit surveyed the damage then took some photographs before returning to his car.

A dog trotted by the slumping Quomuz, paused, sniffed at the motionless man, and then sauntered away. The Palestinian's eyes sank but did not close.

18 November
1130 hours
Military Family Housing, RAF Lakenheath, UK

Young Tyler Mercer slept like the angel he was. His mother leaned quietly against the bedroom door, and gazed at her four-year-old son. The boy had tired very quickly after returning from morning kindergarten, and had dozed off to dreamland on his fluffy new bedspread, replete with designs of teddy bears flying antique biplanes that were dropping "I Love You" hearts. Tyler loved everything about airplanes, and he wanted to be a pilot just like his daddy. But his mother's eyes were now red from the tears that had come shortly after Tyler dozed off.

Carrie Mercer had lost all accounting of time, with no idea how long she had stood there, watching the boy. A cold chill made her shudder and her stomach began to churn. The emotions and imagined horrors of life without her husband overwhelmed her as she slowly sank to the floor. "God..." Carrie thought as she cried softly, "How would I live without him? Damn the Air Force and damn you, Damian Mercer. You could have been killed! Don't you know how much we love you and need you?"

It had been four hours since she'd risen for breakfast and turned on the BBC in the kitchen and heard the news of the Syrian raids. Then the phone had rung. It was another pilot's wife.

"Jesus, Carrie!" the woman had exclaimed, "Did Damian go? Pete didn't tell me anything...Damn him. I had no idea...I thought it was just another damned exercise."

"I don't know," retorted the honest, but programmed answer of an officer's wife about matters operational. Mercer, like all the others involved, hadn't violated the secrecy order about the mission. Not that the squadron wives posed a security risk, but orders were orders. "Besides," the husbands always agreed, "it was best not to worry them." But the women had a different opinion. "And," the husbands also knew, "they always figured it out anyway."

Just as Carrie Mercer did: unsure, scared, and asking herself a hundred "What if's?" Carrie watched her sleeping son roll to the other side of the bed.

A fresh tear and then several more began to flow from the young woman's eyes, as she sat feeling very much alone on the bedroom floor. She set her coffee cup on the desk and slowly, instinctively, crept to her son's side. Her arms found his neck and she hugged him as she had never hugged him before. She buried her face in the back of his neck and her tears moistened his little shoulders; he began to awaken.

"Hi, Mom..." Tyler said, turning happily to his mother. The boy paused, noticing the sadness in the woman's eyes and asked, "Mom, are you OK?"

A double ring from the British telephone interrupted the quiet moment between mother and son, and Carrie instinctively reached to wipe the moisture from her face.

"Hey, hon!" came a familiar voice on the other end of the line. "Hey, you...it's me, your flyboy!"

Carrie, her heart now racing, held the heavy antiquated receiver hard against her ear. The static on the line wasn't enough to mask her beloved Damian's voice and warm joy filled her being at the first concrete proof that her husband was alive and well.

"Baby...Damian, are you OK?" Carrie breathlessly asked, wiping away a tear with the back of her hand and sniffling.

"I'm fine, sweetheart; I'm all in one piece," he tried to sound cheerful.

"How was it? Were you...?"

"Scared? Yeah, scared shitless! But don't tell anyone."

Carrie tried to laugh, amused at her man's childlike ego. "OK. Our secret.... What about Zach? He's OK?"

"Ha! The S.O.B.'s already asleep."

"Everyone else OK? Jenn P. called right after the story was on TV."

Mercer paused. He wasn't supposed to tell his wife anything about the mission, a rule most flyers observed in the breach. "Um...no, honey. One crew missing.... but nobody knows for sure."

The pilot's wife drew a quick breath. "It isn't Coleman, is it? Oh, God. Katie's expecting their second...They just...."

"No, no. It's Lew Sanchez, but..."

"Oh, God...." she said slowly. Carrie Mercer closed her eyes as a new tear began to well for an old friend.

Damian Mercer tried to tell his wife that Sanchez could be safe, that he could be anywhere; that no news could be good news...but Carrie Mercer's intuition told her differently.

"Honey, I gotta go," Mercer said, "Guys are lined up here to call. The colonel made us turn in our cell phones before we departed Lakenheath." He tried to think of words to reassure her, but what words could? Instead, he told Carrie he loved her and Tyler. She replied, "I love you, too, so take care of yourself for me, OK?" Noisy static was the only reply as the connection was severed.

Carrie Mercer hung up the receiver.

"Mom," asked young Tyler, who had listened to

the conversation, "was that Dad?

"Uh huh, sweetheart. He said to tell you he loves you," Carrie replied.

A silly grin just like his Dad's appeared as Tyler said, "I love him, too." His mother hugged him so hard that he squeaked.

"Not so hard, Mom. I might break."

18 November
1645 hours
Washington, DC

The hot glare of a dozen Klieg lights bathed Senator Ann Ruston-Brand as the network production assistant straightened the lavaliere microphone on the politician's neatly-tailored blue dress.

"Thirty seconds to air," came a voice from the darkened backset area, as the production assistant took one last look at Ruston-Brand's appearance and then scampered off the set.

"OK, Senator?" asked the NBC Capitol Hill correspondent, Jon-James Irwin.

"Ready!" came the confident, eager reply from the two-term Democrat from Michigan.

"Gonna start with the Pentagon and the briefing, then to you for re-ax. OK with you?"

"Fine," Ruston-Brand said, offering a practiced smile to the camera.

"Seven seconds to air..." came the director's distant voice. "Cut to net ID...then four, three, two, one...take audio and logo. Camera 2 ready, one stand-by...and roll tape...."

A familiar voice-over announced.

"We interrupt regular programming with this Special Report from NBC News. Reporting live from Washington, NBC News correspondent Jon-James Irwin."

"Good afternoon. This is Jon-James Irwin. A night of air-war in the Gulf...as American planes conducted raids on key terrorist infrastructure in Northern Syria. These attacks, apparently in response to the terrorist bombing in New York, began, we're told, at 7:30 p.m. last night Eastern Standard Time -- about 3:30 a.m. Middle Eastern Time."

"Pentagon sources confirmed that U.S. Naval and Air Forces attacked what is described as an important terrorist headquarters in Syria -- several suspected terrorist training compounds and radar installations. We go now to the Pentagon where NBC correspondent Caitland Myers is standing by, Caitland?"

"Jon, I'm in the Pentagon's press briefing room where we've just been told by Air Force Chief of Staff, General Barton Hatfield, that approximately twenty Air Force F-15 bombers, together with another forty Navy aircraft, have attacked key al Qaeda installations in Syria. General Hatfield's remarks came only moments after State Department officials announced that part of the bombing was an effort to destroy terrorist support facilities, which may be linked to terrorist attacks against the

United States and Israel."

"NBC News has learned that the State Department has also confirmed that the actions were unilateral American efforts, and confirmed that those Air Force planes had come from several U.S. air bases in Europe. Pentagon sources tell NBC News that the Air Force planes may have come from either Italy or Germany. One source told me, Jon, that several U.S. warplanes were lost."

"General Hatfield would not confirm those reports, adding only that all crews had not yet reported in, and that final word on the raid would come only after all American personnel were accounted for. General Hatfield also refused to say whether any U.S. military women were involved in combat operations."

"That's the latest from the Pentagon, Jon. We're waiting for a complete briefing within the hour on all aspects of the attack, and I'll be standing by."

"Caitland Myers, NBC News, the Pentagon."

"Thanks Caitland." Jon Irwin said, turning toward Camera Two.

"With me now, for reaction to the U.S. raid, is Senator Ann Ruston-Brand of Michigan, a junior member of the Senate Armed Services Committee and an outspoken critic of the President's war on terror.

"Senator Ruston-Brand, good evening. An NBC News tele-poll taken just yesterday indicated that eighty-seven percent of the American people thought some form of military reprisal would be appropriate. I'd like your reaction to today's attack. But first, did the President confer with you before ordering this attack on terrorists in Syria?"

"Thank you, Jon, and no, the answer is 'no.' The President did not confer with either me or any other member of the Senate Select Committee on the Status of Women and Minorities in the Military before he undertook this unannounced action, now expanding "his" war against Syria. If, as the President says, this war is about terrorism, then I demand that he explain why he has expanded the conflict to northern Syria. We're not at war with these people, Jon."

The law maker went on, forcefully.

"I am, to say the least, shocked that the administration has undertaken this potentially explosive action. We cannot understand why the administration now threatens to risk war and invite terrorism when a negotiated resolution with the Syrians would have been more prudent."

Irwin interrupted. "But Senator, isn't the President -- as Commander-in-Chief -- entitled to order forces into combat in time of war as he sees fit if he perceives a threat to the nation?"

"Well, technically, perhaps." Ruston-Brand snapped. "But what you need to understand, and the American people must appreciate, is that American service personnel were put at risk by this operation. We have to ask ourselves, 'Is this what we want our Armed Forces doing?' Now that the President has committed forces to the area, I'll be calling for legislation under the War Powers Act forcing him to publicly declare his intentions in the region before taking further similar action. We simply have no proof that Syrians were involved in supporting terrorism. Clearly this illegal attack is all about oil."

The Senator continued. "In fact, that part of Syria is primarily an agricultural region with little in the way of military capability. I am just worried that this action might cause further retaliation against us from around the world, when the whole matter could have been avoided by skillful diplomacy."

"Senator Ruston-Brand, the President and Secretary of State announced only last week that any reprisal would be justified, since our attacks could be launched against the source of state-sponsored terrorism. Do you dispute that many civilians became targets themselves in Israel and the United States? Doesn't the President have the right to act when American lives and interests are at stake?"

"I am not convinced American interests ARE at stake, Jon. After all, no one has any proof that Syria is guilty of sponsoring any international terrorist activity. I'm still not convinced this war isn't about American oil interests!" Ruston-Brand said, pointedly raising her eyebrows into the camera.

"The Administration had better be explaining why we continue to believe we have to be the world's policeman. Wouldn't it be better if we employed those resources here at home, where there is so much to be done? Why aren't our soldiers being used to rebuild America's infrastructure?"

JANUARY

A cadre of young officers walked amidst the thirty or more conscripts who labored to move barrels and crates from the two oversized freight-haulers, newly arrived from the east. Four metric tons of material and supplies had to be quickly opened and hidden, lest prying eyes from above learn clues about the secret.

The men moved awkwardly in their gray-green synthetic suits, and the oversized rubber gloves they wore made handling the weight more difficult.

The soldiers, calling instructions to one another

through protective masks, loaded the material onto small carts and scurried them into the warehouses. Other men inside then began the process of draining the contents of the yellow, blue and green plastic drums into plain black metal drums marked "Heavy Lubricating Oil," while other soldiers repacked the black drums into freshly-stenciled wooden crates marked "Agricultural Fertilizer."

"We've only another twenty minutes before the satellites can see us," a junior officer called out. "Finish that last lot and move those trucks. Hurry!"

Eleven thousand meters overhead, a trio of Syrian MiG-29's circled, providing cover in the event of an unwanted intrusion by the Israelis or the bothersome Americans.

This was the last such shipment the Syrians would receive from their allies.

As the last barrels were unloaded and stored, the ungainly fuselage of a nearby MI-8 lifted from the ground. Inside, a Syrian colonel looked at his Palestinian guest, Mustafa Quomuz, and smiled. "We will ensure a small quantity is safely prepared for shipment as you requested, old friend. Let us hope it serves you well."

Quomuz answered, "And you have made arrangements to ship these materials to the port quickly?"

The colonel nodded, "At night, just as we always have. And the warheads; just as you requested. The other shipments have arrived safely in Africa?"

Quomuz only smiled.

11 January
1700 hours
Leonardo Da Vinci International Airport, Rome

"Rome Center. Libyan Arab People's flight nine-zero-seven requesting instructions and clearance to land," came the transmission, in broken English, from the approaching Russian-built transport plane.

An Italian international approach controller responded in equally troubled English, "Yes, flight nine-zero-seven come left to seven-zero degrees and maintain one-zero thousand."

"OK, Rome Center."

On the tarmac, over three thousand meters below and ten kilometers distant, six Italian Air Force policemen and their officer in charge, a young lieutenant, stood at ease awaiting the arrival of their celebrated American guest. The setting sun sparkled sharply from the highly polished brass work on their uniforms. Each man's dark blue jacket and trousers looked tidy and pressed. Their white leather belts, holsters, and leggings were crisp from hours of polishing and buffing. "Even in January, it is hot in these wool uniforms," one of the men complained silently to himself. It had been a cool day, he thought, but even at sunset the uniform was uncomfortable.

Exhaust from a just-departed jet hung heavily in the air and made breathing difficult.

The roar from a passing Lufthansa flight just in from Munich blocked out other noises, as the honor guardsmen looked up and shielded their eyes against the setting sun, searching the sky for the plane inbound from Tripoli. Above, as the Libyan crew lowered the giant plane's landing gear, a "whoosh" of cool air filled the cargo bay. Those in the rear of the plane tried to free their eardrums of the pain brought on by the pressure change. But Luis Sanchez didn't notice. His head barely moved. The mild buffeting from the drag of the wheels against the rushing slipstream only caused the young captain's head to move slightly. A lock of his black hair fell gently out of place.

In a few days, Luis' mother would cry when she saw her son, her Nino, again. She would, like all mothers of soldiers, see not the man in the neatly pressed and medaled uniform. Rather, she would see the happy face of her youngest son again; the boy with laughter in his eyes and mischief in his heart...

The giant transport came into view and seemed to hang lazily in the sky to those watching from the ground. How large and ungainly the aircraft seemed. "How can it fly with such apparent ease?" one of the young Italian enlisted men wondered aloud. Another of the honor guard pointed at the approaching giant, and told his comrades how his older brother was learning to fly jets, too.

Just then, two official Vatican limousines drew near. The darkly shaded windows on the long, black Mercedes Papal State vehicles concealed the identities of their occupants. The cars then pulled to a

stop and a young black-robed priest stepped purposefully from the front of each vehicle. One of the
young clerics opened the rear door of the lead car,
and out stepped an older, gray-haired monsignor.
The older man spoke quietly to his junior and gestured broadly with his left hand.

Monsignor Enrique Alvarez squinted into the
setting sun and sniffed at the fumes of jet fuel that
permeated the evening air. At sixty, the Monsignor
was one of the top five or ten Vatican officials assigned to the diplomatic corps. His full, thick salt
and pepper hair and deeply tanned skin made him
look like a rich Mediterranean jet setter rather than
a man who had spent forty years cloistered in a
priest's robes. His round face was thinly etched at
the eyes, giving him a well-deserved aura of wisdom. He had been selected for this delicate diplomatic mission over his strong objection.

First, he personally loathed the Libyan regime,
even though that country had recently renounced
terrorism. He feared that even his well-practiced
veneer of diplomacy could not hide that fact. Second, he, like his young American guest, was Puerto
Rican. "This one is a little too close to my heart," he
had protested. But Cardinal O'Banion had refused
to listen. "Enrique," the Chief of Vatican Diplomatic Services offered evenly, "Our most seasoned
foreign affairs officer must receive the boy's body.
Our friends in the American State Department insist
that they will have no public role in the receipt of
the coffin from the Libyans. They want no part of

whatever public relations coup the Libyan government hopes to stage. I then told them that since the boy was a military officer, it would be fitting that at least one Department of Defense official be on hand when the Libyan plane arrives. But Secretary Klein, who is an old friend of yours, says he's worried about security and the chance of violence." The senior papal statesman continued, "The Americans do not wish to be perceived as conciliatory in any way to the madman's amateurish publicity ploy. And finally, Enrique..."

Alvarez knew what was coming, so he politely finished his long-time colleague's sentence with a slightly cynical smile. "Yes, and finally Enrique...you, too, are of the same blood as the captain. Your presence will be of great comfort to the boy's mother and father..."

"Yes," the cardinal from Dublin nodded, grasping Alvarez's upper arm, "you understand our wishes."

Alvarez cast his eyes quickly to the heavens and sighed. He was sorry he'd missed a chance to see his old friend, Eldon Klein.

Both men shared a quiet laugh as the Irishman gently slid his hand up to the monsignor's shoulder. "We toil in the vineyard, my son...." he offered, recalling a bit of old office humor between the two.

The roar of a British Airways jet bound for Frankfurt returned Monsignor Alvarez to the present. Stretching his sturdy, athletic frame, he turned and stepped back into the limousine. Inside its quiet luxury he picked up a cellular telephone and began to speak. Meanwhile, the two younger priests, assistants to the Monsignor, spoke in rapid tones and motioned and gestured quickly. Although the Italian honor guard members couldn't hear the conversation, each knew these were no ordinary priests from Vatican City. The red sash around the older man's solid waist told the guardsmen that these were important men.

One of the two young priests then walked briskly to the guardsmen and asked who the officer in charge was. The young lieutenant stepped forward and offered a salute to the clergyman. The priest nodded his acknowledgment of the officer's salute and pointed to the press gallery fifty yards distant, then said, "You will please do your work quickly, Lieutenant. Please, we wish to avoid..."

Just then a third vehicle joined the already-parked limousines. A dark green hearse with gold lettering on the tailgate, "S.V. Castiglione," rolled up. The driver pulled into line with the other cars. A portly older man rolled from behind the wheel and a younger but equally rotund man appeared from the right. The older man mopped his brow with a handkerchief he had pulled from his right hip pocket as the young priest and the Italian lieutenant approached.

"You are Senior Castiglione?" the priest inquired, offering his hand.

"I am, Father. And this is my son who assists

me," came the reply and a sweaty palm in return.

"You are familiar then with what we will do today, eh?"

"Yes, Father. We understand that there will be a body brought here. We are to process it through customs as quickly as possible and prepare it for transfer to the United States. We have done this several times in the past..."

But the young priest interrupted. "And there are to be no contacts with the news media. The American government is especially anxious that no photographs of the body appear on television or in the newspaper. Please be quick and discreet, Senior Castiglione."

"We understand completely, Father. Please assure the Monsignor that all will be handled as we discussed and thank him for the generous fee."

"You may thank the American embassy for the generosity," the priest said with a wry smile. The older Castiglione looked to the ground with a twinkle in his eye as the young Vatican diplomat turned to attend the Monsignor.

"Marco," the elder Castiglione barked to his son, "there is a grease smudge on the hearse. You will see to it now, eh?"

"Libyan People's Flight nine-zero-seven stay on two-seven-zero and descend to two thousand for final approach."

"OK Rome Center. Two thousand for final," responded the pilot, a Libyan Air Force major. The nearly three-hour flight from Tripoli was almost over. Below and behind the flight deck, the cargo bay lights revealed a serene strength about the young American's face. He had a firm jaw-line and olive skin, and a bushy black mustache complemented his eyes--the eyes which had claimed so many young women--the eyes that had always appeared to dream. A red flight scarf wrapped tightly at his throat was neatly tucked into his green flight suit. A small tuft of chest hair poked from beneath the zipper not fully closed to his throat.

His hands lay motionless at his sides. He had been not quite six feet and his sturdy thighs, made strong by so many years playing at his passion, baseball, still strained against his uniform. A glint of light reflected from the new shine on the toes of his tightly laced flight boots. A small pocket of air bounced the plane and the captain's left foot swayed lazily to the right.

The transport pilot could now see the east end of the international runway drifting toward him. He lowered the giant wing flaps to help keep the plane afloat as it slowly drifted toward earth.

"Rome Center, Libyan People's flight nine-zero-seven on final and landing please."

"Libyan People's nine-zero-seven cleared to land. Crosswinds north at ten knots."

"Rome Center, ten knots, yes, okay."

The Libyan co-pilot began calling a checklist of pre-landing instructions. The pilot called over the plane's intercom to the security personnel in the bay below. In a quick Arabic military voice, the pilot ordered his passengers to prepare for landing. And, as a cynical afterthought, he added, "Please see that our American passenger is comfortable!"

Below in the cargo bay, two Libyan Army officers, a man known to them as Mustafa, and a German exchanged glances and a smile. One of the men and the man named Mustafa walked to where Captain Sanchez lay. The Palestinian smiled in contempt at the American aviator and said, loudly enough for his compatriots to hear, "Your soul burns in Hell, dog. But you will serve Allah and our purpose very well, indeed. God is great." And then, before turning away with a sneer, he spat in the young officer's face. Saying no more, the colonel placed his hands atop the heavy bronze lid and sealed the American's coffin against the light.

Puffs of white smoke and an audible screech of rubber against concrete marked the Libyan transport's return to earth. The big jet's nose wheels touched down just as the pilot called for reverse thrust on the engines and, with the help of his co-pilot, pressed both feet against the braking pedals beneath the cluttered instrument panel.

As the giant, bulky transport began to decelerate, the tower called taxi instructions. "Libyan People's nine-zero-seven turn left onto taxiway six west and proceed as ground control directs."

"OK, Rome Center," came the reply from the cockpit.

The Castiglione undertakers, the Italian guards and their Vatican supervisors watched from the isolated ramp as the aircraft lumbered toward a slow turn. The distinctive green rectangle that was the Libyan national flag came into clear view on the craft's four-story "T" tail. It had been many years since a plane of this size from that nation had landed in Italy.

A single blue light flashed from atop the ground control truck as it led the giant jet toward its pre-planned stop far from the main terminal. The following jet dwarfed the small truck.

As the plane slowed and lurched to a halt, the roar from the jet engines subsided into a high-pitched whine. As each of the engines lost power, the whine gave way to a hiss and soon, the only noises within the hearing of the honor guard were those from the other airliners on the runways nearby. The Italian lieutenant called his charges to attention with a practiced cadence as the three Vatican envoys stood by.

After the airport ground crews placed landing chocks in front of and behind the plane's massive rubber tires, the Libyan crew inside activated the hydraulic lifts to open the cargo door at the craft's rear. A passenger door, too, was opened, well below and behind the flight deck on the port side of the craft.

A lone figure, the Libyan pilot, clad in a khaki flight suit, carefully descended the ladder toward the black pavement. He positioned and re-positioned his flight cap and fixed his teardrop shaped aviator's sunglasses. The older priest and the monsignor walked toward the Arab visitor. He extended his right hand and, over the nearing roar of a jet ready for takeoff, said to the pilot, "I am Monsignor Enrique Alvarez, emissary of His Holiness, Pope Benedict. I believe you were instructed that I would meet you here..." The pilot, per earlier instructions, refused the envoy's handshake.

Unflappable, the Monsignor, a veteran of countless diplomatic missions, continued, "I am ready to receive the remains of the American Air Force Captain Luis Sanchez. I am to take the boy home to our country, Puerto Rico."

The Libyan, under orders to so respond, unfolded a typewritten page and began to read, "God is great. His servant Colonel Muammar Quaddafi returns Captain Sanchez as a gesture of good will from the Socialist People's Libyan Arab Jamahiriya and the people of Syria."

The pilot continued his speech to the audience of one, "You will tell the world that the Arab people, who suffered death and misery at the hand of the American pirates and their Israeli masters, are an honorable people and are always of good will and peace. The brotherhood Arab peoples return to the attackers one of their sons..."

Monsignor Alvarez's face revealed none of the contempt he felt as he listened patiently, as he had done so many times before to so many other martinets.

"You will tell the world how the peace-loving Arab people have been attacked by unholy invaders.

But as the Koran foretold, we shall not be vengeful, for that is Allah's right and His will. And we His people are a people who make this gesture to even our assassins. God is great."

Smiling, the Monsignor folded his hands below his waist. He turned and nodded to the younger priest nearest to him. The younger cleric, in turn, spoke quickly to the Italian lieutenant.

The military escort team snapped to attention at the lieutenant's command. Then, on the lieutenant's command, they formed two rows of three and marched in lock step, to the rear of the aircraft. As the honor guard approached the rear of the plane, the flight crew finished the job of lowering the cargo ramp.

The monsignor and the two junior priests joined the honor guard at the craft's rear. Looking up into the hold, Alvarez saw a complement of four men: two Arabic men in military dress, another in civilian clothing and a slender Caucasian also in western-style clothing. As the diplomat raised a hand to his eyes to shield himself from the setting sun, the fourth man, the Caucasian, turned quickly and disappeared into the darkness of the cargo hold.

"How odd," Alvarez noted to himself. "I wasn't aware so many others would be aboard the flight..."

The monsignor's attentions quickly turned to the honor guard as the airmen took up positions at the end of the ramp. Two uniformed Libyan officers wheeled the casket down the incline toward the waiting pallbearers. The lieutenant called the formation to attention and ordered "Salute." Two parallel rows of white gloves snapped briskly. The officer then called "Order arms," and the gloved hands snapped down as quickly as they had ascended.

The Libyan officers stopped and, with a foot brake, ensured the casket would roll no further. Turning, the pair then casually sauntered back up the ramp and disappeared into the belly of the airplane. On his own command, the Italian officer and a sergeant quickly stepped forward and faced the container. The lieutenant nodded to the sergeant, who unfurled an American flag and, handing one end to his commander, began to carefully drape it over the heavy bronze lid. A gentle breeze ruffled one end of the flag as the lieutenant again called for a salute out of respect for a man he had never met.

In the distance, the lenses on two score video cameras racked in tight zoom to capture the moment. All the world's major television news operations were on hand. It was newsworthy enough that the Syrians had unexpectedly returned the body of an American flyer lost not more than two months before, but the fact that no American official would be on hand to receive the body made this front-page, lead story news. Four Carbinieri strained to hold back the throng of more than eighty journalists and cameramen seeking a better view of the event. Manufactured or not, this was great drama. The television networks called it news.

The United States Department of State had two days before it dismissed the combined Syrian-

Libyan gesture as a publicity ploy -- a vain and futile play for airtime on the world's newscasts. The State Department was right about the publicity ploy, but mistaken about the futility of the gesture.

As the Italian honor guard gently raised the coffin from the trolley, both Castigliones opened the double doors of the hearse and extended the brightly polished aluminum bier to accommodate the heavy bronze case. A small gust of wind toyed with the flag, but the lieutenant smoothed the colors with his white-gloved hand. The complement of airmen again raised the coffin and slid it onto the metal framework and into the hearse. The older Castiglione then gently closed the hearse doors behind.

Then, the Libyan pilot, again under orders, walked from the shadow of the mammoth plane toward the hastily assembled press area and, unfolding his typewritten script, began to read, "God is great. His servant, Colonel Muammar..."

As the media recorded each of the Libyan's tortured English words, Monsignor Alvarez settled himself into the back seat of his black limousine. Glancing at the crowd of reporters, he allowed himself a smile, and said to no one else, "At least the boy will have a decent Catholic burial...."

The three-car motorcade turned a wide semicircle around the press area and headed toward a gate at one end of the runway, past runway lights, radar antennae, and fences for the five-minute drive to the immigration and customs facility. Two Italian policemen waved the limousines past the chain-link gate and quickly locked it after the cars had passed. As the entourage turned onto a secondary road, two marked police vehicles took up positions, front and rear, in escort formation. Television news cameras tried to focus on the procession, but it quickly disappeared behind the huge noise-abatement fences at runway's end.

As had been prearranged, the five cars now headed for an unmarked concrete building adjacent to one branch of the airport's fire protection services. There, they would meet a physician from the Italian Department of Immigration and Health Services. That doctor would perform an examination of the body and clear it for entrance into Italy and also approve its exit to the United States.

The lead police car pulled alongside the cream-colored, windowless morgue as the last rays of sunlight shimmered from atop its tile roof. The sun was now almost halfway below the horizon. It would be dark in another hour. The other four cars in the procession now pulled into neat, parallel formation, usurped parking spaces, and stopped their engines. One of the police officers commented to another that the hearse was the largest one he had ever seen. In the meantime, another policeman stepped quickly into the building and reappeared with the government coroner, a Pakistani, Dr. Rashid.

"I am Monsignor Alvarez," the diplomat introduced himself, still walking to join the doctor and the officer. "We are ready, sir, if you are."

"Yes," Dr. Rashid replied, "but will an American physician join us?"

"No, Doctor. The Americans do not wish to interfere with Italian customs procedures. They only ask that you clear the body for entry and exit as quickly as possible. I am sure that the Americans will have ample opportunity to examine the young man. But that may be some time, and there are not sufficient facilities for the Americans to conduct an autopsy at their embassy. They do not wish to delay a burial by taking the body to Germany where they do have such facilities. So, it has been requested of the government that you perform an autopsy. I do ask, informally, Doctor, that you do so and report your findings only to me."

"Yes, well...then, but I will not be able to release the body until the morning. I will be alone here, until my orderly arrives at midnight."

"Very well, Doctor," Alvarez concluded. "Please contact me when we may make a transfer to the Americans. My assistant, Father Torcelli, has a uniform for the young man. Please have your staff dress him."

As the physician and the monsignor completed the details, Castiglione and son and two policemen busied themselves by hoisting the heavy bronze coffin onto an elevated cart. The younger mortician leaned a broad shoulder into the coffin and strained to make the heavy container roll. His father, aided by one of the young priests, opened a set of double doors leading to an anteroom adjacent to the autopsy chamber. The younger Castiglione rolled the bier up the uneven concrete ramp into the anteroom, through another set of double doors and into the autopsy room as the pair of Vatican limousines slowly pulled away and into the night.

Doctor Rashid followed the undertaker into the morgue. Because his assistant would not arrive for several hours, he asked the younger Castiglione to help him place the body on the examining table. The mortician complied. He quickly lifted the bronze lid and slid his hands under the young man's shoulders. With the doctor's help, they carefully lifted the body of Captain Luis Sanchez.

January 11
2300 hours
Feltwell, England

Two Americans and their wives slumped comfortably in the corner booth near the bar at the Three Bells pub. Both smiled contentedly as the ladies complained in mock seriousness about fighter pilots being unable to hold their liquor. One of the pilots yelled for another round, as the innkeeper shouted back, "Its last call, gentlemen and ladies. Closing time...besides, you'll want to be heading home instead of ordering another pint!" But the rotund, jovial man behind the bar reached for two clean glasses and began to fill them.

Only a few of the natives were still in the pub

when the barkeep called "Drink up!" The good-natured but rowdy Americans had again disrupted the quiet and reflective atmosphere of the pub and sent the locals home to an early bedtime. When the Yanks gathered, the townsfolk agreed, it was better to let them have the run of the place than to try to quiet them. Seldom did any furniture get broken-- but when American fighter pilots and their ladies congregated, they were, in the words of the locals, "apt to go a bit over the top." People all over East Anglia knew the Three Bells was an American gathering place on Saturday nights. Older locals stayed away, opting for more sedate, less "American" surroundings. Younger people, especially younger women, made a regular Saturday night trek to the pub in hopes of finding a dashing aviator for courting.

It was like any other Saturday night and as was their custom since the flying days of World War II, the American pilots and their women gathered in the pub in small huddles of six or eight to relive the week's flying. Most of the flyers wore their one-piece zippered flight suits, "green bags" they called them. Their women dressed in the standard "uniform" of a fighter pilot's consort: provocative tight denims or short skirts with high heels.

A slender, long-haired woman was as much a part of the pilot's equipment as was his helmet and flight suit.

A warm odor of hot cooking grease wafted in from the kitchen and mixed with a hint of tobacco and the musty smell of old fires from the hearth. Those aromas blended with the memories of countless whiskies, ales, and bitters to complete the cozy atmosphere for another party at the Bells. Times were good when the squadron gathered. The talk got louder and bolder as the evening hours wore on, with each pilot bragging on himself until the others interrupted with a raucous and good-hearted cry of "Bullshit!" Then the group would hoist their mugs, as another pilot would spin his tale of heroism in the wild blue yonder! Brave young men so full of life. They were indestructible, and they told themselves they would live forever. Such evenings were the stuff of memories.

Not that General Kilrain's flyers needed an excuse to celebrate, but tonight was special and melancholy. Captain Luis Sanchez was coming home. Most of the pilots in the squadron had known and flown with Sanchez. The deaths of both Sanchez and Barker had been a blow to the "Eagle drivers" of the 48th Fighter Wing. But that was fourteen months ago, during a mission that almost no one mentioned these days. Tonight, the only memories were the good ones. The bar talk about Sanchez was irreverent and funny. About the time he had thrown up on himself during a flight, about the women he had squired, and about his beloved MG Midget. Tonight was a night Sanchez would have loved.

Happy talk, good beer and pretty women.

The few locals who had chosen to remain among the Americans at the Bells didn't mind the din. In many ways, living with the Americans was a source of amusement for the villagers of Feltwell. Their lives were generally so staid, so regular, so very British. Certainty and predictability were the mainstays of life at nearby Lakenheath, just as they were in any one of a hundred such villages that dotted the coastlands of East Anglia. Its few dozen shops of green grocers and ironmongers surrounded the imposing square flint work of the town's centerpiece, the Church of England. There were fish and chips stalls and a pub or two. And most of her people seldom traveled more than a few pastures and fields from the confines of the village. Many saw little reason to wander elsewhere. All that a sturdy East Anglian ever needed was right there along the High Street or near the village green.

Into the midst of the English pastoral tranquility were thrown rowdy, raucous, vivacious young colonials - much as their grandfathers had been in the world's last full war in the forties. The mix made for an interesting cultural clash.

Americans and Englishmen, so very different despite the common heritage and mother tongue. Yet each was amused and bewildered by the other. Most of the Americans who flew those big, noisy jets were a source of constant amazement to the British. The Americans, it had always seemed to the villagers, were always so full of life and hope and promise. They were viewed as overgrown, overindulged children. The townspeople, the Americans said, were odd: at once quaint and punk, proper and coarse.

And the warm beer; or more precisely, beer served at room temperature-- well, that took some getting used to. "But one could," a seasoned navigator pronounced, "with practice," as the barkeep served up the last round of the evening.

No one particularly noticed when Tracie Pruett walked into the pub. The small gaggles of Americans were engrossed in their own conversations and good liquor and did not notice the entry of another pair of shapely legs and high heels beneath a too-short black leather skirt. Her blonde hair, with a whisper of strawberry hue, was cut close, almost in a pageboy, and large silver spangles hung from her ears. She looked around the room and found a lone figure sitting at the bar talking with the tavern owner. "This might be interesting," the young woman smiled to herself, and zeroed toward an empty stool near the aviator. Before she could sit down, the clicking of her heels against the stone floor caught Zach Pollard's ear. He turned, his eyes meeting hers. Pollard, caught off guard by her stark, intense beauty, smiled nervously but didn't speak.

Tracie Pruett smiled in return, and then asked the tavern keeper if "A gentleman wouldn't buy a lady a drink on such a cold evening?"

Pollard turned and stammered uneasily, "Uh, yeah, uh, sure. Sit down, OK?" His pilot's mystique and aloofness melted in the face of an attractive woman. Then, with an almost school-boyish grin, he said, "Hi. Uh, my name's Zach. What's yours?"

"My, you're quick with a cheeky line, then, aren't you?" The woman smirked sarcastically. "I thought you Americans were all real ladies' men."

The awkward Pollard averted his eyes and smiled, "Well, I...."

But the young woman interrupted. "My name's Tracie." She extended her slender but firm hand to the man, she continued, "And I'm quite afraid I've run into a spot of trouble with my car. I've just parked it outside. But it won't run. I saw the lights and thought a little warm conversation would help."

Across the room in the corner booth, Carrie Mercer elbowed her slumping husband. "Is that OUR Zach actually talking to a woman? She's cute. Damian, who is she?"

Damian Mercer grinned, and not inconspicuously eyeing the scene at the bar, retorted "I don't know, but I'd better go help him out. You know how slow Zach is when it comes to women. Better let a pro handle this one. You know white men can't...."

Carrie Mercer rolled her eyes and mockingly gestured to the woman, "OK, Superfly, go for it. But how are you going to explain to her why you fall asleep after five minutes?" With that zinger, the two couples erupted in laughter as Carrie Mercer and the other woman at the table swapped high-fives.

"Fighter pilot studs!" The other woman laughed. "Boy, if we'd only known the truth when we picked these two losers up off of that barroom floor..."

Quiet giggles erupted again as Carrie and Damian Mercer exchanged a happy peck on the lips.

Neither couple noticed as a grinning Pollard slipped out of the pub closely behind his new British friend.

As the pub door quietly closed behind Zach Pollard, Damian Mercer ran a playful hand up his wife's skirt. His grinning entreaty was met with a quick jab to the groin from Carrie. Across the room, the newest lieutenant in the squadron was getting a hard education in the pilot's universal game of "crud" at the pool table. Two pairs of pilots took turns trying to sink a colored ball by rolling a cue ball at the colored ball and never letting the white ball stop rolling. All was legal in crud, from body-blocks to profane insults.

Losers buy the bar, laughter all around. Luis Sanchez would have felt right at home.

12 January
0100 hours
Customs Morgue
Leonardo DaVinci International Airport
Rome

The physician pulled the green surgical mask from his face and began to pluck, finger by finger, the soft, latex gloves from his hands. It had taken him most of the evening to complete the autopsy requested by the Vatican. He had worked by himself, slowly and methodically.

When he had finished stitching the last suture, the doctor was tired. He sat down at a folding metal table just beside the cold porcelain-coated slab where Luis Sanchez lay, naked and cold. Reaching for a foam cup, the coroner took a sip of the jasmine tea he had nursed throughout the evening. Finishing the sip, he took fountain pen in hand and began to draft the official cause of the young officer's death. He printed each word, carefully, in English. He did not let the fact that he was angry with this assignment affect his work. He was unsure why he had been assigned to this cloak-and-dagger task. He had protested the fact that the body would not be taken to the central municipal morgue in the heart of Rome. There, he would have had at his disposal the proper facility, the proper instruments, and help from a number of assistants.

But the coroner's protests were in vain. The decision to handle the matter in this way had been made at the highest level. The Vatican was involved, the American Embassy was involved, and his own government was also involved. Although a physician, he was a civil servant and civil servants followed orders.

"It made no difference," the physician said to himself. "The world's evils," he resigned himself, "were all due to politicians and lawyers." But had the doctor been more politically adept or more current in his readings about the world, his findings would have been of greater significance to him.

"Drowning; within the past seventy-two hours." The doctor wrote in the space indicated for cause of death. He continued, "Asphyxiation and deprivation of oxygen to the lungs, heart and brain." Then, as an afterthought, he noted, "I shall add a footnote, which might be of some importance to the American doctor who will read the report." Rashid checked his notes intently, and then returned to the report, "Approximately 750 milliliters clear, non-saline solution in tracheal plexus. Released for embalming."

Luis Sanchez had recently drowned in fresh water. This fact was not remarkable to a man unaware that the American's plane had been shot down over the sands of Syria more than a year earlier. The doctor's final entry on the official autopsy form would go unnoticed for several days. Although the coroner completed his report, a stenographer would not type the document and prepare it for official transmission until Monday, two days hence. By then, Luis Sanchez would be home.

As he replaced the cap on the fountain pen, the doctor walked from the autopsy chamber into a small, adjacent office where he found the orderly fast asleep on a badly worn couch. A quick turn of the light switch awakened the sleeping man, who had arrived for work just after Dr. Rashid had made his first incision.

"I am finished, Carlo," the doctor indicated. "Please dress the body with the uniform we were given, and I will help you replace it in the coffin.

Did you sleep well?"

"Si, Doctore," came the groggy reply from the couch.

"And, Carlo, you will find the coffin in the ante-room where the mortician left it earlier today. Please retrieve it, eh?"

The orderly wiped the sleep from his eyes as he made his way to the brightly lit autopsy room. He scanned the far wall and found the small refrigerator. A can of Coca-Cola would wake him sufficiently to perform his unappealing work. Carlo was thankful the government was paying him double overtime tonight, but mere money was slight compensation for the fact he had to handle the body of a dead man in the dark of night. The job was difficult enough in the middle of the day. Nonetheless, he set about the task of redressing the body, as the physician busied himself with cleaning his surgical instruments for the next day's work.

It took Carlo about thirty minutes to dress the body and comb the hair. When he had at last straightened the captain's tie a final time, he turned and walked to the double doors leading to the outer room where the casket had been stored during the autopsy. As the wide aluminum doors swung open, the orderly noticed that the outside double doors to the room were ajar. "The undertakers forgot to close the doors," he said, only slightly annoyed. But no matter. The outer room where the casket lay was dark, except for the glare from the nearby streetlights beaming in through the slightly open outer doors.

The Italian coroner turned his attention from the autoclave where he was sterilizing his surgical tools to his aide as the orderly pulled the casket alongside the examining table.

"Where is the one the body came in?" the doctor quizzed his helper.

"I don't know what you mean, Senior Doctore, this was in the next room. There is no other..."

The coroner did not understand. The American had arrived in a heavy, expensive bronze casket. But the coffin Carlos had wheeled in was built plain and wooden as if for a pauper's grave.

12 January
0400 hours
Feltwell, England

Daylight was still two hours away from the rolling fens of East Anglia when Zach Pollard unwrapped himself from the bedclothes and stumbled toward the bathroom. His size thirteen feet shuffled to the small water closet of the four-room row house. There, leaning against the wall, eyes closed and half-dreaming, the American found his target. Pollard relieved himself, then pawed for the pull-chain on the old gravity-flush toilet, and yanked hard.

The remnants of the squadron's pub party swirled around the porcelain bowl, down through red-rusted iron pipes and into the sewers beneath the village that Pollard and the other Air Force aviators called home. From there, the dregs of one-too-many Greene King lagers mixed with the run-off from the brickwork streets, then ran into the nearby River Ouse, past neatly trimmed farms and villages, and flowed, eventually, into the North Sea.

It had been a pretty good party, a wake, of sorts; the squadron's traditional way of greeting new pilots to the fold or mourning the passing of a lost comrade. Besides, Luis Sanchez had always loved a good party. So his return from Syria -- via Libya -- was sufficient reason to remember his raucous good nature and to recall that night over the desert...

Shaking himself one last time, Pollard leaned away from the wall and turned sleepily toward the hallway. His six-foot-four frame lumbered back to the bed, and, laying down, he reached to encircle the sleeping figure of his new, petite friend, Tracie Pruett. He smiled as he felt his heart still racing. He had not been with many women and although he had only met her hours before, he wondered to himself if she might finally be "the one."

The British girl with the funny accent turned away from him and buried her nose deep into the pillow.

Outside, a passing lorry bounced along the uneven cobblestone surface of the village streets. Its rumbles and groans broke the pre-dawn silence as Pollard drifted back to sleep under the influence of new emotions, strong lager and even stronger memories.

12 January
0430 hours
Rome

Even in the early morning hours, the narrow streets of Rome were busy. Not even after dark did the notorious Roman traffic abate. One drove on Roman streets only if guile and daring rode along as passengers. Street signs meant nothing; the only rules of the road were one's wits. Amidst a sea of darting, weaving cars, the unwary or unseasoned could easily perish. Marco Castiglione's feet furiously worked the clutch and gas pedal of the small, light-blue Fiat van, as the young undertaker approached the storied Coliseum. He looked left, then right, as he drifted into the busy circle of traffic that surrounded the ancient ruin. In the back of the small trade-van, the empty bronze coffin shifted slightly and began to vibrate against one side of the vehicle.

Marco's chubby hands tried to grip the steering wheel, but his sweat made them slip. He was far more nervous than he was cold, as his mind raced over the few facts he had been given three days before. What at first had seemed like an easy way to make some money to him and his father now seemed like a venture far more dangerous than the money was worth.

"I don't like this, lying to priests...making a delivery in the middle of the night. And why do we deal with this German. I don't know, Santa Maria, I don't know..."

But Marco's father had made all the arrangements, as he had always done. The younger recalled his father saying, "When you are older, my son, you will take over this business and you will make the decisions. But I am the father and this is my business and you will follow my instructions in this matter...." The elder Castiglione had directed his son this time as he had many times before.

"Why in Christ do I steal a coffin that has already been used? It is empty. Could they not have a new one? And why do I deliver it at this hour? Why does my papa do this thing?"

To be sure, the younger Castiglione had helped his father in some questionable business before. Like the times when he collected and delivered bodies to the university for the use of the medical students. So what if the State had paid them to bury those wretched souls in simple, municipal graves for the poor. No one was the wiser, Castiglione and Son had told themselves. There had seemed some honor, some purpose in that. Even the police had looked the other way.

But tonight was far different. "They do not want even the body...only the coffin," Marco Castiglione again questioned himself. As he drove through the sea of red and white and amber lights, he felt as though a thousand eyes were watching him. Surely, the police must be watching his every move.

"Oh, Papa! How will you explain this to my wife when they arrest me?"

Suddenly, a taxi veered in front of the van. Marco

at once jammed on his brakes and turned sharply to the right. "You whore. I spit on you..." shrieked the wide-eyed, rotund mortician at the top of his lungs. But no one could hear the curse as he sped off into the night. His heavy load shifted again, this time with an audible "thud" against the sidewall of his van.

In the distance, he heard the high-pitched whine of a police siren and the sound made his heart race faster. "The police are surely on to me now," Marco was convinced. His eyes were glued to the roadway as he looked for his turn onto the road leading north to the Tiber and his prearranged meeting place.

Marco sighed in relief as the siren disappeared into the hurried distance. "Perhaps, I am lucky to-night," he thought as he turned the small truck northwest onto the Via dei Fori Imperiali. Just ahead, on his left, he saw the gleaming white monument to Victor Emmanuel II, a tourist attrac-tion to the many thousands of visitors each year. He slowed as he neared the landmark, allowing a young couple to pass in front. Slowly accelerating, he watched another group of late night revelers wander happily in the streets nearby. He drove on, four more blocks, past the Pantheon and then sharply to the north toward the Tiber.

Soon, his eyes fixed on his destination. Just ahead lay one of the many bridges over the storied river, this one illuminated by two rows of lights. Marco had been told to approach this bridge, the one closest to the Castle St. Angelo, bathed in light on the far riverbank. Marco approached the end of the bridge, but just before driving up onto the structure, he turned sharply to the left and drove along a narrow brick road, which followed the south bank. He could see the St. Angelo clearly. How beautiful it appeared, reflecting off the dark waters of the famous river. Marco then recalled that he was to look for a larger, canvas-sided truck parked near the bridge.

The two men in the parked truck saw the blue van before Marco had turned off the main road. "Go ahead," the man with the German accent said to his compatriot, "Signal the driver. Flash the lights once." Marco's eyes caught the prearranged signal immediately. He depressed the clutch and let the van coast to a stop just in front of the larger truck. As Marco killed his headlights one of the two men in the truck, a swarthy man in workman's overalls, jumped down from the cab and ambled toward the young Castiglione.

"You are exactly on time, Senior Castiglione. Do you have the casket we ordered?"

"Yes, yes, it's in the back," replied Marco, recognizing the man who had made the arrangements with his father three days earlier.

"Very well then, you can help us load the box into our truck, no? You see, I have a very bad back and my friend and I could not lift it without your help."

The man's apparent ease and gentle tones reassured Marco. He managed a nervous smile and replied, "Of course, my father has the same complaint. 'Marco,' he says, 'Marco, come lift this, come pick up that'..."

"Ah, yes, fathers are that way, are we not?" laughed the man in the coveralls, patting Marco on the back as the other man from the larger truck joined them.

The three opened the back of the Castiglione van and hoisted its contents onto their shoulders. The darkness of the evening made them all but invisible. Likewise, their meeting place was well obscured from public view by the riverbanks, buildings and the bridge traffic overhead.

As he lifted his end of the casket into the back of the larger truck, Marco Castiglione began to feel more at ease. The older man's voice and demeanor had made the young man feel comfortable. The swarthy man in the coveralls laughed with Marco and the other man as they strained to lift the box into the truck. "This is going to be easy money," Marco thought to himself. "You had nothing to worry about. Papa was right about this job."

MARCH

15 March
2330 hours
London

"Tracie, you are about to get the thrill of a lifetime. You know that?" The woman half-smiled and swatted away Pollard's playful paw that grabbed her buttocks. A more than slightly tipsy Zach Pollard laughed, leaning heavily on the petite but oddly strong woman as the pair made their way through the lobby and into the elevator of London's Royal Air Force Club. It had only been a block along Piccadilly from the Hard Rock Cafe, but the American had drunk more beers than he should have and walking took the concerted effort of the pair in order to navigate their way to bed for the night.

The evening had been filled, as usual, with Zach's happy babbling about his airplane, the squadron and happenings at the base. Tracie, ever attentive, listened patiently and prompted Pollard's rambling with the occasional pointed question. Their dating had been sporadic, much to Pollard's dismay, since their meeting at the Three Bells only two months before. Tracie, Zach had complained, just vanished for days on end--something to do with her job as a buyer for several stores in the Midlands--and then she'd just reappear, without notice, for a few hours of passion.

Damian Mercer had opined that she had another lover and that Zach had better watch himself. But Pollard was smitten. He lacked the easy way with women that so many of his comrades in the squadron seemed to enjoy. Zach Pollard was an affable, happy young man and seemed destined to wander naively through life. No, Tracie Pruett was his first serious romance since college and he dreamed, secretly, that one day he'd marry her.

The elevator ride to the third floor rooms ended quickly enough and Tracie found the room key in her purse. Pollard leaned over to kiss her, but his aim was off center and his mouth found an earring and a lock of hair instead.

"In you go, then, my large American."

Pollard belly-flopped almost straight for the bed then rolled over to unlace his shoes and ready himself for a night of passion with his English rose. Tracie had almost instantly slipped into the bath area and Zach heard water running behind the closed door.

After what seemed like an hour, Tracie emerged from the water closet. Only the dim bulb above the sink provided backlighting to her slender, half-naked form. She stepped slowly toward the foot of the bed. Pollard, lying on his side, raised his elbow to support his spinning head.

Slowly, deliberately, she ran her hands down both sides of the black camisole that gave definition to her firm breasts and waist. She raised her foot and placed the toe of her black, high-heeled slipper atop the bed. Her hands found the lacework of the garter belt Pollard had given her earlier, locking her fingers inside of her panties. Slowly, tauntingly, she slid the panties down over her well-rounded bottom and athletic thighs. She stopped, as her index finger began to caress her moist, inner thigh.

"Mister Pollard," she teased, now in a deep, throaty purr. "I'm quite afraid it's YOU who are in for the thrill of a lifetime."

Pollard could not answer. His heart was beating wildly as every muscle in his body tightened. Before him stood his living fantasy, an erotic blond goddess so perfect in her sexuality that he might climax just watching her tempt him.

The woman now removed her panties and gently tossed them toward the young flyer, who caught and held them to his lips. Her scent was strong and he closed his eyes and tasted her.

Tracie leaned forward and began to inch her way along his massive frame. Her tongue found his toes, then atop his foot and up along the inside of his thigh. Zach moaned, "God, Tracie, I want you..." His massive hands reached down beneath her arms and with one motion lifted her above him. He held her tightly as their lips and tongues met. Pollard was so excited that his breathing turned into heavy panting. He found her shoulder straps and hurriedly slipped them over her petite but muscled shoulders. His kiss was warm and wet upon her neck. Her back arched, exposing her firm cleavage to his mouth. His hands now rose to cup her firm breasts as her slender fingers toyed and tickled his hair and ears.

Her nipples were sweet and warm and she moaned as he encircled each gently with his lips...her bottom now swayed rhythmically up and down as her excitement built toward his. Pollard raised his leg so that her bottom massaged his upper thigh and torso. Now, his pulse raced as if upon the wind. He could stand the teasing no longer and quickly he reversed their positions so that he could easily enter her. But just as quickly and with equal sexual ferocity, the trim blonde rolled him over and pinned his arms above his head. Pollard tried to protest, but she buried his words with another long, hungry kiss.

"Not yet," she panted. "I'm not ready..."

The woman's eyes were afire: her nostrils widening with every breath. Her jaw set firmly, as if she were about to embrace in mortal combat. Pollard was held almost motionless by her animal intensity as the woman slid her torso toward her partner until he could taste her warmth. She demanded that he please her. Pollard, completely within her control, obeyed. As his kisses found their mark, her form writhed and pushed hard against his face, the back of his head buried deep into the pillow beneath. She reached down, fingers encircling his head, and pulled him more deeply into her. "Faster, damn you, faster..." she commanded, now fully in control of her lover's actions.

"Ja, mein Gott...Ich...."

16 March
0900 hours
London

Zach Pollard's arm encircled only an empty pillow when he awoke from the night's passion. After a slow awakening, the young officer gathered enough consciousness to realize he was alone and that Miss Pruett had, once again, vanished. But Zach Pollard was too tired and hung over to do much more than sigh.

18 March
2000 hours
Nairobi International Airport

Farouk Ayugi almost swaggered as he walked into the airport terminal. In his left hand was a canvas bag holding a new laptop computer. Slung over his right shoulder was a knapsack containing three days' change of clothing.

The thirty-year-old Fulani Muslim had spent the past decade in Nigeria serving the Islamic jihad against Christians. He had paid his dues both in the bush and in the streets of Lagos and Kano, and now had been elevated to more responsible duties. In his party's armed struggles, he had made some convenient political allies. To Farouk and his compatriots, even the devil would have seemed less objectionable if he would have helped end the Christian oppression of their people. That's why Farouk, a man with a university education, had agreed many years earlier to act as a courier--a smuggler--for his cause.

The mission was always simple: fly to Uganda, Chad, the Sudan or the Central African Republic. Carry a portable computer to London, Paris or Amsterdam, in exchange for ten thousand dollars.

Like always, Ayugi had no idea of the significance of what he carried in the case or for whom it was intended. If captured, Ayugi could not compromise his unknown client's interests. He could say with a straight face that he had no idea what he was carrying. Ten thousand dollars was a cheap price to pay for confidentiality. And Farouk's unknown masters had only insisted on security. That is why they only utilized college educated, English speaking couriers, such as Farouk.

The London trip was the young African's eleventh assignment as a courier. He had never been caught, although there had been a close call in Paris the year before. He had quickly learned that one of the cardinal rules was to look very much at home wherever he was sent.

Today, he played the role of a wealthy student heading back to university in the United States. London would be just a layover to see friends and visit a number of tourist attractions. His attire made the story all the more plausible: high-top athletic shoes, bleached button-fly dungarees, a New York Hard Rock Cafe tee shirt and a brightly-colored Adidas warm-up jacket. He topped off the ensemble with a bright red Chicago Bulls hat. Tucked inside his jeans was an ambassadorial passport stolen and forged a week earlier for this mission. His cover story was simple. He was the son of an employee of the Nigerian Embassy in Nairobi. He was en route to school in the United States.

Farouk's command of the English language was good enough that, together with his attire and cover story, he looked very much the part of a modern globetrotting youth. His costume was neither un-usual nor out of place; such was the pervasive im-pact of American marketing. Everyone in the world wanted to look like they were born in the United States.

Farouk hadn't had the slightest trouble passing through the x-ray scanners and metal detectors when he passed through security screening at Nai-robi Airport. The security guards on duty had been alert enough to demand that he power up the port-able computer Ayugi carried with him. He'd even commented to the guards that he approved of such security and that he "felt much safer knowing all passengers were subject to the same scrutiny." His broad smile and cooperative attitude were all the more convincing to the gate security personnel who ushered the young man past their checkpoint and down the concourse.

Only the deep-set eyes of Chief Inspector Joshua Otunga saw through the youth's practiced facade.

Otunga had been thirty years a policeman. He had begun his career as a nineteen-year-old patrolman on the docks of the port city of Mombasa. It was there that Otunga had developed his keen ear for languages and dialects, for most of the half-million Indians who lived in Kenya had emigrated through the port of Mombasa. More than a hundred thousand Arabs--from Syria, Iran, Oman and the other Islamic nations-- had come through there, too. It seemed to his superiors that Joshua Otunga had the best ear for languages in the department. He'd earned his way into the officer corps by hard work and an uncanny nose for evil play. He'd even earned a university education during his tenure and had spent a year-long sabbatical working in Paris and London with Interpol.

Otunga was a professional; a cop's cop. He had nabbed more than a few would-be criminals based upon nothing more than instinct. Unhampered by the strictures of probable cause that slowed his western counterparts, Otunga had made a name for himself in the national police force by solving the "unsolvable" cases. He, himself, couldn't explain his talent. But he had often joked that it was the sense of the hunter he'd inherited from his ancestors of the Lo tribes.

He slouched his giant six-foot-seven frame back away from the inspection station as the security guard examined the young courier's goods. Otunga gave the appearance of yet another overweight, dozing civil servant. The yellow sweat stains on his wrinkled white shirt, the loose Windsor knot, his sagging trousers completed the image to the unwary. But the sleeping crocodile's senses missed nothing. With half-closed eyes set deep within a large, round, almost purple-black face, he watched the practiced smile and happy banter affected by the younger African. Otunga listened carefully to each word, each laugh, each phrase uttered as the cover story was played out in casual detail for the unwary inspectors. He focused on the young man's body language and his gestures. Each movement was a clue, each word told a story.

"This young boy is hiding something," Otunga assured himself, his mind instantly ablaze with interest. And then, slowly rising to his feet, he spoke in quiet tones to the security officer. "A moment, Daniel, if you please." The large inspector walked behind his subordinate and, looking at the laptop, then toward its owner, said, "I'm sorry, young man. Is this your computer?"

Ayugi, suddenly sensing danger, smiled

broadly and offered, coolly, "Sir, yes. Is there a problem?"

Otunga, the master hunter, responded in equally relaxed fashion. "Perhaps; there has been a report of a stolen computer much like this. Will you please step around the counter and join me in this office?"

When the two men were inside the cramped office, Otunga spoke. "I am quite certain there will be no delay in boarding your flight. But, if you please, I need to ensure this is not the stolen item that was reported to us only a few minutes ago. You quite understand, don't you?"

"Why, of course, but you will find that the computer is mine. It is a gift from my father," came the collected response from the courier. And then, reaching into his jacket for his diplomatic passport, "My father is with the embassy," bluffing that any interruption of his travel plans would result in unpleasantness for this impertinent, overweight civil servant.

Chief Inspector Otunga only smiled and nodded his head. He had been threatened by much more powerful men and he had never flinched. Besides, this was no time to flush his quarry.

Then, taking the laptop under his arm, Otunga offered, "I'll return shortly. I simply need to run the serial number through our computer data base. Please make yourself comfortable."

The giant inspector then disappeared behind a double-thick door into an adjacent office. Taking a penknife from his pocket and removing the backplate screws, he scrutinized every detail of the internal mechanisms of the computer, paying particular attention to the wires held in place with small welds. Once again wielding the penknife like a surgeon, the detective opened the back of the floppy drive and quickly opened the sliding door.

Otunga saw immediately that the space was filled with soft black foam rubber. "Odd," he thought to himself, wrinkling his forehead. He deftly slid his right forefinger between the foam and the computer casing, and, pulling gently, heard the faint but unmistakable rattle of glass.

Although his curiosity was piqued, Otunga slowed his movements, taking care to protect whatever fragile contents lay inside. As soon as the foam case was free from its tight confines, Otunga allowed himself a moment to survey the contents. "Four clear test tubes...sealed and corked with a red and black rubber stopper and marked with a small red skull." Inside each vial, a clear, colorless liquid that looked like water, only more viscous.

The large man's brow wrinkled. "God in heaven.... chemicals; and I don't think its drugs! This isn't hashish oil...I wonder who he's working for!"

Otunga had to think fast. As he replaced the padding and the foam that held the first vials, he turned his attention to the power converter wrapped neatly inside the carrying case. "Let's have a look," he whispered to himself. Again, he handled the knife with swift, sure-handed skill. It took only a moment, and quickly, he'd removed the back of the small black box to find four smaller sealed vials, also wrapped in thin black foam.

Otunga rapidly analyzed the emerging situation. He'd uncovered what he thought was a shipment of toxic nerve or blood agents. Otunga was no longer worried that the young black man in the outer office was planning a hijacking or even the destruction of the British Airways jet. Yet he did know from experience that the Nigerian was a runner and he was probably working for someone important in one of world's terror organizations. "But who?"

There was no time to waste.

A man with less experience would have arrested the courier on the spot. Certainly, there was enough to make a prosecution stick. But the people who were waiting in London for these chemicals would be warned. "And if I don't act now," the chief inspector considered, "We might not find them until it's too late. Even the slightest delay might warn them off."

Chief Inspector Joshua Otunga had to make a tough choice. "If I'm wrong, these chemicals might find their way into a municipal water supply and I might have stopped it."

Otunga gently lifted one of the test tubes from its cushion and slipped it into his pocket. He then took extra care to replace the foam lining and the back cover, adjusting it carefully so as to leave no clue it had been disturbed. Still, he knew he was running a risk.

But Otunga's instincts told him he was right. In

his career, he had made hundreds of similar decisions balancing the known destination of the contraband against the chance of catching both the courier and the recipient. But Otunga totally understood the chance he was running. He would allow the younger man to board the flight, and then call an old friend at Scotland Yard. The officer quickly re-assembled the casing, and once having replaced its back cover, returned to the outer room where the courier sat with apparent patience.

"I am so very sorry, very sorry indeed, my young friend," the officer apologized. "It seems that these old eyes are not as observant as they once were. It appears that I have been mistaken. Yours is not the computer that was stolen. Indeed, they have already recovered the missing one. Can you please forgive me?" Handing the computer back to its owner, Otunga offered a handshake and repeated his believable apology once more.

"No, sir," offered Ayugi, "You have nothing to apologize for. Please, accept my gratitude for your service. I was not troubled in the least."

"Then, you will at least allow me to ensure you reach your flight on time?"

And, walking out of the office and into the corridor, Otunga summoned a passing electric cart and ordered its driver to ensure the passenger with the laptop got to the gate immediately, and that he should not be required to undergo any further security screening.

"And again, my young friend, please accept my

sincerest apology..."

With a sigh of relief, Farouk Ayugi quietly congratulated himself as he was whisked past the last inspector and toward the London-bound flight. "That was close, but they suspected nothing," he mused silently. And, with a touch of arrogance that befalls a man whose luck has saved him from peril, he thought to himself, "This is too easy, Allah be praised!"

After Ayugi disappeared onto Flight 2376, Joshua Otunga quietly returned to his office and made his way toward a secure telephone. Not sure that his young target did not have confederates still watching in the airport, Otunga continued to play the role of a slothful civil servant with nothing more on his mind than a nap on a secluded couch.

Farouk Ayugi was still smiling in self-congratulation as he settled himself in the coach class seat of the British Airways flight. Time now to sit back, sleep, and enjoy an uneventful flight. He told himself that, once again, his wit and guile had outwitted yet another unsuspecting government fool.

"Secure line, please. Chief Inspector Joshua Otunga," came the request in nearly perfect English diction, as if he'd been educated by the dons at Oxford.

Having secured an encrypted government line, Otunga asked, "Yes, Scotland Yard please. I can hold."

The clicks and beeps from the headset told Otunga his call was beaming from a microwave tower, into space, off a British Telecom satellite, into a receiving station near the English coast at

Dover, through an encryption computer and into yet another microwave link to the headquarters of Scotland Yard.

The familiar double ring of a British telephone told the listener he'd gotten through.

"Reserve desk," came the quiet answer.

"Yes, this is Chief Inspector Joshua Otunga in Nairobi. Is Chief Inspector MacHugh available?"

"One moment, hold please."

Otunga grew impatient. Big things were in the offing, and he needed to talk to an old friend in a hurry. Then a woman's voice returned to the line, "I'm sorry, sir. The Chief Inspector is not available this evening. It is rather late, sir. Perhaps he can call you in the morning?"

"Madame," Otunga spoke distinctly and with authority, "this is a Red Alpha communication. It simply cannot wait. A matter of some national concern, terrorists, I believe, so I must talk to Harold at once!"

The woman on the British end of the call knew that no one called Sir Harold MacHugh by his first name unless the caller was a person of great import himself.

"Very well, sir. The Chief Inspector will be contacted. May I have the number where you can be reached?"

It was almost four hours before the phone rang in Joshua Otunga's office. He'd fallen asleep at the battered wooden desk. The ringing startled him, but his big hands nimbly found and clutched the handset.

"Inspector Otunga..."

"Please hold for Chief Inspector MacHugh."

A few moments later, in full jovial and robust tones, MacHugh's voice boomed: "Joshua Otunga, you old lion! I'm in Scotland. I'll wager your conscience drove you to it...am I right? You've called for mercy. I am right, aren't I?"

"Harold, I wish it were a social call. But, old friend, my lost wager on the test match will have to wait. I've some business for you and I am quite certain you'll be interested..."

Just after he'd finished a mid-flight snack, the courier reviewed his plans. Once off the British Airways flight, he would replay his story about life as a university student to the officials at Passport Control. The courier didn't want to rely upon the ruse of officialdom - such a confrontation might arouse undue suspicion. He felt secure in his fall-back plan, though. Customs officials seldom bothered important persons carrying diplomatic passports. He knew from experience that more than one unexamined diplomatic pouch had carried contraband through the world's airports. He'd then make his way to the luggage pick up, where he would retrieve his knapsack, and he would then declare the value of his computer.

"No sense in being tripped up trying to escape paying duty," he'd been advised.

The courier would make his way past the carousels and into the "Goods to Declare" section. There, he would gladly display his laptop, certain the Customs people would be lulled by his openness. "After all, would a smuggler openly declare ill-gotten goods? Of course not!" went his reasoning. It had worked many times before. It was an application of the old saying, "If one wanted to remain unseen, it was best to hide in the open." It was so often true!

Safe in the knowledge that he'd remembered his instructions, Farouk Ayugi reclined his seat and, pulling his cap down over his eyes, slipped into a shallow sleep.

19 March
0400 hours
Gatwick Airport, London

Colin Blackford's hands were covered with smudged newsprint and nicotine, telltale signs of another long and uneventful night perusing the infamous British tabloids. He sniffed at himself and winced at the odor, the smell of too many cigarettes and half-dried, oily sweat. Blackford scarcely resembled the once-fit military officer he'd been only two years before. "Four more hours 'til knock off..." he sighed to himself as he turned past the well-endowed girl on page three, in search of a story concerning first-division football.

The airport office of Scotland Yard's Special Branch was bathed in flickering fluorescent light. Too bright for the early hour, Blackford thought. The irritating buzz from a tube above his desk annoyed him as well. He'd mentioned the problem twice before in a memo to maintenance. But, as usual, there had been no response, especially since Blackford was only "temporarily assigned" with the Metropolitan Police. The staccato from the dying light offered a frayed counterpoint to the low tones of a 1940's ballad playing on the BBC on a corner radio.

Blackford scooted his wooden chair back across the chipped tile floor and, placing both feet atop the gray, scratched metal surface of his government-issue desk, patted himself in search of another John Player Special. His face was an ashen pale, typical of so many inhabitants of the British Isles. Too little sun, plus too much lager and smoke, had rendered the once-strapping, six-foot-three Blackford a near physical wreck. He fumbled the cigarette into his dry mouth and leaned forward to find his almost empty butane lighter. He lit up, sucked the smoke deep into his lungs and watched a slender curl rise from the end of yet another early morning sin. The captain's baggy and bloodshot eyes returned to the paper, looking for football news. As he glanced through the financial section, he caught a glimpse of his father's picture. And, shaking his head at the photo, he noted the caption described how the elder Blackford had been named manager of the second-largest portfolio on the London Exchange. It had been seven months since the two had spoken.

Now thirty-one, he could easily have passed for forty-five. Blackford cursed himself for letting the sins of smoke and drink sabotage his combat-ready physique. There had been a time, not so long ago, when the captain could outrun his entire squad of men up any hill, bearing a full field pack and rifle.

"Damn. The old man was right. I was never destined for the City and I was a damned failure as a soldier." He swore to himself again. Another long drag on his sweetly foul cigarette helped quell the rumblings of early morning hunger. Blackford coughed to himself and swallowed a small shard of phlegm. Another pull on the cigarette. Again, he inhaled the smoke and held it deep in his lungs. He closed his eyes and ran a grimy hand through his shaggy brown hair. He began a long, slow exhale as his partner, a Scotland Yard detective, Sergeant Derek Fox, walked in from the adjoining office.

Fox greeted his young associate. "Early morning, mate. The Nairobi flight is in. They'll be off-loading in about fifteen." For some reason known only to British immigration officials, inbound flights from Africa landed in London only during the early morning hours.

Fox, scanning a sheath of papers held loosely in his left hand, added, "And a blue fiver says we nick at least one wog with candy in his knickers." Blackford let go a wry chuckle at the sarcastic suggestion that at least one passenger would be carrying heroin into the country. The Americans called them "mules," Blackford recalled, but the reference was lost on the Englishman.

Just as in New York, Chicago, or any other

modern megalopolis, police work in London was ninety-five percent drudgery, especially for those assigned to the graveyard shift in the international terminal. Although Blackford and Fox were technically assigned to counter-terrorism duties with Special Branch, the two plainclothes men spent the majority of their time helping Her Majesty's Customs and Immigration nab small time drug dealers and black marketeers. Blackford's most memorable arrest during his tour of duty at Gatwick was the African woman who tried to smuggle a monkey into the country. The woman had dressed the primate as an infant. Blackford still hadn't lived down the ribbing from the other officers as a result of the chase scene through a series of food vendors' stalls. It was hardly an auspicious chapter in an otherwise uneventful tenure with Scotland Yard.

"If only I'd kept my damned mouth shut in the brigadier's office," Blackford swore at himself.

How many times in the past two years had Blackford worked the Customs Division? How many midnight-to-eight shifts scanning African and Asian passengers for the signs of illicit drugs? Blackford had often mused to himself that his responsibilities were akin to watching paint dry on a wall. How many more nights would there be?

"Why in hell couldn't you keep your bloody mouth shut?" Blackford reviled himself behind closed eyes. He repeated the curse, recalling the altercation with his last commander that had landed him in the Gatwick doghouse.

"Bastards," Blackford swore silently to himself, "Those bastards had it coming...they cost me two men!"

The assignment to civilian law enforcement was Blackford's penalty and everyone in his SAS regiment - and at Scotland Yard - knew it. It was hardly a fitting assignment for a bold young officer with an enviable combat record, from a moneyed background and a private school education. He had been rated as "superior" during every mission he'd served with the SAS until he'd failed to curb his tongue.

Blackford's tart mouth, however, had kept him at odds with those who could have helped his career the most. He was a young man with a satin sheet upbringing trying to make it in the coarse-hands world of Army counter-terrorism. His school chums all worked in the City at brokerage firms or were now junior barristers at the Temple or Gray's Inn. But, as was befitting a square peg jammed into a round hole, he neither wanted the world into which he was born nor was he generally accepted by those in the world in which he chose to live. His life-long battle for recognition with his emotionally-distant father, a corporate financier, had left him angry, combative and frequently alone. Such were the reasons the solitary life of a soldier had appealed to him. But the self-imposed exile had not been without cost. The one woman he thought he loved had abandoned him years before....there had been only a few lovers since.

Sergeant Fox took a swig of half-cold tea from the thermos on Blackford's desk. Graveyard hadn't been much kinder to Fox, either. But the older man was only three years away from a pension and the bungalow in the Cotswold's.

"Come along, Colin," Fox said, taking a friendly swipe at the younger man's elevated feet. "Queen and Country, lad; Queen and Country."

Blackford half-chuckled a friendly "*Get stuffed*" to his partner as his feet found the dirty tiles below. After all, it wasn't Fox's fault he had been sent to work the graveyard shift at the airport. So, Blackford pulled his tie together and reached for the crumpled jacket hanging on a nearby chair.

Fox was already out the door as the younger constable grabbed a portable two-way radio, flicked off the lights and headed for the escalator.

"Queen and Country," Colin Blackford sighed. "Sod it!"

British Airways Flight 2376 from Nairobi was perfectly on time. The nose of the Boeing 757 stopped right in front of a huge set of Plexiglas windows as the ground crew chocked her wheels and swung the passenger jetway into position. From inside the terminal, the rushing whisper of the two turbofan engines dissipated into a gentle whir and then into silence.

Up the inclined jet way trudged Farouk Ayugi and two hundred other sleepy passengers in a startling array of colorful tribal cloaks and headdress. Many of the women carried large fishnet sacks with clothing and food inside. There was nothing special about the attire or behavior of these passengers. In fact, theirs was the norm for international passengers arriving from the African continent. But to the uninitiated, the throng seemed a circus--a stark contrast to the stayed and conservative British daily attire. Even the Americans, from California and Texas with their brightly-colored Bermuda shorts and printed tee shirts, seemed subdued compared to these travelers. Mixed in with the mostly African throng were a few Indian and Pakistani businessmen in three-piece suits and turbans--no doubt headed for the London financial markets.

Blackford and Fox were still several hundred yards away in another part of the terminal, as the crowd made its way in groups of threes and fours through a maze of corridors, stairways and escalators. Then they mixed with passengers from a score of other just-arrived flights. The international passengers finally arrived at a large central receiving hall, where they were segregated by prominent brown and white signs into "European Community" passengers and "Other International" passengers. Each group then formed long lines or "queues" while they waited for their turn to file through a narrow gate and a conversation with an immigration agent.

High atop the receiving hall, and virtually unnoticeable from the floor where the new arrivals stood in line, were a series of one-way mirrors. Behind the smoke-colored glass sat two of Her Majesty's

Customs and Immigration agents in "the perch." Each was armed with binoculars and hand-held radios. From their vantage position, the agents could scan each newly-arrived group for certain telltale signs of smuggling. Like their counterparts in all the world's major air terminals, Her Majesty's customs officers had honed their skills of observation into a fine art. An experienced officer looked for the subtle clues that the untrained eye would miss, like the cut of a man's hair, the way a woman's nails were trimmed, and whether a suit was newly purchased or two years off the rack. Language, too, was a giveaway. The trained ear could detect, for instance, a French accent cloaked in an Irish brogue. But to most agents, it was the eyes. The eyes of a guilty man revealed all, no matter how practiced or trained they might be. At least, that's how the customs officials felt. In short, the agents had developed a "gut test," a "feel," for the kind of person who was up to no good. Often, very often, their instincts served them well.

As the passengers from Nairobi filed into the central hall, agents Todd Morrison and Jayne Peterson, perched high behind the glass screens, surveyed the crowd below. "Nothing unusual today," Morrison opined. "A school group, some young marrieds, several in on business, and it looks like a family or two." Peterson sighed her unspoken acknowledgement, whilst sounding rather bored.

As she was looking over the incoming group from Istanbul, Peterson made mental notes about a man carrying a black briefcase. She immediately radioed her concerns to another agent below. "I doubt it's much, but give a look, will you, love?" she asked her colleague.

"We'll check it out. Over," came the tinny reply on the handset.

Morrison now chuckled, reaching over to tap his partner on the arm. "Look in Queue 4, halfway back from the front. Young woman, schoolgirl I'd guess--what's she fidgeting with?" he queried.

Peterson, swinging her binoculars toward a teenage black woman, focused on a large white mesh handbag. As the girl fussed with the bundle, a small, furry head popped out from beneath a green shawl. "It's a cat. Love, we can't have that, can we?" Peterson suggested.

Both the officers shared an early morning laugh. The British were extremely fond of animals, which was why they had enacted the strictest animal control laws in the world and had eradicated rabies from their island fortress. Unemployment might be high, rail workers could go on strike and the price of a pint of bitter Might double, no matter---but let rabies find its way onto the island! Well, the Queen might as well abdicate. It was that serious an issue to the average Englishman.

"Shall I call it in or will you?" Morrison asked his eagle-eyed partner.

"Go ahead, but tell Nigel to be gentle. It's probably a pet. Have to be quarantined, though," she observed.

"Break the girl's heart," Morrison offered.

"Yes, but we tell them before they board," the ever officious Peterson replied.

Back on the receiving floor, passengers in the Customs Hall would normally stand in line for at least an hour before spending a few minutes with an immigration agent who reviewed their passports and visas. The agent interview was the real first line of defense. This was where the seasoned officers had a chance to closely scrutinize the newcomers for those telltale signs of wrongdoing. These professionals were subtle and understated in their questioning, even though they might be misperceived as slow and unwitting. But beneath their practiced exterior, agents would mentally receive and compile hundreds of bits of information about a given passenger. More than one smuggler had been tripped up by seemingly innocent questions posed by the officer.

Ayugi, though, was cool to the scrutiny. With a certain arrogance, he reminded himself that he'd beaten these civil servants plenty of times before.

After each passenger was cleared through passport control, it was up yet another set of escalators and to the baggage receiving area. Again, agents were poised behind carefully placed screens so that they might watch the travelers without detection. Now the agents looked for the way passengers handled their luggage--again on the lookout for incongruities. It was a dead giveaway, for instance, if a young man in shabby dress picked up a single expensive leather suitcase.

Once passengers had collected their belongings, they were again divided into separate "Nothing to Declare" and "Goods to Declare" passageways. Here in these narrow hallways that looked and functioned like cattle pens stood Detective Fox and Captain Blackford along with their counterparts from H.M. Customs. The officers and agents trained their eyes on the passengers and their luggage. This was really the last opportunity for the government to screen any contraband before newcomers left the Customs Hall through the giant opaque glass doors and departed into the terminal.

No system was perfect, of course. And some smugglers did escape detection. The sheer weight of numbers operated against the Customs Division. There just wasn't the budget or the necessary manpower to stop and frisk every newcomer to the country, to say nothing of the uproar the liberals would raise in Parliament. So it was up to the men and women of the Division to make the system work. "One must have a certain amount of faith in the basic decency of people," Peterson had often told her subordinates. "That, together with a sharp pair of eyes, a keen sense of smell and good intuition." Despite the best efforts of H.M. Customs and Immigration, however, a few bad ones did get away.

That's what Farouk Ayugi had planned.

As British Airways Flight 2376 emptied its cargo of passengers, the large flight information boards above Colin Blackford's head clattered and buzzed the arrival notice of the gathering crowd in the terminal.

An unanticipated series of quick beeps from Blackford's pager could barely be heard above the public address announcing the arrival. "Who the hell wants me now?" an irritated Blackford asked the air. "Shit," he muttered, as he held the radio close to his right ear and pressed his left index finger hard into his other ear to listen. A hurried instruction from the paging operator told him to go to the nearest police cubicle to take an urgent, priority phone message.

Someone in London wanted to talk to Colin Blackford in a hurry.

Blackford quickly found his way up the nearest escalator, past a newspaper shop, two food areas and a gift store. He darted into an unmarked door and asked the woman police constable on duty where he might find the nearest "Class A" telephone. Stepping into the back room, he quickly lifted the receiver and relayed his name and badge number to the airport police security telephone operator.

"Captain Blackford," the operator responded, "Please hold for Sir Harold MacHugh."

"Damn!" The young Army officer, freshly out of breath, gasped to himself.

"The old bastard would love nothing better than to catch me napping. It's why he sent me here."

But before Blackford could finish talking to

himself, the polished voice of Sir Harold Malcolm DeBrassure MacHugh, Lieutenant General, retired, came on the line.

"Blackford?" the head of Scotland Yard's Special Branch counter-terrorism unit boomed.

"Sir!" Blackford snapped. No sense maddening the old bastard any further.

"Blackford, I haven't much time to discuss entirely the implications of what I am about to tell you, but you are immediately needed on a matter of some particular importance."

"Sir," Blackford answered sharply again.

"Blackford, I know you haven't particularly enjoyed your present duties, and I haven't enjoyed sending you there."

"Like hell you haven't," Colin Blackford thought to himself.

"But, Blackford, we believe that someone, perhaps a courier, is arriving from Nairobi this morning. We believe he's carrying chemicals, perhaps nerve agent, but as of the moment, we know little more. Do you follow me, Blackford?"

"Sir, I do. But..."

"There isn't much time, Blackford, so I'll finish. The chap is a young black; he'll be coming in from Nairobi. He'll be carrying one of those notebook computers in a black canvas bag, Blackford. That's got the crucial bits in it. The plane should be landing soon and I need for you to identify and follow him. When he's dug in, you call for assistance. He'll be dressed very much like an American. You know, wearing dungarees and the like. I suspect him to be about twenty-five or so, medium height, carrying a diplomatic passport. So, Blackford..."

"Sir, shall we apprehend?" Blackford interjected, wishing to sound attentive to procedure.

"You most certainly shall not!" MacHugh shot back. "Under no - do you hear me, Blackford? Under no circumstances are you to apprehend. Nor are you to alert the subject to your presence. You are to follow him, Blackford, nothing more, and certainly nothing less."

Before the young captain could respond, his superior continued forcefully.

"Don't muck this one up with your usual bravado, Blackford. Just track him and report. Do you understand? You simply must hurry now!"

Blackford was crestfallen; he had sensed an opportunity to free himself from the kennel by making an important apprehension. All he could muster in response, though, was an obedient, "Sir. I do, sir."

MacHugh eased for a moment toward his junior. "Finally, in case you're wondering, we shan't make an arrest just yet. We think he's part of something bigger. So this fellow is just a courier. Am I very clear on this, Blackford? We don't want this grouse flushed." Without taking so much as a breath, Sir Harold continued.

"Blackford, you understand that I'm giving you an opportunity to serve your Queen and Special Branch. Don't make a mess of it."

Before the young officer could respond, Sir

Harold MacHugh, military hero and veteran of the Falklands War, had hung up. "Damn," Blackford swore to himself. "Damn."

With little time to act, Blackford slammed the phone into its cradle and bolted from the Special Branch office. He fairly darted down the corridor, knocking a cup of hot tea from a secretary's hand as he ran toward the up escalator. There were few people in the terminal at this hour, or the race would have been a dodging steeplechase. He made his way back to his partner in short order, but the cigarettes had taken their toll. Blackford was almost fully winded when Fox inquired, "Hello! A bit early for physical training, isn't it?"

"Listen Derek, something's up. We've got to work fast. Come with me," Blackford panted.

Taking the older officer by the shirtsleeve, Blackford found an empty customs office and, still breathing hard, began.

"Has the Nairobi flight deplaned yet?"

"Yes, they'll be in Customs Hall by now, why?"

"I've just spoken to Sir Harold MacHugh."

Fox quickly interrupted, "You're having me on, right? Come on, it's too early for pranks."

"No, damn it, listen. I'm keenly serious. There's a courier arriving on the BA flight from Kenya and he's carrying a shipment of chemicals. I have no idea what it is. Care is the word, eh? We've got to follow him. Scotland Yard is arranging backup, but until then, we're to handle this matter. Black male, late twenties. Carrying a laptop computer, black case. Dressed like an American, too."

"But surely there are other agents and backup personnel? Why us? Why alone?" Fox, worried that the game might involve violence, asked nervously.

"I don't know. Sir Harold doesn't think the chap has anything sticky in mind just now. He believes our man's bringing in some heavy chemicals and we're not to spoil the show just yet. They want to catch all of them, I suppose. Look, Derek, you go up to the perch above the Customs Hall. The Kenya passengers will be in there for at least another twenty minutes. You target the chap and then you radio me. I'll pick him up after he clears the baggage claim area. We're supposed to track him until we find out who his contacts may be."

"Right, then. You have a radio, too?"

"I'll get one. Usual the tactical channel. Make sure passport control doesn't muck this thing about. Make sure Peterson's people pass our man through straightaway."

"Right-O," Fox replied, and as he turned for the door, added a note of humor. "And you said, Colin, that nothing of interest ever happened on this shift." Blackford, excited at the prospects of such a chase, flashed a sarcastic grin and the two men headed out the door and on their separate missions.

In the customs hall, meanwhile, Farouk Ayugi was a study in serenity as he stood in line waiting to present his credentials at passport control. He made small talk with the other weary-eyed passengers. To the casual observer, Ayugi was a happy-go-lucky young student, full of the excitement of the world.

Derek Fox made prompt work of the two flights of stairs to the perch above Passport Control. Once inside the narrow room concealed behind the one-way glass, he found shift supervisor Peterson eyeing the throng below. "Jayne," he began, "We're looking for a young chap, black, late twenties, carrying a notebook computer. Black bag, I think. Have you seen him?"

"No pet, haven't been looking--we've been rather busy rounding up stray cats," the woman replied in mock seriousness. "But let's have a look." It only took the experienced agent a few moments scanning the crowd, when she exclaimed, "Ah, there's your chap. American, is he?"

"Not really sure, but he's got the attention of the Chief Inspector."

"Special Branch on the lookout for computer thieves these days, Ducky?" taunted Peterson, in semi-serious reference to the occasional bureaucratic squabbling between Customs and Scotland Yard over turf. Peterson and Fox had known each other for years.

"Listen, pet," Fox chided, "be a love and clear him straight through Passport Control. He's probably carrying a forged or stolen passport, but that's of little concern. Who knows, he may be a courier for the drug cartels, and our intelligence is that he's carrying something very expensive. Can you lend us a hand, then, love?"

"Oh, Ducky, anything for you," she teased. And

with a slight giggle, Jayne Peterson picked up a gray intercom telephone and punched a lighted button. Down below, on the floor of Passport Control, all of her subordinate agents picked up their handsets and listened as Supervisor Peterson relayed the "not to be disturbed" order.

One of the agents soon added, "I see him. He's in my queue, not to worry," then averted his eyes and went quickly back to the passenger before him, a rotund woman from Uganda.

Farouk Ayugi now feigned frustration for the benefit of his fellow line-standers as the family ahead of him was called to the passport control station. He shared a glance with another passenger, a businessman, perhaps, and rolled his eyes and sighed as if he, too, were put off by the wait. Five minutes later, the family ahead of him cleared the Immigration desk and disappeared beyond a partition.

"Next, please!" called the passport inspector. The agent, a man in his mid-forties, was dressed in a rumpled white uniform shirt with black and gold epaulettes. He carefully avoided eye contact with the courier, and, in a monotone, asked, "Passport, please."

"Yes, certainly." Ayugi cooperated, adding a wide grin to put the agent off guard.

Then, as if to assure the target that he was not being watched, the agent recited the litany of droll questions that all international travelers themselves could recite.

"How long will you be in England, Mister...ah, Mister Marambi."

"I will be in your country but three days before I return to the United States to university."

"What is the purpose of your stay?" came the next mechanical question.

"Oh, I hope very much to see the Tower of London and Buckingham Palace and a few other attractions."

"Then the purpose of your stay will be tourism?"

"Yes, and to see friends."

Without so much as lifting his eyes from the desk, the agent stamped Mr. Oliver Marambi's passport, returned the booklet to its owner and called, "Next..."

Ayugi again smiled broadly at the "unsuspecting" government agent and, with a shove of his left hip, spun the turnstile and walked toward the escalators and the baggage claim area. But as the young courier disappeared behind the partitions and up onto the escalator, the passport inspector glanced up into the perch and smiled faintly into the one-way mirrors high above. Jayne Peterson, who had been watching the transaction, nodded and then turned to Derek Fox and said, "He's all yours, Ducky."

"Thanks, love!" Fox said as he fingered the transmit button on his two-way radio and called a coded signal to Blackford, "The kettle's on, mate. It's off to tea. Mark him, bag on the left shoulder, red cap."

In the Duty-Free section, Blackford heard and understood his partner's transmission. The rest of the operation belonged to him.

A full fifteen minutes passed before Farouk Ayugi found his luggage and made his way past his fellow travelers and their luggage carts and headed for the "Goods to Declare" and "Nothing to Declare" lines. He selected the "Goods to Declare" line, just so British Customs wouldn't feel the need to open and inspect his computer. Two times in one trip might be stretching even Ayugi's luck.

As Ayugi rounded the corner to join the "Goods to Declare" queue, Colin Blackford caught the first glimpse of his mark. Blackford had been astute enough to remove his identification badge and had stored his two-way radio beneath a counter. He would make himself as inconspicuous as he could so that his man, Ayugi, would not remember him.

Once at the customs cash register, Ayugi again played his role, this time in full voice. "I feel I must declare this gift from my father." Although Ayugi knew full well that he would not be obliged to pay any duty on the computer, he was hoping that the customs official on duty would quickly usher the young student through without paying. As the uniformed cashier queried the courier, Blackford took up a position, partially obscured by a large, round pillar, so that he could memorize as much of Ayugi as possible in a very short time.

"No, young man," the agent at the cash register cheerfully responded. "You needn't pay tax for that item. Since, as you say, you are only passing through. Next, please."

Farouk Ayugi smiled again as he reached for the laptop, and, turning, walked through a pair of large glass doors into the main airport terminal.

Colin Blackford watched from a safe distance as Ayugi prepared to board the British Rail express train bound for Victoria Station in downtown London. Ayugi walked at a leisurely pace as he made his way down the concrete platform to his assigned car, swinging the shoulder bag to and fro in his left hand. Over his right shoulder was draped a backpack. Because it was still early, the usual rush of passengers had not yet begun. Blackford looked around to find the next vantage point behind which to hide as he followed the courier's movements.

Ayugi finally stopped at the eleventh car in line. He waited for a group of three women to pass and then laid the computer case on the concrete and reached for the door handle on the compartment door. A British Rail conductor passed by and offered a nod to the black man as he stepped into the car and found a seat in the cabin. Two businessmen, a priest and a cadre of Royal Navy enlisted men soon followed. But seating was ample on the long car, and Ayugi soon found that he had two bench seats to himself. He placed the shoulder bag between his hip and the side window and tossed his backpack over the arm of the adjacent seat.

Meanwhile, on the platform outside, Blackford continued the stealthy chase.

"Eleven is closer to the engine, so I'll quick jump into ten. I want to be behind him when we arrive," Blackford reasoned. As the captain boarded the tenth car, a gaggle of American students followed, making a raucous noise in celebration of their high school trip to England. Blackford was glad for the camouflage. He sat close to the group as if to appear he was an adult sponsor for them. The young people had barely settled in their seats when the train lurched forward, signaling the start of the thirty-minute trip into the city. Blackford avoided looking forward into the next car; concerned that Ayugi might spot him. But when he finally allowed himself to look, Blackford saw clearly through the car doors that the black man had done nothing to try to lose any possible pursuer.

Farouk Ayugi only pulled the bill of his cap down over his eyes and leaned against the window and began to sleep.

"There you sit, my friend." Blackford spoke soundlessly to himself. "You're a cool one. Or you're bloody inexperienced. You should have doubled back before boarding; just to keep me on my toes...You could have had a look at the others getting on the train. Surely you'd seen me get on with no luggage."

Blackford's quiet observations were quickly interrupted by a sharp "THWACK" on the side of his head from a tennis shoe, launched by one of the American teens in a game of "keep-away." "Damn!" Blackford shouted, his ear ringing from the blow. His surprised and angry cry was quickly met with a chorus of giggles and an insincere

'Sorry, Mister,' from one of the teens. But Farouk Ayugi had heard and noticed nothing. He was mentally lost in the arms of a woman he'd never met.

Colin Blackford, rubbing his reddened ear, muttered "Queen and Country; bloody hell! Why could you NOT keep your damned mouth shut?"

19 March
0730 hours
New Scotland Yard
Counter-Terrorism Branch

Sir Harold MacHugh looked up as the elevator doors parted, his suit jacket draped over his left arm, a coffee cup in his left hand. At sixty, he stood square and strong. His five-foot-nine-inch frame carried a hefty one-hundred-ninety pounds. His hair was almost fully silver, with specks of auburn still revealing the origin of his famous temperament. A native of Scotland's west coast, near Oban, MacHugh looked every inch the sturdy highlander.

He greeted two uniformed officers as he walked briskly down the hallway of glass and chrome and soon found his office in the main directorate of the division; his name was stenciled in gold leaf on the double glass doors leading to his spacious office. His deputy, Police Major Arnold Brewbaker, greeted him at the door "Sir, was the flight from Edinburgh pleasant?" Brewbaker inquired.

"You know damn well it wasn't, major," The

chief complained with a slight grin. "It's a conspir-acy, and you're at the head of it, Brewbaker. You and that accursed Otunga; every chance I've taken to land a Highlands salmon, you and al Qaeda or the FBI or some junior minister manage to muck it up! It's a plot, I tell you, and I will tolerate it no fur-ther...."

"Yes, sir; perhaps you're right. It is a plot. How is Inspector Otunga, by the way?"

"He's well and sends his regards. Is the team as-sembled? We've got some quick thinking to do."

"Right, sir; in the secure conference room."

Twelve men and women stood in almost perfect military unison as MacHugh entered the room. He'd come to expect such protocol from his subordinates over his twenty-eight years as an officer and soldier in the British Army. Although the men and women on his staff at first resented the pomp and circum-stance, time and experience had shown them that Sir Harold was worthy of such a show of respect. Although he had long since retired from the Army, he was their leader, and they were, after a fashion, "his" army.

"Please be seated, ladies and gentlemen."

The lights quickly dimmed, and the group took their seats around a large, smoked-glass oval table. Upon Sir Harold's command, a projector displayed the face of the courier to the assembly.

"This man is Farouk Ayugi, a Nigerian opera-tive for, well, that's the question of the hour! He ar-rived in London now some three hours ago and he's carrying with him what may be the beginning of a terrorist weapon of unspeakable horror. We fear the poison he's carrying is Sarin, Soman or VX. It may be destined for the streets of London!"

MacHugh's mention of the deadly chemical hushed the gathering.

"This next picture was taken a year ago. It's the same man. This picture was taken by INTERPOL in Paris. Ayugi is a courier. As you know, Nigeria sells the services of some of its people to transport, shall we say, sometimes sensitive materials for certain clients. As a rule, these couriers are not particularly well trained and are easily tracked. Their clients are willing to run that risk because of the deniability it gives them. Certainly, our Arab friends can be spotted at a distance...so people like Mr. Ayugi come in handy. And, of course, the Nigerians need the cash, what with the never-ending struggles in that country."

"I wouldn't normally be troubled at the prospect of a Nigerian courier...and certainly I would NOT have interrupted my fishing safari. But this lead comes to us from Chief Inspector Otunga in Nairobi."

The members of Sir Harold's team exchanged knowing looks.

"Yes. And you all recognize that Inspector Otunga has been a great friend of Scotland Yard over the years. This lead came from him personally. He's one of the very best and I value his counsel. Lights please, Brewbaker."

"You have in your dossiers information, including that which was provided by Inspector Otunga. I want suggestions, ideas. My own thoughts are that this is no normal terror operation, or if it involves the Islamic extremists at all. Take nothing for granted at this point. Assume nothing. We're waiting on final lab results from Otunga. Further analysis might tell us where the stuff was synthesized. After the initial survey on the stuff, Otunga's people will hand-carry the tube to our embassy and we'll fly it to the Army chemical warfare center for testing. Of course, that'll alert MI-5…" MacHugh's reference drew a series of unhappy looks from around the table.

"But we shan't have to wait too terribly long for the results, I'd think."

One of those gathered at the table spoke the fears of all, "Soman. VX. God. I would have hoped with the UN Chemical Conventions we Might have seen the last of that."

MacHugh interrupted. "Hardly! International treaties bind only law-abiding nations, not rogue states or criminal organizations. Right, that's why we could all use a brush-up on the stuff…Tony, a few words on the subject, if you will."

A scientist from the Special Branch chemical-analysis laboratory rose to speak.

"Right, well, then…our original fear that this liquid was chem-war was on target. We have a tentative thought from Inspector Otunga that it is VX. But let's not assume things and jump the gun. He's whisked it off for testing. Deadly stuff, this is. It's a clear, colorless liquid with a fruity smell, not unlike camphor oil. We field tested the stuff with the Americans back in the sixties and built chemical warfare clothing to combat it.... Thank God we never had to find out if it worked. We do certainly know," the chemist added, "that Saddam Hussein used some of this against the Kurds in the late eighties. And al Qaeda may have hidden some stockpiles around the world, we just can't be sure where. Lord knows who has their hands on the stuff now!"

He drew a breath, surveyed the room, and continued.

"Here's how it works. Vapors make the pupils contract rapidly, followed by blistering of the eyeballs, resulting in quickly diminished vision. The toxicity is much greater when absorbed through the eyes than through the skin. But it is nonetheless lethal, even if absorbed only through the skin. Immediate and I do mean immediate decontamination is required for even the smallest droplet. Let's all be reminded. A small dose on the skin or in the eyes can be lethal in less than fifteen minutes and it isn't a pretty death. I've brought a rather graphic film taken from the Iraqis of the effects. I have no idea when or where this was made. I hope I never find out...uh, let's run that strip, if you please."

The silent black and white film splashed against the pull-down screen. The grainy picture revealed an emaciated Arabic male about fifty years of age sitting on a wooden bench in an otherwise empty room. The film revealed a splash from above the man's head, and almost instantly he began rubbing his eyes, nose and face. After three minutes of almost frantic tearing at his face, the subject seized his chest and rolled onto the floor, obviously unable to find breath. The camera focused on his face and mouth and the grotesque mask now fully filled the screen. As the man half rolled toward the camera a sickening mixture of dark fluid, probably blood and vomit, erupted from his face. The unfortunate soul began to twitch and convulse spasmodically into a violent contortion that forced many of MacHugh's staff to avert their eyes. The surreal black and white images only increased the horror.

After they had watched the victim's ten minutes of horrible agony, MacHugh called for the lights.

After a long silence, Brewbaker asked softly, as if he did not want to have his fears justified, "Al Qaeda, sir?"

"Well, of course," MacHugh responded, clearing his throat and collecting himself in the wake of the ghastly scenes. "Ah, normally, they deal in explosives. But this isn't the normal fare even for the Jihad or Hamas. Generally, it's too risky from a public relations standpoint. That's why I feel we have to look elsewhere for our culprits." MacHugh felt reasonably certain a new Palestinian government, run by Hamas, wasn't behind this…whatever "this" was.

A deputy chief of counter-intelligence quickly voiced the fears of all, "My guess, its VX, but a relatively small amount. I suspect they'll try to aerosolize it…. the stuff wouldn't work particularly well in water. So, look here, we might presume that they'll want to spread it out quickly, so they only need -- what, ten to twenty pounds of explosive to disburse it over a five, ten-square-mile area. Am I correct, Des?"

Harold MacHugh studied the deputy intensely.

Des continued, "We know that a damn bomb would be relatively simple to build, if they have the right components. It's not the explosion that'll do the dirty work; it's the aerosol effect of the poison or the splash effects or residual pools where the unwary might step."

No one else at the table spoke; they didn't have to. The deputy's insight was well founded. He paused, but MacHugh bade him continue.

"Pure terror weapon; sickening death. We have to admit to ourselves we could be facing a catastrophe...." the deputy's thoughts trailed off, before collecting himself.

"So, let's refresh. The key to maximizing the terror value is that they have to set off an explosion to vaporize it. I estimate it takes only about twenty pounds of high explosive, packed tightly around the vials--and set off at just the right time. But of course, I'm just surmising, here."

No one in the room said a word as the projectionist illuminated the central Middle Eastern region on the map.

"Where did they get the damn stuff?" a voice called out from the darkened room.

The deputy chief of counter-intelligence again

pointed to the next slide. "Here it is, in Syria, then. This is where an educated guess would say our chemicals are coming from...but then, again, uh, let's have that other slide please, yes. I suppose any place here along the eastern slope of the Urals. Old Joe Stalin built lots of chemical warfare assets and uranium enrichment plants there, you know. And our Russian friends have absolutely no control on these things anymore. Russian mafia steals it, sells it on the black market to the highest bidder."

The speaker returned to his seat and caught McHugh's attention.

"So it's really a matter of supposition, then, isn't it? We must suppose that our courier has the VX or Soman still in hand and he's waiting to join forces with another accomplice or two who have enough explosive and the detonation devices. Our Nigerian won't build the bomb, so he must be making contact with others who have already set a plan in motion."

"Now, as for our ultimate quarry, the bomber, well, he'll also need transportation," Brewbaker injected quickly, drawing a picture of their unknown nemesis. "I'd say a small lorry or a trade van is all they need to deliver the thing. Could easily be detonated by remote control."

All in the room considered Brewbaker's suggestion, and then one officer opined, "Sir Harold, I'm sorry to be the bearer of such a solemn idea. But it may well be said that we're up against the possibility of a threat to large sections of the city. We have to believe it's possible, if not likely. Shall we alert for a possible evacuation?"

MacHugh's staff looked gravely around the table and then turned to their leader, who did not immediately answer.

MacHugh didn't answer the inquiry directly, but, after pausing to collect his thoughts, Sir Harold drew a deep breath, and then summarized. "All right, then, our theory is that this is a chemical bomb. Possibly Middle Easterners built it, but we shan't know that for some time. We're guessing a bomb, and not yet completed. But we don't know why or for whom. Then again, the plan may be to drop the nasty stuff in a water or food supply. We must presume our adversaries have the technology and ability to complete construction and effect detonation or delivery. We have the option of snaring our courier right now, but then we'd be off the game, wouldn't we?"

MacHugh knew he was taking the gamble of his career and if he was wrong or missed a step, hundreds, even thousands might suffer or die.

"I'll notify Ten Downing immediately. We're maintaining primary surveillance, at least for the next six hours. We must get a lead on who our courier is working for and just how far they've progressed and who is financing them. I've got young Blackford out there on point with the surveillance team. A few nights standing in the rain will calm his impertinence."

Those in the room laughed quietly. All knew Blackford and recognized him as the young, temporarily-assigned Army officer with proven potential, but instantly questioned whether this most urgent situation did not warrant more seasoned, professional police handling. Blackford's insubordination to his Army superiors was known throughout Scotland Yard. His impertinence had set him back in the eyes of the SAS leadership. It had set him back in the eyes of all, save Sir Harold MacHugh, a former SAS officer himself, who felt a kinship with the young Blackford.

"We've got video surveillance throughout the city, thanks to Westminster CCTV. They have cameras; thousands of them. I want video of this man's every move. But more importantly, young Colin won't let this one slip by. He's a stubborn young man. He's a Scot. I'd have no other than him watching our man. Have him relieved after midnight and I want to see him here in the morning. Constant updates, do you hear me? Constant; nothing is too trivial in this one!"

19 March
2330 hours
Port of Zeebrugge, Belgium

A gentle breeze from the south rippled across a calm sea. "A calm crossing," the loadmaster of the Sea Link Ferry thought to himself. He took a short drag from a cigarette, and then flicked it into the black water below. Beneath his galoshes, the great ship's steel hull and decks vibrated from the rhythm of four giant diesel engines running at station keeping. Her propellers churned the brine into little froths of white foam as the Captain, high atop ship's bridge, held the vessel hard against the dock, in order to keep the loading ramps in position. It would be a heavy crossing, with so many cars and vans and lorries boarding from the continent, bound for Felixstowe, England.

Mustafa Khalil Quomuz eased his left foot off the clutch on the small, canvas-sided Volvo truck and inched the vehicle forward to the drive-up passport control window just inside the ferry terminal. He smiled broadly through his large, bushy black mustache and greeted the Belgian customs officer in fair conversational French, "Bonjour, monsieur, I am late for the midnight crossing, no?"

"Mais, no, monsieur," the attendant responded. "You are on time. Your passport and visa, please? Your destination?"

"Birmingham, England."

"And the purpose of your crossing?"

"Oh, yes, I drive these funeral coffins from Brussells to England. They sell very well there."

"You are Turkish, it says here..."

"I have a Belgian visa and work permit."

"Of course," the Belgian official agreed, thinking to himself, "another Turk who had come to Belgium and stolen jobs from us." He stamped the Turkish passport and the Belgian visa, and, handing the document back to the driver, curtly said, "Pull forward until you see the man in the blue sweater. He will tell you where to go next."

"Au revoir."

"Merci."

Quomuz pressed the gas pedal and drove slowly until he came to the ship's second mate. The Englishman, whose weathered face had seen more channel crossings than could be counted, gestured with a sweeping left hand and said, "Line number 9. Have your boarding card and ticket ready." The driver complied, and, as he accelerated, hit a speed bump in the asphalt, jarring the lids on the ten caskets stored carefully behind. Soon, he was well in line behind another, larger truck bearing furniture from Holland, destined for Wales and Ireland.

The ferry traffic on the English Channel and the North Sea was still considerable, for the Channel was the highway between the continent and the British Isles, the Channel Tunnel notwithstanding. The load aboard M.V. *Vollendam* this night was further testament to the gathering economic strength of the union between the Western European nations. "No one will even think to bother me," Quomuz thought to himself. "There are so many other trucks and vans boarding tonight."

There were very few barriers to transportation between the continent and England, Quomuz knew. The European Community leaders, so intent upon lessening trade restrictions, had made passage between all borders virtually free from interruption. Long gone were the extensive passport and visa reviews, because business and the economy did not tolerate delay. Gone, too, were the thorough inspections of all cargo-bearing trucks that crossed these borders. Political pressures to keep goods and commerce flowing had won out over concerns for security, despite the practical concerns voiced by the likes of Sir Harold MacHugh. He'd testified before select Parliamentary committees that the lessened trade restrictions had made a terrorist's job all the easier. Of course, there were random, perfunctory inspections by customs agents. But the volume of traffic and the limited manpower available to inspect the thousands of trucks and vans which crossed the channel made crime detection virtually impossible. Every new day simply meant that smugglers had carte blanche to do their evil business without fear of interdiction.

Quomuz had correctly made the assumption that he was never in danger of detection as he drove his coffin-laden truck up the corrugated steel ramp into the ship's hold. His papers appeared in perfect order and the port's customs agent lacked both the time and the inclination to inspect his truck.

The ship's hold was awash in bright light as Quomuz followed the hand signals from the loadmaster who arranged the trucks and cars in a balanced order so as not to weigh the ship to either side. Once he was nestled in tight behind a truck carrying dairy products from the Netherlands, Quomuz turned off his engine and pulled up hard on the handbrake. Outside the cab of the truck, Quomuz listened to sounds so foreign to his native Palestine, the noise of prosperity; the crashing of

JONATHAN BRUCE

heavy chains against the steel deck, the shouting of
men as they rearranged the hundreds of cars within
the ship's hold, and the deep-throated rumble of the
massive ship's engines deep below. The sounds angered him, for it was not this way in his homeland
nor, he doubted, would it ever be. He was, he believed, like so many of his forefathers, the victim of
a conspiracy between the Jews and the Western
powers. "They have stolen the money and the land
and it is we who suffer. But again, Jewish pigs, you
will soon feel our sorrow."

As Quomuz reached down to the floorboard to
gather his jacket, his mind flashed to the time his
mother had died in a "tactical operation" at the
hands of the Israeli Army. That was the horrible
scene that replayed incessantly in his memory. It
was in the summer of his fifteenth year, when his
father's modest home, ten kilometers southeast of
Jerusalem, in El Walajeh, had been raided by the
soldiers and razed by bulldozers. The nightmarish
memories of that August morning were razor sharp.
To this very day, he secretly feared the soldiers; the
ones who kicked down the door only minutes before
dawn. These were angry, shouting men with guns
and bayonets.

*He tried to fight. But the boy, then barely fifteen,
was thrown to the ground. When his older brother
ran to protect him, a swift blow from a rifle butt
sent the elder sibling sprawling into the dirt. "We
hide no one! We have wronged no one. Please!" his*

father screamed, as the intruders threw their few belongings into the street. "Please. Please. We have done nothing wrong! The small, frightened boy struggled against the boot against his neck, as his brother was kicked repeatedly until he no longer moved. That's when the bulldozers began their terrible, crushing work.

It mattered not that it was a neighbor who had secretly lied to the Israeli soldiers that Quomuz's family was harboring PLO terrorists. It was irrelevant that the neighbor was seeking revenge for a business deal gone bad with Quomuz's father. It was of no consequence that an Israeli commander had later come to the family and explained the mistake and offered money to the family.

The images of the day repeated themselves in his mind's eye in slow, incessant, agonizing detail. The memories had haunted him and possessed him for years. Quomuz would remember that his brother had lingered for three days in a poorly equipped Arab hospital before internal bleeding and infection took his life. Three days Quomuz had sat by his brother's bed, changing gore-soaked dressings and swabbing away urine and feces from the motionless form. Once, at night, in the midst of half-sleep, he thought he'd heard his brother's voice murmur and he'd hated himself for not being attentive enough to capture his brother's wishes. In the days following the attack, he'd stored enough hatred to motivate himself for several lifetimes.

But for the attack that killed his brother, Quomuz might have been a shopkeeper like his father and uncle before him. There had never been any love for Israel among the Quomuz household, but, before the raid, there was no serious motivation to take up arms against the Jewish state.

The raid changed all of that, and thereafter, Quomuz's life was given over to an all-encompassing purpose: revenge. His anger had driven him to service in the Hamas and other like-minded organizations and a career of violence. He, like his enemy, had become a weapon of vengeance that had ended the lives of other children's fathers. He reasoned away any hypocrisy the situation might have suggested. But he reasoned his cause was the more just, simply because it was his cause. After all, he knew that Israel and its American ally had no misgivings about killing Palestinians. As he recalled a horrid past, his thoughts turned to more recent events and the feelings of terror and rage at how his own life had nearly ended when the Americans had attacked that night in Syria.

The endless right of reprisal would be his and the time for revenge was drawing near. The nearly four hundred pounds of plastic explosive, hidden beneath the satin lining of the coffins, would provide enough of a blast to ignite the Soman bomb the fundamentalist engineers had designed. With luck, his weapon would trigger larger secondary explosions from U.S. bombs held in storage bunkers. Those blasts would be big enough to shatter steel and crumble concrete. More important, Quomuz thought, would be the rain of nerve agent and chemical waste scattered for miles around the English countryside. The international political outrage would be ten times greater in effect than the deaths and destruction that would surely follow.

Even though Quomuz and his allies would provide the poison, the international press would quickly seize the notion that the chemical fallout had come from an American air base. The English political left would be reinvigorated. Renewed calls for British withdrawal from the Middle East and total chemical and nuclear disarmament by NATO would follow, Quomuz believed. The Americans themselves might be forced to withdraw from the British Isles under the pressure. Certainly the Israelis would suffer, if only indirectly, from the explosion, for surely, Quomuz reasoned, critics in America would more closely scrutinize transfers of weapons technology to Israel. "The media is a wonderful ally," Quomuz reassured himself.

One shipment of the gas was already in place, following a daring run by smugglers across the Irish Sea. If all was on schedule, as Khalil Quomuz hoped, the second shipment of chemicals had also arrived in London, via the Nigerian courier.

There were men waiting for him in England, men skilled enough to prepare the bomb and trigger the explosion. Many enemies would die, and

Quomuz knew his life, too, Might already be forfeit. But for the moment, there was nothing to do now, other than to find some wretched British food and a reclining chair on the passenger deck for some rest.

The crossing to England would be nearly six hours.

20 March
0145 hours
Central London

Colin Blackford wiped his eyes with his shirt-sleeve and wondered whether his promised relief would ever show up. He hadn't slept in almost thirty-six hours and the fatigue was about to consume him. He could not help but let the events of the past twenty-four months replay in his tired brain. "If ONLY I'd kept my damned mouth shut," he swore, remembering the day he'd returned to his Headquarters at the fabled British Army Special Air Service, from Afghanistan…

Returning to the present, Blackford cursed himself for his own intemperance. After a moment of further reflection, he again shook himself and reasoned that Ayugi had been almost too cavalier. He'd made no efforts to disguise or hide his movements. It had all been rather easy to track him, too easy, perhaps. Regardless, the African hadn't made a sinister move since he'd left the London Underground station at Russell Square and walked five blocks past the British Museum and over to the five-story walk-up St. Margaret's hotel.

The area near the St. Margaret's was filled with inexpensive tourist accommodations, so Blackford had no trouble securing a room in a hotel on the opposite side of the street with a view facing the front entrance to Ayugi's hotel. A quick telephone call to the St. Margaret's front desk revealed that the courier had taken a room facing the street, thankfully, opposite the window where Blackford had sat for the more than twenty hours since the stakeout had started.

Another Scotland Yard operative had taken up a position in the alley behind Ayugi's hotel, parked in a small, white Vauxhall van with darkened windows. The third, a Woman Police Constable, had registered as a guest and taken a room two doors down from Ayugi, near the common bath, and a fourth officer stood post on the rooftop of a building next door. The quartet was connected electronically.

For Farouk Ayugi's part, the chase had been no chase at all. He was wholly unaware that his movements were being watched. And so, following his instructions to the letter, he, too, waited. But unlike his pursuers, the courier could afford the luxury of sleep. The single bed was not to his liking--much too soft. But sleep was sleep and it was well to gather some when one could, he had sighed before dozing off to sleep.

"Two-seven, has the bastard moved at all?" Blackford radioed his associate in the alley van.

"Not an inch, mate," came the exhausted reply.

Before Blackford could respond with tired sarcasm to his partner, there came three gentle, almost silent knocks on his bedroom door. In stepped a detective sergeant, a man named Drummond, and a veteran of countless late-night stakeouts himself. The sergeant sarcastically chided Blackford, "Oy! When do they serve breakfast in this place?"

"God," Blackford shot back, not taking his eyes from his binoculars and Ayugi's window. "You're an hour late. Where the hell have you been? Damn. I haven't eaten in hours!"

Drummond answered, "So sorry, mate. Got hung up at the Yard and I had to take the tube. Listen here, I am supposed to tell you the chief inspector wants to see you in the morning. Eight-thirty, sharp."

"Right, then. Sod; that gives me a whopping five hours sleep. I wonder if he minds if I shower and shit in the meantime?" Blackford answered, still irritated.

The sergeant slung his jacket onto the bed and loosened his tie, then lit a cigarette. Blackford ran his fingers through his oily mop of hair and began to brief his relief man on the tactical lay out. As the Sergeant assumed the watch, Blackford bade him a sarcastic good morning, and then headed down the hallway. Several turns down the carpeted stairs later, Blackford slipped out the front door of the hotel and headed for the underground tube station. "They could damn well have sent a car around. Old bastard. Making me find my own way back," the detective muttered to himself.

A quarter of an hour later, Colin Blackford slumped against the window of an empty London Underground carriage. He dug deep into his coat pocket searching for a cigarette, but the last had been smoked hours ago. It seemed he hadn't eaten in a week. He was even too tired to sleep. Maybe a hot shower would help.

Fifteen stops later on the Piccadilly line he'd be home, grab some quick sleep, then head back to Metropolitan Police Headquarters, better known to the world as Scotland Yard.

20 March
0830 hours
Rural East Anglia, England

Quomuz wrestled with the steering wheel of the left-drive van as he negotiated the narrow British roadway. He was worried that driving on unfamiliar roads might cause an accident that would end the plot he and his compatriots had devised. He swore at a passing British motorist who had flashed his lights angrily at the Palestinian. The English had little tolerance for those who menaced the orderly flow of traffic.

Taped to the dashboard was a hand-drawn map sent a month earlier by two members of his small cadre. The men had also come to England with false Turkish passports and had found jobs at common labor in Cambridge. The location was ideal because, as a university town, the mix of races and cultures would allow the men to live and work in the open without fear of discovery. Their created identities were an effective ruse. Turks and central Asians were familiar enough throughout the United Kingdom. It was common knowledge that menial jobs were more easily gotten in England than on the continent. Hence the flow of Asians to the British Isles.

Soon, Quomuz came to yet another confounding English roundabout. There were very few intersections on British highways. Rather, at the point where two roads met, road engineers had placed traffic circles. One entered the circle and drove around it until the appropriate exit came into view. The trick, however, unknown to Quomuz and virtually every other foreign driver, was whether to stay to the inside or outside of the traffic flow. A sudden jolt from the back of the van shocked Quomuz into the realization that his left wheels had bounced over the curb which lined the island in the center of the circle. He quickly jerked his wheels to the right and again bounced both himself and his volatile cargo. Quomuz quickly prayed to Allah that his driving would not end his mission before it began.

He was close to his destination, a house not far from Cambridge University.

Thirty minutes later, he found the address written on the map. The building was a two-story white brick affair with a small garage located at the back and accessible from both the street and a narrow alleyway in the rear. Quomuz pulled up off the street and into the dirt and gravel drive. He came to a stop just in front of the closed garage doors and honked the horn three times, as planned.

Tariq Bashir quickly emerged from the back of the building and greeted Quomuz in Arabic.

"I will open the garage. It's large enough for the van. Hurry."

Quomuz drove the van quickly into its hiding place and his lieutenant closed the doors behind. "Come into the house. Mohammed is there. You have our essentials?"

"Yes, my friend." Quomuz laughed at his operative's eagerness. "But first I also need to eat and shit. It will be my first shit on the English...but not my last."

Both men laughed as they entered the empty building.

"This building is owned by the people who hired us. It is never used and we were told we could sleep here. It has been a perfect choice for us."

Surveying the structure, Quomuz agreed.

After he had eaten some bread and meat prepared by one of his men, Quomuz began to detail the plan for which the men had been selected.

"Our sons and daughters have been murdered by the Jewish pigs and their American masters. A year ago, after the Americans attacked our camp in Syria, we and our al Qaeda compatriots devised this attack to repay both England and America and the Jews for the deaths of our people. An old friend in Libya also helped us. The colonel well remembers it was the same American air pirates that killed his child many years earlier in Tripoli."

"I have brought a bomb for the Americans, but a very different bomb than we have been using. Inside the truck I drove into this place is a large bronze coffin. In the coffin are the weapons. You have the plastic explosive?"

"In the boxes in the attic above," Bashir indicated. "But what of the detonator and the timer for the bomb?"

Quomuz answered. "A nearby brother shall be here soon."

"Then you have heard from our brothers in London?" Bashir asked of the team leader.

"Only yesterday," Quomuz responded. "All is as we planned; we will soon have our first diversion to occupy the London police. We will then make and deliver our bomb to the Lakenheath base, the very air base where the American air forces began their attack on our camps. The British gave permission for the attack to begin from this base and so they must pay, too. This bomb will contain a small quantity of nerve and blood agents. We have transported them in several, separate quantities. Our purpose is to explode the bomb and scatter the chemical weapons about the American compound. We haven't exploded such a weapon in a long time and this first use will teach us how to make better and bigger chemical weapons in the future. This is the thing that the West fears most."

Quomuz continued.

"We still have support from our friends in Europe. They wish very much for such an explosion to take place because they wish to encourage the anti-American sentiment here in this country. An accident or even an intentional explosion which releases even a small amount of chemicals will cause political embarrassment to the governments both in England and the United States."

Mohammed asked, "And how do we come by these chemicals?

"Our benefactors, including Sheik bin Laden, helped procure them from our friends in Iraq. We were receiving small quantities even before the Americans invaded. As the United Nations busied itself chasing the weapons in Iraq, we were busy smuggling them into Syria and then into Africa. Bin Laden's money speaks loudly in every country where he has friends. But the Americans themselves have provided the means to transport it here. We arranged for the purchase of these chemicals some time ago, but we could not devise a way to deliver them. However, the missing American pilot we held captive provided us with the solution. We waited for the right moment to return his body to his family, and placed the body in an expensive casket purchased in Spain. When the body was flown from Tripoli to Rome, we were able to retrieve the coffin. That is the same coffin I brought with me here today. It contains the chemicals, sealed in lead. The entire world focused on the body, when it was the container they should have been worried about."

Quomuz expressed amusement. "It is the same story we were told as boys. How the servant lived in the rich man's home. Every day, he would lead the master's camel out of the gate and tied to the camel was a bag made of silk. The master's guard each day would demand the poor man open the bag, but he would find only stones, and would let the servant pass. The fool never realized that the servant was the wiser man, for he was stealing the rich man's camels!"

The trio shared a laugh.

"We have also ensured that a small quantity has come into England with the help of other friends. Those chemicals will arrive here soon."

Quomuz concluded. "We will rest today. Our contacts are in place near the American air base. We await the wire transfer of more funds from Switzerland via our al Qaeda banker in Milan. We will meet tomorrow. In three days the wrath of Allah will destroy our enemies. God is great."

20 March
0845 hours
New Scotland Yard
Counter-Terrorism Directorate

A slightly rumpled Colin Blackford combed his hair one last time with his fingers then reached down to ensure his shirt was tucked properly inside his trousers. He'd managed to find his best suit in serviceable condition and had run a hot iron over his last clean shirt before speeding to the Yard via the tube.

A short elevator ride landed Blackford on the chief inspector's floor. Upon entry to the cavernous outer office, he was directed by a stern-looking aide toward the adjacent briefing room. Approaching the imposing oak-paneled room, Blackford blinked the last sleep from his tired eyes and then pushed against the heavy double doors. The room was bathed in bright white light. A high gloss on the massive conference table reflected perfect mirror images of the faces that sat behind each microphone.

"Ah, there you are! Come in, Colin," boomed the robust Chief Inspector Sir Harold MacHugh from the far end of the giant oval. "Find a seat. I believe you know everyone here."

Blackford looked around the table. No fewer than thirty faces of power from each of the Yard's key operational departments were present: counterterrorism, international ops, electronic surveillance, and special weapons. Impressive people, the lot!

"Ladies and gentlemen, you know young Blackford. Worked that spot of trouble some months back for us on the Rubens Hotel bomb. Good work, that was!" MacHugh pronounced.

"Been doing a bang-up job at the international terminal ever since," MacHugh said a little too loudly. Both the young man and the group knew Blackford had been in the doghouse, so Blackford pretended not to hear and averted his eyes from the group. He made his way toward an unoccupied seat. MacHugh continued. "That's why I've brought him aboard for this one. He's been following our Mister Ayugi since he arrived from Nairobi."

MacHugh paused and smiled. "Right, then, does everyone have tea?"

Blackford worked his way to a second row seat behind the large shining oval. As a temporary officer, protocol dictated he sit behind the department and section heads gathered around the table. Here sat some of the brightest and most experienced minds in international police work. Never at a loss for words during lower-level staff meetings, the normally self-assured Blackford felt slightly cowered by the present gathering. He'd keep his mouth closed and eyes open during this meeting. It was his mouth, after all, which had landed him in MacHugh's service.

His eyes had only adjusted to the glare of the conference room lights when the Chief Inspector pressed a button at his console and the room went black, save for the opaque light on the rear screen projector at room's end.

"Some developments since we last met….this is the man we've been talking about, Ayugi. He started as a courier for several of the red political parties in Nigeria. Kept his hand in the business of running documents for a variety of causes in Africa and the Middle East. We normally wouldn't be so concerned about his movements; usual trade is in low-level diplomatic documents, guns, that sort of thing. He never gave us reason to bother with him. Next screen, if you please."

"Right. Our friend Otunga now says the computer he was carrying dealt more than just solitaire. What we're following, as you know...well, it's Soman. Otunga's people confirmed it. Slight odor, but then, if you're whiffing it, well, you're already in trouble...aren't you?"

MacHugh couldn't resist a bit of understated levity.

"And this is a photograph of the nasty bits our gentleman was transporting. Small vials, certainly, but the chemicals carry quite a punch. Well, then, I suppose they must," MacHugh smiled broadly at the group. "These vials of chemicals...not the usual fare for our local terrorists. This material came from someone who commands a high price and expects to cause a big problem. We could have seized it at the airport, but we would be off the game, then, wouldn't we?"

MacHugh leaned heavily upon the table, making careful eye contact with those surrounding him. His normally upbeat tone turned grave. MacHugh, then rising, placed his massive hands on his hips said, "This is a big risk we're taking. Bear with me, if you will. Let's see the next picture, please."

MacHugh continued.

"This poor fellow was found floating in the Tiber River with two gunshots to the head. Chap's face was utterly obliterated by nine millimeter rounds. Perhaps Soviet or Warsaw issue, but no slugs were found. Italian forensics, well, at best,

they have found only a small fragment of the pro-
jectile."

"Who is he, rather, was, he?" came a voice from
the second row.

"A mortician, actually. We thought a professional killing at first. Italian police regarded this as
a street homicide. You know, robbery or drugs or
some sordid affair. Then the man's father, also a
mortician, came forward with some interesting details. It seems that he and his son were hired on
rather short notice by the Vatican to receive and
transport the remains of an American military pilot
shot down during their big raid against Syria over a
year ago, the one launched from up in Anglia at the
US air base. Oddly enough, it was the Libyans who
returned the body to Da Vinci airport and the Vatican received the body with the help of the mortician, a Mr. Castiglione and his son. That's our dead
man, the younger Castiglione."

"The curious aspect is that the coffin that transported the young American was stolen shortly after
its arrival in Italy. We think just after the autopsy by
Italian customs."

The members of the group exchanged glances.

"Why on Earth would someone want to steal a
dead American from an Italian morgue--when a live
one would have been so much less trouble?"

Opined another voice in jest, "Yes; we have
several to spare. One can always find an extra
American outside Buckingham Palace."

Mild laughter around the table softened the serious air in the room. But a prompt "Steady on," from MacHugh returned the group to the matters at hand.

"No, it appears the thieves didn't want the pilot. That's where Signori Castiglione comes in. The older man finally came forward last month after someone tried to shoot him. They missed, fortunately. So, out of fear, perhaps, he contacted the Italian authorities and said that he and his son had been visited by a man the day before the Libyans delivered the body to Rome. He had been promised extra money to steal the empty coffin and deliver it to two other men--one of them an Arab."

"Apparently, the younger Castiglione lived up to his part of the bargain and paid dearly for it. From there...yes, the next picture please...from there, the trail gets icy. We can only surmise that the coffin was used to smuggle something onto the continent. One can only speculate, perhaps, that our friend Mister bin Laden or his people are up to no good. Although that's a stretch. I have no more facts than those I've given you."

Sir Harold MacHugh turned on the conference room lights once more as Colin Blackford scratched a sleep seed from the corner of his tired eyes.

"This has the attention of Ten Downing and the White House. The Prime Minister is quite interested. And he's signed on for our handling of Mr. Ayugi. Recall that he approved the use of our airfields in the attack against the terrorist camp in Syria, just as the Tory government under Mrs. Thatcher authorized the use of Lakenheath as a staging area for the raid against Libya back in 1986, to say nothing of old debts from Desert Storm AND the current mess in Iraq."

The political weight and risk of the matter was not lost on the assembly. As the Chief continued, pens flew busily over yellow pads and fingers caressed laptops as messages were passed from senior division heads to their subordinate branch superintendents.

"MI-5 agree that we are risking reprisal. The back-benchers in Parliament will have a field day if there is retaliation and any Englishmen die. So, here's the line: We theorize there's a possible connection between our dead Italian mortician and Mister Ayugi. The only problem now is that we have a cold trail. Lord knows what became of the coffin or its contents or whether it is actually related to Mister Ayugi and his chemicals. It may be nothing, but Number Ten wants to know, and that's what I want you to find out."

"Are the Americans involved? Have we notified the FBI, CIA? After all, the raids did come from their air bases."

"Only generally. We've told them where Mr. Ayugi is at present. No need to worry them yet. You know how they overreact. They'd send in their usual lot of clever experts. No, we may have precious little time to uncover this mischief. We shan't have time to nursemaid the Americans. We'll let them know when we've done the real work," MacHugh grinned broadly.

Another small titter of subdued laughter arose from the group. The American and British intelligence communities worked often and well together. But cultural differences between the two groups often made for unsettling relationships. American enthusiasm was sometimes taken by their British counterparts as "cowboy" recklessness and British patience and attention to detail was wrongly interpreted by U.S. operatives as inept lethargy. For now, this would be a wholly British investigation.

"I'll want a full report on how each of your departments plans to attack this situation by one-o'clock today. No, make that two. I'm at Whitehall for lunch. Two it is, gentlemen... and, er, ladies."

As MacHugh's team rose and gathered by the doors to exit, the Chief Inspector called out, "Blackford, a moment, I have something special in mind."

The room emptied, and the elder Scot extended a burly arm to envelope Blackford's shoulders in a slightly patronizing "father and son" way that irked the younger man. The Chief's warm smile, however, put Blackford at ease. "There is an opportunity for some good work here, Colin. You're trained in counter-terrorism, and your service record in Afghanistan was first-rate! And now, I'm going to play a hunch," MacHugh began, quietly and firmly.

The Chief began to speak and Blackford began to sense that the kennel doors had just been opened.

21 March
0930 hours
Cambridge

Quomuz affected a familiar but carefully pre-pared image for his outing in the famous university town. Tonight, the air of affluence was the perfect disguise, he knew well. Westerners would not allow themselves to suspect that a man in an expensive Austin Reed suit could be a terrorist, even if he were an Arab. He looked very much the son of another wealthy Saudi oil family. Quomuz fit the part well, from his expensive leather shoes to the massive Ro-lex watch--his mustache was neatly trimmed and his fingernails were lacquered.

Traffic was busy along Castle Street as the Pales-tinian walked from the front of his temporary home. "Many cars tonight," Quomuz noted. "Too many Westerners, too much money." Turning right, he stepped onto the sidewalk and headed toward the center of the city, his steps were measured and slow, for Quomuz was ever on guard that his movements were being watched. He would, therefore, adopt a cool, slow gait. A casual glance at his watch indi-cated that he was right on time. A ten-minute walk would place him in front of the St. Giles Church, where he would meet an old compatriot in the strug-gle.

Quomuz allowed himself to stare across Castle Street, past row houses and down a grassy slope to the Cam River. Colored lights strung along its near

bank shimmered in the evening darkness and reflected upon the black, flowing ribbon of water. Music and happy party sounds buzzed from atop a boat
house pub on the far bank. Quomuz would not allow
his mind to consider such simple pleasures. There
was a job to be done. And these were the sights and
sounds of his enemy.

At the Palestinian's approach, Petra Voss
coughed a gentle signal to her colleague. As planned,
the woman rose from the steps of the church and
embraced the taller man. They kissed, as if lovers,
and kissed again. He ran his fingers through her hair,
and then reached behind the small of her back and
held her to his side. The couple began walking, careful, practiced, and measured. Happy lovers, or so
they were to appear to the casual observer.

"Are you hungry?" Voss asked in Arabic.

"Yes, but there is little time. How are you?"

"I am well. Did our possessions arrive safely?"

"Yes. This will be a small test of our new capaci-
ties. We don't have the means for a full-scale delivery....yet," Quomuz paused, "but the amount we will
disperse in this attack will be enough to send a message to our enemies. We shall use what we learn in
this attack for more lethal operations."

"Very well, then. All is on schedule. Dieter is
ready. I have found an isolated area for staging the
assault. We will rendezvous on the A-11 motorway
and proceed to the preparation area." Voss reached
into her pocket and slipped Quomuz a small paper
with directions to the meeting point along the high-

way, near Great Eversden. "We will meet you there before first light, Monday morning."

Taking the small folded note, Quomuz nodded. "Good. Bashir and Mohammed are ready. What of our man in London?"

Voss smiled. "He is in place and ready to serve us when we call. He has been conspicuous. We are sure the British have seen him and are watching. For all of their famous subtlety, these British are clumsy and obvious. What of the helicopter?"

"Bashir has arranged a flight. There is a civilian airport here in Cambridge. We will eliminate the pilot and meet you. It is a short flight to the coast. A friendly ship awaits us in the channel off Folkestone...."

The pair rounded a corner onto a busy street near Trinity College. Students and tourists crowded the busy sidewalk, jostling in and out of shops, restaurants and pubs. Quomuz and Voss blended neatly into their surroundings. The busy streets provided the perfect cover. They appeared as yet another pair of lovers enjoying the charm of the famous city.

"Blundering English," Quomuz continued now in well-practiced German. "It is unfortunate our African associate was not told of all our plans for him. But then, perhaps he would not have been so willing to assist had he known, shall we say, the depth of his involvement," Quomuz mused.

"Don't concern yourself with him," Voss added tersely. "His people will be well paid. They always are. They will not complain. And on the subject of payment, Quomuz...."

"That has already been arranged," the Palestinian assured his comrade. "Bin Laden has been most generous. Our relationship has always been....profitable, no?"

Petra Voss said nothing in return.

Satisfied that plans were all well in hand, Quomuz again swept the woman into his embrace. "Now that we have finished our business. What of pleasure? It has been quite some time since last we...." Quomuz said, his eyes wide in anticipation.

Petra Voss stood on her toes and quickly bit the lips of her compatriot and took him by the hand.

Their casual stroll now quickened, replaced by urgent, rapid paces. They walked down the busy walk and across the high street, past a pub on the right and down an alley to an unlit doorway, and up a flight of metal stairs to a flat above a greengrocer.

Inside, Quomuz smelled the familiar, sickly sweet odor of burning hashish. American jazz played on a stereo in the corner of the sparsely furnished room. A red-haired woman sat cross-legged on the torn couch, reading a French magazine. She did not speak when Voss and the Arab entered. Rather, she exhaled a long, bluish cloud and, peering through the smoke, eyed Petra.

"You are late. You know not to displease me!" the red-haired woman named Sandrine said in a condescending and domineering manner.

Without so much as a word, Petra Voss removed her short leather jacket and walked over to the woman. She narrowed her eyes, and then slapped her fiercely. Quomuz focused intently...watching the drama before him. Yet in the next instant, Voss reached out, her hands embracing, caressing the taller woman's face, and kneeling beside the couch, kissed her with the same intensity she had displayed moments before with the Palestinian. The women's fingers clawed at each other's hair and clothing--- not losing their oral embrace for an instant. It was like two animals in heat.

Quomuz became instantly aroused at the women's passion; he reached over to the wooden table and picked up a half-empty bottle of Prusser's Navy Rum. He took a great swig, never letting his eyes wander from the drama playing out before his eyes. When both women were stripped to their bras and panties, Petra spoke in a half, husky whisper. "Sandrine, my friend will enjoy our company, yes? Let us entertain him."

The redhead again did not speak, but took another long drag on the burning pipe and held the smoke deep in her lungs. When she finally exhaled, she spoke in halting English. "Enjoy...Join us, yes."

22 March
1645 hours
London

The sky was remarkably clear and an unusually warm breeze blew in Sergeant Drummond's window from the south. Good weather was a rarity in

England, and even a hint of warmth was welcome. "Time to check in with the others," Drummond noted to himself.

"Two-Six from Keeper. Two-Six?"

"Two-Six here."

"Any sign of life from our man?"

"Nothing. I've relieved Two-Seven from the first shift. The only movement all day has been routine delivery through the alley."

"All right, then. Keep sharp. Four-Seven, are you on? Come in, Four-Seven," Drummond called to junior plainclothes W.P.C Gayle Richardson.

"Four-Seven, sir. Nothing at all," Richardson reported drolly. "Housekeeping services within the past twenty minutes made the rounds, but nothing unusual. She knocked on each door."

"Housekeeping services, Four-Seven? Isn't it rather late for the maid?" Drummond asked.

"I wouldn't know. She came to all the rooms," Richardson continued. "Turkish looking woman; perhaps Pakistani."

"Did you hear anything unusual, Four-Seven?" Drummond asked, pressing.

"Nothing, sir; not a peep out of him. I'm only two doors away. And he'd have to come by this room to get to the loo and the stairs," the W.P.C. observed.

"Has he gone to the loo today, Four-Seven?" Drummond continued.

"Only once, after mid-morning, sir. He must be waiting for a contact. Shall I casually walk by his room, pick up some sound or something?" she queried.

"Hold on. Not worth compromising our position. Stay where you are for the time being. Listen up; keep your eyes and ears open, Four-Seven. I'll check in with the main office straightaway. Keeper out."

22 March
1700 hours
492nd Fighter Squadron
RAF Lakenheath, England

Tracie's answering machine once again infuriated Zach Pollard.

"This is Mildenhall 80010. Cheers; I can't come to the telephone right now, but leave your name and a number and I'll ring you ..." came Tracie's prerecorded voice.

"Goddamn it, Tracie!" Pollard swore as he slammed down the receiver.

"Dude, it's like I told you, she's gettin' busy with another guy somewhere," Damian Mercer teased, hitting his co-pilot on the arm, "and he's probably a tanker pilot, too."

"Fuck you, Zulu," Pollard responded, more seriously than Mercer would have guessed. "And fuck her, too. She's a master of hide-the-ball. It's like we only do things on her terms; never on mine. I don't know if she got burned by someone or what, but I am tired of this shit."

"Hey, brother, chill. She's been doing you this way for months. First she shows up and then she disappears for God knows how long. She's either playin' you all the way to the altar or..."

"Don't say it, asshole. Forget it. Let's go get a beer."

23 March
0445 hours
Rural East Anglia

The headlights from the blue Fiesta sprayed evenly over the black surface of the A-11 highway. It was early enough; even the usual throng of lorries had not yet begun to choke the narrow roads to and from London. Only the rumbling of an occasional horse trailer headed for the barns at Newmarket broke the morning quiet.

A steady drizzle drained the low-hanging cloud-bank that hung over the English countryside like a pall. Beads of wet, chilled air clung to the wind-shield and evaded the wiper's futile sweep. Inside the small Ford, Petra Voss lit another cigarette and swung into the right-hand lane to pass a slower moving lorry. The warm smoke that filled her lungs fought a losing battle against the cold morning chill.

"We're almost there. Another thirty minutes," Voss said to her comrade, Dieter Koln. Koln, older, was a fellow countryman and also a former member of the Bader-Meinhof movement. "The sun will not come up for another hour," she said. "We meet

Quomuz shortly. He assures me all is prepared. His men are ready."

Koln, unshaven and clad in black leather, considered Voss's assurances. "And your American 'friend,' he suspects nothing?" The German man snarled contempt for the flyer he'd never met.

"No, the oaf! He is like so many of them, stupid and slow-witted. He has not compromised me."

"And what of him, your American," Koln sneered, "was there no farewell?"

Voss took another long drag on her cigarette and quickly flicked it out into the moist morning air. Exhaling, she answered, "I tell you, it made me sick to lie down with him. I should have killed him. But there was no need to call attention to our plans. He served our purposes well."

Koln did not answer, but turned his gaze out the car window into the wet, dark countryside. He reflected only momentarily on the dismal English weather. But his thoughts soon turned to the bomb he would shortly build with his Palestinian comrades.

Meanwhile, still thirty kilometers to the north, Mustafa Quomuz dozed in the front seat of the utility vehicle he'd driven in from Cambridge on the A45 the night before. In the back of the canvas-sided truck, his two Palestinian lieutenants slept, crammed between a wooden crate filled with weapons and ammunition and the coffin brimming with its three hundred pound cache of explosives.

Quomuz had parked the truck among a group of

heavy lorries beside a stand of pine trees just off the road near the Lakenheath air base. British truckers favored such overnight "lay-bys," and the local police generally ignored them, Quomuz had learned. He'd even shared a pot of tea with one of the drivers earlier in the night. The Welshman had readily accepted his story that Quomuz was a Turkish immigrant.

"Even if the man had been an insipid bore, at least his tea was hot," Quomuz thought. And he had appreciated the chance to stretch his legs. But his men in the back were not so lucky, for their orders forbade them from making as much as a sound throughout the night.

Quomuz was startled from his shallow sleep by the engine noise from the next truck over. A big diesel was grumbling to life. For an instant, his heart raced and his breath quickened. He glanced at his watch as he quickly regained his memory. The Palestinian shook his head to jostle the sleep from his brain, and for a moment tried hard to remember where he was. He reached for his eyes to clear the crust away and paused, holding his face in his palms. His back and arms tightened against the morning stiffness.

Just as the nearby truck pulled out from the lot and onto the narrow two-lane road, the headlights of Petra Voss's car illuminated the row of trucks where Quomuz had parked. The unexpected brightness hurt his eyes and he shielded them with the crook of his arm. Voss, not instantly finding Quomuz's truck, drove quietly into the lot and turned off her headlights, so that only her parking lights could be seen.

"Dieter, can you see it? It has a red canvas covering its side."

"It's too damn dark. Turn on the lights again."

"No. That's not the plan. We'll have to wait until there is more light. We'll not call attention to ourselves. Wait. Try some sleep."

Koln shrugged and leaned his head against the cold glass. "A few more minutes," he agreed, "mean nothing."

Half an hour later, the sun slowly climbed from the frosted fields that surrounded the truck park. A heavy mist still enveloped the countryside, diffusing the light and making it difficult to see.

"Dieter, wake up. It's time!" Voss commanded, tossing yet another cigarette from her half-open window.

"Do you see them?" Koln asked.

"Over there, third from the end."

The woman started the small car's engine and, without turning on the lights, pulled to a stop in a space next to the red-sided truck. She rolled down her window, and the olive-skinned Quomuz promptly recognized her.

"You are on time," Quomuz said calmly in German. "The American school buses will be on the road in less than two hours. We are ready. Pull onto the roadway. We will follow you. Are you sure the location is secure?"

Voss nodded, then shifted the car into reverse

and began the drive twelve kilometers distant where the final preparations for the assault were to be made. Quomuz followed at a modest distance, careful not to call attention to the vehicles traveling in tandem.

There was still very little traffic this early. Only once did Voss slow her pace to accommodate an oversized carrot truck turning from a nearby farm. But fifteen minutes and several turns later, the woman guided the car down a quiet, muddy, one-lane road obscured by a canopy of overhanging trees and a tall hedgerow. Soon, Quomuz and his men turned as well and followed the German couple. Quomuz downshifted to ensure his truck could negotiate the muck.

Voss had selected the location because it led to an abandoned barn in the wooded valley between two small hills. No one could see the meeting place, either from the main road or from the air. The only risk was of some farmer accidentally happening upon the terrorists as they armed their explosives. But the calculating Voss had quickly dispatched that concern. "What would it matter if another damned Briton died? It would be his bad luck, the meddling bastard," she'd told Koln.

Voss pulled the car off of the road and onto a narrow grassy spot that served as a shoulder. Only a few feet ahead, and partially obscured by hedge, sat another car she had parked there a day earlier. She stepped quickly from the Ford and hurried over to the first vehicle. "All is intact; no one has touched anything. The damn English, they are so trusting. They are like sheep."

Meanwhile, Quomuz, too, had pulled off of the rutted muddy road. Once out of the cab, he walked to the back of the truck and quickly began to untie the cord that secured the canvas covering. His eyes suddenly met the barrel of an assault rifle held by one of his men. "Easy, my friend; save your shooting for a better target." The man smiled and lowered the weapon.

Koln and Voss soon joined the Palestinian at the rear of the small truck. Then quickly, and without instruction, Quomuz's lieutenants, Bashir and Mohammed, began to open the crate that held the weapons.

"I'll give you a pistol and a rifle. The rifle magazine holds fifty rounds," one of Quomuz's men told Koln in broken German, who nodded his understanding of the Kalashnikov's use.

Voss eyed the truck's interior and, seeing the bronze coffin, inquired, "Quomuz, the Semtex is well packed?"

"Nearly three hundred kilos; it will make a great noise. A very great noise!" The Palestinian laughed.

"What of the chemicals?" Voss asked.

"Ah…yes. Our chemical surprise for the Americans; it is placed here in this container," Quomuz continued, laying the padded metal box inside the coffin near a bulge of plastic explosive.

"And the detonator?"

"It's in the front of the truck."

"Dieter will help you prepare it."

It took just over an hour for the team to attach the detonators to the explosive. The blast would have to be strong enough to lay waste to any security door on the American bomb depot. With luck, the blast would shatter the Americans' weapons storage berm and the bombs that lay inside. The chemical package would likewise shred into countless microscopic droplets and disperse into the air of the surrounding area, depending upon the strength and direction of the wind.

Koln first drilled a hole into the side of the coffin, just large enough for two fingers to fill. Then, reaching into the box, he gently extended the detonator wires, and packed one end of the charge in two handfuls of plastic explosive. A long trailing black wire was left exposed, which the German passed back through the hole to Quomuz, who slid it through an opening in the metal paneling and into the cab.

Koln then scooted out of the truck bed and into the cab and, finding the detonator wire, connected it to an electronic actuator, the trigger. If all went as planned, a firm push on the button would actuate a three-minute timer that in turn, would explode the destructive mass.

"The crater might be a hundred meters wide," he mused. "We will see if the price we paid our black African friend was money well spent."

When the bomb was completed, each member of the team was fully armed and issued extra ammunition. Quomuz then gathered them together to review, for the last time, their plans.

Quomuz spoke in his native tongue for the benefit of the Palestinians, Voss and Koln understood Arabic better than Bashir and Mohammed understood German.

"These are the aerial photographs and here is the map we were provided by our comrades from the former KGB. Notice how the air base is divided in half by a common highway. The section of the base that lies to the south of the highway is unsecured."

Quomuz, pointing at the photograph, advised. "This is where the Americans live. There are many houses for their military personnel. That is where the school is and where the buses will unload the children. Now look just here...that is the secure portion of the base. It is to the north of the road, in this area." Quomuz continued, "There is the main runway, these are hangars for their aircraft, and now look here to the west. See these bunkers where the munitions are stored? A wire and chain fence surrounds this entire north section. Another wire fence surrounds the munitions storage area. But that is all that separates the base from you. Two wire fences. Perhaps the Americans did not listen well to their Jewish masters about security."

The Palestinians shared a laugh as Quomuz continued. "The whole area is large, but patrolled by inexperienced security forces, military policemen still in their teens. Remember, this is where their weapons are kept, stored in these concrete bunkers. This is your target. You can see that your entry point is on the far west side of the security section and only a few yards from the bunkers. The fence at your entry point is covered with trees. But the security is very poor. You should easily breach these defenses."

"We are in three teams. Mohammed and Bashir will have the truck with the explosive. Petra and Dieter take the school bus. I will provide air recon and the escape flight as planned. The helicopter stands ready in Cambridge. Now, look at your watches. The American children arrive at the school in just over an hour, but there are several points along the road leading to their school where the bus can be stopped and boarded."

Voss unfolded a detailed British highway map. "We will stop the bus here with our car. After we have boarded, we will proceed to our planned rendezvous where the helicopter will be waiting. We will then come for the two of you, Bashir, and will radio you when we are within range. That is when you trigger the bomb. We then fly quickly across the English Channel, where we have friends waiting in Belgium who will meet us at Zeebrugge. Our transit out of Europe has already been arranged," Quomuz added.

"Dieter, my friend, once you are in command of the vehicle, you will not allow the bus to stop moving at any moment. So long as the bus is kept moving, the police, the British Army and the Americans won't attack you. The children are your best protection--but do not hesitate to shoot one of them and throw the body onto the roadway. In this way, they will take you very seriously. Their buses have two doors, front and rear."

Dieter Koln nodded in understanding.

"Petra, position yourself at the rear of the passenger compartment near the back door. You will have a clear view of everything from there and can also watch the road behind you. Dieter, you will stay right behind the driver so you can clearly see the highway ahead."

Voss smiled knowingly as the team leader continued.

"You must proceed quickly to our rendezvous. Remember, the bus and the children are expendable. Time is not. You must be at the meeting point at 0830, just one hour after our operation begins. We cannot allow them to organize a reaction. We must escape before they understand what has happened. Do you completely understand?"

"Of course," Petra Voss agreed. "No one will open fire upon us so long as we have the American bastard children. We will take one or two of them into the helicopter, yes?"

"And then," Quomuz added, "we throw them into the sea. The murdered children of Palestine will be avenged."

"So long as we are paid, Quomuz," Voss, ever the mercenary, added coldly. "So long as we are paid." Quomuz elected to ignore her remark.

"Mohammed, the arming mechanism gives you

only three minutes..."

"We are prepared to die," Mohammed assured his leader. "Allah will receive them well in Paradise for their sacrifice, those who die in His name. My older brother Nawaf was one of the martyrs who carried Allah's wrath to the Zionists. I honor his sacrifice and am ready to join him."

Without hesitation, Quomuz continued. "You have studied the aerial map of the airbase and have seen for yourselves the fence on the west end of the weapons compound. The American security guards will be distracted when our comrades seize the bus loaded with their children. I anticipate that all available forces will be brought to bear upon the moving bus and their attentions will be diverted."

"Petra, you and Comrade Koln will radio me when you have taken the bus. Then I will radio you, Bashir that you are to begin the assault on the base. That is the moment when you will drive through the wire fence and toward the bomb supply depot."

"The Americans are such fools. You will encounter only slight resistance from their Air Force security personnel. They only have small arms and are not trained for real warfare. Some of their forces will even be women. Slaughter them, the infidel sluts. There is no dishonor in killing them, for they are the enemies of Allah. Kill them, just as we have killed the Zionist women."

"After you have driven the bomb into the weapons supply area, radio me. I will be only moments away from you. Then trigger the detonator. You must only push the red button on the box that is in the front of the truck. Then, you will have time to save yourselves. I will be waiting there for you in the helicopter and we will go together to a hero's welcome in Palestine."

The strike team all nodded. Dieter Koln reached into the pocket of his leather jacket for a package of cigarettes and offered one to each of the others. Quomuz declined, and walked toward the second car Petra Voss had hidden earlier. He opened the right-hand door, but before entering, he turned and gave a knowing smile to the two other Palestinians and said slowly in Arabic, "Revenge is ours this day. God is truly great!"

23 March
0645 hours
Feltwell, England

Zach Pollard zipped his flight suit and reached down to turn on the television. The antique British set crackled to life as he made his way to the kitchen for some coffee and a peanut butter sandwich. Two brisk rings from the telephone startled him...

"You up?" Damian Mercer inquired.

"Yeah, thanks. What time we take off?"

"Nine, but we gotta mission plan. The BBC says there's some weather over Scotland. How's Tracie?"

"Don't know; I tried her all last night. Not a

word!" Pollard sighed, resigning himself.

"I'm telling you pal, there's another guy...." Mercer pestered.

Pollard, not yet awake, was in no mood for fun. "Uh huh. Listen, I'll see you at work."

"That's a roger," Zulu Mercer answered.

23 March
0730 hours
Cambridge, England

The Cambridge-Anglian Flying Service had been open for half an hour when the scheduled customer, an Egyptian student, a Mister Karabak, was to arrive for an early morning photo session over the University. "A low ceiling this morning," the pilot thought to himself as he straightened his tie.

The Englishman smoothed his optic orange flight suit one last time as Quomuz drove into view. "There's our Mister Karabak now. Spot on time."

Quomuz parked some fifty yards from the lone, waiting Jet Ranger helicopter, and seeing the pilot standing near the craft, called a hearty "Hello" and offered a sweeping wave of the arm to put his quarry at ease. Alighting from the car and walking toward the boot, Quomuz again waived, receiving a return gesture from the pilot. Quomuz wasted little time retrieving an oversized nylon camera bag from the trunk. Inside the bag were radios, hand grenades and magazines for his 9-millimeter handgun. The pistol and silencer were tucked carefully in the waistband of his trousers and were further concealed by the leather jacket he'd chosen. The Palestinian affected a broad smile and a happy wave as he approached the helicopter--in turn, the pilot boarded and began his pre-flight preparations.

As the two-bladed rotor slowly began to turn, the pilot looked up at the passenger-side door to see the smiling face of his morning's fare, Mister Karabak. "Good morning! Cheers! Ready for your flight, sir?" he yelled, in order to be heard above the rising engine noise.

"Yes!" Karabak responded, bending down. "Just let me lift my cameras into the helicopter."

"Right-O...Won't be a moment 'til we're airborne," the pilot added and looked down once again to study the collection of gauges and dials on the console of the craft.

The Englishman's happy words were his last. A silenced shot from the pistol to the Englishman's temple snuffed the life instantly from the sandy-haired father of two. The blast rocked the pilot's head and sprayed the side pilot's window with a spider's web of blood, hair and brain.

Quomuz stepped quickly to the pilot's side door and, opening it, unharnessed the lifeless form and let it fall to the soft, wet grass below. The assassin grabbed a roll of paper towel sitting on the copilot's seat and wiped away the blood from the window as best as he could. With a quick toss, his satchel-arsenal landed with a plop in the craft's back seat.

Quomuz hopped aboard, and without waiting to fasten his restraint, revved the engine and planted his feet firmly upon the rudder pedals.

As the Jet Ranger lifted into the wind and rain, Quomuz shot a glance at the dial of his watch. "Seven thirty-eight. On schedule...."

23 March
0745 hours
Central London

Maureen, the floor maid at the St. Margaret's, was a sturdy East Ender with arms and wrists as strong as any Cockney man's. Trudging slowly along the corridor, her shoulders slightly stooped from many years in domestic labor, she pulled a heavy canvas laundry bag behind her as she had almost every morning for the last twelve years at the hotel. She was the chief upstairs domestic, and although the work was backbreaking, she was glad to have it. Any job was a good one, she believed, if it paid; especially in these tough times.

She gave a perfunctory rap on Farouk Ayugi's wooden door and announced "Maid, sir...." There came no quick reply. Accordingly, the woman found her passkey from amidst a noisy jangle and slid it into the lock. Again she called out, "Maid for the room, sir." Again, there was no answer.

Maureen entered and found the room to be fully dark. "Here...what's this? Morning, and no one's opened the curtains?" She slid her hand along the cool plaster wall for the light switch. When the ceiling lamp above her splashed the room with light, her eyes filled with horror. There, spread-eagle on the bed, lay a half-naked black man--the right side of his head missing. His half-face was bloodied and grotesque. His remaining eye stared blankly at the woman and the sheets were soaked with a dark red and purple blood.

She stood, horrified, unable to speak.

After what seemed a silent eternity, the heavyset woman cried out, "Bloody Hell..." then screamed loud enough to wake those on the floor above her.

The Woman Police Constable, sitting but two rooms away, jumped to her feet. "No time to worry about the cover, something's wrong," and, keying the microphone on her two-way, called her male counterpart. "Keeper, this is Four-Seven. Trouble...." But before Drummond could answer, WPC Richardson was out the door and bounding toward the maid and the dead man.

Entering through the open door, she couldn't believe her eyes. There hadn't been as much as a sound from Ayugi's room since she had assumed surveillance duties the day before. The constable grabbed the shrieking woman by her broad shoulders and pulled her from the room. At the same moment, she reached again for her radio and called a hurried message to counterpart, "Keeper, our man's been shot. Get over here quickly. Repeat, he's been shot! Call forensics. Jesus...."

It took the plainclothes detective only a minute to radio the uniformed members of the Metropolitan Police on standby support duty. He raced from his perch and into the street; his lungs nearly exploded as he bolted into the lobby of the St. Margaret's and up the stairs toward Ayugi's room. Already, a small group of hotel residents had begun to gather outside the dead man's chamber.

"Get the goddamn hell away..." Drummond screamed hoarsely.

"Police business. Get the hell out of my way."

In the distance, the cacophony of approaching sirens intensified.

When the detective burst into the room, he found WPC Richardson hunched over the dead man's body. "What the fucking hell happened here?" the sergeant demanded. "I thought you said you had heard nothing?"

The woman turned, angry, at the near accusation. "I didn't hear a damn thing, Sergeant, not a damn thing! Not so much as a bloody sneeze!"

"All right," he paused, collecting his breath, his heart still beating too fast. "No one's accusing you. Jesus fucking Christ! There will be hell to pay for this one.... Let's keep people back, now, all right?" The small group of residents continued to career for a better glimpse of the goings-on.

The woman constable pushed two men back with her hands on their bare chests. "All right, gentlemen," she huffed. "Police business; nothing to do with you." Two uniformed officers suddenly appeared in the hallway and took control of the maid and the patrons still gathered in the corridor.

The WPC reentered the room and now saw her counterpart leaning over the corpse. He looked up at her for a moment, and then suggested, "Let's take a look before there's a real crowd in here. Let's not lose our heads or any crucial evidence. What do you make of this?" the sergeant asked, pointing at a tell-tale bullet hole in the wall next to the dead man's bed.

She answered, "Looks like high-velocity blood spatter and tissue on the wall and window. From the looks of it, the shooter was standing about halfway between the door and the bed. Must have been a bloody cannon; probably a silenced .45 caliber automatic. Just look at the poor bastard's skull! Jesus. Someone wanted this bloke dead, that's for certain." The conversation was sharply interrupted by a series of high-pitched beeps from a two-way radio.

"Keeper here," Sergeant Drummond answered. Then, in slow, methodic tones, came the voice of Chief Inspector MacHugh. "Keeper, this is Tower. What is your situation, Keeper?"

"How in the hell..." the man swore into the air before keying his microphone. The pair exchanged knowing looks. Raising the handset to speak, the detective answered, "Tower, our man's been killed. We have little else at this time."

"That is exceedingly unfortunate..." came Inspector McHugh's measured, restrained response, and then he added with emphasis, "...for you both!

Secure the area and report to me immediately. And above all else, find the contraband. I repeat, find and secure the contraband. Tower out."

The handset went dead.

"Christ!" the detective swore. "Let's get the uniforms to clear these people from the hallway. Bloody fucking sod! Let's have a quick look about for our man's luggage."

Outside the St. Margaret's, a full two dozen marked and unmarked police units were already blocking the street, and a crowd of curious tourists strained to get a view of the excitement. Soon, the building would be overtaken by a swarm of investigators. None, however, would find the laptop or its lethal content.

Her Majesty's government had wanted Mister Ayugi alive, the chemicals traced and the collaborators found. There would be hell to pay.

23 March
0755 hours
Bury St. Edmunds, England

Gerald McCrory steered the oversized bus off of the four-lane A45 and onto the smaller B1065, a two-lane road toward the American primary school at RAF Lakenheath. McCrory's "coach," as the English termed a bus, was large even by American measure. It was larger even, than a standard Greyhound bus. Some were even equipped with television and video to keep the usually boisterous school crowd at bay.

But all was quiet this morning. The American school children he'd picked up in Bury St. Edmunds were still sleepy enough that they hadn't begun the morning's free-for-all. McCrory looked over his left shoulder and smiled as he saw mops of brown and blond hair just over the tops of the high-backed seats. A few had fallen asleep again during the half-hour ride from home. Not all Americans lived within the confines of the air bases in England. Most, in fact, chose life "on the economy" rather than live in the cramped base houses. That made for a long series of bus rides to and from school each day--but most service families preferred the American schools to the local ones, even if it meant early mornings for the children.

"The day is yet peaceful enough," McCrory thought to himself as he slowed for a curve. "Another ten minutes and the U.S. Air Force will take to the roads..." he chuckled. McCrory had driven this route for thirteen years and had come to know well the habits of American drivers and their early morning routines.

McCrory was soon within sight of the air base. Another bus, then two, appeared a half-mile distant, approaching from the opposite direction. "There's Cameron and there's Andy. Both right on schedule," McCrory told himself, recognizing the other drivers he'd known for years.

The coachman was suddenly startled as a

small blue Ford Fiesta pulled slowly from a hidden dirt siding onto the roadway just ahead of the school bus. "Hello...What's this?" McCrory asked himself, slightly irritated at the driver's actions. He quickly applied the brakes to slow the larger vehicle.

"Mind you," McCrory said into the windshield, "I'd have gone by soon enough. What's the hurry, then?

The blue car puttered along slowly, causing McCrory to downshift once again. As the tandem approached the crest of a small hill on the narrow road, the car suddenly stopped dead in the roadway. McCrory, too, footed the brakes and the bus came to a halt only feet behind the blue Fiesta.

Gerald McCrory turned to answer one of the children who asked why the bus had stopped, but Petra Voss suddenly sprang from the front seat of the car. With a fluid sweep, she brandished the AK-47 assault rifle and sprayed a quick burst into the windscreen of the parked bus.

McCrory turned on instinct as the windshield just in front of him splintered into a thousand tiny pebbles of glass. Just then, Dieter Koln let fly a concussion grenade, purposely aimed to the side of the bus. The blast shattered the dozen windows along the right hand side of the bus-- glass and dirt and rocks spewed from the shock and slammed into tiny faces and blasted an eight-year-old boy, bloodied, into a small friend's lap.

The driver was too dazed to react as the German woman ran for the door and blasted another volley up and into the cab. Thirty metallic pings tattooed against the roof as Petra Voss kicked open the door and stormed up the step and onto the landing next to the cowering driver. McCrory's right hand reached down for something. The East German lowered the muzzle of the automatic weapon and pulled hard on the trigger.

McCrory's body jolted and shook as if he were being battered by a crowbar. The first bullets ripped his face away from the skull, as small bits of his smashed jaw spewed onto the seat behind. Blood spattered against the window and seat.

Then a chilling silence, as the children, their young minds unable to comprehend the events that were unfolding about them, stared in utter disbelief. Voss kicked at McCrory's limp figure and yelled for Koln to join her.

On the highway behind, Reg Savidge also stared in shocked horror. He had pulled to within a hundred yards behind the scene when Dieter Koln took aim and coldly shot at the second bus. One round found its mark, hitting the driver in the left upper arm. But Savidge, acting on instinct, quickly rammed the unwieldy coach into reverse and stomped his foot down on the gas pedal. Dieter Koln raced for the bus door where Petra stood, panting hard like a wild animal. "Petra, goddamn it, you've killed the fucking driver!" Koln raged from a surge of adrenaline.

"Damn you! He was reaching for a weapon. Now get on and throw the goddamn body out. You drive."

The German woman's voice temporarily shocked some of the children to their senses and they began to scream wildly. Others cried for their mothers.

"Shut up, damn you all!" Voss screamed in frightening English. A ten-year-old black boy nearest to the woman hid his face and cried loudly.

"Come here, you little black bastard. Come here!" Reaching for the boy, Voss dug her fingers deep into the child's throat and held his face close to hers.

"Do you want me to kill you right now? Is that what you want, you little bastard nigger?"

Then, turning the frightened child's face toward the others, she again screamed, "Is that what you all want? If you want, I will kill all of you now. You will shut up and do what we tell you!"

Gerald McCrory's head made a sickening, hollow thud as the bloody mass hit the pavement. His lifeless arms flopped like a rag doll and he fell into a grotesque and mangled heap. Dieter Koln wiped a bloody hand off on his pants leg and planted himself where the dead driver had sat only moments before.

The engine was still running as the terrorist quickly surveyed the clutch and shift. He planted a heavy foot on the gas and engaged the clutch in the lowest gear. The bus lurched forward, slamming the small Ford off to the side of the roadway, as thirty sobbing children cowered close to each other amid the blood and glass.

As he continued pulling back, the wounded Reg Savidge managed to key the microphone on his two-way radio. "Central. We've got an emergency here. I am shot, I tell you. I'm shot! A bloody madman has taken Gerald's coach and the children with it...."

Two minutes later, the Suffolk Constabulary was on the telephone to the American air base. Another minute later, General Jack Kilrain ordered his security forces onto full alert and called out to his vice commander, "Get HQ Third Air Force. Urgent..."

Dieter Koln's bloody hands slipped as he oversteered the ungainly bus down the narrow two-lane highway. By now, the morning rush of traffic toward the American bases at Mildenhall and Lakenheath had begun to slow traffic in all directions. In the rear of the bus, Petra Voss swiveled her head back and forth, scanning the highway behind, looking for the first signs of the British police or American service personnel.

"Keep going straight, Dieter. Look for the signs to Brandon and stay on the road until I tell you to turn."

The children were now huddled in groups of three and four, their arms interlocked, faces hidden. Many were crying and some had even crawled onto the floor of the bus beneath the seats to hide from the bad people that had scared them so. Papers and books were scattered everywhere and blown about by the wind as it streamed in through the shattered glass on the front and side of the bus.

Passenger cars now passed the damaged bus. Drivers and passengers craned their necks and pointed at the bullet holes and broken glass, wholly unaware of the evil so near.

"Remember, drive slowly. We must give them time to react to us. Quomuz must have time to reach the rendezvous point by helicopter...." Voss commanded. Koln braked, quickly downshifted and found second gear. The vehicle slowed to less than thirty kilometers an hour as still more passenger cars passed.

In the distance, Voss heard the warbling wails from an approaching armada of police cars. Overhead, a Royal Air Force helicopter beat the air heavily as the moving surveillance took shape.

Now twenty-five kilometers away, Quomuz banked to the right and dipped the stolen craft toward a roadway and clearing in the midst of the Thetford Forest. The skids bumped hard against the uneven surface of the clearing and mud from the wet ground soon caked the undercarriage. Quomuz slowed the blade rotation, but did not shut the engine off. As the blade slowed, Quomuz opened the pilot's side door and with a powerful two-way radio in hand, stepped into an inch of mud below. He stretched the telescoping antennae to its full length of four feet and toggling the "on" switch, pressed the microphone key.

"Bashir? Can you hear me? Bashir? Respond..."

"I hear you," came the clear reply from not more than nine kilometers away.

Bashir and Mohammed had concealed themselves in a grove of bushes, roughly halfway from the nearest road and the wire fence that surrounded RAF Lakenheath.

"What can you see? Bashir, tell me."

"There are sirens, and a helicopter has flown over but it not returned. We see on the other side of the runway, American forces are running like wild dogs. There are small vehicles everywhere. But they are at least a kilometer away, maybe even two away. We see the bomb depot as in the picture. There are only two guards. We are ready."

"Hurry! The bus has been taken and the Americans are in confusion. Make your entry and trigger the bomb when you have entered a storage bunker. Then radio me as we have planned. Allah goes with you."

"Quomuz," Petra Voss shouted into her radio in Arabic. "Quomuz, we heard your transmission. Quomuz, respond!"

Although Quomuz clearly heard the German's transmission, he smiled and called "Godless Whore" into the air as he collapsed the antennae of the two-way radio and stepped back to the cockpit of the Jet Ranger.

"I will let the Americans and the British have you as small payment for our visit. Your death," Quomuz thought, "will cover my escape well."

SEVENTH PSALM

23 March
0820 hours
Royal Air Force Lakenheath

A few short kilometers away, the Palestinian assault team made ready their attack. The team leader, Bashir, crept back into the clump of bushes that obscured the canvas-sided truck. Mohammed returned from the back of the truck and joined his compatriot in the cab.

"The rifle and grenade launcher are ready. The bomb detonator is armed. Allah is with us..." Mohammed's hands began to shake hard enough that his fingers lacked the strength to turn the ignition. His compatriot reached across to steady his grip and, twisting, started the truck's engine. "Go ahead, my friend," Bashir exhorted, "as we have trained many times."

Mohammed raced the engine and released the clutch, as the truck's rear tires began biting into the soft earth and spinning mud and grass behind. In an instant, they lurched forward and began the two-mile dash for the wire perimeter. Trees, bushes and stumps hurried past the windows of the truck as the vehicle gathered speed.

Bashir cocked the bolt on the Kalashnikov assault rifle, and then released the safety of the Chinese grenade launcher. The terrain was bumpy and the truck bounced almost out of control as their speed built. Suddenly, the weapons storage area loomed into view. Ahead, beyond the barbed wire fence, were the large concrete bunkers that were believed to house the American nuclear weapons; their low, thick concrete roofs rose only a few feet from the surrounding earthworks. "There on the left, Mohammed," Bashir shouted. "Aim for the large, brown door--the one on the left. Hit it, knock it open."

The deafening wails of the warning klaxon wavered through the hallways of the 492nd Fighter Squadron.

"Jesus Christ!" Damian Mercer yelled. "What the hell?" He covered his ears and raced for the hardened section of the squadron bunker. Mercer was quickly joined by a dozen other officers and enlisted, each yelling above the siren's roar. "We're not scheduled for an exercise...What the hell is going on?" one officer yelled. Another said, "This couldn't be a joke. Nobody screws around with the warning klaxon. Maybe a malfunction?"

Suddenly, two fully-armed security policemen burst into the room, M-16's locked and loaded. A uniformed staff sergeant barked sharply, "Sir! This is for real! You officers get down! NOW!"

Mercer's eyes swept the room and found Pollard. Both, wholly startled at the rush of events, dove for the floor beneath the heavy wooden tables the pilots used to spread their flight maps upon. "What the hell is going on?" one of the new lieutenants shouted to no one in particular.

The Security Forces NCO quickly gave instructions to his subordinates, as they placed their hands against the massive steel and concrete vault door and pushed hard. As the door slowly swung on its titanium hinges, the sergeant rotated the case-hardened steel wheel lock, and then reached up high on the wall near the door and pushed a hand-sized red button. The wailing klaxon silenced and Zach pulled his hands away from his throbbing head. "Man, what the hell is happening out there?" Pollard asked his crewmate, Mercer.

Came the reply, "Don't know, but it looks like we're in here for a while."

On the far side of the base, the terrorist attack was well underway. Small arms fire from the American sentries impacted on the hurtling truck only a few seconds before it hit the wire security fence. M-16 rifle rounds from the squad of four camouflage-clad security forces riddled the ground and raised a shower of mud.

Bashir felt the first rounds smash into the hood and roof as the speeding truck neared its collision. A quick volley ripped across the face of the windshield, splintering glass in tiny shards that flew into the driver's eyes and throat.

"Are you hit, Mohammed?" Bashir screamed as he lowered the grenade launcher toward the American patrol. The bouncing seat made aiming difficult, but the terrorist found his aim and let fly with a loud "Koosh." It took only a millisecond for the round to explode into one corner of the storage bunker as chips of concrete and steel rained down on two of the American security detail, a unit of National

Guardsmen from Iowa. The blast knocked a third Guardsman off her feet as Bashir aimed the AK-47, fired, and raked the position where two sentries had taken cover.

Just before impact, Bashir grabbed hard for the bomb-activation device. He placed it squarely in his lap and ducked below the dashboard as the fence came racing toward the cab.

The double-stranded barbed-wire fence collapsed into a tangle from the force of the blow dealt by the speeding truck. The high-pitched scream of popping, snapping wire relieved of its tension matched the constant staccato of automatic gunfire. Bashir turned his weapon out the side of his window and let fly another volley. Pings and thuds of copper-jacketed lead ricocheted off the cement face of the bunker as Bashir tried in vain to answer the fire from the U.S. forces. He exhausted one banana clip and quickly inserted another. One American guard ran toward the vehicle, his weapon ablaze. A stream of fire riddled Bashir's door and smashed into his upper thigh and stomach. Blood squirted hard from deep wounds to Bashir's femoral artery and gut.

Lowering his muzzle and sighting along the overheating barrel, the terrorist's aim found the young American. The Arab's adrenaline masked the pain as he squeezed hard on the trigger. Five quick rounds smashed into the young man's upper chest and arm and he dropped to the ground, writhing and screaming in agony.

A staccato of lead crashed against the truck from the American security team, now only thirty yards distant. A quick radio message from the team leader, a junior sergeant, ensured more firepower would be quickly on the way.

"The door, the door...." Bashir screamed at the driver, who slammed the truck into reverse and re-aimed for the bomb-dump door. "Now, now!" Bashir screamed, "The door..."

Nineteen-year-old Airman First Class Barbara Hatley lifted herself from the grass-covered roof of the bunker. Her left arm was numbed from bits of steel and concrete that had flown from the blast of the Arab's grenade volley. Quickly surveying the rapidly expanding chaos, the young woman's eyes fixed upon the driver, Mohammed, and she formed a hurried plan of attack. Petrified, Airman Hatley didn't allow herself time to breathe as she jumped ten feet to the concrete pad below, her M-16 cradled firmly in her arms. Hatley landed hard on her right ankle, something snapped, and she rolled awkwardly toward the truck as Mohammed released the clutch and began a death crash toward the shelter door.

Suddenly, from above, the Jet Ranger helicopter swept in for a closer look.

But Hatley, now only yards from the truck, managed a glimpse of the hovering aircraft above. There was no time to deal with that... She pushed herself up on a bloody arm and managed to gain her feet. The truck's wheels were now spinning wildly and gaining speed. Hatley raised her right hand, and without sighting, crushed the hand grip and trigger. Seven fast shots traced a line into the steel just beneath Mohammed's window. "Christ!" the young woman shouted.

As the truck sped toward the door, Bashir fumbled vainly with his left hand to find the bomb's trigger.

Hatley quickly reloaded, slamming another magazine into the semi-automatic and aimed again. Squeezing evenly this time, her blast was true and rocked Mohammed's head and shoulder. The Palestinian slumped toward his bleeding partner, his left arm in the steering wheel, his foot fixed to the accelerator.

The truck careened off its path, and, gaining speed, slammed headlong into the steel-reinforced concrete bunker--just wide of the entryway door. The crash slammed Bashir hard against the dash. Dazed, Bashir shook himself and reached for the Soviet-built rifle and began to open fire through the splintered side window. His human targets were now only scant yards away, some crouched behind concrete works, while some lay prone against the ground.

A wild, swinging arc of fire from the terrorist's gun found Barbara Hatley's left leg and she crumpled to the pavement. In sheer agony, she rolled against the concrete buttressing to find shelter from the fire. Short bursts of lead sprayed from the weapons of young Air Force security forces. Many of their uneven shots fired wide, wasted on account of fear and nerves. More experienced combat troops might have dispatched the terrorists quickly, but these were air base defense forces, unseasoned and untested. But despite the team's collective innocence and fear, their previous training steadied their inexperienced hands. And quickly, the Americans coordinated their fire and directed it upon the cab. Sergeant Turkula, in command, yelled to steady his small band. And suddenly, a merciless volley from the ten fully automatic rifles shredded the aluminum cab and finally smashed the life out of the man once known as Bashir.

The digital electronic timer slipped from the bloody-slick seat and onto the cab floor...

Barbara Hatley clutched her bleeding thigh and screamed to her sergeant, "Look! What about the chopper? Look at the chopper!" The sergeant whipped his head around and seeing the helicopter, yelled, "It's not ours. Repeat. Not friendly. Open fire...open fire!"

As the first shots sped toward him from below, Quomuz climbed and banked away from the shooting. He was a sitting duck in this slow-moving excursion craft. As for his bleeding comrades on the ground, he could do no more than watch helplessly. He reached instinctively for his pistol. "Perhaps a few shots will kill some of them and buy Mohammed some time..." But as more fire from the ground hit his rotors and undercarriage, Quomuz thought better of it. This was no time for bravery. "There are many more battles to be fought," the Palestinian rationalized to himself. "I must save myself to continue the struggle another day." Pushing the throttle and turning toward the English Channel, he continued his acceleration and climb. "Mohammed is now with his martyred brother; they and Bashir rejoice with Allah. They are martyrs and heroes. Perhaps, one day, I will die as bravely...but not today!"

Enroute to a security conference at RAF Mildenhall, Colin Blackford keyed the microphone and called out over the high-band security radio to Scotland Yard. "I am in pursuit. The coach is about five kilometers distant and the Suffolk Constabulary is positioned to intercept and block upon our orders. Over."

"Roger," came Sir Harold's dispassionate reply. "Do not close. Repeat. Do not close on the carriage until I arrive. We are airborne and should be at your location within twenty minutes. How are our American friends holding up?"

"In the hunt. I am correct, sir, that we have jurisdiction?"

"Yes. That's been coordinated. Their security forces are subordinate to you. Is that clear?"

"Roger."

Blackford floored the accelerator of the Range Rover in hopes of glimpsing the hijacked school bus. The four-wheel drive vehicle responded with a lurch. Blackford rued the fact that he could only muster about ninety-five kilometers per hour in the specially outfitted vehicle. But then his quarry didn't generate much speed either. The coach was doing no more than fifty-five. Thus, Blackford could keep up, followed by three marked Suffolk Constabulary chase cars--their blue lights flashing. Switching to a tactical radio frequency, Blackford called out to the nearest marked car. "Right, then, keep this pace. Come no closer."

"Roger, Metro," the uniformed officer answered.

In the far distance, a procession of marked Air Force security vans and cars sped to catch up. In the lead American vehicle were four armed agents of the Air Force Office of Special Investigations. Counter-terrorism was, supposedly, an AFOSI specialty and it galled any American to take orders from a Brit.

"It's their country..." General Kilrain had ordered over the radio, just a few minutes earlier. "You work for the Brits in this one. Is that clear?" The agent had offered a correct, "Understood, sir," but he hadn't liked the order. These were American kids on that school bus. And if British intelligence had been so damned good, one agent complained to the other officers in the van, "...why the hell was this terror-drama being played out now?"

"Longstreet to Blackford," the ranking American agent called out on the radio. "Longstreet to Blackford."

"Blackford here, over."

"We're only four, maybe five klicks behind you. What's your exact position?"

"Approaching two kilometers out. Hold your position for further orders. He's not showing any signs of letting up. Stand by."

Back aboard the hostage bus, as the cold, wet wind streamed through the shattered windows, amidst a wail of children's cries, Petra Voss scanned the sky above, seeking out the promised rescue helicopter that was nowhere in sight. The German woman began to sense betrayal.

Keying her hand-held radio, she screamed into the transmitter, "Quomuz, Quomuz. Where are you? Over. We are near the rendezvous point. QUOMUZ!" But the hoped-for answer from Quomuz was not forthcoming.

"The radio works. Something else is wrong, Goddammit!" she yelled to Koln, who screamed back, in a near hysteria, asking for directions to the planned rendezvous site.

"It's the next right turn, that large field," Voss screamed. "Where is the fucking helicopter?"

A few kilometers distant, there was a sudden quiet at the bomb depot as Bashir's head and shoulders fell against the cab door. The young American sergeant ordered a cease-fire and strained his eyes to catch a glimpse of motion coming from the truck.

Stillness was the only reply.

"Hold your fire. Stay low," Staff Sergeant Turkula rasped, now hoarse from the countless hurried commands given in the firefight. "Hatley! Where the hell are you?"

"Over here. I'm shot to shit, Turk! You gotta get

me some help!" Hatley unbuckled her webbed belt and, fashioning a crude tourniquet, tried to put pressure on the gaping hole in her upper left thigh. "Goddammit Turk!"

"Hold it!" Turkula yelled. "Don't move. Who the fuck is near Babe? Can anyone get to her?"

"No, Sarge," a voice called. "She's behind the other bunker. This asshole's got a clear shot if one of us breaks into the open. Fuck it. I'm gonna go for her."

"Fuckin' hold your positions. You hear me Airman Rees? I don't know what the fuck this guy is up to," Turkula yelled. "Babe, stay cool. We're comin' for you. Just hang tough."

"Command Post. Tiger Two. Tiger Two. Over."

"Go, Tiger Two."

"We're at cease-fire, but I can't see the guy. Babe's down. I got two others wounded."

Before the Command Post could answer, three hundred pounds of high explosive ripped against the cement blockhouses and sprayed debris in every direction. The concussion hit Tim Turkula, lifted him off the ground and sent him sprawling in a heap against a concrete revetment. The blast tore his helmet off and it disappeared into oblivion. At least three other security team members, who had rushed to the firefight, were also caught and catapulted in the wake of the blast, their arms and legs wounded by shrapnel and the searing heat.

Babe Hatley's eardrums shattered from the overpressure of the blast and her lungs quickly emptied their air. The shock wave should have killed her, but the concrete buttressing had saved her from the full force of the explosion. The day went black as she was knocked unconscious; her leg was still spurting blood. Everyone not as well protected as she, was dead where they lay.

"Here, sir," Colin Blackford radioed back to a suddenly tense Harold MacHugh.

"Blackford, there's been an explosion at RAF Lakenheath. Hold."

MacHugh quickly switched frequencies, reestablishing the communication link with the American Command Post.

"This is General Kilrain. We've had an attack. Secured area. Strategic munitions. Over."

Sir Harold MacHugh, his eyes widened by the news, swore to the pilot next to him, "Damn the lot! That was their plan!" Then, changing frequencies and keying the mike to communicate with Jack Kilrain, he offered up news no one wanted to hear. "Roger, General. I'm quite afraid I have disturbing news to offer…it may be that your attackers had access to chemical weapons. Over."

"Damn!" Kilrain swore. "What else can you tell me? Over."

"General, my team is after the bus. Can you manage at that scene? I'm calling the Prime Minister. Over."

"Roger, MacHugh. Please proceed. We've gotta take a look at the scene. Thanks for the word on chemicals. Out."

Jack Kilrain quickly surveyed the Command Post, and urgently barked directions. "MOPP condition 4. Condition Black. I want everyone, I goddamn mean EVERYONE in chem-warfare gear now. Explosive Ordinance Disposal to the weapons storage area."

"Sir," came a question from one of the majors assigned to the Command Post, "Shall we flash priority to the Pentagon and Air Forces Europe?"

"Get on it!" Kilrain shot back. "I want a message for transmittal in one minute. No, wait. The Red Phone. Now!" The General reached for the direct line to the U.S. Air Forces in Europe Command Headquarters in Ramstein, Germany.

Meanwhile, a small, redheaded boy aboard the hostage bus began to scream uncontrollably, fueling Petra Voss's rage all the more. She jumped back across the seat and smashed her fist into the child's teeth, knocking him to the floor in a sprawl of tears and blood.

"Quomuz," Voss blared into the radio, "Quomuz...Goddammit, Dieter. We are dead. The bastard has stranded us. He has stranded us."

"What will we do, Petra?" the German man yelled in anger.

The bus careened up and over a small rise in the uneven road as Koln turned onto the dirt road that led to a field that was to have been the helicopter landing zone.

Colin Blackford slowed and, grabbing the microphone, ordered his convoy to slow and halt its approach, only a few hundred yards behind the captive bus.

"Sir Harold," Blackford spoke. "The bus is coming to a rest in a clearing not five klicks from the airbase. Clear field of fire, but the children..."

"Steady on, Colin," came MacHugh's measured reply. "Let go with a red smoke to signal your position. We'll land there."

The bullet-riddled bus came to rest on a slight incline in a clearing amidst some tall pines. The earth was soft beneath the massive vehicle's several wheels and its weight caused the undercarriage to begin to sink slowly into the moist ground. The clearing was about a hundred yards in diameter and was not fully visible from the roadway behind, where a cavalry of British police and American military vehicles had now assembled.

Colin Blackford and his American counterpart, Special Agent Longstreet, quickly met. Blackford ordered Longstreet to deploy his men into the nearby wood and to encircle the bus. No man was to approach to nearer than fifty meters, Blackford had insisted, and no one, absolutely no one was to open fire without Blackford's express command.

"Listen, damn it," Longstreet protested, "Those are American kids on that bus, and no one is going to tell American forces they aren't going to open fire if an opportunity presents itself."

"You'll bloody well curb your temper, Mister Longstreet!" Blackford shouted pointedly, emphasizing his words, "and do exactly what I tell you."

"Those may be American kids, but they are going to be DEAD American kids if you and your cowboys go off half-cocked. We're going to handle this via British protocol and you WILL follow our orders. The only authority you have here is that which I give you. Am I perfectly clear, Mister Longstreet?"

"Fuck you, pal. I haven't got time to argue with you...." Agent Longstreet shouted angrily as he checked the safety on his M-16 and ran off into the nearby trees.

Blackford snarled in exasperation and, turning back to his car, ran smack into the square, imposing figure of Chief Inspector MacHugh, who had been listening to the Anglo-American discourse only a few feet behind.

"Well played, Blackford!" MacHugh judged. "I see you appreciate the difficulty of command. Especially when one commands, I believe your term was a bunch of 'cowboys'? Steady on, then," MacHugh concluded. "Let's check our tactical frequency. Can't help but wonder when MI-5 will drop by to give a so very helpful hand."

Colin Blackford shook his head and walked quickly to a platoon of Suffolk County Constables who had now gathered on the scene.

In the clearing, Petra Voss lifted herself from the floor of the motionless bus and peered out of the shot-shattered windows toward a stand of trees not fifty feet ahead. In her hands, she clutched the assault rifle still loaded with exploding ammunition.

Dazed and terrorized children huddled in clumps of twos and threes behind the seats, too frightened or too shocked to whimper or cry. Voss's partner, Koln, sat beneath the driver's wheel, his back against the seat. His breath was short and heavy and his nostrils flared each time he exhaled.

"Dieter, they are moving into position around us."

Koln didn't respond.

"Dieter, can you see anything? Look into the trees closest to the bus. Is there anything there?"

But thirty-three kilometers distant, to the northeast, Quomuz looked up and over his shoulders in an effort to spot any pursuing aircraft. The skids on the Jet Ranger skimmed only inches over the trees below. The slightest miscue and the hurtling craft would catch a skid and flip wildly onto the forest floor below. The approaching coastline gave the Palestinian a momentary measure of relief. Once over the water, he'd drop down to wave-top level and hope British or American radar would not "see" him as he made his way to the waiting merchant ship.

Suddenly, to the left, there was a clearing---a beach and a landmark. The lighthouse he'd planned for. A sharp dive drove the jet-helicopter to within a few feet of the sand and a flock of gulls was startled into flight from the wash of the spinning rotor blades whirling overhead.

"Ocean Enterprises..." Quomuz called in prearranged code. "Ocean Enterprises, this is 2 RK 7."

"Roger, 2 RK 7. This is MV *Ocean Enterprises*," came the response in stilted Arab-English. "We have you. Come right ten degrees and hold course and altitude. You should see us on the horizon. We have you in radar contact."

Back on land, the school bus was fully surrounded by armed American and British soldiers, plus Suffolk Constabulary policemen.

Overhead, four British Army helicopters swooshed in tight circles, guns pointed at menacing angles from the open bay doors. Although it was still midmorning, a gathering overcast blotted the sun and gave an appearance of dreary afternoon.

On cue from Sir Harold, Blackford called to the bus on a bullhorn.

"If you can hear me, then raise a signal. I repeat, raise a signal if you can hear my voice."

Inside the bus, Koln and Voss exchanged stares. They were trained to expect this and knew instinctively that time was the ally of the British and that the longer they waited the more their own advantage -- if any -- dissipated.

Terror and surprise were Voss's only weapons. Negotiation only aided the British. It provided the British and Americans with time to reinforce their position. They could employ time to supply themselves with food and drink and fresh personnel. The British could afford to wait and hope for a terrorist mistake.

The objects of concern--the children--were huddled and dazed by the stark terror of the moment.

One child, a seven year old, wet his blue jeans rather than ask the scary lady for help. His sister wrapped a ten-year old arm around his head as he began to cry. "Mommy would be mad at me if I made a mess..." he sobbed to his sister.

"We must act quickly. Quomuz has abandoned us or he is dead or is taken," Voss half-whispered in German to Koln, who looked nervously for a cigarette.

Koln then answered. "We each take a child and force ourselves to a car. Perhaps..."

"Perhaps. But go where? We're fools. We're dead fools. We are on an island and our 'friends' have abandoned us. Perhaps we should kill as many of these Americans as we can..." Voss threatened.

Blackford took up the bullhorn and again called, "You are completely surrounded. No hope of escape. Give yourselves up. You will not be harmed. Do you hear me? Let the children free and you will not be harmed."

"Only to spend our lives rotting in a British prison?" Koln observed to his female counterpart.

"No. Not in a British prison!" Voss agreed.

Suddenly, matters took a dangerous turn.

Koln reached for a shivering child crouched nearby. "Come here, you miserable little fuck," the German man growled in heavily accented English. And, clutching the child by the hair, he nodded to Voss who, likewise, grabbed a small boy into her arm and began to stand.

"You out there!" Voss announced.

"We will kill more of your children if you do

not obey us! One movement from any of you and these wretches all die."

MacHugh and Blackford, who lay prone behind low bushes near the bus, exchanged worried looks.

"Bring a car near this bus NOW! Leave it."

Blackford handed the bullhorn to MacHugh. The Chief Inspector took a deep breath, paused, and then called out to his enemy. "No. You shan't have any car. We know full well who you are. Your comrades are dead at the air base. Your mission has been spoiled. Do you hear me? Your comrades are dead."

Voss spat, "Bring the fucking car NOW or we kill another child! Do you want that, you British bastard? Do you?"

"It's a quick call!" MacHugh took the lead. "We'll give them the car. At least that way we free most of the children…. I know it's a risk..."

Before MacHugh could finish, Blackford turned and pointed to a nearby constable, motioning for the officer to bring a car forward. "I'll take it in, sir," Blackford offered.

"No. Steady..." MacHugh began to answer, but his words were cut off by the roar overhead. A British Lynx helicopter zoomed past, not fifty feet above the hostage bus. Its pilot blasted the scene below with an intense rotor wash and the deafening roar of his jet engines.

Voss quickly screamed, "Move that damn helicopter. NOW! And bring us the car! You have no more warnings!"

The two-way radio lying near MacHugh blared: "Blackford, this is Longstreet. We're only twenty yards from the bus. We're now in position. I've just gotten word from my command to take the bus. Repeat. We're taking the bus. Have your people stand clear."

"Good hell!" MacHugh shouted. "If this isn't a cock up! Blackford, tell that damn American if he so much as moves...."

A short burst from Voss's automatic weapon shattered the face and skull of her young captive. The terrorist grabbed the lifeless, bleeding corpse and heaved it from a window. "You are wasting my time you fuck-pigs!" Voss screamed.

"Bring the fucking car or another dies."

Special Agent Longstreet and his squad of four armed Air Force personnel stood and trained their weapons on the bus door. "On my command," Longstreet ordered. "When the last one comes off the bus, we hit. We can't wait for the fucking Brits. Aim high if you can. Try to hit 'em in the upper body to avoid the children. But no matter what, we gotta take these bastards out."

Longstreet knew he was ordering the possible deaths of more American children. But Voss's action had proven the terrorists were not to be reasoned with, and Longstreet guessed that the longer the Brits talked things over, the less likely it was that ALL the children would escape unharmed. It was a bad set of choices forced upon the Air Force special agent, but this was no time for timidity. Action demanded action.

MacHugh didn't waste words or time with the Americans. He waved his hand sharply at Blackford, telling him to move toward the bus with the car.

Colin Blackford put the vehicle in gear and pulled the car even with the front door of the long motor coach. He quickly turned off the engine and removed the keys. "No sense giving them an advantage," Blackford reasoned. He noticed that the petrol tank was only one-quarter full, and smiled. "Another small bit of luck...."

Suddenly, a woman's voice from inside the bus called to him and demanded he leave.

Before exiting the car, Blackford felt his right pants leg and retrieved a hidden service-issue Beretta. "It may come in handy," he mused.

"Now, leave, goddamn you!" Koln's voice pierced the silence.

With no options, Blackford crouched low and began to duck-run away from the car and bus.

Voss, who had surveyed Blackford's exit, now took another child by the hair and kicked her to the front of the bus. Koln and his captive crowded in behind. Now, with each terrorist holding a child as a shield, and the foursome began the slow, awkward descent from the bus. Voss then raised her weapon high and spattered the roof of the bus with another burst...a warning to anyone who might attempt a rescue.

Just yards away, another British Army helicopter hovered over the tree-rimmed clearing and dipped its nose slightly toward the bus. Longstreet quietly called to his men. "Wait until they put the kids in the car...that's when they're most vulnerable.... Their hands will be busy."

Dieter Koln and the now-screaming child stumbled out of the door and toward the right-hand driver's seat. Petra Voss opened the left-side door and began to maneuver herself in first--keeping the child between her body and danger.

"Shit!" Longstreet thought to himself, "No time to waste." He bellowed "GO! GO! GO!" as he led his men forward.

On command, four camouflage-covered agents spread and rushed the car. Voss had expected an attack, but the spontaneity of the charge caught her off balance. She swung her captive fully in front of her and leveled her gun on the child's shoulder. She squeezed hard and a burst raked the air high over the heads of the on-charging agents.

Jim Longstreet lowered his M-16 to hip level and squeezed hard. His blast zipped the ground short of the car, but sent dirt spewing into the face and eyes of Koln and the flailing, terrorized child.

"Bloody Hell!" screamed MacHugh, as Colin Blackford stood, instinctively, and raised his pistol toward the back of Dieter Koln's head. Another volley from Petra Voss caught a charging American fully at mid-sternum, not five yards from her position. The heavy thuds of lead slammed into the agent's chest. Not even the flak jacket he wore could wholly protect him, as the force of the blasts knocked him from his feet, unconscious.

Blackford didn't pause to breathe. He quickly sighted the German man and gently pulled three shots from his handgun. Koln's head split in an instant.... blood and brain matter exploded and showered the child, who fell to the ground in shock. Dieter Koln's dead body collapsed atop the motionless boy and the gun he had clutched moments earlier fell quietly from his hand.

Meanwhile, the Americans were almost on top of Petra Voss when she squeezed her final burst into the sergeant who had been just ahead of Longstreet. A sickening series of "thwaps" tagged the NCO's legs and lower abdomen and the shock of the blast knocked him to the ground. Just as the burst played out, Longstreet raised his arms and jumped onto the German woman, the child and the car all at once. Voss slipped his tackle and began to crawl away. Longstreet saw the child was now free of the vile woman's clutches and he instinctively covered the child's body with his own.

Voss quickly reached into her trousers, hoping to find a concealed pistol. But her fingers barely felt the cold metal when Blackford fell upon her and, jamming his gun barrel deep into her throat screamed, "Just give me a reason, bitch...one fucking reason to send you to Hell!"

Voss froze, her eyes glaring deeply into Blackford's -- their faces close enough to taste the other's breath.

"I need help here!" Blackford called to the

others around him, his heart pounding from the action.

In an instant, an American agent joined Blackford atop the captive woman. He buried his right knee hard into Voss's gut, knocking the wind out of her. The American quickly pinned her hands above her head and Blackford seized her gun. Colin was short of breath and his chest heaved with each breath. He was angry...more so than he'd ever been in his life. "I should kill you straight fucking now, you heartless cunt," the captain screamed, as his nostrils flared and his face burned red with rage.

A firm hand now rested on Blackford's tense shoulders. It was MacHugh. The grip was reassuring. "Well played, Blackford. Well played!" Sir Harold spoke softly and proudly.

Blackford, though, was still flush from the hunt, and a cold tremor quickly ran up his spine. His sense of reason began to return and, knowing the terrorist was well-secured, he began to withdraw his body from hers...but not before a final sense of justice compelled his right hand to deliver a savage back-fist pistol-whip to the terrorist's jaw. Pieces of tooth and skin and bone exploded from the hard, sickening thud, knocking Voss cold.

As Blackford's volley found its mark and the air filled with silence, all the players held their position, as if frozen in time. The battle was over. It was a full thirty seconds before anyone made a sound.

"Right, then," Chief Inspector MacHugh offered, in a calming, almost detached and neutral tone. "Let's get cracking. There's work to do. Bring the ambulances forward and attend to the children."

Blackford stood with his wrath still afire, his gaze fixed on the unconscious woman sprawled at his muddy feet.

"You've earned your bob today, Colin!" a sincere MacHugh proclaimed.

Blackford only nodded in response to the praise from his superior. "Go back to the Chief Constable's car. Open my attaché case; you'll find a pack of Player's Specials, plus some single malt in the flask. You've earned a smoke and a wee nip." A uniformed constable approached MacHugh as Blackford walked slowly away.

"Sir, there's a call for you on tactical band. I believe its London."

The Chief took the wireless military radiotelephone from the officer and moved to a quiet area away from the others, who were busy collecting the children and wrapping them in coats and blankets. Scotland Yard's head-of-section plugged a finger in his unoccupied ear to muffle the sounds of new crying and screams from the children. With the tension relieved, the young ones could begin to let go.

Special Agent Jim Longstreet approached Sir Harold from behind. There were several scores to settle with Her Majesty's finest.... But pausing, he could make out MacHugh's now strained responses in what was, very apparently, a one-sided conversation.

"No, sir. We've the situation in hand."

"Yes, sir. Several children. One confirmed terrorist dead here. One alive. The woman. Two dead at the air base."

"Immediately? But...Wouldn't we rather.... Perhaps we could..."

"British Army, sir? Minister, this is a police matter! Sir, I must protest. Jurisdiction for this matter rests squarely with the Metropolitan Police. My chaps have been working...."

It was obvious to Longstreet that MacHugh was losing the battle. Whoever was on the other end of the line had more horsepower. Suddenly, Chief Inspector MacHugh straightened to attention and briskly offered, "Yes, Prime Minister! The Army Barracks at Colchester. Straight away, Minister!"

MacHugh disconnected the phone and quietly swore into the sunless sky, "Damn."

Turning, his eyes met Agent Longstreet's with an unexpected fire, so much so that Longstreet was held speechless. Forgetting his anger for the moment, the American began to query his counterpart, but the taller Scot stepped briskly by the Air Force officer and shouted to a half-dozen uniformed policemen standing nearby.

"Fuck it," Longstreet sighed, now walking toward his own men gathered in a semicircle around Koln's almost headless corpse. "The deal's done."

23 March
0930 hours
Royal Air Force Lakenheath

Kilrain's order had taken immediate effect. The non-commissioned officers on the base-wide disaster response team had quickly responded, donning protective chemical warfare gear, masks and gloves, and had ensured that the entire base population had done the same.

No one was certain as to the extent of the damage, nor whether any chemical agents had been freed following the blast. But procedures dictated that the military presume the worst.

"Make damned sure your masks fit tight!" called a chief master sergeant from Ordnance to his team of bomb handlers. "And Ray, check those gloves..."

Within moments, the entire base complement of more than four thousand had donned their drab spacesuit-looking chemical protective gear and dispatched a fleet of busses to the family housing area several kilometers distant in an effort to ensure that the family members were safely transported from the danger area.

Kilrain ordered his senior staff and the ranking enlisted members to the Command Post for an emergency briefing on disaster procedures.

"OK, folks, settle down" came Kilrain's voice from his filtered bubble-mask. Speech was difficult in the chemical gear, but frequent training had prepared the base for the problems at hand.

"First order of business," Kilrain called. "Security?"

The Security Forces commander, a lieutenant colonel also fully clad in chemical gear, stood and addressed the staff. "Base perimeter sealed, family evac plan underway as we had planned. Sir, there's no indication at present that any fallout made its way to the housing area...Pretty well contained to the flight line and the weapons storage area. Suffolk Constabulary is helping cordon off a ten-mile radius around the base. Thank God this is farming country...no civilian villages of any size in the radius. I guess the next thing is to pray for rain!"

Kilrain rose, grimly. "Good, Doug, now...Let's review the decontamination procedures...OK, Doc...take it."

The ranking medical officer on base stood and addressed the group.

"OK, folks...we're in MOPP-4. All pressurized buildings on reverse flow to keep any germs or radioactive particles out. We're in full alarm black conditions until otherwise announced. We've got a chem-protected ambulance team en route to the attack scene. They are fully protected, and I've ordered that they put M8 paper on their arms and legs – that way we can detect any chemicals."

The command flight surgeon continued, raising a black rubber-gloved hand to emphasize the point. "Dirty patients will not be transported to the hospital. We have established a triage area for potential contaminees on the far end of the runway…"

"Now, the rest of you…. remember to watch your folks and particularly the M8 paper," the security forces commander interjected. "Watch the M8 paper strips for a color change. Identify potential contamination by comparing any color change on the M8 paper to the color chart in the booklets each of you have in your chem suits. Remember, a yellow-gold color indicates the presence of nerve agent, a red-pink color indicates the presence of blister agents and a dark green color indicates the presence of a blood agent."

The staff had heard the briefing before, but the morning's events had generated new urgencies.

"Now, let's quickly review symptoms," the doctor said, raising his voice through his respirator mask.

"Let's hold off telling people to inject antidotes. We'll keep a close hold on those hypodermics, but General Kilrain, we have plenty, so no worries there."

The doctor continued, "Folks, again, we don't know exactly what we're dealing with here, if anything. But, remember, if one of your people is exposed to a low dose of nerve agent, characteristic symptoms include increased production of saliva, a runny nose and a feeling of pressure on the chest. Check their pupils. Look to see if they become contracted. Another symptom is that their short-range vision deteriorates and the victim feels pain when he tries to focus on a nearby object. Watch for headaches, tiredness, slurred speech, hallucinations and nausea. Now that's for a low dose."

The staff exchanged worried glances.

"OK, medium exposure… Symptoms from the skeletal muscles are common. Moderate poisoning may present itself by muscular weakness, tremors or convulsions."

The flight surgeon continued.

"It's important that you note the symptoms and report them to the medical team. The degree of exposure dictates how we treat. OK, exposure to higher doses can lead to difficulty in breathing and to coughing. Pains in the gut may develop; watch out for cramps and vomiting. Especially be on the lookout for involuntary discharge of urine and fecal material. Under NO circumstances do you remove the chem suit, no matter what. In high doses, your victim may suffer convulsions and lose consciousness. Any questions?"

The group sat silently.

Jack Kilrain stood and called for the ranking enlisted person on the disaster team, a barrel-chested chief master sergeant who, after checking with his subordinates at the attack scene, put down his radio.

"Thanks, sir…Remember the drill… make sure all of your people wear gloves and respirators until the 'all clear.' Disaster team scrubbers and medical rescue personnel must wash any suspected victims with soap and water at the scene. We're already setting up a decontamination center on the flight line…We have no reports of chemicals yet, but if the M8 paper indicates, remember that victims of VX and other nerve agents should be cleaned with alcohol. We've got plenty!"

An emergency radio call for General Kilrain ended the meeting. "Folks, I want a status report from division heads and section chiefs here in one hour. If everyone does their job and keeps a cool head, then we'll get through this."

Kilrain's words did little to calm the fears of these military professionals, who instantly returned to their tasks. Outside the command post, the four thousand men and women in Jack Kilrain's fighter wing busied themselves with the task of saving their comrades.

Several kilometers away, in the American family housing area, Carrie Mercer pulled a sweater tightly around young Tyler amidst a throng of other military wives and their children. A score of busses had arrived just minutes before, and the families of the military members were herded onto the transports by active-duty military members dressed in their chemical-protection gear and masks.

"Would someone please tell us what is going on?" a young wife asked a taller man in his protective suit, who tried to speak clearly through his respirator.

"Ma'am, there's no time to explain, but there has been an explosion on the base…"

The families had always known there might be times when an emergency evacuation would be necessary. On arrival in country they had all been briefed on the possibilities, but no one ever really considered that such an emergency would take place.

"This is just a drill, isn't it?" another woman asked as she hurried up the stairs and onto a waiting bus.

"Why are you guys wearing gas masks?" someone else called out, sensing that the exercise was more than just a drill.

"Just precautionary, ma'am…" came the tinny reply from the NCO with an M-16 slung over his shoulder. The sergeant tried to reassure the woman, but his own fears belied the urgency of the situation.

"Ma'am, I think this is a real-world emergency and we're doing our damndest. The general says we have to evacuate you folks as far and as fast as we can."

"Katie? Honey, is that you?" Carrie Mercer called out to another pilot's wife, "You OK, where's your little boy? Where's Charlie?"

"Carrie," the young woman cried out, "He's at the day care on base. I had a doctor's appointment…. I am worried sick and the cops can't tell me anything."

"God, Katie…." Carrie felt heartsick as she tugged her own small child close to her on the bus bench seat. "Come on, sit here with me…I'm sure it'll be OK."

As Carrie Mercer's bus fell into line behind another bus laden with frightened family members, a tall, black, barrel-chested NCO took a microphone from the driver and addressed the bus as best he could from behind the gas mask.

"Ladies…ladies, can you hear me OK?"

A woman in the back waved her hand, indicating that he was heard and understood.

"OK, ladies…I'm Chief Maynard…Oh, to hell with this thing," the senior enlisted man said, removing his gas mask to the relief of the women on the bus.

"Whew, that's better!" the chief smiled, causing a few on the bus to return his smile.

"OK, here's what we know," the chief began to explain. "I won't lie to you, but it's bad…."

"We've been attacked, some kind of terrorist thing. There were some shots and an explosion out near the far end of the runway. We have no word on casualties, but we don't think that many of our people were involved."

"Thank God for that!" another woman called out.

"Yes, ma'am," Chief Maynard continued. "You folks know the drill. And you are all pretty brave so I gotta hand it to you! You are being evacuated. We're headed over to Alconbury to the old base there. There is a temporary hospital there that we keep for emergencies just like this one."

"What about our husbands?" a younger wife called out.

"Ma'am, it's too early to know anything…I really am sorry about that. But what I DO know is that the entire base immediately went into protection mode. My guess is that they are all safe and secure…and the minute I hear something on the radio, I'll tell you! But I think you can feel pretty safe. Those guys know what to do…. so try not to worry!"

The chief continued. "Now I know that many of you are concerned about the kids at the day care. Don't worry. The Chaplains and their staff have two special busses and they are picking those kids up right now. Those busses will have a special police escort and the kids will join you over at Alconbury. OK?"

Carrier Mercer reached out and held Katie Smith's hand as both women breathed a slight sigh of relief.

"One final thing. We'll be setting up temporary shelters for the night and there will be food…I'll PERSONALLY see to the food, 'cause as you ladies can tell, old Chief Maynard don't like to miss too many meals!"

The chief master sergeant's purposeful comment had its desired effect, for he had provided assurance to those who needed it most and lessened the fear of danger with a bit of self-deprecating humor.

There were times, and this was one of those times, when the idea of "Air Force Family" was more than an advertising slogan.

23 March
2030 hours
Royal Air Force Lakenheath

A nearly-exhausted Jack Kilrain walked into the command post followed by the senior enlisted ranks and, laying his gas mask atop one of the computer desks, sat down in a swivel chair. "Chief," he said, tiredly, "please get me the secure line to HQ USAFE. I must give them a status report."

Five minutes later, Kilrain was on the line with General Glen Benson, Commander, United States Air Forces Europe.

"Sir, this is an update on our condition. You already know about the dead. We've secured the base perimeter area and the civil engineering crews have already replaced the wire fences. Security Forces patrols have been tripled and there is no, repeat, no evidence of additional munitions or enemy fighters."

"What about the weapons storage area, Jack?" came the urgent voice on the other end of the line.

"Looks like we caught a break there, sir." The truck bomb did not, repeat DID NOT breach the concrete bunkers and the earthen berms. Our munitions storage area took superficial damage only. None of our weapons were compromised."

"That's good news. What about the chemicals?"

"More good news, sir," Kilrain half smiled. "Our detection gear found only miniscule traces of nerve and blood agent. Not really enough to kill anyone and it was confined to a very small area no bigger than a few square meters. My guess is that the explosion incinerated the chemicals they were carrying. It certainly didn't spread like they may have hoped. Our decon teams cleaned the area quickly and we brought in flame-throwers to burn off whatever small amounts might have landed in the grass as a precaution."

"Anyone showing symptoms?"

"None, General. Our med people deployed quickly and, like I said, the decon teams did their work as trained. The flight surgeons tell me there was zero chemical injury. Zero."

"That's a relief. Good work, Jack. Can't help but wonder what these crazies thought they'd accomplish with the chemicals. Looks like it backfired on 'em."

"Sir, I'll update you in another hour. I need to check on the wounded and get with the Chaplains to notify some next of kin."

"I don't envy you that task, Jack. Tell your people 'well done' for me! I've got to brief the President ASAP."

"And I don't envy you THAT task, sir," Kilrain said, laying the phone back into its cherry-red cradle.

26 March
1100 hours
Lakenheath, England

No fewer than a dozen hastily-painted bed-sheet banners angrily demanded the immediate withdrawal of American forces from the East Anglia countryside.

"American Chemical Bombs Kill Children," one sign read. Another said, "U.S. War Criminals Caught!" A third called for the end of "American Air Piracy," and flapped in the steady breeze as a small throng of forty protesters chanted and yelled their demands behind a cordon established by the local constabulary.

Nearby, a dozen reporters from the London media were on hand to record the protest organized by a coalition of anti-war and anti-Israel groups.

Holding a bullhorn and railing into the drizzling air, an aging nun decried the "American cover-up" of the illegal chemical weapons that had been "discovered" at the Lakenheath base following the terrorist attack.

"We call on Her Majesty's Government to immediately account for its knowledge and participation in this clear violation of the United Nations conventions on banned chemical weapons," the nun, an active member of the nuclear disarmament movement yelled to the small crowd. "There are inhumane crimes being inflicted upon the Palestinians. Under a ruse of self-defense against the war on terrorism, our Government, the Americans and the Israeli state are working an ethnic cleansing program against the Palestinians and the takeover of more and more of their land for the exclusive use of Israeli Jews. It is the utmost hypocrisy for our Government and the Americans to justify their insane invasion of the Arab homelands in search of that which they, themselves, so willingly keep and deploy. We will fight these Nazis with every fiber of our beings."

As the nun continued her harangue, other members of the various movements handed pamphlets to the press describing the horrific discovery of chemical weapons at the U.S. Air base.

"We Sisters of Peace make it known that we harbour no ill will toward the many thousands of Americans who work and make their living at RAF Lakenheath. We know that most of the enlisted men and women don't really believe in what they're forced to do by their leaders. We've comforted these young people who are upset about the mothers and children they've killed during the illegal invasions of Iraq and Palestine. Many in the armed forces are on food stamps themselves. We join them in their struggle to overthrow their Pentagon oppressors."

Three news cameras then caught several of the sisters holding what appeared to be blood-filled baby bottles as two local constables approached to prevent the protesters from blocking the narrow village streets.

"Oy, you stop that!" one of the constables yelled as the women began to spray the officers' faces and uniforms with the red liquid. The melee was on as several women constables wrestled the offending nuns to the ground amidst the protesters, who chanted wildly and attempted to prevent the officers from restraining the sisters.

Several hours later, video images from the protest were broadcast over two of England's news networks, while the voice-over identified the "discovery of the American chemical weapons" as the reason for the protest. Later in the day, the images had been edited and transmitted to the major network newsrooms in New York.

27 March
1600 hours
AFOSI District Headquarters
RAF Mildenhall

Zach Pollard fidgeted with the zipper on the left pants leg of his flight suit and looked nervously at the bare, pale brown walls around him. It had been at least an hour since Lieutenant Colonel Riordan had "escorted" him to the headquarters of the Air Force Office of Special Investigations in the United Kingdom. Pollard sensed that Riordan had taken some perverse pleasure in the task. He'd used only the fewest of words when he had called the captain in from the squadron briefing room and tersely commanded: "Captain Pollard, you will come with me!" Riordan had strangely emphasized Pollard's rank, "captain."

"Why? What's up, Colonel?"

"I don't think it's appropriate for you to speak, Captain."

Riordan maintained a stern, official bearing. He had again particularly emphasized the word "captain," as if Pollard needed to be reminded of the difference in their pay grades.

"Well, sir, do I have time to call home? I just need to..."

"Enough, Captain. Say nothing more and come with me. That is an order."

The drive from Lakenheath to the Mildenhall OSI building had taken just over fifteen minutes, marked by Riordan's stern silence. Upon entry to the red brick fortress, Pollard noted the steel bars on the windows. He'd never been in an OSI office before, and his only connection with the law enforcement agency had been in reciting the usual humor about the organization. None of its members ever wore regular blue Air Force uniforms, although all held military ranks and titles.

Rather, OSI operatives referred to each other as either "Special Agent" or "Agent" to disguise their true ranks from the uniformed population of the service. Most Air Force people regarded the OSI as something of a necessary evil, an occasional nuisance, and the source of some humor. Perhaps it was the polyester "leisure suits" they wore, or the pseudo-secret manner in which they investigated everything from espionage to adultery. It was their penchant for "investigating" the latter that earned them liberal doses of derision.

Suddenly, there was no humor in this situation, for Pollard was wholly without a clue as to why he was now apparently being treated as a criminal. More maddening was the fact that no one, not Riordan, not even one of the agents, had told him why he was here.

This was too cruel even for some of the pranksters in the squadron. No, Pollard was sure, this was no joke.

Pollard sat uneasily in a gray metal, government-issue chair. The faded green leather seat was coming unraveled at the corners. More than one "suspect" had squirmed in this seat. "Government issue from the fifties, no doubt," the flyer offered to himself in nervous disgust.

On the far side of the room, an old gray metal desk with an ancient, manual typewriter completed the sparse furnishings of the interrogation room. Pollard thought the room looked like a set on a low budget movie.

Unable to sit still, he stood for the fifth or sixth time and walked toward the locked door. As he had done before, he pressed his ear to the cold metallic surface of the door in an effort to hear any approaching footsteps or speech. Although he knew by now it was a futile gesture, he reached for the knob and tried hard to twist it open. Again, no luck.

This time, uneasiness and fear began to take its toll--and he slammed his fist hard against the wall adjacent to the door. Returning to his seat, Pollard wondered aloud, "Where the hell is Tracie? She's probably pissed that I'm not home right now."

Just then, Riordan and an unfamiliar plainclothes man entered the room. The latter, a stocky, muscular figure, carried a briefcase and a small tape recorder. He walked past Pollard and hopped up on the desk, his legs swinging freely beneath. Pollard thought the man's casual air odd, given the current situation.

The captain was surrounded, front and back.

And he didn't much like the feeling.

"Sir," Pollard mustered the words from a dry mouth, "would you please tell me why I am here? Am I under arrest or something?"

But Riordan didn't answer. The heavyset man spoke instead.

"Captain Pollard, I am Special Agent Jim Longstreet. I am the district commander of the Air Force Office of Special Investigations. I have been in contact with the Federal Bureau of Investigation and the Defense Intelligence Agency. Each will be sending agents to interrogate you shortly."

Then, reading from what appeared to be a three-by-five note card, the agent continued:

"I am investigating certain offenses under the Uniform Code of Military Justice of which you are suspected. These offenses include Conspiracy to Commit Espionage under Article 77, Murder under Article 118, and Espionage under Article 106a…"

"What!" Pollard, now more angry than frightened, jumped to his feet and screamed. "What? ME? Murder and Espionage? That's horseshit and you know it, Colonel!"

"Shall we also add Conduct Unbecoming an Officer, under Article 134, CAPTAIN?" Riordan yelled back, again, sarcastically over-emphasizing Pollard's rank.

"Sit down, Captain Pollard. I must advise you of your rights under Article 31 of the Uniform Code of Military Justice."

An enraged Pollard again stood and, pointing a

finger at the agent, screamed, "No way, pal. No fucking way! I'm not saying a damn thing until I get to talk to a lawyer. I don't know what the fuck you guys are after, but I'm not having any more of it. Am I under arrest? Because if I'm not, I'm walking." Pollard stepped toward the closed metal door, but as his hand found the locked knob, he knew his protestation was pointless.

"Captain Pollard, if you even want to think of staying out of Leavenworth for the rest of your life, to say nothing to about ever flying a jet again, you'll park your ass right now and shut up!" Riordan yelled, his faced reddened.

Pollard, sweating, sat again and squeezed the sides of the chair so hard his fingers hurt. He swallowed and looked to the far side of the room.

"Now, I will continue, Captain," Longstreet advised.

"You have the right to remain silent, that is, to say nothing at all. You also have the right to have an attorney present before any questioning. The Air Force defense counsel is provided to you free of charge. However, you may obtain a civilian lawyer to represent you at no expense to the Government. Finally, if you give up each of these rights as I have explained them to you, any statement you make can be used against you in a court-martial or other disciplinary proceeding. Do you understand each of these rights as I have explained them to you?"

"Like I said, pal, I want to talk to the ADC right now!" Pollard demanded, in reference to the mili-

JONATHAN BRUCE

tary defense lawyer on base.

"Pollard, let me give you some advice," Riordan
seethed. "No little-league Air Force Area Defense
Counsel is going to do you a bit of good. You've
gotten yourself into a big-time mess here and I'm
here to tell you that the CINC wants some answers
and he wants them now. That's your only hope."

"The CINC?" Pollard, his throat now tight,
cracked as he demanded, "What the hell are you
talking about, sir? The Commander-in-Chief, U.S.
Air Forces in Europe wants me to tell him what?
What the hell are you talking about?"

"All right, Pollard. What we're talking about is
this..."

Longstreet opened the briefcase and retrieved an
eight-by-ten black and white photograph of Tracie
Pruett. "Jesus!" The young flier exclaimed. "What
have you guys done with Tracie? What the hell has
she got to do with any of this?"

"You call her Tracie, is THAT right, Captain
Pollard?" Longstreet asked, checking to see that the
tape recorder was operating.

"Yea, Goddammit. That's her name. What the
hell of it? What? Am I accused of sleeping with a
British girl? Is that a crime? Jesus!"

"No," Longstreet answered, "You are accused
of conspiring to commit treason and murder and destruction of government property with a terrorist
with connections to the old socialist Red Army Faction. Her name, as you well know, Captain, is Petra
Voss." With a quick flip, Longstreet slid a color

eight-by-ten photograph across the desk to Pollard.

The photo, still moist from the developing process, revealed in sharp, grotesque detail the rear-ranged face of Tracie Pruett, courtesy of Colin Blackford's sharp right fist. Now, her close-cropped blonde hair was matted with blood, her left cheek and eye socket swollen and engorged with black-blue blood. Her mouth hung open, revealing several teeth that appeared dislodged or broken. Dried blood was crusted on her slackened chin; her eyes were glazed half-open and lifeless. Her skin seemed a pale, bluish-white, and she well-resembled a cadaver.

Jim Longstreet felt it might be to his advantage to amend the truth of matters. "She's dead, Captain."

Zach Pollard stopped breathing. His chest felt ready to explode. His hands and body began to shake -- he felt disoriented, confused and scared. At the same moment, Longstreet slid another photo across the desk. This one displayed Dieter Koln's sprawled corpse, in a pool of blood surrounded what remained of his head and shoulders.

"This one, too. Was he a friend of yours?"

Pollard's stomach wretched and, unable to control its churning, the young captain vomited. His body, now racked with fear, bent double and shook violently. Tears now ran down his face and into his open mouth, Pollard, unable to draw a breath, heaved again as yellow-green bile splattered the legs of his flight suit. A searing cold swept down his back and his stomach lurched again...

Riordan turned his head and looked toward Longstreet. The agent smiled wryly. Captain Pollard had reacted as the agent hoped he would.

Rising, Longstreet tossed a handkerchief to Pollard, who was still doubled from the pain. Longstreet motioned to Riordan, and spoke calmly. "When you are ready to tell us what you know, Captain Pollard, we'll be ready to listen."

Pollard tried to right himself and scream, "Tracie!" But instead, he gagged on his own sputum. He grabbed at his gut again and bent double. Slipping to his knees on the cold tile floor, he was so consumed by pain he could not have heard what the agent had offered. But Longstreet, now almost through the doorway, called to one of his junior operatives, "Get the Area Defense Counsel. Tell him he has a client who needs to see him. And get a towel for Captain Pollard. He's made a mess in here."

27 March
1915 hours
Office of the Area Defense Counsel
RAF Lakenheath

The sun had been down for almost two hours and a cool, wet breeze had begun when attorney Jared Hurst, Captain, USAF, made it back from his temporary off-base home to his hastily assembled office in a WW II-era Quonset-hut. His enlisted assistant, Sergeant Karlene Summers, hadn't told him much in their hurried phone conversation—just "get back to the office and don't bother changing into a uniform," she'd said.

"It's an officer case, sir," the paralegal had said. "A pilot, too, and I think he's in big trouble. You better hurry."

Sergeant Summers had led a shaken Zach Pollard into Captain Hurst's office and had found him a can of warm orange soda. He smelled of the dried vomit on his flight suit and his hands were shaking. By now, Pollard was numb. He'd spent all of his emotion on the floor of the OSI interrogation room and now he was drained and exhausted.

Upon his hasty return to his office, the lawyer spoke a few words to the sergeant in the outer office before making his way into the room where Pollard sat. Closing the door behind him, Hurst extended a hand to Pollard who only returned the offer with a hollow stare.

"Can I trust you?" Pollard seemed to beg.

"Yeah, but first things first, Captain..." Hurst said, trying to interpret the man's slack expression. "I guess I'd better do some talking first. I'm Jared Hurst, the base criminal defense lawyer. I don't work for any of the commanders. They aren't my bosses. If you want me as your lawyer, well, then, you are my boss. OK?"

"OK," followed his listless reply.

"Next, don't believe any of that crap you've heard

on TV about military lawyers. Yes, I'm a real attorney. Six years ago I earned my law degree from the University of Nebraska; the Harvard of the Plains. I was a criminal prosecutor in Colorado for two years before joining the Air Force. And no, I'm not here because I can't get a real job, either. I'm a military brat. Dad was Regular Army; a thirty-year man. OK?"

Pollard sat silently and nodded.

Hurst continued. "Now I don't know what kind of trouble you're in, but first we have to get to know each other before you decide if I can help you. First thing I gotta tell you is that whatever you tell me dies with me unless you say otherwise. You got that? Good. Now, you're in the 492nd?"

"Yeah, I'm a Wizzo. You know, weapons systems officer? I was at Mountain Home before here." Hurst smiled briefly and reflected back to his first two years in uniform at Mountain Home AFB, Idaho. He fondly remembered one raucous evening spent with some fighter jocks at Scrubby's, a popular off-base BBQ spot.

Hurst, slowly maneuvering his new client into a more relaxed state, leaned back in his chair and asked, "You know 'Stoves' Coleman? He's an old friend."

"Yeah, I fly with the Stovepipe. He's a good shit. How do you know him?"

"Hmmm, better let Stoves tell you; it's a matter of attorney-client privilege," Hurst laughed. "Let's just say he and I have been through some scrapes together. But ask him about a certain bachelor party at Scrubby's a few years back that got a little wild. Ask him to tell you about a dancer named 'Blaze,' and her can of whipped cream. Give him a call if you want to check me out, fair enough?"

"Fair enough; but for now, they've ordered me not to talk to anyone except a lawyer and they weren't too happy about that. But I'm in some deep shit..."

Hurst reached for a yellow legal pad in the top left drawer of his ancient, government-issue oak desk. "All right, what's the story?"

"OK," Pollard let loose a long, nervous sigh and sat back in the chair. His eyes glued on the young attorney. "The best I can figure out is that they think...the OSI, I mean, and my commander...that I was responsible for the attack on the weapons storage area and on those kids..."

Before Pollard could continue, Hurst's face broke into an almost half-laughing stare of disbelief. "What the hell?"

"No, listen. I was dating, that is I was, you know, involved with this British girl. She slept over a few times. Her name is Tracie. Tracie Pruett. I met her in a pub where the squadron hangs out and stuff. We've been going together, although she has a place in Bury St. Edmunds. They...well, she. Fuck. This is hard, Captain."

Pollard began to cry again, and as he did the Air Force lawyer looked around for a tissue.

"Thanks. That's OK." Pollard said, wiping his face with the sleeve of his soiled flight suit. "Anyway, they shot her. They say she was part of the attack and that she's some kind of terrorist. They told me that Tracie's not her name. Petra something, and that I am part of the attack. Jesus, man, can you believe it? Me? First they kill my girlfriend and then they say I'm a terrorist. Can they do that?"

Hurst didn't answer for several minutes. He couldn't. He was both dumbfounded and amazed. This case wasn't his usual fare. He was accustomed to representing young enlisted troops in misdemeanor cases. Nothing this big had ever walked into his office before. But collecting his thoughts, he began asking a standard series of questions, wondering if he was equal to the task before him. This might be "the" case of his very young military career.

"You didn't tell them anything, did you?"

"What do you mean?"

"I mean, you didn't tell them anything. You didn't admit anything to them about yourself?"

"Man, what the hell kind of lawyer are you? What the hell kind of question is that? I didn't tell them anything because there isn't anything to tell. I'm no damn conspirator. They killed my girlfriend and you're asking me if I told them anything!"

"Hold on a minute, Zach. I'm real sorry about your girlfriend, but right now, my main concern is you. It sounds to me like they're putting together some kind of big case against you. And believe me, anything you say--I mean anything you say--can be turned against you. In case you forgot, those terrorists turned this entire base on its ear...not to mention England, most of NATO and the White House."

"Yeah, but they said if I don't talk to them they said I'll never be able to fly again..."

"Listen, man, not flying again is about the least of your worries right now. You'd better be worried about spending the rest of your life at Fort Leavenworth, Kansas. We both know that the best Army post sucks when compared to even the worst Air Force installation."

"Where do you come off with this shit, Hurst? Where do any of you?"

"Settle down, Zach. I'm on your side. But we're playing in my arena now. This isn't an airplane, so you aren't in control. You gotta trust me and believe that I've got reasons for the things I say and the questions I ask. OK? So let's just start at the beginning. Just tell me about you and this woman."

The attorney began to take notes as Zach Pollard took an angry swig from the soda can and began to recall the night he'd first met the slender British girl with the funny accent.

27 March
2145 hours
Addenbrooke's Hospital
Cambridge

Nearby at Cambridge, in the Addenbrooke's Intensive Care Unit, Airman First Class Barbara Hatley slowly began to awake from the anesthesia. Her second surgery in four days had completely

wracked the young woman. The chemical decontamination process at the base had delayed emergency attention to her wounds, and she had lost
even more blood during the ambulance ride. "But
the prognosis is better than just 'fair'...even good!"
her English surgeon had reported to General Jack
Kilrain after the operation ended.

She'd been drifting in and out of a dreamless state
for the past several hours, wholly unaware of her surroundings or her condition. As the morphine began to
wear off, Hatley began to sense a sharp pain in her
legs and stomach and, in a semi-conscious state, tried
to reach her heavily bandaged thigh. Wrist restraints
prevented her from ripping the intravenous tubes from
her arms and Barbara Hatley began to feel confusion,
fear and frustration....

Hours later, at midnight, a nursing shift change
brought fresh, tender hands to care for the young
security cop, who struggled to regain consciousness.
"So, how's our heroine?" a matronly British nurse
asked the supine woman -- not expecting much of
an answer.

"Uhh..." was all Hatley could manage.

"Oh, you're back with us," the smiling nurse
noted, as she quickly toggled the intercom to the
nursing station. "Call Dr. B! Our patient is coming
around."

Barbara Hatley, still confused and groggy, began to gag on the tubes the surgeons had placed in
her nose and throat. She couldn't breathe deeply,
and her eyes opened to a blur of blinking amber and

blue lights that seemed to surround her.

"Onnngh."

"Hold on, Barbara...the doctor is coming right now. You're all right, dear, you're going to be fine."

And stroking a warm, reassuring hand along the wounded woman's cool forehead, the nurse smiled and offered, "Just hold on."

It would be another week before Barbara Hatley's National Guard squadron teammates would be allowed to see her, armed with a dozen roses, funny balloons and a Playgirl magazine.

Even then, Airman Hatley would hurt too much to laugh.

27 March
2230 hours
Royal Air Force Lakenheath
Office of the Area Defense Counsel

Captain Zach Pollard finished telling lawyer Hurst about his involvement with the woman now known as Voss, just as Sergeant Karlene Summers entered.

"Captain, the OSI guys are here and they've got some other civilian suits with them. Are these guys FBI or something?"

"Probably...up from London, would be my guess," Hurst ventured to Pollard as the flyer's eyes lifted from the floor. "Zach, you hang on here for a minute while I see what these guys want."

Hurst stood and walked into his outer office and was quickly greeted by a half-dozen cold stares. Longstreet, the only man in the group Hurst knew, spoke first.

"Captain, this is FBI Special Agent Murtry. He's head of the London office and is heading up the investigation into the attack and counter-espionage."

The tall, black agent, fifty-ish Hurst guessed, nodded as if to cut short the introduction by Agent Longstreet. Murtry fixed his intense gaze upon the young Air Force attorney, and then stepping forward, began to speak.

"Captain, we don't have time to dance around with niceties..."

The agent's bearing and tone took Hurst aback.

"I need information and I need it fast. Your boy in there is in a lot of trouble, and what he doesn't need is for you to try to dazzle us with your legal brilliance." His disdain for lawyers became apparent, even though Murtry, himself, held a law degree from Howard University.

Hurst, buying time to collect his thoughts only answered, "Go on. I'm listening."

Murtry sensed he could intimidate the younger man by virtue of his presence, age difference and the ominous sound of his title, "Chief, Counter-Espionage, London District." He attempted to assume control of the lawyer by affecting a suddenly patronizing, relaxed air.

"What we need, Captain, err, Hurst -- may I call you Jared? What we, I, need are the full details. There may be more violence planned. We need to know where your boy's team got the bomb. We want to know their suppliers and who paid the freight. This IS a matter of national security...."

Hurst, slightly offended by the older man's obvious shift in tactics, remained solid.

"First, Agent Murtry, let's keep this on a professional level. I am a Captain in the United States Air Force and should be addressed as such. Second, my client is not a 'boy.' Hurst emphasized the point, taking aim at the older black man, knowing full well that the term was derisive to both.

"Now," the young attorney paused, not fully sure he could seize the upper hand in this hurried, hallway negotiation, "Agent Murtry, I understand your problem. You've got dead people, you've got terrorists with big weapons, you've got heat from the White House on down, and worst of all, you've got CNN standing outside the main gate -- probably armed with more facts than you have."

Hurst's blood was pumping hard, and, not knowing if he was in Murtry's league or not, pressed the attack.

"Now I'm equally sure you know I'm not some hot-shot 20th & K Street silk-suited lawyer you guys always deal with back in D.C. But I'll tell you what, none of those silk-suits even knows what the inside of a military courtroom looks like."

Murtry interrupted. "Excuse me, captain; this is

no longer a military matter. This is looking like a federal civilian prosecution. You're in way over your head, young man. Federal prosecutors from the Justice Department are on their way here now. That means they've already contacted the federal public defender's office, who will probably send in a team straight away, and you'll have no more to do with this case. So, you'd better work with me before our government and the British government negotiate extradition or even prosecution before the Crown Courts. And may I remind you, Captain, the English have no Constitution for you to hide behind!"

Hurst, his heart racing loudly in his own ears, quickly seized upon Murtry's threat, and, realizing the agent had overplayed his hand, answered coolly:

"No, Mr. Murtry, you guys will never give jurisdiction over Captain Pollard to the Brits on this, so don't even try to convince me otherwise."

Hurst was right on target and Murtry knew he'd lost a small point to the younger man. Hurst pressed on.

"And it may very well be that the feds fly him outta here to the U.S. for incarceration and prosecution. But for now, he's my client, and…" Hurst paused for effect, "he's not talking to anyone." The Air Force lawyer knew he was about to step onto thin ice, but sensing a tactical advantage in the conversation, he continued. "I'll tell you what, Mr. Murtry. I'm sure you've already made plans to extradite with the Justice Department…."

"They'll be here in the morning," Murtry

quickly shot back.

Hurst had guessed correctly.

"True enough, you can probably have him off this base in a heartbeat, and I've got no way to stop you...."

Hurst paused to bait the trap.

"But if, indeed, Pollard does have anything to tell you, you'll want to hear it from him.... here and soon! Because if he can help you, and if I'm willing to let him, you'll need him to give you locations, names, phone numbers...right? And if you ship him to some stateside federal prison for pretrial confinement, you'll have lost a good witness, time and information. Besides, Mr. Murtry, he's still my client -- so you'll have to send me, too. I could use the vacation back home, and I still won't let him talk! So, Special Agent Murtry, if you really DO want to find out who's behind this attack, you'd better leave my client here for now. Got that?"

Murtry squinted hard at the feisty young man and considered both his boldness and his offer. There was some sense in what the attorney had said. The agent looked quickly at his team, who, to a man, shrugged and nodded as if the logic of Hurst's bargain was unassailable. Even a slim chance to talk to Pollard was better than no chance at all. And, time was of the essence. The trail might still be fresh.

"All right, Captain Hurst," Murtry conceded, knowing full well that he'd been bettered in the debate. "We'll give your client forty-eight hours here in the U.K. before we take him -- and you -- stateside. Forty-eight hours. That's all."

"Seems fair," Hurst added, quickly sealing his temporary victory. "But one more thing..."

"Go ahead."

Hurst glanced at Agent Longstreet's focused eyes.

"Immunity; I want a grant of full immunity from prosecution for anything he gives you; and I do mean anything. And that immunity runs to any and all prosecutions, state, federal, foreign or military!"

Murtry shook his head. "Sorry, I have no authority, and at the present, no inclination either."

Hurst couldn't help himself. His competitive nature wouldn't let him drop the matter there.

"The hell you don't." Hurst's voice raised a full octave. "Listen, you guys don't give squat about Pollard and you know it! You want the people, the terrorists, and the government, behind this attack. Pollard is, at best, a small fish...."

"Now hold on a minute, Captain, you're asking way too much here..." Murtry responded angrily.

Hurst immediately knew he'd stepped too far. He quickly pulled back and, after a long, thoughtful pause, he smiled and said, "Well... it's late and this has been a tough day for all of us. Let me talk to my client. Then you and I can talk in the morning, say, 0900; my office?"

"Make it 0900 in Longstreet's. And no other deals have been made, understand?"

Hurst nodded, knowing he had at least planted a seed with the FBI about a possible immunity. The young counsel also thought he'd better call his boss in Germany. The chain of command hated it when a young defense attorney went solo on big cases.

Longstreet concluded the conversation.

"Captain Hurst, the Commander has ordered your client into pretrial confinement here on the base. He'll have to go with us tonight."

Hurst knew there had been no confinement hearing, and he could have correctly objected to such an imposition. But he relented on the point, knowing Pollard would at least be better off for a night in the base confinement facility. The attorney had enough troubles. He didn't need Pollard doing something stupid out of desperation, like taking flight or attempting suicide. It had happened before.

"Okay. Give me a moment with him. In the meantime, he needs clean clothing and a shaving kit."

Longstreet nodded and raised his portable radio to call instructions to his deputies to find a suitable uniform, sleeping apparel and a shaving kit for the new prisoner. Jared Hurst turned from the group without shaking hands, and, opening the door, found Captain Zach Pollard in tears.

The FBI agent motioned to Longstreet and his subordinates and the gaggle turned and walked out into the street.

"Who the hell is this kid?" Murtry asked Longstreet, half-smiling.

The Air Force investigator paused, and then smiling in admiration of a fellow military officer, said only, "I told you...he's very quick. Some big firm stateside will grab him quick when his tour is over."

Murtry chuckled. "Sometime soon, let's hope. In the meantime, I've got forty agents and their British counterparts looking under haystacks for info on Pollard. I could use a few of your OSI team if they're available."

"Okay. I'll have to up-channel the request. You know, federal law, the Posse Comitatus Act. I can't surrender military assets for use in civilian matters without approval. Besides, it isn't clear who'll prosecute this one...."

"We will, Mr. Longstreet," Special Agent Murtry said confidently. "Bet the farm on that one."

"Maybe. But my hunch is that you're gonna find that Pollard was duped from the get go."

"I know that. The Brits know that. Hell, that was my guess when I first learned an Air Force officer was involved." Murtry conceded. "But we can't leave any possibility uncovered."

28 March
0700 Hours
RAF Lakenheath Confinement Facility

Zach Pollard's first night in jail had been an understandably sleepless one. Although he had been provided with underwear and a new flight suit and a shaving kit, he still bore the morose look of a trapped man. His mood was bleak when his lawyer entered the spartan cell.

"Hey, Zach. How are you feeling?" a still-tired Jared Hurst inquired.

"Not very good, counselor. You know all those things I told you last night about Tracie? Well, they were all true. I mean, I really love her."

Hurst could see the obvious pain in his client's eyes.

"What..." Hurst tried to ask, but before he could complete the question, Pollard continued. "I mean, she's dead. You know. Dead! I can't deal with this!" Pollard began to cry for the hundredth time. "Do you understand? And now all this shit...."

The lawyer wanted to say he understood but, of course, he didn't. The whole scenario was too bizarre. Hurst stared at the crying man. And, after a few moments of awkward silence, punctuated only by Pollard's sobs, Hurst continued.

"Look, Zach, I'm on my way to a meeting with the FBI agent I told you about last night. I'm going to try to work some sort of deal to keep you out of this mess. I mean, if you are telling me the truth and there's nothing to the idea that you were involved in all this, well, I want to make sure you don't get caught up in someone's political agenda to crucify anyone and everyone potentially involved. But YOU, Zach, have got to get your shit together. I don't need you falling apart on me. OK?"

"OK...But, you gotta believe me. I had no idea she was anything but what I thought.... And I still don't believe what these guys are saying...."

"Well, we can work that out later, but for now, I

just wanted to stop by and make sure you were all right. OKAY?"

Pollard was too consumed with grief to answer.

At the same instant, at base OSI headquarters, a red-faced Longstreet slammed his fist down onto his desk and shouted into the telephone.

"He's...what? What do you mean he's...?"

The OSI agent had just been told that his FBI counterpart, Murtry, had left for Washington at 0400 hours local time and would be away from London "for an indeterminate time."

"That's just fucking great!" Longstreet complained.

"You guys come rolling in here, claim jurisdiction in the investigation, put an Air Force officer in pretrial confinement, then your head man leaves the country. Do you have any idea what problems that causes us here? I don't suppose you guys appreciate that we have a speedy trial clock ticking. He's in pretrial, damn it! We gotta prosecute the guy within 90 days or we gotta cut him loose. Guilty or not guilty! Damn it!" Longstreet paused as his deputy stuck her head into the office and whispered that defense attorney Jared Hurst was in the building for his meeting with Longstreet and the FBI.

"Look," Longstreet yelled into the phone, "I'll call you back. I've got the defense counsel here and he's going to have a fit! And I don't blame him...."

Longstreet slammed the receiver down as Captain Jared Hurst entered the room.

"Have a seat, counselor. Uh, coffee?" Longstreet

was stalling and, despite the mental fog of an early morning after a late night, Hurst immediately sensed something was wrong.

"Okay, Jim, spit it out. Where are Murtry and the rest of his henchmen?"

"Called out of the country," came a terse, if not embarrassed, reply.

"What? When?"

"Early this morning, about three hours ago. London FBI won't tell me more than that."

"Well, I guess I should say I'm surprised, but I'm not," Hurst added evenly. "We've both seen this before. Someone in Washington farts and the entire universe goes ballistic. I guess I should be pissed off," Hurst noted, "but your speedy trial clock is ticking and we both know it, don't we? Regardless if it's a military or federal prosecution -- not that you have or ever will have any evidence -- you gotta get him formally charged and tried within eighty-eight days from today. Good luck," the lawyer concluded sarcastically.

"Jared, I must confess, I thought you'd be pissed." Longstreet smiled.

"Hey, you guys are helping me out. Why should I be pissed? But any guesses why Murtry flew outta here so quickly?"

"No idea," said Longstreet.

"But you'll, I mean the OSI, will still investigate, correct?"

"Oh, you bet," Longstreet hastened.

Jared Hurst thought to himself that Pollard had

better be telling the truth that his involvement with Tracie or Petra was no more than an innocent liaison, at least from Pollard's perspective. Hurst's knowledge of the military and the law told him that if that were the case, his client was already a free man because an investigation would reveal nothing. Pollard's career, however, was over. Pollard had found himself, albeit accidentally, in the middle of an international news story and that meant embarrassment to someone. Thus, Pollard's career would end for no official reason. Captain Hurst knew the story by heart; he'd already seen it a hundred times.

A lukewarm comment by his commanding officer in Pollard's next Officer Performance Report, and that would be it. It was a sure bet that Pollard would be marked down in the judgment block. Now Pollard could not remotely hope for a "Definitely Promote" recommendation when his records went before the major's promotion board in four months. He would surely be passed over for promotion, and ushered out of the Air Force with a meager severance package. But Jared Hurst couldn't deal with the vagaries of the political system in the Air Force. He could only deal with the criminal aspects of the case at hand. He returned to his thrust and parry with the agent.

"Very interesting problem you have there, Jim. The FBI takes jurisdiction, leaves you out in the cold, but you are compelled to investigate a crime that didn't occur and which will never be prosecuted."

And rising from his seat, the lawyer couldn't resist a dig, "But that's what you get paid all the big bucks for, right?"

Longstreet only shook his head and thought to himself that Captain Zach Pollard had a very smart lawyer representing him.

28 March
1100 hours
Raleigh, North Carolina

Carrie Mercer stood in the living room of her parents' North Raleigh home, portable phone in hand, talking to her husband overseas.

"And the weird thing is, I can't find Zach anywhere…"

"Did he get hurt?" Carrie asked.

"No, no. I was with him during the attack. But as to where he is now, I have no clue. Colonel Riordan said he was doing something for General Kilrain. He'll turn up, eventually. The idiot!" Damian laughed.

"Any problems at home? Ty OK?"

"No, honey. Ty is fine…a little worried about his Daddy, but we're fine! In fact, he's napping with Grandma right now."

"Jesus, babe…" Damian Mercer said, speaking from the bedroom of his recently evacuated base house.

"Sure is lonely here since you left me…" Mercer tried to interject some humor.

"Looks like nobody touched anything...but then, I guess they wouldn't. The sky cops had the housing area sealed off about ten minutes after you guys left."

"God, I don't even remember if I turned the VCR off...." Carrie Mercer laughed, making the best of the situation.

"Um, no...actually, you didn't." Her husband laughed. "TV was still on when I got off the base the next day...Sorry I didn't get to see you before they herded you on the C-17."

"Now THAT was an experience...about ten thousand crying kids and moms...we left Alconbury the very next morning. God, I got my period. What a mess. Thank God one of the women on the flight crew helped me out. We didn't have any change of clothes, but the Air Force had lots of blankets and food and stuff...and they got us a commercial flight to Raleigh as soon as we landed in Dover. Was there, like, any other problems at the base? The news has been full of stuff about germ warfare..."

"No, they cleaned that mess up quickly. But the area where the attack was is still quarantined. I think some Army guys are there, really decontaminating the place to make sure."

Pausing, the pilot added sheepishly, "Um, Honey...I really am sorry I got you into this mess," he offered, sincerely. "You didn't bargain for this when we got married."

"What the hell, Damian?" the woman chirped. "At least it isn't boring. None of the girls I went to Leesville High with ever had THIS much fun," she added semi-sarcastically, as her own father ambled in from the kitchen with a cup of coffee in hand.

Damian Mercer smiled. He was lucky. He had married a very brave woman.

29 March
1100 hours
Washington, D.C.

"Welcome back to a special edition of 'FACE THE NATION.' Hale Gardiner of the Baltimore Sun joins us now with questions for Senator Ann Ruston-Brand of the Senate Armed Services Committee and a leading advocate of reform in the nation's armed services. We're talking about the buzz on Capitol Hill this week - America's armed services abroad."

"Senator, you were one of the few outspoken opponents of the recent air raid on Syria, and you have been an outspoken critic of the President's war on terrorism. Now it looks like your prediction of retaliation has come home to roost. Any 'I told you so's!' for the President?"

"Most certainly not, Hale," the senator answered, feigning a look of deep conciliation.

"I am sure the President could not have possibly

foreseen the tragic and terrible consequences at the air base in England. That's why I have called for a complete investigation of the incident by an independent agency. I am concerned that the President wasn't told the whole story by the military. Why, for instance, were we storing chemical weapons at that base? And I have to wonder why our military intelligence community wasn't ready for this attack. I am taking particular interest in the failed leadership on the ground at our air base at Lakenheath, England."

"Any idea who was behind this attack, Senator?"

"Well, Hale, as the Post reported the day before yesterday, two Germans were killed. If I were to venture a guess, I'd have to say this administration has no idea how many enemies we've made. Probably an effort to embarrass both the U.S. and the British governments in the eyes of European Union. I might add that the point was well made. Perhaps we needed to be embarrassed."

Ruston-Brand affected one of her trademark squints into the camera to punctuate her point. "Of course, the President has made such a point of aligning himself with an 'extremely conservative' element in British politics. Perhaps they share some of the blame as well. All of which is clearly overshadowed by the very real threat that a nuclear explosion might have killed millions of innocent people, to say nothing of the chemical and germ warfare contamination that was spread all over the English countryside."

New York Times columnist Kendall Porter then asked, "You've been strongly critical of our continued participation in NATO, saying that it's too costly and potentially threatening. How can you justify that in light of the efforts of former Eastern-bloc nations to develop democracy and free-market capitalism? Isn't this a dangerous time to turn isolationist?"

"Kendall, the Pentagon and the White House have been preparing for the past fifty years to fight a war that we've already won. The Communist bogey man was a myth perpetrated by big business and the military to keep pumping billions of tax dollars into an inefficient and wasteful rat hole. Look. The Soviet system crumbled from its own weight across Eastern Europe. Frankly, the Soviets would never have developed a nuclear capability if we hadn't threatened them first. Today, there simply is no foreign military threat to our security. I'm not wholly certain these 'terrorists,' as you call them, aren't a convenient excuse for our colleagues on the other side of the aisle to ensure big spending for their benefactors in the defense industry. We need to refocus our attention and our strength back here at home. Our roads, highways and cities are in shambles. My God, how long will it take before the Administration finally cleans up the Gulf Coast? Why not take some of that youthful military might of ours and point it toward fixing problems at home?

"But Senator, the Majority Whip from Georgia takes strong issue with that. He's called for reductions, true enough, but said in yesterday's New York Times that strength abroad is needed -- especially in uncertain times. Your reaction?"

"Well the senator would be expected to say that, wouldn't he?" Ruston-Brand chuckled, throwing her head back. "His whole state is military dependent! But he knows as well as I do, that sooner or later we're going to get off of this military footing and finally put the Cold War to an end. There simply are no major threats abroad that justify the massive expenditure of money we don't have. I'm quite certain the Russians have no offensive plans. That makes us the one remaining superpower. Who else is out there? This 'terrorist' thing is overstated; it's the President's bogey man. My God, the Administration has even renewed the 'Star Wars' hysteria again. I'm told that next year's budget earmarks billions for technology that doesn't even exist. Just one tenth of that money could shelter this nation's homeless for a generation.... No, Hale. That's why I'll be co-sponsoring a bill with Senator Frye calling for new reform in the military. It's the Domestic Military Service Act and it calls upon the President to employ our service personnel in domestic nation building when we're not engaged in combat operations. We feel strongly that...."

APRIL

2 April
0400 hours
Kattegat Strait
Off the coast of Sweden

Mustafa Quomuz stood on the foredeck of the slowly-plodding trawler, *Georgi Zhukov*, as it rounded the Skagen, a slender cape on Denmark's northernmost tip. To protect himself against the North Sea wind, he gathered his heavy woolen coat against his throat and quickly returned his hands deep into his pockets. He'd not come above deck since his fast aerial boarding after fleeing the East Anglian countryside. Only the darkness outside allowed Quomuz to venture into the open air. The terrorist leader still couldn't believe that luck alone had saved him. He had been most fortunate to elude a hail of gunfire at the American air base, and evade British and American radar. Surely, he thought, this must have been the will of Allah. Or simply that the British and Americans had been taken so completely by surprise that they'd lost his helicopter on radar.

Not that British and American intelligence had forgotten Quomuz. Quite the contrary. All NATO nations had been placed on alert and had undertaken massive search efforts for the helicopter and its pilot. Sadly for the Americans, only a submarine could find the missing Jet Ranger now, for Quomuz and his rescuers had quickly scuttled it to the bottom of the sea moments after the Palestinian had landed on the Latvian trawler.

Just last night, a flight of two Danish F-16 aircraft from the air base at Alborg had made a nuisance of themselves...repeatedly flying past the *Zhukov*, with surveillance cameras on full...hoping to find some reason to justify a boarding in international waters. Since Quomuz had been safely stowed below decks, there was nothing for the Danes to see. Even so, the former East German skipper steered the *Zhukov* on a course on the Swedish side of the water. "Just as well to avoid Danish authority," Quomuz reasoned.

"If all continues well," Quomuz believed, "four more days and I will be safely in Wismar, just off the northern coast of Germany. There will be warm food, safety, and, perhaps, a woman. Then on to my friends in Hamburg."

3 April
1045 hours
Addenbrooke's Hospital
Cambridge

"...Dear Barbara, happy birthday to you!"

"You guys sound like shit, you know that?" Barbara Hatley mockingly criticized a hospital roomful of her fellow enlisted security force team-mates, "but I'm sure as hell happy to hear it!"

Barbara Hatley's review of her fellow guards-men's *acapella* choir's first, and last, public per-formance met with rousing good cheer, evidenced by whoops, yells and "hoo-ahhs!" Even the nurses had joined in the fracas, obeying doctors' orders to keep the patient's spirits high.

"Hey," a familiar voice boomed from behind the small crowd. "Can't a one-star get to have his pic-ture taken with a real Air Force hero?" Jack Kilrain was popular with his troops, just as he was with his officers. Elbowing his way through the small throng, Kilrain made his way to Hatley's bedside, where the young airman had propped herself up on a couple of pillows. She tried to straighten her yel-low nightgown, but Kilrain couldn't resist.... "You still out of uniform, Airman?" Hatley giggled. It was rare, in fact discouraged, for officers and enlisted to share many social moments together. It was known as "fraternization," and officially it was believed to undermine discipline.

But Kilrain disdained the notion that he was

"fraternizing" with his troops. He'd been a constant figure at Hatley's bedside during his off-duty hours. He'd even given standing orders to several junior officers in the Wing to "see to Airman Hatley's needs." They'd all happily complied, and the entire base had taken notice. Barbara Hatley not only survived the attack on the weapons storage area, but also had been credited with helping repulse the invaders. News of her heroism had spread quickly, thanks to a very efficient Defense Department publicity machine. TIME and NEWSWEEK had run color photos and several television networks had asked for interviews.

Even key politicians had wanted a piece of the action. One nurse had reported to Airman Hatley that Senator Ruston-Brand's office in Washington called, asking for a chance to fly to England to 'visit' the wounded young woman...with the press corps present. Hatley had been put off by a letter from Ruston-Brand suggesting that the airman ought to serve as a role model in the feminist struggle for equality.

Barbara Hatley had not joined the Air National Guard to make a political statement or to prove a point. Like so many others, she'd wanted to serve her country and earn some money for college. Now she was worried that undue publicity would single her out, "and that's not what I want, sir," she'd told her Wing Commander. "I just did my job along with the other guys on the team. We lost some people that day," Hatley recalled. "I'm just lucky to be alive and I don't see any heroism in that."

General Kilrain reached for Hatley's shoulder-length hair and tousled it. Looking across the bed at her father, a retired thirty-four year Army sergeant-major who had been flown to England for this occasion, the general cleared his throat and began to address the gathering.

"Hold on a minute everyone. Sergeant-Major Hatley.... I guess you all know how proud we are of your daughter, Barbara...ooops! Sorry, 'Airman' Hatley. But, Barbara, I cannot and will not tolerate your continuing breach of military courtesy and protocol."

Kilrain's face suddenly affected a faux, stern gaze, catching everyone, including Barbara, off guard.

"Over the past days, I have heard you and people around you repeatedly refer to you as 'Airman.' As you know, assuming an unauthorized rank is a violation of the Uniform Code of Military Justice and I won't stand for this any longer!" the General chided. Kilrain had the ability to make the hairs on the back of a troop's neck stand on end, even when he was jesting. Just the effect he'd wanted for this group of Hatley's peers and comrades.

Just as Airman Barbara Hatley was prepared to respond with a "But, sir..." Kilrain interjected, "So, as punishment for your blatant misbehavior, I am forced to impose the following punishment. If you please," Kilrain turned to the young woman's father, his co-conspirator, "Sergeant-Major Hatley, read the punishment order." Beaming, the young woman's father rose from his bedside chair. Slowly unfolding a typewritten paper, he began to read aloud and barked:

"TEN HUT! Attention to orders.

By order of the Secretary of the Air Force, and in recognition of her devotion to duty, Airman First Class Barbara Gayle Hatley is, effective this date, hereby promoted two grades to the rank of Staff Sergeant, United States Air Force, with all the rights and privileges to which such a non-commissioned officer is entitled. By Direction of Jack Kilrain, Brigadier General, United States Air Force."

The crowd let go a collective "Whoop!" and tears filled the eyes of the elder Hatley as a now-grinning Jack Kilrain reached into his pocket and produced a pair of brand new staff sergeant stripes and began to fix them to the young woman's pillow. "By the way, 'Sergeant' -- Kilrain emphasized the word -- "I understand there's a medal or two coming your way. The package is on the Secretary's desk. They'll probably want to pin them on you in Washington."

The crowd again responded with a happy "Atta Girl, Hat!"

And, for the first time in a long time, Barbara Hatley began to blush.

There are moments in the military, like this one, when people in uniform warmly share the sense of being a part of something bigger than themselves, part of a hard mission in hard times under hard conditions. True enough, people in uniform have died before and would die in the future, but today, not one man or woman in that hospital room -- a long way from home -- would have been elsewhere for a million dollars.

Standing just outside the patient's room in the famous children's hospital, a handful of doting British nurses smiled.

3 April
1330 hours
Houses of Parliament
London

The European media was in a frenzy and the political consequence of the attack was only now beginning to manifest itself. At "Question Time," the tension had spread quickly through the Commons.

"Would the Prime Minister give his assurance," a bearded opposition back-bencher bellowed, "that the illegal, and dare I say, immoral, chemical weapons stored by the Americans and exposed in this unfortunate raid were present without the Prime Minister's knowledge and acquiescence?"

Rising amid heated shouts and catcalls, the PM smoothed his trousers, fastened the middle of three buttons on his jacket and, taking the measure of his antagonist, bore in. "My right honorable friend knows full well that neither this government nor our allies, the Americans, either manufacture or store the chemical weapons that my friend alludes to. The traces of the chemical weapons were brought here by those very forces who laid on the attack!"

Unbowed, the opposition Member of Parliament responded. "Then will the Prime Minister and his government not concede that it utterly failed to discover these chemicals in advance of the attack. And that his government has failed, and continues to fail, to take adequate measures to prevent a similar occurrence in the future?"

The Prime Minister, now on the defensive, promised a thorough investigation by both the Ministry of Defense and by the Lord Chancellor's office.

Another opposition back-bencher took to his feet and echoed a dire sentiment. "Will the Prime Minister now agree that this nation's subjugation at the hands of the Americans must finally cease? Will he not instruct the foreign office to begin discussions with the Americans which will lead to the eventual withdrawal of their forces from this island and to the end of the threat which they pose by their presence here?"

Before the Prime Minister could answer, a raucous chorus of cheers and boos filled the great hall.

The noise would not abate for several minutes, and by the time it had subsided, a truth had been distorted to a worldwide television audience in the hot lights and noise of the political frenzy.

Watching the proceedings from afar, Quomuz smiled. His message had been clearly delivered.

4 April
0945 hours
New Scotland Yard

Chief Inspector Harold MacHugh's anger remained unabated since his department had been stripped of jurisdiction over the "Voss-Koln Incursion," as the terrorist reprisal attack had come to be known in official British intelligence circles. Neither he, nor any of his operatives, had been allowed to interrogate the captive woman, and MacHugh had made sure his displeasure had been made known in the halls of power throughout London. His persistence proved an embarrassment at Whitehall and among certain backbenchers in Parliament. It was feared the Times of London had caught wind of MacHugh's disenchantment.

The government didn't need yet another political fiasco this season to compound the crisis at Lakenheath, and only one month after an embarrassing episode involving a rash of illnesses brought on by shoddy government inspection practices in the nation's dairy industries. Thus, MacHugh had earned a summons to Number 10 and a session with the Prime Minister.

"Sir Harold, there are crucial interests of national security to be considered..." he'd been told, in patronizing terms.

"Thus we..." the PM's voice asserted.

"Damn you and your royal plural," the stalwart Scot fumed to himself.

"Thus, we must allow the authority most suited to these matters to handle the issue. I'm quite confident that both the Home Secretary and the General Staff agree with me." It was obvious the battle had been lost before it had even begun, so MacHugh, reckoning he could lose little else, pressed the issue.

"The PROPER authority, Prime Minister? Scotland Yard IS the PROPER authority. You cannot seriously suggest that either MI-5 or MI-6 is the correct agency to handle this matter."

"Frankly, Harold, you've put Her Majesty's government in, well, an embarrassing position. We understand that your field operatives could have taken the African courier. But the trail went cold and you lost the game! The Tories and the Liberal Democrats have been having a field day with us. I presume you saw last week's "Question Time" in the Commons! They'll be making hay out of this well into the next election.... and I have Scotland Yard to thank for it! I'm told the press and the BBC are considering coverage regarding your handling of the matter. Imagine!"

"Pardon me, Prime Minister," Sir Harold McHugh, Knight Commander, Order of the British Empire, retorted. "But you approved our handling of Ayugi and this was clearly an act of foreign espionage and terror. If Military Intelligence were on their game, this wouldn't have happened. As it was, my lads caught the scent at the airport -- well within OUR jurisdictional authority."

MacHugh looked sternly at the British Chief Executive, raised his voice another decibel, and continued:

"MI was nowhere to be seen! The male bodies we later took were Arab and German. The woman is German. I should rather suggest that this was an MI-5 cock-up. Or were they too busy playing spies with the CIA? Where were MI-5 and their fabled domestic intelligence? Where were their deep cover operatives? And for that matter, where the bloody hell was MI-6? Why didn't they act? They have responsibility for foreign intelligence. No, Prime Minister, Scotland Yard is apparently the only agency alert and on duty, and it was damn lucky we found the courier as we did."

MacHugh had hit several nerves, damning in one breath the Prime Minister's acquiescence in the plan and a series of noted intelligence failures attributed to both MI-5 and MI-6. A number of serious compromises in internal security at both agencies had embarrassed the Crown during and since the Cold War.

"We find your lack of perception in this matter disturbing, Chief Inspector!" came the Prime Minister's angry reply. "The matter is decided. Scotland Yard will divest itself of any further responsibility in this matter." The Prime Minister's stern expression remained unchanged, and rising to show him the way out, curtly thanked MacHugh for his view.

"This is the course we have chosen and we shall follow it. MI shall have your support...your full support, Harold, and we'll have done with it."

As MacHugh left the room, there was no friendly handshake with the PM He knew an order when he heard one, and he was none the happier for it. There would be no reconsideration of the Prime Minister's policy. Scotland Yard would neither hinder MI-5 efforts nor investigate the matter further. Any additional investigative steps by the Metropolitan Police would result in "significant administrative repercussions," the Prime Minister had assured MacHugh.

Sir Harold reached for the handle of his car that had been brought to the front door of 10 Downing Street and turned to see the PM standing in the open doorway, his prize West Highland terrier at his feet.

"And Harold," the Prime Minister called, smiling broadly, "Do remember that unity is key to any team endeavor! I'm sure you recall that from your Sandhurst days."

MacHugh, angered by the Prime Minister's order of silence and his demand for cooperation, said nothing as he slid into the Bentley and quietly ordered his driver to return to the Yard. The domestic criminal case, as far as Her Majesty's government was concerned, was closed.

Officially, at least.

MAY

2 May
0930 hours
Room SH-216, Hart Senate Office Building
Washington, DC

Eldon Klein adjusted his reading glasses and returned to his prepared text. The Secretary of Defense was asking the Armed Services Committee for more money than any of his predecessors, all combined, had ever sought for a single contingency operation. This was lead-story grist, and every major news media outlet was present in the gallery.

"Mister Chairman, the greatest long-range threat to American security is neither a bomb, nor a bullet, or even a gun. It is poverty and its corollary, starvation." Klein paused and looked the chairman squarely in the eye, over the tops of his half-glasses.

"Our world will add another billion people over the next ten to twelve years. At least ninety percent of that increase will occur in what we euphemistically call 'developing nations.' The population explosion continues unabated! In fact, some twenty million of the world's poorest people migrate to urban areas each year."

Taking a sip from the lukewarm glass of water in front of him, Klein continued. "But these 'urban areas' aren't necessarily on maps. Such include eroded and barren hillsides, deforested and dried-up wetlands, fields that no longer bear fruit, fouled water supplies and nonexistent sanitary conditions. Economic progress in Africa and the Middle East simply cannot keep pace with population increases. Such conditions strain what meager resources and infrastructures exist in these, the poorest of nations. Corrupt, inefficient governments are simply unable to cope. The result: instability, ethnic and religious tribalism and warfare. Lawless safe-havens supplant legitimate, democratically-elected governments, and anarchy reigns supreme. The time for action is now. I will be happy to respond to your questions or observations."

"Mister Secretary, that's all very well and good. But sir, I must say," the junior senator from Oklahoma began, "aren't we talking about a lot of money here? The State Department has estimated more than forty-six billion dollars in relief aid over the next three fiscals alone and I am certain the Pentagon will ask for at least twice that amount."

"Senator, there's no question we're in Africa to stay. If we're going to prevent another 'Afghanistan,' we must be proactive! Terrorism grows in the bellies of hungry men and the only way we can beat this thing is to feed it to death. If death today is preferable to living another day in squalor, then the radicals have a ready-made army. That's why we've got to beat the fundamentalists by reaching the people before they do. But we simply cannot send in aid workers unescorted or unarmed. The State Department is negotiating leases with Nigeria and Mali so we can give the UN and the various relief organizations some protection. I need not remind any of the panel about the horrors of Somalia, where an ill-equipped expeditionary force was decimated by local warlords who were hoarding the humanitarian relief supplies. Now, imagine that on a ten-fold scale. Even as we speak here today, in Darfur, Sudanese militiamen kill the aid workers before they get a chance to set up food distribution centers. So we've got to have fast-start forward operating locations to meet 'contingency' operations."

The Chair next recognized the senator from Michigan who likewise read from a position paper her staff had prepared:

"Although it's not well publicized, we've had a small US force deployed in Djibouti since just

after 9-11. It's important because we've been following the terrorist's trail. We know they're infil-
trating and exploiting the poverty and misery on
the eastern half of the African Continent. I understand that we picked Djibouti because it's located
in a strategic spot where the Red Sea meets the
Gulf of Aden. My military advisors tell me that it's
only a short flight from our base in Djibouti to
Yemen, which more than a few al Qaeda leaders
call home. It's also close to both the Sudan and Somalia, two other locations where Islamic fundamentalism runs wild. But Mister Secretary, my concern
is this: Are we building another expensive 'Club
Med' that we'll have to leave behind when the political situation becomes untenable, just like we left
so many expensive bases in Saudi Arabia?"

Klein rose, and holding a pointer stick, he indicated a small spot on a map.

"Senator, the current US Combined Joint Task
Force-Horn of Africa, is located here at Camp Le
Monier. There is not much more there than some
cinder block buildings, a scad of tents and a runway. But it gives us a presence and quick access to
the places we need to be. These are bare bones and
relatively inexpensive. Not much nightlife, to be
certain! I think the money is being well spent."

"Really? 'Relatively inexpensive?' Is that how
you term it, Mister Secretary?" Senator Ann Ruston-Brand began, genuinely surprised that the
"hawkish" Defense Secretary had expressed himself
in unusually humanitarian terms.

SEVENTH PSALM

2 May
1030 hours
Camp Le Monier, Djibouti
Combined Joint Task Force-Horn of Africa

The Senate would continue its public and partisan wrangling over the Secretary's budgetary requests for another two months.

Two oceans away, however, Air Force Staff Sergeant Erica DuPree sat cross-legged on her cot and, using her laptop, typed to her blog, "AFDozerGurl" via satellite uplink. Outside her forty-person tent, which overlooked the Gulf of Aden, hundreds of service personnel from several nations busied themselves noisily rebuilding an airport and support facilities. DuPree was grateful for a few moments of contact with her twenty-first century world as she labored to help transform an ancient one.

"We're doing more good here than people at home are ever told. We're fighting this terrorism thing w/ a sword in one hand and food in the other. Just last week, our civil engineering squadron rebuilt a school for like 1,800 kids. They were sooooooooo thankful! ☺

I am working my butt off. 12 on and 12 off, just like everyone else here. But like, when a TV news producer stopped me the other day she didn't want to hear about the good we do. She wanted me to tell her how I felt about all the GI's who have been killed over here. See, its like, I don't know anybody who has been killed here. She didn't even want to hear about the school. She didn't want to hear about the medical care we bring. In fact, the base Vet even takes care of this farmer's donkey! Dudes, I'm tellin' ya, we're doing good things here. I think the CIA is here, too. They launch UAVs at night. Waaaay cool. But we're not supposed to know about that. LOL

One of you e-mailed me and asked if you could send me some T's and Rainbows. Too funny. We have BDUs for casual wear and Kevlar for formal wear, 24/7! My helmet is da' bomb.

See ya in the chat room later. Aim High!"

Outside, Marine Corporal Donnie Morales of the 3rd Provisional Security Company adjusted his sunglasses and peered into the engine of the half-ton as it sat idling at the makeshift motor pool. "I dunno, Captain, Lieutenant," the corporal from south Los Angeles yelled over the din of a half-dozen cranes and bulldozers. "What did you sirs put in the gas tank last night? Sounds like you got some sand in there. That's why she's running a little rough. Guess I'd better pull the filter."

Had the sprawling site not been patrolled day and night by heavily-armed and well-trained Marines, the camp might have resembled any construction project in the world. The newly renovated ninety-acre base, once used by the French Foreign Legion, had become the expeditionary headquarters of the Combined Joint Task Force almost overnight.

"CJTF-HOA" as it was known, was now temporary home to soldiers, airmen and marines, all part of the growing multi-nation presence in the Horn of Africa, in support of humanitarian and counter-terrorism operations across the region.

"Get that palletized generator over by the hospital," Army Captain Jennifer Marrs called into her walkie-talkie to the Air Force engineer at the controls of the crane that hoisted the massive generator lightly into place. "That's it. Gently, gently….lower…lower…."

The bustle of activity would continue well into the flood-light illuminated darkness…and into every night thereafter until the makeshift base was fully operational. Four British transport planes were scheduled to arrive day after tomorrow and the runway landing lights weren't working properly. Command had made the runway a priority. Time, everyone knew, was short.

There were tons of food to be distributed, medicines to be administered, and dangerous, armed men to be found and fought.

JULY

3 July
1100 hours
British Army Barracks, Colchester
East Anglia, England

Petra Voss remained in dark isolation a full story below ground in a rock-cold vault with only a stainless steel cot and toilet for companionship. No windows, no bars. Just twelve-inch-thick concrete walls and one door, sealed shut. A single, bare bulb caged in thick wire starkly illuminated the vault. Her prison clothing consisted of only a pair of heavy cotton trousers and a pullover shirt. No undergarments, no shoes, no belt and only a thick processed-paper sheet for her bedding. Her personal accouterments were equally sparse: No cigarettes, no books, no magazines and certainly no visitors -- save the daily, fruitless "chats" with one or more "information extraction" officers, courtesy of MI-5.

Despite its energetic efforts to encourage "meaningful participation," MI-5 had learned nothing from terrorist Voss. Not a request for food, not even a request for bathing facilities. She'd learned early in her KGB training that an accent could aid an enemy by revealing one's nationality and thus, one's training and sponsorship. She'd eat only meager amounts of prison food, lest, she feared, she'd be drugged. Sodium Pentathol had proven ineffective as well. Her allergic reaction - anaphylactic shock, the doctors called it - had frustrated even the more extreme forms of interrogation. Her violent reaction had placed her in the infirmary for ten days. Ten days lost to her interrogators.

Voss's Teutonic heritage, her indoctrination and combat training made her an impossible woman to break. She volunteered no information about herself and would answer none of the simplest questions. Voss was a pro, as all concerned had instinctively known from the outset. No dramatic gestures like hunger strikes or suicide attempts. She sat, trance-like, on either the floor beneath the light or prone atop the cot. Day in, day out, for the past three months; never so much as a word passed her lips.

It became something of a game to both sides. MI-5 would ask the questions, Petra Voss would not answer. And so on, twice a day, seven days a week...

Not that MI-5 hadn't been forceful in its effort

to make her talk.

British Army doctors still hadn't removed the stainless steel sutures from her jaw, a result of the blow she'd suffered at Colin Blackford's hands. Freshly bruised, Voss had earned "a bit of a rough up," as one interrogator had described his subsequent attempt to gain information from her. Such treatment of a prisoner would never be tolerated in the United States. But here, there were no Constitutional niceties to get in the way of an efficient investigation, British agents thanked themselves. It would be at least two more months, the doctors had said, before she would be able to fully open her mouth. No matter; for now, she could take nutrition through a straw.

There would be no trial for Petra Voss, at least, not in the near term. There was far too much information to be gotten from her. A trial would stem any efforts to gain crucial information from the woman, so it had been agreed there would be no trial and no information leaked to the press that the German perpetrator was even alive. Official reports had described the woman's death after the firefight with British and American agents. The photos of her unconscious body - courtesy of Colin Blackford's right hand - had convinced the press that the unknown woman had died from wounds suffered in the battle. Had they only been more discerning, they would have noticed a telltale lack of bullet wounds.

But the clock was ticking. Sooner or later, word of Voss's captivity would slip out. The American press would have a field day and the rout would be on! The Allies needed information and they needed it fast.

Luckily enough, British Army intelligence officers had, early on, taken fingerprints, DNA samples and photographs of the woman. Those efforts proved the most helpful, for Interpol's data banks had, at least, revealed Voss's name and basic information.

"VOSS, Petra. Aliases: unknown. Age: 35; born near Hamburg. Educated in the Staatschule. Believed recruited by remnants of the Bader-Meinhof Gang while in her teens. Languages: German, Arabic, English, and Dutch."

They'd even considered asking the Americans for help. "We need not bother the Americans with this just yet," one Whitehall scion had reasoned. "Let our chaps learn all they can before we are forced to contend with the American press." Even if the CIA or FBI knew anything," according to prevailing wisdom, "they probably wouldn't share." A discreet query of Interpol revealed no record of her. "Surely," one MI-5 agent reasoned, "this wasn't her first operation. She's had some experience, perhaps in the Middle East. Let's check with the Mossad."

But, it was ticklish getting information from the Israelis, as everyone in the British secret services all knew. The Jerusalem government still remembered the harsh British occupation of Palestine and the land now known as Israel. They also knew that they often had to invoke the assistance of the Americans for such information...but in doing so, they tipped their hand to the ever-nosy Yanks.

Most frustrating, of course, was the knowledge that the terrorists never hamstrung themselves with notions of chivalry. Rather, a western agent was as good as dead upon capture...unless he/she could be used as a chattel in a quiet, international body bargain.

Despair, MI-5 had hoped, brought on by the unrelenting sameness of her solitary captivity would eventually fracture her silence. Certainly, the technique had worked before, most recently in Afghanistan. Even the sturdiest of men, physically fit and emotionally hardened, had broken under such treatment. But Petra Voss was no ordinary combatant, for hers was the strength borne of an unyielding devotion to the socialist ideal. As if that were not armor enough, she had been newly steeled by the sense of utter betrayal at the hands of her one-time comrade, Mustafa Quomuz. Vengeance, it seemed, proved an effective antidote to the daily British dosage of interrogation.

Not that Voss was devoid of any human need or want. Indeed, there had been days when she wondered whether her compatriots had forsaken her or whether they even knew she was alive. Perhaps it was her fate to die in the bleak anonymity of the steel walls around her, she allowed herself to consider on more than one occasion. But whatever her secret thoughts, Voss had not allowed her tormentors to sense her fears.

"They have kept me alive for a purpose," she had reasoned to herself. "That's why the beatings stopped---I'm worthless to them dead, so they must have a reason."

9 July
1432 hours
Dirksen Senate Office Building
Washington, D.C.

General Jack Kilrain scooted his chair closer to the microphone. He'd arrived from the United Kingdom only hours before, hastily summoned by the Chief of Staff. Behind the row of senators on the Armed Services Committee, staffers scurried back and forth, pushing papers and pouring cups of hot coffee as the panel convened for a third straight day of hearings into the attack at the American air base in England.

Senator Ann Ruston-Brand whispered to a young male assistant and, taking stock of all the camera positions, readjusted her chair to ensure that the lighting was the most beneficial to her for the nightly network news.

Although the Air Force Chief of Staff and a host of other Pentagon luminaries had already testified, Ruston-Brand had saved most of her venom for Jack Kilrain.

"General…" the senator began, "When I concluded yesterday with the Chief of Staff, I was inquiring about Air Force preparations for the attack, which cost the lives of several young Americans, plus the one young woman who totally victimized by horrific violence. Your boss, the Chief of Staff, didn't seem to want to answer my questions, so, now, I want to know--exactly--what steps you took, General, to prevent the attack."

Kilrain bristled at the notion that he, or any other peacetime commander in a foreign nation, could actually prevent such an attack.

"Senator, if I may, I'd like to correct a statement in the Washington Post article which may have influenced your question. That article, dated last week, incorrectly states that a January intelligence report warned of security flaws at the Lakenheath base complex."

"In fact, the three-hundred-page report entitled, *Increased Overseas Security and Force Protection in the Aftermath of Abu Du'an*, describes measures that had recently been taken to improve protection of the munitions, operations and residential compounds. Those measures were not, I underscore, were not taken on account of a security alert. The report was a summary of protective steps that British Ministry of Defense officials had taken in response to security observations made by U.S. and British officials in recent months..."

"But, general," Ruston-Brand cut Kilrain short, "I'm asking what security preparations YOU made...not your assessment of British failures."

"Senator, the airbase at Lakenheath is a Royal

Air Force facility. The British government owns it. We don't. The British government owns the land and we pay rent."

"But General, American tax dollars pay that rent and pay your salary. Do you mean to tell me that you abandoned security planning and precautions to the British? Is that what you are telling the parents of the dead young men and women?"

Before Kilrain could answer, Ruston-Brand affected her trademark squint as she turned full face into the hearing room camera, and then continued. "And wasn't it your negligence that allowed one of your pilots, an officer, to provide information to one of the terrorists, a woman with whom he had been living?"

Kilrain was angered by the cheap shot, but held his tongue and carefully composed his response.

"Senator, that matter has been fully investigated and no evidence was found that implicated the officer in ANY way!"

Having scored a minor point, Ruston-Brand changed topics. "Let's return to the issue of training, particularly the young women under your command. I am particularly interested in what precautions you had taken to avoid injury to women like Airman Hatley. Would you care to comment?"

"Senator," Kilrain responded carefully, "The Security Forces wounded at the Lakenheath attack were not, I repeat NOT, active-duty personnel. They were National Guard augmentees sent in to replace the active-duty people who were deployed in the Afghan and Iraqi theaters of operation."

"So now you're scape-goating the National Guard?"

"No Senator, I'm saying that National Guardsmen are trained by the Guard and the quality and quantity of that training varies from state to state. I'm saying that these particular Guardsmen from Iowa served particularly well, given that they had only been in the UK for a few weeks before the attack. I'm saying that much of our American defense capability is borne by the Reserves and the Guard and, in spite of the best efforts from all concerned, it takes time to integrate the Guard with the active-duty mission."

The Michigan Senator, now angered, pressed her attack.

"General Kilrain! Do you now resort to blaming the good women and men of our Reserves for your own failure to anticipate and guard against the attack that did SO much damage and cost SO many lives? Do you? Do you?"

It was nearing mid-afternoon, so the several teams of network reporters and producers turned off their cameras and lights and worked their way out of the hearing room and off toward their video editing booths. They had their talking heads and sound bites for the lead story on the evening news.

Few broadcast reporters stayed long enough to hear Kilrain's answer. Neither did Senator Ruston-Brand. She had scored her points with a convenient foil and had assured herself of coverage in the top section of the news. With her entourage in tow, the senator stood grandly, smiled sarcastically at Jack Kilrain, and left the hearing room, pausing only long enough to excuse herself with the Committee Chair, explaining that "pressing constituent obligations" necessitated her departure.

Kilrain, angered by the obvious publicity play at his expense, answered for the record.

"Senators, we rely upon the civilian intelligence community, both American and British, to advise us of the potential threats. We rely upon Congress to provide the personnel and equipment needed to accomplish the missions given us. Even though organized terrorist groups had been reported generally targeting U.S. and other allied personnel around the globe, Her Majesty's Government felt, in light of domestic anti-western sentiment, that enhanced security efforts were, at that time, unwarranted. The reports did not point to any indication that organized terrorist groups were targeting specific U.S. or other personnel in the United Kingdom. As for the officer referenced by Senator Ruston-Brand, I repeat, there has been no proof of any illegal or improper conduct on the part of that officer."

Despite his rational explanation, Jack Kilrain, the Air Force and Zach Pollard had suffered severe body blows in the hot lights of television and public opinion.

Senator Ruston-Brand's internal memo, written two months later, to the other members of the Armed Services Committee ensured that Jack Kilrain had seen his last promotion.

13 July
0900 hours
AFOSI Detachment
Royal Air Force Lakenheath, England

Special Agent Longstreet kicked back in his chair and crossed his feet atop his desk and looked attorney Jared Hurst straight in the eye.

"Well, counselor, you asked for this meeting. Your client wants to confess?" Longstreet chortled. He'd known the defense lawyer for the two years both men had been assigned to the installation. Hurst's well-earned reputation as a tough defender in court had been supported by his handling of the FBI agents shortly after the attack on the base and the school bus. Longstreet knew Hurst was more than a worthy adversary. On at least two courtroom occasions, the young ADC had cross-examined the agent, secured an acquittal for his clients, and had won the agent's respect as a hardball player.

"Spare me the cop talk, Jim. You and I have known each other long enough not to bullshit with each other. Right?"

"OK, that's fair enough. What's on your mind?"

"Just this. What are you planning to do with Pollard? You guys have investigated this case pretty hard and have been keeping him in pretrial confinement ever since the attack. What I'm getting at is this: Are you guys going to charge him or not? And if you are going to charge him, what the hell are you going to charge him with? You know I won't let you talk to him or the FBI or anyone else..."

Longstreet's eyes lit up at the challenge.

"Hey, your boy was fucking a German terrorist. She masterminded the most daring attack on an American military installation in history. Remember, American kids got killed, she's part of a conspiracy to build and detonate a WMD that could, in all probability, have killed YOU, counselor, and you saunter in here and make demands! Pollard may be a conspirator and a traitor."

Hurst responded, "Jim, 'may be' won't cut it in court!" as he sharply returned the agent's hard stare.

Longstreet continued. "There are a lot of people...and I mean a lot of important people, who want everyone involved with this deal either dead or in prison for life. You got that?"

"Longstreet, that's your problem. Remember, you must 'prove' Pollard was involved and you can't do it. The FBI, and the Brits, couldn't. They've dropped Pollard like a hot potato. You can't prove shit. All you got is shit!"

"What we got, counselor, is motive and opportunity," Longstreet raised his voice, in a bluff.

"Motive?" the young lawyer shouted, "Motive? What motive? Pussy, for Christ's sake? You think this guy sold out his country for pussy?" Hurst raised himself out of his chair. "P.S., Jim-old-buddy, I got news for you! Motive and opportunity aren't elements of a crime. You gotta prove the ELEMENTS of a crime, not your cop-show 'motive and opportunity' horseshit."

"Hey, it's happened before, pal," Longstreet's voice raised several decibels. "The guy was a loner; didn't date much. Then in walks this woman and she turns him every way but loose. Never know what a man will do after he's had his brains fucked out."

"Give me a break. Yeah, I'll admit he was sleeping with the woman...but what the hell does that mean? Did it ever occur to you geniuses that the poor dumb bastard got used? I talked to his crewmate, what's his name...Mercer, yeah, Damian Mercer. He laid it all out for me. Said this woman played Zach like a fish. She kept him on the string all the time, broke up with the guy once or twice, and then took him back. She showed up at a few of the squadron wives things, asked a few questions, usually about deployments. Then she'd bolt. Truth be told, the wives, innocently gave her more intel than he ever did. Wives start talking about deployments, day care, new families, etc., and Voss could piece together the entire operational picture. I did some other checking, too. All the way back to flight school Pollard's instructors say he'd have cut off his right arm to wear a green bag and earn those wings. So I don't think he'd sell his country or his wings for some snatch. And I don't think a jury will buy it, either. So, what else you got, man? Because what you got now is pretty lame."

"Your man want to take the box?" Longstreet offered, vainly hoping the attorney would consent to a polygraph examination. Longstreet knew the investigation had revealed nothing to incriminate Pollard. The query was nothing more than a wild shot in the dark.

"No way! You know the court says you can't use the results and neither can we." Hurst pointed a finger toward his opposition. "So what's the point to that? Forget it."

Before Longstreet could respond, Special Agent Kelley, Longstreet's deputy commander, stuck her head in the door and called Longstreet to an "emergency meeting."

Longstreet rose and extended his hand to his adversary. "Sorry, counselor, we've gotta continue this discussion another time."

The attorney just shook his head and headed for the office door.

Longstreet, grinning, couldn't resist another dig. "Why don't you give me a call when your guy wants to plead? It'll help me get promoted..."

Jared Hurst, sizing up the agent for a clue to his intent, and laughing, answered with a half-serious "Fuck you. I'll see your sorry ass in court. In the meantime, I want him released. Now! Oh, and tell the front office we're looking at civil damages for wrongful imprisonment."

Hurst was ushered to the security-locked door by a junior agent.

After the lawyer was out of earshot, Longstreet walked into Kelley's office and plopped down in her overstuffed easy chair.

"Whoa, thanks for the rescue. Our resident Perry Mason was all over me."

"Tough, huh, boss?" Kelley asked. "I could hear him bearing down on you in there. He can be a buzz saw. Remember that forgery case he beat us on last November? He had me on the witness stand for three hours!"

"Yeah, we're screwed and he knows it. We haven't got shit on Pollard. But I didn't want to let him know that. I was fishing for something, hoping he'd slip. Hell, on second thought," Longstreet laughed, "He probably figured me out, too."

"I know what you mean," Kelley answered. "So what if our Captain Pollard was sleeping with this woman? What the hell does that prove, anyway? We took statements from every guy in the squadron and, to a man, they swear Pollard is as loyal as a dog. I talked to some of the wives, too. They say our little German was a cool customer. She came to a few of the wife things. She'd listen politely, add a few innocuous comments...but mostly she'd just listen. They also say this, what's her name.... Tracie, Petra, what the hell.... didn't come around the pilots, though. If she was looking for secrets, she didn't dig very hard. You know how hard it is for a pilot to keep his yap shut when confronted by a nice pair of legs. Guess she got what she needed from the wives, particularly about school bus times, drop-offs and such."

"That's our other problem. She could have gathered all the intel she needed simply by driving around the outside of the base or talking to the local Brits. Hell, ninety-nine percent of our operations are visible to every car on the highway outside the base. There's no indication she used anything Pollard could have told her, anyway. All his classified knowledge is related to flight operations. And the grade school kids, the bus.... Hell, that's been a security disaster waiting to happen for years. We've been an obvious sitting duck."

"So, what was her angle? Why Pollard?"

"Who the hell knows? Cover? He gave her entry to the wives' organization. Guess she picked up enough loose conversation to help her formulate a plan. She scouted some of the turf without anyone noticing. The FBI tells me they figure Pollard was likely just the camouflage. They're probably right."

"Well, what about the Brits? They know any-thing?"

"If they do, they ain't saying. Besides, all we got for a witness is a dead German and a few people who know that Pollard and this woman were boinking."

"Boinking, Jim? Boinking? That's a new one. Where did you come up with that? You make a lady blush!"

Longstreet laughed.

"So, boss, what are we gonna do? The Justice Department doesn't want this guy. We've got to tell the interim Wing Commander that we've got noth-ing upon which to base a prosecution and soon, too. The whole Air Force is up in arms over the deal. In fact, the Pentagon is pretty consumed with the Sen-ate hearings. Looks like General Kilrain will be the scapegoat. The FBI played us pretty good, too, I'd say. They rush in here three months ago, begin this big field investigation. We're left on the sidelines, but they get us, the Air Force, to put Pollard on ice for ninety days, maybe illegally, and the Feds never take the hit for it. We're the ones who will catch heat!"

"I know. But one thing's for sure. Whatever pans out, Pollard's career is over. So is Kilrain's. You know the Air Force. They want a scapegoat to punish, even if there isn't one. You know how it is in the modern military; to be accused is to be convicted!" Longstreet shook his head. "As weird as it seems, Zach Pollard is taking a bullet that was headed for the Pentagon."

"I'll file my report with HQ this week. I'm going to recommend that no action be taken. But who knows. It's up to the new commander and the generals at USAFE. They could go court-martial, but there's no evidence; they could go administrative discharge, you know -- lesser standard of proof, but there's no real value there either. Or, they could drop the whole thing. If we even try to prosecute Pollard and his lawyer will replay those Senate hearings in Technicolor. He'll fry Kilrain for causing the attack. Jesus.... what a mess," Longstreet swore. "But I'll bet that even if we drop this, Pollard's chances of promotion or retention are 'Slim' and 'None.'"

"And, as we all know," Agent Kelley smiled calculatingly, sipping a soda, "Slim just left town."

AUGUST

Gerhard Allmenroder exhaled a long plume of smoke from his lungs and closed the window overlooking the streets of what had once been East Berlin.

"It is good to see you, my old friend. One hears many stories of the grand sheik these days. I am glad he has not forgotten his friends from our years together in Hamburg. But I am saddened by the loss of our Petra. Her death came as a blow to us all…at least, those of us who are still left."

Quomuz looked the German squarely in the eye. "She died well. I was at her side when she was wounded. It was all I could do to leave her, but she insisted. Both she and the other one, Koln, fought valiantly."

"It is too bad, indeed," Allmenroder continued. "In another time, when we were strong, we, the true Red Army Faction, could have saved her, perhaps. Our threats and bombs spoke loudly once. Maybe the operation might have gone differently. Alas, she is dead, and the reports of the operation were limited to what I saw on the television and read in the press."

The Palestinian looked out the window as Allmenroder continued.

"Time and politics have moved against us, my friend. Just look out there. There is no more stomach for revolution, no fire, no passion. Once, we were the vanguard of the new socialist revolution. The people would have marched with us to overthrow the fascists."

"Perhaps..." Mustafa Quomuz spoke, in perfect German, pausing to reflect on world events since the remnants of the Bader-Meinhof gang had died or given up the struggle. After a moment of thought he answered his long-time German contact. "You should have offered the people food for the belly. A hungry man will fight, but a man cannot eat principle. And the Jew. He has seen to it that your people, and mine, have starved."

"Yes, Quomuz. The Jew. What of the Jew? Your Zionist friends seem to be in complete control of the West."

"And laughing at us both!" Quomuz said sternly.

"But, we digress. You have come to ask me for help if you strike again at the Israeli. What you ask is difficult. In these times, especially."

"I need security and access. I am here to purchase equipment for the struggle. Al Qaeda's 'charities' have generated money. But I need old friends to help me acquire the goods I require from certain manufacturers. I have the chemical weapons but not the means to use them. That the technology is here, in Hamburg, I know. You can help me, no?" Quomuz asked.

"Look outside, I tell you, the Polizei watch us day and night. They have long memories," Allmenroder said, gesturing toward the closed window. "Look beyond this city. It is all over Europe. The Serbs, the Slavs, and the Czechs. Damn the Poles as well!"

Smiling broadly, Quomuz continued, "Ah, so here is our chance to repay your enemies. Our first attack in England was successful. But to be effective over a wide area, the chemicals need special equipment and special handling. Our next attack will be on a larger scale. We will launch the chemicals in artillery shells, but this will also be only a precursor. I want to be in a position to bring an entire city to its knees. So, I seek certain spray equipment and larger artillery shells from German manufacturers. They will not so willingly sell to an Arab man. But you, Gerhard, or the men you know…you can help me find these items. We...I...must continue the fight. You must help me. You can honor the death of Petra, a socialist hero."

Allmenroder cut him off.

"But how can I help you if I cannot help even myself?"

Quomuz did not answer immediately. He rose and walked to the second-story window and continued. "Let us find workers who drive the trucks and labor at the port. Surely their loyalty can be bought. I have the money, you know the workers. But I must have your help, my old comrade."

"Look, let me see if I can help. I can arrange transportation and a house for you," Allmenroder offered. "A flat in Hamburg, perhaps where we were students together. But I will have to work slowly to find the men you need. Let me know the exact equipment and where it is to be found. This will take time and the task will be difficult, but your money will be....persuasive. After that, then transportation; perhaps a ship. I know men on the docks at Hamburg. They will be discreet. Then we can get your equipment to the Sudan."

"Allah blesses you," Quomuz laughed at the man he knew to be an atheist. "I will bide my time in Hamburg. There are faithful followers there to help me."

"Sadly, beyond that, I cannot support your cause," Allmenroder said, stubbing out the remnants of his cigarette. "I haven't the people. What few are still loyal to our cause lack the inclination. Petra was a rare one. She was possessed. There are very few like her -

at least still in Germany. Forgive me, old friend. We are busy suffering from the disease of Western capitalism. And besides.... you have always had friends in the Middle East, no?"

"Yes. Allah has been generous and so have you. I value the sanctuary you offer, and I will not forget your loyalty. Then perhaps, when the time is right, I will ask you to arrange my return to Syria. There, our brothers will finance our Jihad against the American and his Zionist whore."

Allmenroder laughed. "You mean the Zionist and his American whore."

"There is a difference?" Quomuz sneered.

"But come," Allmenroder offered. "I recall that my friend Mustafa had a certain affection for our blonde German women. Perhaps an evening of pleasure will remind you of the old times."

"Infidel!" Quomuz shot back loudly with a laugh. "You shall burn in Hell for your wickedness, dog."

"Ah, my friend has not forgotten the old times after all," a smiling Allmenroder said as the men rose to leave.

6 August
0900 hours
New Scotland Yard

Chief Inspector Harold MacHugh stood unexpectedly and offered Colin Blackford a warm handshake as the younger man was ushered into the senior's office.

"Splendid to see you, Colin!" The greeting seemed genuine.

MacHugh appeared glad to greet Blackford, only recently promoted to the rank of major in the Special Air Service, British Army, following the bus hijacking. Things had changed remarkably since that violent day in Thetford Forest when Blackford had taken Petra Voss prisoner. In addition to the promotion, and upon MacHugh's personal request, Blackford had been permanently assigned as an SAS liaison to Scotland Yard's counter-terrorism branch. Unlike the last time he had been summoned into MacHugh's office, Blackford, too, was genuinely pleased to see his superior. It had only been a few months since Blackford had languished in the obscurity of night duty at Gatwick airport, but since the events of March at the American air base, it seemed that years had passed.

Only the day before, Blackford had finished a brief and hurriedly arranged detail to Antrim, Northern Ireland, where he'd studied police counter-terrorism techniques. The assignment had been acknowledged by Blackford's contemporaries as a success and served to separate young Blackford from any taint which came about as a result of the mishandling of the African courier by other Metropolitan police.

Much had transpired since the Lakenheath attack and much was yet to come. Colin Blackford was a changed man since the day he'd chased a bus full of terrorized children and had nearly come to blows with an American officer. To his civilian colleagues, and even to himself, he seemed to have found a new sense of purpose and dedication. He noticed himself agreeing more with policy and doctrine and holding his famous tongue when he disagreed with his superiors' orders. Daily workouts in the gymnasium had helped him return to the fitness he'd enjoyed years before.

In the intervening months since the attack, Blackford had come to understand why Sir Harold was the powerful man that he was. MacHugh, it was agreed in quiet conversations, had a reason for everything he did. It was also known that the Chief Inspector took care of his people, even though there had been times, particularly on the graveyard shift at Gatwick, when Colin Blackford would have bet long odds against MacHugh's loyalty. But Blackford, the young hothead, was no more.

MacHugh had, early on in Blackford's tenure with the law enforcement agency, recognized spirit and drive in his junior. "Just perhaps," the Northern Ireland station chief had recently confided to Blackford, "that's why Chief came down so hard on you. Better have him a friend than an enemy. He's tough and smart, Colin; he's Army just like you and a Scot as well. Perhaps he sees some of himself in you, so bide your time here well. You've been given a reprieve, thanks to the terrorists. Make the most of it, mate."

To his credit, Blackford recognized his new

stature and had done some shaping up since he was freed from the sidelines; and, as he said, he had put himself "into the match" against the team that attacked Lakenheath. He had spent the past several months honing those skills he'd lost while checking passports in the air terminal. He'd smoked his last cigarette and had spent a good deal of time getting fit by running several kilometers a day and retraining in hand-to-hand combat and special weapons. He'd even gotten a fresh military haircut and was a frequent visitor to the post gymnasium.

Now, sitting in the Chief Inspector's office, Major Blackford felt very much the professional soldier he'd hoped he'd become when he first joined the Army ten years ago. "A bit more mature," he'd admitted to a friend. "After all, one needn't make any more enemies if one was to have a career in the Army!"

And there were enemies aplenty in a civilian bureaucracy like Scotland Yard. Every new day, every new issue, created a new turf fight between departments and spats between divisions within departments. It was important, therefore, to have friends of influence. Those on the rise had sponsors in power both within and without the Yard. Sometimes, very important friends at Whitehall, Parliament, the Conservative Party, even Number Ten Downing Street.

That was a valuable lesson Blackford had learned the hard way. It was a lesson MacHugh knew from hard-fought experience.

That's why Harold MacHugh had to be careful now, especially now. Following the debacle at the

St. Margaret's Hotel, there were powerful influences arrayed against him in and out of Scotland Yard. More than one critic in Parliament and in the United States had called for MacHugh's resignation. Even MacHugh's closest colleagues were quietly vying for his throne. MacHugh inaudibly reviled them as self-interested serpents poised to strike for their own political gain. MacHugh, who had no ambitions beyond his current station, was motivated only by his sense of duty to the nation and to the Crown. Among his peer group, he was a rarity.

MacHugh knew the perils his country faced in the so-called "post-Cold-War world." He had dismissed as "utter folly" the notions suggested by the press that the end of Communism suddenly meant a world free of conflict. "Indeed!" the eloquent Scot had proclaimed, criticizing the lust for disarmament among some English and Americans. "The world is a far more dangerous place today than it was even five years ago. Al Qaeda proved that. We can ill afford to slacken our resolve just yet."

MacHugh's words, oddly, had infuriated many people of influence in England and abroad. His stern warnings were not in vogue and several politicians and the press alike decried him as a relic. Fortunately for MacHugh, he was still held in high esteem in Downing Street, notwithstanding the harsh exchange with the PM over Scotland Yard's involvement in the Voss matter. The Prime Minister needed a man of MacHugh's character on his team, even if it was politically costly to keep him there.

MacHugh, undaunted, would continue his pursuit of Quomuz. But, he needed an ally. Most of his contemporaries either lacked the steel or the interest to keep up the fight. Surely, he could have accepted another honorary title and retired comfortably to the Lake District. Others had already done so. That's why he now had to trust a younger man, a man very much like himself: rugged, spirited, dedicated and, above all, loyal. Best of all, MacHugh knew, Blackford was Army and had no political ambitions in Scotland Yard.

And so Colin Blackford now sat before the Chief. His presence was no accident nor was it an occasion for a friendly chat. MacHugh began to unveil his course of action to the young major.

"Your tour in Northern Ireland, was it what you had hoped for?" MacHugh inquired.

"Indeed, sir. I learned some new tricks. Polished some old ones; I had become a bit rusty," Blackford grinned.

"All right, Blackford, I'll be straight with you. Chelmsford-Gray sent you to me and I sent you to Gatwick to teach you a lesson. You spoke the truth back at Credenhill. Arthur knew that, and so did I. But unfortunately, in the Army, the truth is a bomb that can kill its bearer. You were right in what you said to your Brigadier. You were dead wrong in how you said it…and to whom. Army officers of your junior rank do NOT report to the Commons!" MacHugh smiled, knowing his junior had already learned that lesson.

"By the way, were you aware that Arthur Chelmsford-Gray and I were at Sandhurst together?"

MacHugh grinned broadly upon seeing Blackford's genuine surprise at the revelation. "You're damn lucky you had friends at Credenhill before someone who outranked you cut you loose! Let this be a lesson to you, son...everyone who smiles at you is not your friend, nor is everyone who takes you to task your enemy. You'd be well-advised to remember that! "

A truly-repentant Blackford lowered his eyes in acquiescence as MacHugh smiled warmly and genuinely.

"Sir, you don't owe me an explanation. I was a prat and deserved a good thrashing...which, I got!" Blackford shared an honest laugh with his chief.

"Of course, I agreed with all you said. Damn military intelligence and damn politicians anyway, but your timing was dreadful. There were, and are, policy considerations that, often and strangely, obscure common sense. It wasn't the place for an SAS captain to make that point. Arthur was way ahead of you on that. He'd already carried your message to the Chief of the General Staff. What he didn't need was an impertinent officer to echo the refrain! That's why you found yourself working for me. Arthur simply wanted to give you some cooling off time. He and I know you have the makings of a cracking good senior leader one day!" MacHugh wasn't lecturing, but rather, seeking understanding now from his new protégé.

"Look Colin, when this affair is all over, remind me to tell you of a certain young Army lieutenant who showed a similar lack of discretion in the face of a certain Ministry of Defense bureaucrat on Cyprus." Blackford returned a knowing smile.

"Well, enough of THAT...on to the present! We're in for it now, you and I. And I shan't mince words with you. I've got a posting for you that could cost me my career and you," MacHugh paused gravely, "your life."

"Quomuz? Is it Quomuz? It is, isn't it?" Blackford excitedly quizzed.

"Spot on, lad!" MacHugh said, pleased with Blackford's intuition, "Spot on!"

"Let's get on with it, then," said the Chief as he ushered Blackford to the conference table and opened a sealed folder.

"MI has been stingy with information since the attack at Lakenheath. I'll wager there was hell to pay in Whitehall, even before we had our Miss Voss in custody. They really dropped the ball, despite secret American warnings to them that a reprisal was in the offing."

Blackford's attention was sharply focused on his leader's every word.

"You know of Quomuz, of course, from the BBC reports. MI, looking to recover some lost prestige after the attack, shamelessly provided that information to Broadcast House. And you know that the woman -- Petra Voss -- was taken after the attack. MI-5 has tried, somewhat in vain, to let it out that she died. Perhaps it's for American consumption. But too many people saw otherwise that day, including you, Colin."

"So who, or WHAT, is this Petra Voss?" Blackford inquired.

"You're a bit young to recall the Bader-Meinhof gang, Colin," MacHugh observed, affecting the role of professor. "They were a group of radicals back in the early seventies. They actually called themselves the 'Red Army Faction.' They thought, wrongly of course, that the German government was secretly run by Nazis, so they planned and started a terror campaign to force the government to respond with overwhelming force. They believed, oddly, that the old West German government would suspend civil liberties, just like Adolf Hitler did in the 1930's!"

Blackford winced hard at the preposterous notion, as MacHugh continued. "The gang assumed that the citizenry would rebel if their government was exposed as a Nazi resurgence! They thought, again, wrongly, that all of the coal miners and factory workers and railroad workers and the like would rise up and overthrow their oppressors, just as predicted by Karl Marx! This lot wasn't short on hubris, or on self-delusion to be sure, because they truly believed THEY would lead the revolution and overthrow the government...and THAT is the garden our Miss Voss was grown in!"

"God, she's a zealot, then, isn't she?" Blackford exclaimed.

"Indeed. And there's more. We think that when she was a young woman, she fell under Quomuz's influence. He was an itinerant student in Hamburg in those days. His preachy notions of oppressive governments and jack-booted invaders caught the ear of Miss Voss. She's been a warrior ever since!"

Blackford nodded. "What more can you tell me about Quomuz?"

"Nasty bloke, that one!" MacHugh exclaimed. "The CIA and our intelligence services reveal that Quomuz has a great deal of personal expertise in the use of bio-weapons and that he's trained others how to use gas for possible attacks in Europe. He's been up to no good for years. Giving the Israelis fits. He's known to have organized a hotel bombing in Amman, but the Jordanians tell us Quomuz was actually planning to release a chemical bomb. The bomb exploded, but not the vials of nerve agent. As luck would have it, they found the chemicals unexploded. They arrested four of Quomuz's people who had built the damned thing. Quomuz got away, but he was convicted, in absentia, by a Jordanian court and sentenced to twenty years in prison, plus two death sentences for other earlier crimes he'd committed. You already know about his forays here and in Israel. But finding this man is like picking a star from the Milky Way on a cloudy night."

Blackford considered what his superior had just revealed, and then he pressed on. "And what of the Voss interrogation?"

"Nothing. Nothing at all. She's a tough bitch,

I'll grant her that. I only know that because an infantry colonel at Colchester and I.... Well, let's say that another school chum from Sandhurst hasn't forgotten me."

Blackford nodded thoughtfully.

"Right, then. It was no accident our man Quomuz made his escape cleanly that day. Royal Air Force radar had him all the way. He could have been taken or shot down quite easily. The RAF even had a Tornado covering his escape. They could have easily knocked him down. But, at the last instant, Downing Street took a hard decision on the advice of the American Department of Defense. And, I'll add, a most incorrect one. He was there to be taken and for reasons that still escape me, we let him go."

The major now furrowed his brow, indicating his confusion.

"I understand your concern, Colin. Why let the bird fly? From the PM's perspective, the government wanted to know who provided his support. Quomuz is a talented, ruthless man…"

"All the more reason to kill him…" Blackford interrupted.

"Precisely! But MI-5 wanted to know who was holding his leash. Could it be al Qaeda, Syria, Iran, or even operatives in the Sudan? So they let him go on the chance they could track him and take out the lot. There was talk that your old mates at Special Air Service were planning a strike against both him and his supporters."

~ 363 ~

Blackford, confused, interjected, "Then why not do so now…he shouldn't be that hard to trace. Doesn't MI have…?"

"Ah, there's the sticky point. The Americans and our government are heavily involved in Iraq right now. Damn few in Parliament or in Washington have the nerve to undertake another offensive operation, on an overt basis. Washington and the PM have their hands full with political opposition. The President and the PM both fear a new conventional military offensive will undo the so-called 'peace process' in Israel with the new Hamas government and…in Iraq. Of course, what they don't want to understand is that our Mr. Quomuz is no doubt planning to do exactly that; end the peace process."

"So, Colin, here's the essence of what I need to tell you. Quomuz has got to be stopped quietly, and carefully. The Americans just don't have the right people close to him and neither does our own MI. They'll never catch him. He's savvy. He's daring and effective. I'd not want to face him one on one."

Blackford's eyes widened slightly.

"He has a fatal shortcoming, however; it's his arrogance. Our friends in the Israeli Shabak lost him for a couple of weeks after the raid, but he later surfaced in Berlin."

"So where is our terrorist friend now?" Blackford quizzed.

"Syria. Quite possibly south of Damascus, at the new commando training center financed by al

Qaeda. It's been relocated since the Americans bombed Abu Du'an over a year ago."

"Let me go on. There's more," MacHugh said, pointing to a map of Israel and the West Bank. "Quomuz is a Palestinian. Here is his home, near Jerusalem in the West Bank. Now Hamas has taken over the government and many people on both sides don't want to see the Palestinians and the Jews make peace. Mustafa Quomuz is one of those people."

MacHugh continued, gesturing. "If you'll take a look at this map, you'll see where Israel is sticking her chin out -- just inviting her neighbors to take a swing at her." MacHugh pointed at the locations of a number of Israeli farming communities built in the West Bank region. "Here, too," the chief pointed near the Golan Heights, "those stubborn Jews are really asking for trouble."

"Where's the connection, sir?"

"The Shabak and Mossad think Quomuz is up to something again. Remember, he's a driven man. He hates the Israelis and wants to strike them hard, again and again. We know he's been looking for sponsorship and may be training a new cadre. Perhaps he was getting ready to strike Israel when the Yanks bombed Abu Du'an. We think Quomuz may have been near Abu Du'an and we are almost certain our Miss Voss was, too."

"So," Blackford began to get the picture, "Deduction has it Quomuz is planning to strike again. Perhaps planning to hit an Israeli settlement in the

West Bank. Very tempting! That would be an easy target. And it could have the effect of reigniting a new war between Israel and the Hamas Palestinians."

"Very perceptive, Colin," MacHugh smiled.

"But what's our interest, sir? Can't the Israeli Army or Mossad handle this? Why is this, and you'll excuse me, sir...I mean, is this a British concern?"

"Good question, Colin. Good question. And here's your answer. But it's a complex one. First, the Americans are putting keen pressure on Israel to forgo preemptive strikes into Palestine or any Arab nation. The Congress is threatening to cut off funds to Israel if she doesn't work toward the peace plan. So the Israeli armed forces can't be involved beyond any defensive action. I can tell you they hate that role. They know a defensive posture is an invitation to defeat..." Sir Harold paused to let the words sink in.

"There's more. Number 10 is very concerned about British Jews who have migrated to their 'homeland,' so to speak," MacHugh said, indicating his disapproval, "and they are very much at risk. Technically, they're still British citizens. Number 10 has officially ordered Scotland Yard to stay out of this mess, but the PM still wants a measure of revenge for the attack at Lakenheath. On the one hand, Number 10 can't seem to be overtly involved, but then, we can't sit idly by. Thus, any action against Quomuz must be on the quiet. Given the new Hamas 'government' in Palestine, and Israel's point blank refusal to negotiate with any of them,

Quomuz and his people will feel emboldened to start something afresh."

MacHugh paused, and then continued, "But the real center of this situation is the WMD issue. We know Quomuz has access to nerve agents and probably a lot more. We are certain he knows who has them, and where; and he has the financing needed to pursue their use."

Blackford stared hard at his senior.

"The Americans created a political nightmare, advancing WMD as the sole reason for attacking Iraq. Not that the old bastard didn't have it coming, mind you. But who ever said Saddam Hussein actually kept the nasty stuff in his country? If you ask me, he'd scattered his assets across the region!"

Blackford interjected, "You know, sir. I recall that old Hussein flew his entire air force to Iran during Desert Storm. No one in the West understood that move, either. So your fears, sir, may be well grounded."

MacHugh nodded in agreement. "Hence your tasking, man. Find Quomuz, and I'm certain you'll find the trail of the WMD and relay that information to me. Imagine," the Scot said, smiling. "The finest law enforcement agency in the world answers the world's biggest riddle. Good sport, what?"

Blackford smiled broadly.

"So, Colin, here's your chance for a real piece of work. I'm asking you to find Quomuz; we don't want him brought back for trial. Well, then, the fact is... he is to be eliminated. And most importantly,

JONATHAN BRUCE

find those chemicals. You're equal to it, I gather?

Blackford beamed,

"So, first step, the Holy Land!"

Major Colin Blackford straightened himself and inhaled deeply, then nodded. "It'll be good to get a crack at the bastard. Shall I be going to Israel soon? I presume HQ SAS has approved the posting."

"Indeed, your posting has the approval of Credenhill and you're on the next plane out!" MacHugh laughed. "Do you suppose you can find your way to the international terminal at Gatwick?" MacHugh grinned, rubbing good-natured salt into his young friend's old wound.

"I'll just leave that one alone, sir."

"You HAVE changed, haven't you, Major?" MacHugh laughed aloud.

The pair shared a smile.

"As for ground support, you'll be met in Tel Aviv by Deputy Director Chaim Aran of the Shabak. We've known each other for years. He's aware you've tangled with Quomuz before and that you were keen to be made part of the action. You'll go to Tel Aviv and get the lay of the land. Make yourself available for dirty details. Use your nose. Cultivate relationships. Certainly the Israelis can handle much of this themselves. But they would surely appreciate Quomuz being taken off their hands for trial. That way they don't infuriate the Palestinians more than they have to. Besides, they'll never refuse an honest gesture of help... especially if things get dicey."

Blackford couldn't mask his excitement as MacHugh continued.

"You're not on holiday, Colin. Don't forget that Quomuz killed at least two of our countrymen, and I want him dead! Remember the coach driver and the helicopter pilot in Cambridge. The chap left a widow and two small children. MacHugh's eyes brightened, "Besides, if you're on the hunt and bag this bastard, think of the leg up we'll have on MI! Perhaps the PM will invite me to Crufts."

Blackford stood and, buttoning his jacket, thanked MacHugh, who sincerely wished he were making the trek alongside Blackford.

Saying little else, MacHugh again extended a firm hand, which Blackford grasped. The two men's eyes met.

"Godspeed, Colin. Godspeed!"

9 August
1615 hours
Shabak Headquarters
Tel Aviv

Major Colin Blackford stood before a modern glass and chrome desk. From behind the desk the short, wiry, graying man arose and extended a firm hand. "Welcome, Major Blackford," Deputy Director Chaim Aran said. His perfect English came as a surprise to the flight-weary Blackford. "Our mutual friend MacHugh speaks well of you. Damn little impresses that old Scots duffer! If you impressed him, then you've impressed me."

Blackford could only interject a polite "Thank-you," before Aran continued.

"We'll discuss classified matters tomorrow after you've had a good meal and some sleep. When you're fully briefed, you'll join a patrol unit north of here in the Port of Haifa. We've selected a host officer for you, my former aide, Captain Reisner. She's there undercover, serving as part of the uniformed harbor police. But enough talk for the moment...We've reserved you a room at the Hilton. Suffice it to say we both have strong interests in the, er, subject of your visit. But that is for tomorrow. Now, go get some rest. We'll get you fully briefed tomorrow."

Colin Blackford was glad the greeting was brief. Rest in a quiet room was exactly what he needed.

9 August
1925 hours
Terrorist training camp
Southeast of Damascus

It had taken some time to gather the needed weapons for the planned assault. The American air attack at Abu Du'an had damaged more of the terrorist operation than many had believed. The American reprisal raid had seriously depleted the stockpiles of weapons, ammunition, and other materiel. His friends in Germany had been of little help for this operation, and even the Syrians had been more cautious than normal. Damascus didn't want to openly risk another American air strike, but it had provided some munitions and money; especially since this newest planned attack would strike the interior of their hated neighbor to the south, Israel herself.

Rehearsal for attack had gone well, Quomuz believed. This would be a classic commando operation and he had chosen a trio of fanatics for the task. Fast, simple, and bloody. The logistics were uncomplicated; a covert trek across the Syrian frontier, followed by a swift approach to an Israeli farming commune near the borders with Lebanon and Syria. This would be followed by a rapid retreat back into friendly territory, with the attackers eventually melting into the caves and hills of southern Syria. The retreat would be covered by a mortar barrage of chemical-laden artillery shells. If conducted properly, the terror value would be maximized and the Israelis would not know who to blame: Shiite fundamentalists, Jihadists, or even a militant faction of the Hamas.

Indeed, Quomuz hoped, the Israelis might suspect any number of the countless Arab-extremist groups in the region. It mattered not to Quomuz, for the results would serve his end.

First, many Israeli settlers would be killed and a hostage might be taken for future barter. Second, his men would prove the utility of chemical weapons on a larger scale. The raid in England was a first, cautious step. This attack would be far more lethal and would serve as a precursor to larger, more deadly attacks in Europe and America. Third, the Israeli Army and Air Forces would conduct a swift reprisal, which, in turn, would bring more hatred upon Israel. Perhaps the entire Arab world would rise in Jihad against the Jew. If handled properly in the Western press, Israel could be made to appear the aggressor. And with luck, Quomuz hoped, the never-ending circle of death would widen to engulf more friends of the Zionists.

Even certain influential American politicians could be counted on to call for the end of aid to Israel, despite its own war on terrorism. Americans, after all, had no real stomach for death. They could be counted upon to run from a prolonged fight. Even their economic support to Israel might dry up if Israeli military action became politically inconvenient for the United States. "It is also true," Quomuz thought, "the Americans have backed out on every friend since its war against the people of Vietnam...Except when it came to saving Jewish interests in the Gulf."

The raid into Israel would require a small team. The keys to success would be speed, mobility and flexibility, Quomuz knew. He had chosen from the best fighters among those assembled at the camp: Palestinians, Yemenites, disaffected Saudis and any number of Islamic fundamentalists from North Africa, as well as central and southern Asia. The current batch of recruits even included a few of the faithful who were citizens of the European Community.

At least three from Belgium, one from the Netherlands, and two French Muslims were undergoing training. But these volunteers would not be accompanying Quomuz on this mission. These men would serve the cause more effectively during a future bombing campaign currently being planned against major cities on the Continent.

The new Syrian complex was larger and far better equipped than the one destroyed over a year before. Best of all, the facility enjoyed virtual immunity from Western attack. Such were the niceties of international hypocrisy, for although the West loathed Syria, there was no stomach among the NATO allies for sustained bombing of President Assad's military infrastructure. Additionally, this new facility was conveniently located near a suburb of Damascus, wedged between two hospitals and several mosques. The belief among Syrian military planners was that the fear of collateral civilian casualties would preclude an American attack. Thus, despite the ubiquitous "legitimate military target" designation it may have been rightfully called, this facility was deemed off limits to American bombers.

Of the many lessons Quomuz had learned in his years of fighting in the shadows was the need for absolute blood-loyalty from his cadre. So, he chose his strike team carefully and trained them with intensity. There would be no mercenaries along this time. The attack was upon an ancient enemy who had violated the will of Allah and stolen the Palestinians' land.

"Your older brother died a hero's death. A real martyr; he died well!" So spoke Mustafa Quomuz to his new lieutenant, twenty-year-old Hassan Merzhed, in the mess hall of the new training compound. Merzhed would lead the raid upon the kibbutz. "You have trained well and it is now time that I tell you of our mission against the Zionists…Your brother Bashir died for Allah, and he rests in paradise with Allah this very day. I will now tell you how bravely your brother fought and died in the Jihad…"

The younger man was consumed by Quomuz's every word. He listened in quiet awe as Quomuz spoke of the raid at the American air base in England in almost reverent tones. As he spoke, Quomuz could see passion swelling within the younger brother; the same fire and passion that had driven the elder brother on his suicide mission against the Americans.

"He killed many American pig-bastards. He killed many of those who bombed our brothers in Syria, Iraq and Libya. Do you have his courage? You will need it, for Allah calls you to the Jihad, young one. Will you avenge your brother's death?"

Mesmerized, the young Palestinian began to feel like a warrior in a holy cause. He clenched both fists and declared his bravery and invincibility to the famous hero of the Palestinian people. Quomuz smiled faintly, knowing he had won the soul of another young man eager for battle. The speech had worked so well, so often, before. It was the same one that had enticed the older Bashir to join Quomuz in the raid against the Americans. It had worked on Merzhed, a younger Yemenite named Issam and a third man, Mohammed Qadir.

"Then if you are ready, we leave in the morning. The trip will be long and difficult. We must be careful in our movements, for there are agents of the Mossad everywhere. Your blood is on the rise, Hassan, but tonight sleep well. Rest in the bosom of Allah. His will is great."

Hassan Merzhed stood and looked at Quomuz bravely, just as had the young Ali al-Said before his "rendezvous" with Allah. Quomuz nodded quietly as the young shaheed-to-be walked away.

"Another true believer," thought Quomuz. "Another martyr at my disposal!"

9 August
1700 hours
Kibbutz Gilead, Northern Israel

Standing in the bright glare of a generator-driven floodlight, fifty-nine-year-old Miriam Glodz reached back to rub her lower spine. The ache she felt came from a hard day tending one of the many irrigation pumps that provided precious, life-giving moisture to the desert, pumped from the fresh waters of the Jordan River. The retired teacher from Scarsdale was happy to feel the soreness, because she believed it a sign that she'd spent another day doing what her God had intended.

Kibbutz Gilead had been begun life in 1975 as a Nahal[2] outpost. It had become a civilian settlement about ten years later, with a population of only twenty young families, some of them former soldiers who had spent their military service on the military outpost and stayed on; its population had grown every year since. There were nearly sixty families at the farming commune tonight, together with some older single members and a handful of young unmarrieds. They came from varied backgrounds, and all had reasons for choosing the kibbutz way of life. They all were united in the struggle to survive on this very ancient and unforgiving land. This world of the kibbutz was arid and rough, rocks and sand. Before the great irrigation projects began, only a few scrub bushes and grass grew here, Miriam had learned. Only irrigation from the Jordan, mixed with the sweat of men and women, brought real life to the region and the commune.

It was backbreaking labor, sustaining life here. But somehow, there were rewards quite apart from the bountiful crops the farmers had routinely produced. There was meaning to life, here, in this ancient soil. Meaning intermingled with continuity; a distant history, that was joined with hope and promise for the future.

Hope was the daily watchword among the kib-

---

[2] Hebrew acronym for No'ar Halutzi Lohem – Pioneer, Fighting Youth

butzniks. Hope that there would be enough warmth in the growing season, enough water, enough fertilizer, proper equipment; and, most of all, hope that their ancient enemies would leave them in peace.

Miriam straightened, arching and stretching her back and, placing her hands on her hips, she let out a sigh and surveyed the last of the setting sun as it disappeared in the west. She let her thoughts wander to where the sun's rays now shone brightly, "Perhaps somewhere over St. Louis," she pondered. That's where her daughter and son-in-law had lived with their children for several years. "Oh, Marvin," she whispered to her late husband, "Who would have believed it? Miriam the Kibbutznik, no less!"

Miriam was happy, perhaps much happier than she'd ever been since her husband's death four years earlier. She'd never felt better in her life, especially since "there was only one doctor here," she'd told her daughter. "So, no one can afford to get sick." There was little time for ailment, either. The work was unrelenting. The planting in spring, tending the vegetable crops all summer, and then the fall harvest. Winters were cold in northern Israel. Even so, there was work to be done every day, repairing equipment, installing new pumps, and preparing for the coming spring. Miriam even shared teaching duties when she wasn't pressed into service driving a truck into the nearby villages or repainting or performing the thousand other endless tasks that came with life on a farming commune.

She chuckled to herself, not yet fully believing

where her life had taken her. "A kibbutz? In Israel?" Thinking back, she recalled the irony of how she had protested when her daughter had first suggested the idea. "My own daughter wants me to be a farmer, for God's sake! I'm an old woman."

But how the four years had passed, and quickly! Miriam had found a new meaning to life. Hard work, she'd learned, didn't age one. Rather, it gave one new energy and purpose. At Gilead, she'd found a home. Surely, the language barrier had been difficult to cross. There were Jews from all over the world here, finally coming home to work the land of their ancestors. There could be found German Jews, Russian Jews, and African Jews. There were Jews from Canada and South America. And the Weinmanns, a nice couple from down the Jersey shore who had befriended her upon her arrival and who had become closer than family now.

Teaching the children was special on the kibbutz; there were no mandatory state-imposed curricula, no teacher's unions or strikes. Teaching here was what she had wanted to do all her life; it was simple one-on-one, and more satisfying than anything she'd ever done before. She could see each youngster grow and change as part of the kibbutz community. And the kids loved the time spent with "Savta[3] Miriam."

After four years as a farmer and teacher, Miriam's daughter couldn't get her mother back home to the U.S. -- even for a visit. "There's so much to do, so much to

---

[3] Grandma

learn..." Miriam had protested. "If you want to see me," she had e-mailed recently, "bring your husband the lawyer and get your hands dirty here!! But I'll bet you can't keep up with this 'old' lady!"

The evening's reflections were interrupted by a familiar voice. "Miriam, come to dinner!" called a friend from the communal dining hall.

"In a minute, Sonia!" she shouted back in Yiddish, "I've got a leaky valve here and it needs a bit more work!"

Miriam Glodz looked back to her pump and then back over her shoulder to see families and friends and hear the happy noises of children laughing as they filed toward the evening meal. She watched their silhouettes as each passed from the darkness and into the brightly lit dining hall. The air was cool at night, even in August. And the beet harvest would be a good one this year, Miriam thought to herself. "Enough profit, perhaps, to buy a new pump!" She said aloud to herself as her spry wrists strained to tighten the gasket collar on the aging pump. "One more turn and... Ouch!" Her wrench slipped its grip and her elbow cracked against a cold steel pipe. Eyeing the stars in the sky above her, she complained, "So, Marvin, nice of you to come help a girl in trouble. On second thought, forget it. You had trouble changing a light bulb."

The ache in her back began to subside as Miriam knelt once more beside the leaking pump and set herself to the chore of saving even a few drops of precious water from waste in the sand below.

10 August
1600 hours
Shabak Headquarters
Tel Aviv

Chaim Aran smiled as his fingers snapped the seal on a three-inch thick dossier and called for an assistant to dim the lights. "Major Blackford, my friend MacHugh tells me you were rather suddenly thrown into this chase. Even as a special operations man, you wouldn't have much experience chasing this particular vermin. So, let me reintroduce you to Mustafa Quomuz. He's a complex and resourceful man and he has plenty of reasons to hate us. Some of this may be new information to you."

Blackford sat back in his chair and focused intently upon the projected images of Mustafa Quomuz on the briefing room wall.

"This much you know," Aran smiled. "Quomuz is a Palestinian-born Islamist militant, guerrilla leader, and he has a long history with al Qaeda, although we're not certain he's fully allegiant to that group."

Blackford cocked his head, not fully understanding the Director's words.

"But I want you to get a sense of the fellow. So, let's go back in time, shall we?" Aran said, "Our man was the son of a shopkeeper. He grew up poor, not far from Jerusalem. His circumstances very modest." Aran continued, "Unfortunately, when he was fourteen or so, his mother and brother were killed during a raid we launched to capture some escaped terrorists they were hiding in their family home. When our defense forces arrived, Quomuz and his father were given time to gather what possessions they could carry, and then we razed his home. Doubtless, the loss of his mother and brother led to his father's suicide shortly after and cemented the lust for revenge in his young heart."

Blackford nodded.

"From there, the trail goes cold for a few years. We know that he attended local Islamic schools, found his way to Europe and made friends among certain sects of fundamentalists in the Turk community in Germany."

Blackford interjected, "Thus, the connection with our Miss Voss."

"Exactly," Aran shot back.

"We know that when he was in his twenties, in Hamburg, he made connections with the members of several radical organizations in Europe, including the Bader-Meinhof gang or the Red Army Faction as it was known then. And speaking of Ms. Voss, you know, of course, that her mother was an active member of the Red Army Faction, which the press dubbed the 'Bader-Meinhof' movement. She was killed in a car-bombing in Düsseldorf in the late seventies when Voss was no more than eight or nine years old."

Blackford shook his head.

"Sometime in the mid-eighties, Quomuz disappeared. It's believed he may have fought in Af-

ghanistan with bin Laden and his crowd. Other reports had him setting up terrorist cells in Pakistan,
Morocco, and India...and CERTAINLY back home
in the West Bank. To the people there, he's a living
legend!" Aran added for effect.

"Then after the Soviets tucked their tails and left
Afghanistan, Quomuz traveled to Western Europe
in the early nineties and joined the underground al-
Tawhid militant organization. That group is devoted
to establishing an Islamic government in Jordan."

"A busy man," Blackford offered.

"A VERY busy man," Aran replied.

"We lost him again in the late nineties," Aran
winced, "but he resurfaced just after the September
11th attacks. We know that Syria is one of his favorite haunts, because he was seen both in Syria and
Afghanistan and, interestingly, was reportedly
wounded in a U.S. bombardment. We traced him to
Iran to reorganize his friends in the al-Tawhid and
we know he traveled frequently to Baghdad in 2001
to have his wounds treated at an Iraqi military hospital with the blessing of Saddam Hussein."

Blackford replied, "Well, that's not what the
news media would have us believe."

Aran replied with a disdainful grunt.

"Our friends in America haven't handled the
media well in that regard. When the U.S. was preparing for the second war against Iraq, Quomuz was
singled out as an example of Saddam Hussein's
support for terrorism. They were right, of course,
but now that the air is filled with so much rhetoric,

the truth of these matters has been long lost on the American electorate."

Blackford shook his head. "Politicians and politics; damn them all!"

Aran smiled. "So, here's the man today. He bills himself as an Islamist militant! True enough, he rallies the faithful against us and America and claims to want an end to a Western presence here and throughout the Arab world. At the same time, we know he has a fondness for whiskey and a certain type of woman. Major, it appears that our Mr. Quomuz is a profound hypocrite who will fight for anyone who will pay him!"

"All the more dangerous," Blackford reasoned.

"Indeed," Aran agreed. "His loyalties are not necessarily with the brotherhood of Arabs. As recently as 2005, he declared "total war" on Shia Muslims in Iraq, and has already helped several al Qaeda suicide bombers target those Shiites. One cannot help but wonder how his financial benefactors in Tehran feel about THAT," Aran emphasized his last words, indicating the irony of the relationship.

Colin Blackford slowly closed his information book as the lights came on in the briefing room and Aran called for the operator to turn off the slide projector.

"So, that is the 'short course' on our enemy. Now a few words about our operations here. You know that our problems are, well, unique. We must never, ever, let our attention be diverted from the constant threat of terrorism. It is the Arab's weapon. He knows he cannot defeat us in a conventional sense. But he can attempt to intimidate us and stop the support we receive from the West."

Blackford reached back and toward the ceiling with both arms and stretched. The briefing had been a thorough one.

"But Quomuz; what of Quomuz? How do we find him, this jackal?"

"We don't," the Director offered. "He finds us. Oh, certainly, the Mossad is also looking...it's looking for ten dozen or so terrorists, not all of them Arab. If this were a normal situation, either we or the Mossad could handle this nicely without you. And if the Mossad found him, well, that would be the end of it. Mossad gets help from the CIA and MI-5...well; at least that's how it's supposed to work. But like us, the Mossad's hands are tied. There is an official "no assassination order" from the Knesset. That means we must be in a purely reactionary mode. Our normal intelligence function generally prohibits us from preemptive strikes. We haven't the manpower to go chasing the man around the world, and we have civil order to maintain here. So, we wait for him to come to us. And, Major Blackford, we'd rather not get involved in the messy extradition business. We'd rather you took him home quietly as your prisoner, and we can disavow any knowledge or participation in his capture...That is, if we're, er, you're lucky enough to find him or him us!"

Blackford nodded his understanding of the situation. "What are the chances he'll strike here - in Israel - I mean?"

"A very good question! It's an educated guess," Aran explained. "Quomuz is a hard core Islamic fundamentalist Palestinian, remember. He believes we stole his home. He believes old Arafat cost him his birthright. So, this is where he wants to hurt us. Whether it is now or next year.... he'll hit us. It could be in Tel Aviv or maybe the West Bank expansions...who knows exactly where?"

Blackford only shook his head. "I don't think either Scotland Yard or the Army will tolerate my absence for a year."

Aran cast a somber glance at the Englishman. "I sincerely doubt you'll have to wait that long, major."

Blackford rose, anticipating the meeting's end.

"So, let's get you on the front lines," the Israeli counterpart to Sir Harold MacHugh said, clapping his hands together. I'm assigning you duty with the Haifa harbor police. Not very glamorous, but it is a potential target. It's easy to hit from the sea. But now, it's time for you to rest up. Tomorrow you'll meet your new partner, Captain Reisner.

17 August
2030 hours
Along the Syrian-Israeli Border

Quomuz sat behind the wheel of the all-terrain vehicle he'd used to cross the vast span of desert between

JONATHAN BRUCE

Jarananah and Izra. He carefully unfolded the map and, holding a flashlight in his left hand, began to coordinate landmarks on the horizon with the myriad symbols printed before him. He traced his finger to the narrow border Israel shared with Syria. There lay the Sea of Galilee...then north along the Jordan to Lake Hulah. Three of Quomuz's young lieutenants, Issam Banazir, Hassan Merzhed and Mohammed Qadir listened in silence.

"Here," he said, looking at the trio, and then pointing to the map. "My young brothers; on the eastern shore of the Hulah is where we will make our final preparations."

Hassan Merzhed leaned in close to the map and looked hard as Quomuz continued.

"Our target is called 'Kibbutz Gilead.' The Zionists' blood will flow there very soon!" Quomuz announced. He pointed to a red spot on the map. "The agricultural commune lies roughly six kilometers north of the Sea of Galilee. So, we will attack and return to Syria within the night."

The three members of the strike team listened intently to Quomuz's instructions: "I have been near this kibbutz many times. It is well armed, but precautions have become lax. Let me show you."

Reaching into a canvas haversack, Quomuz produced a dozen black-and-white photographs from a recent recon "visit."

"There are twenty buildings in total. All of them are cement block and reinforced with steel. They are all one or two-stories; the entire lot.

These are the blocks where the unmarried men and women live... these here are family homes ... machine shops ... these, here, are the buildings where the sugar beets are taken and processed."

Mohammed and Banazir nodded, noting several machine-gun bunkers near the members' living quarters.

"The entire compound is surrounded by wire and is patrolled. But in the last few months, the pigs have become lazy and complacent. I have noticed that at the hour of the evening meal, the guards tend to loiter near the communal dining hall, right here."

Quomuz continued, pointing to a picture of the main gate to the kibbutz compound.

"This is the main gate. It consists of two points of access. But, recently, both have been left open until nightfall. Here is where we will make our entry. The crops will mask our incursion. There is no clear field of fire or vision from the main gate. You simply enter from the fields just after dusk."

"Very well," Hassan Merzhed agreed.

Quomuz went on, "Hassan, you and Issam will enter; kill as many Zionists as you can. Maybe you'll be able to take a prisoner...and leave. Mohammed will cover your retreat with mortar fire and return to Syria. The chemical warheads will spread the poison quickly. So, Hassan and Issam must retreat very, very fast," Quomuz then predicted, "Not even the Jew is bold enough to invade Syria and risk total war. He may be brave enough to violate Lebanon, but he isn't willing to push Syria."

"But," Banazir recalled with a smile, "that doesn't mean our Syrian brothers are unwilling to help us in our efforts!"

Hassan Merzhed and Mustafa Quomuz nodded in agreement.

The plan of attack was simple and straightforward. The team Quomuz had selected would approach Kibbutz Gilead just before the evening meal. Dusk would conceal their movements over land. Security would be lax as the members finished their work for the day and sat down to eat. The attack would catch them off guard.

"In just forty-eight hours," Quomuz promised Hassan Merzhed, "your brother's death will be avenged! But for now, rest, check your equipment, and make ready. I must leave you to prepare the next phase of the battle; but I will watch and rejoice…as will Allah. I will rejoin you after you have been victorious."

18 August
0700 hours
Port of Haifa Police District

From on high, the Bay of Haifa looked like a busy city intersection at the height of rush hour. Ships of every flag imaginable anchored in the seaward waters of the Bay, each waiting its turn to trudge slowly to the berthing areas, pushed and prodded by swarming tugs, missing the next ship by only feet. Departing ships, too, awaited the attention of the smaller boats, as their massive hulls were maneuvered into position to begin the sail homeward. Haifa was a precious nerve center of activity in the Israeli economy, for so much of her livelihood streamed in and out of the famous port. Because she was so small, Israel relied upon seaborne foreign trade to receive virtually all of her consumer goods like autos and appliances, and raw steel and iron. Even the petroleum to power the imported cars had to be brought ashore in massive tankers from other Middle Eastern nations and the United States.

The air on this bright summer's morning was filled with the sounds of the sea: the low-throated churning of huge diesel engines, the pitch of whistles and alarm bells, and a host of toots and groans that all rose intermittently from dockside. Massive cranes hoisted freight containers from the decks of cargo ships and swung them onto the docks below, where idling lorries and trains waited for loading before departing into the Israeli countryside. The cacophony was joined by the horns of the landsailing trucks, cars, trains and busses.

Captain Magda Reisner, the new first shift patrol chief, surveyed the busy morning traffic through binoculars from one of several observation platforms high above the din. She slowly panned the waterfront, first left, then right, then back again. Any unusual action might give her cause to dispatch a harbor patrol unit to respond. In the near distance, one of the Toyota

Fleet, the S.S. *Yorimoto Maru* began offloading, as a giant gangway was hoisted dockside by a massive elevated crane. Several piers over, a smaller freighter, the M.V. *Mariner Star,* took on a load of cotton and tobacco products bound for the Philippines.

"Oops! Look out," Reisner noted aloud to herself, and, keying her radio, called, "Four-Seven?"

"Four-Seven here, Ma'am."

"Four-Seven, you are closest. Pier 93; looks like some trouble. A cargo net has slipped its lines; crates are spilling all over. Looks like a mess. Can you respond?"

"Four-Seven, on it. Stand by in case we need the ambulance. Out."

"Thanks, Four-Seven. Standing by."

Magda Reisner's back was to the door as Chaim Aran and Colin Blackford entered.

"Captain Reisner!" Aran greeted his former aide with a cheery entreaty.

"Oh, forgive me. Didn't hear you come up. Hello, Director Aran!"

"I'm...."

She caught Colin Blackford's eye, and reaching a firm hand in greeting, said, "And you must be our guest from Scotland Yard. Welcome!" Reisner's electric blue eyes sparkled as Blackford smiled a little more than he thought a reserved Englishman ought to have. Blackford was caught off guard at Reisner's accent. It sounded almost British.

"Cheers!" Blackford managed, grinning.

"Captain, I believe you've been briefed on our exchange program with Scotland Yard and Major Blackford's background, particularly in counter-terrorism."

But Magda Reisner's attention was diverted from Aran's words. Blackford had instantly proved a distraction, a fact not lost on the Director, who could not resist a jest amidst the obvious attraction.

"Colin, I'll leave you in the captain's capable hands. Do be on guard, though, she has a black belt in two forms of karate and judo. I'd watch my step."

Blackford, who began to turn a light shade of red, caught himself. "Thank you, sir. I'll do my best to enhance relations between our two nations."

Aran was not yet out the door as Blackford refocused himself on the well-muscled woman's short light-brown hair, which turned up at her chin. Her neat, khaki uniform evinced an attractive combination of a true professional and a healthy, athletic woman.

Magda Reisner began to explain the layout of Haifa in police terms and turned to sweep the horizon with a long, tanned arm. Blackford bravely fought the urge to remain fixed on her eyes and skin and began to listen as the captain detailed local operations in the busy port city.

"We're very dependent upon this port," Reisner explained. "That's why we guard it so closely. Unlike Felixstowe and Liverpool -- I've been there on assignment -- where your chief concerns are theft and civil disorder."

"Right," Blackford nodded, recalling some bruised ribs following an ill-advised punch-up in a pub with some dockside thugs early in his Army career.

"Our biggest concerns are terrorism and arms smuggling. This is virtually an open city. You'll recall that cache of automatic weapons we found shipboard not long ago. We have only a few of the needed safeguards in place at land border crossings or in the airports. We're stretched pretty thin, actually. These ships are so large, and there is so much territory to cover. This is a natural point of entry and even a better target. We've always feared that a well-placed bomb in the hold of a ship could sink that ship in the harbor entrance. This place would be jammed up for a month."

"I see. Yes. So how do you keep the lid on things, then?" A genuinely interested Blackford asked.

"Good intelligence, good sources, good eyes and most of all..."

Blackford could finish her sentence, as could any seasoned policeman.

"...and most of all, good luck."

"Good luck, indeed!" Magda Reisner smiled.

The two had again made lingering eye contact and would have enjoyed a prolonged gaze, but for a call from patrol unit Four-Seven.

"Captain; Four-Seven here. We think you should join us here. This accident has proved more interesting than usual. Guns, Captain. Several hundred of them. And in crates marked 'Agricultural Tools.' Chinese-made if I had to guess. Wonder who ordered these? Also, Ma'am, please call for backup. No emergency. But tell them to bring a flat bed."

"Very well, Yitzhak. We're en route," Reisner replied, grinning.

Blackford, who had a sense of things, smiled and said, "We were talking about luck, Captain. It seems I've brought you some."

"Perhaps you have. Tell you what," the captain offered, "let's get you indoctrinated right off. Here," she said, handing him the keys, "you drive. First course in dockside maneuvers coming up."

As the pair left her office, Blackford admitted to himself that he was taken with his guide and counterpart. She was obviously confident, yet not 'brassy.' She was also professional, intelligent, tough, and very attractive. "This is going to be an interesting assignment, indeed." Blackford smiled to himself, as the pair headed down the metal stairs to the patrol car parked in the street below. Blackford found the following ten hours extremely rewarding, both professionally and, oddly, personally.

18 August
2000 hours
Haifa

The meal she had prepared was delicious. Yet things seemed to move too quickly, perhaps, for a new relationship between Blackford and this intelligent, lovely woman, and certainly too fast for a relationship between professionals from different worlds.

The day had been splendid. First, there was the

lucky discovery of contraband arms. One of Reisner's team had guessed they were destined for an extreme right-wing nationalist group of West Bank Jewish settlers. Second, there had been that fight between Taiwanese merchant mariners and some dock workers later in the day. "You really were super! I mean that!" Blackford exclaimed, recalling Captain Reisner's handling of the situation. "The poor bastard didn't know what hit him until you were full on top of him."

Reisner smiled and looked up from the glass of wine.

"No, those dockworkers are brawlers, not very skilled fighters, really. Just a well-placed palm thrust to his nose. Probably unconscious before he hit the ground," she added with half-joking modesty.

"Well," Blackford beamed at his new friend. "That took the starch out of the lot of them before things got really ugly. I might have had to step in and save you."

"And I might have needed saving," Magda replied. "I'm a pretty good fighter when I have to be," she said, smiling, "but there's something to be said for brute male strength. You might work out as a partner, so long as I do the thinking..." Reisner smiled coyly.

Blackford almost choked. He had never been adept at the banter of flirtation and the double entendre had caught him short. The words Reisner spoke suggested police work, but the way she said it promised more. Blackford was about to reach for her available hand, when she continued, "But not tonight, Colin."

"Look," the woman reasoned, "it's pretty obvious we get along well. And I admit I'm attracted to you...but we've only just met. I think we're both feeling the same thing, but this is all very sudden. And, of course, there would be, well, complications."

Blackford, both nervous and annoyed with himself that he could be so reasonable at a time like this, agreed. "I, well, uh, am not really used to such candor. I find you so totally refreshing...and so lovely, too. I shouldn't want to spoil something either."

"I'm far more trouble than you realize, Colin." Reisner smiled. "This nation, this struggle....my career are important to me. I've paid a great price for my position."

"Oh?" a genuinely curious Blackford asked.

"It is nearly impossible for a woman to advance in the ranks in our defense forces. Although all women, that is except those who are married or have children, must serve twenty-one months of military service. Until very recently we were generally relegated to office work and support roles."

"Oh, God," Blackford laughed. "Don't tell me you're another woman trying to prove she's a better man than I!"

Reisner bristled at the patronizing suggestion.

"No, you arrogant bastard!" Reisner laughed in

return, gently tossing her fork at his head. "The only thing I'm trying to prove to the terrorists is that NONE of us can be frightened and that ALL of us will fight!"

"OK, I'm sorry. Point taken. After all, I did see you handle those stevedores."

"Seriously, women served in the Hagana in Israel's War of Independence, but, since then, nothing. I was one of the first women, three years ago, ever to serve alongside men in the Matcal – the GHQ Reconnaissance Unit. We patrolled the borders with Jordan and Egypt. We freed up other males for duty in the West Bank and elsewhere. I'll have you know that I was appointed the Matcal's first female Company Commander."

Genuinely impressed, Blackford raised his hand and saluted through the candlelight.

"It's not an easy task, but our army has recently created predominantly female companies to patrol our borders for drug smugglers and the occasional terrorist infiltrator. A girlfriend of mine has been accepted into the Air Force's pilot course. She'll do well. Her father taught her to fly when she was ten!"

"So does this mean you'll be wearing jump boots the rest of your life?"

"Colin, I'm a woman, and I like being treated like a woman. But I'm also a patriot. And I'm a soldier. Every combat soldier wants to serve in the most dangerous area; you know that. That is why we serve; it's why we command. Right?" Reisner queried.

"Yes, command." Blackford's thoughts drifted back to Afghanistan. "I have commanded men in combat. But I must confess…I failed once before with a woman. You are damned exciting, Magda…but I'm on uneven ground here."

"You have no one? No girlfriend?" Reisner asked.

Blackford looked down into his wine glass.

"I was married, before. She left me for….well, that doesn't matter. He was there, I wasn't. I've tried to pretend that my duties as an officer got in the way, my deployments to Afghanistan. But truth is, I never was there for her."

"Look, you needn't tell me all of this at once," Magda said softly.

"No, oddly, I want to. I need to. I was never close to my mum, and my father, well, he was always busy. I guess I never, well, learned how to get close."

"Then we shall have to take this slowly." Reisner said, smiling warmly.

"Slowly, yes. But…"

"Then we understand each other, quite intimately, yes?" Reisner said, in a low and suggestive tone, as she reached across the table and gently took Blackford's hand in hers. Slowly she raised his fingers to her mouth and gently kissed them. "So we understand each other. I think this could be wonderful for us both."

"A-a-agreed!" Blackford half-stammered his answer. "Then let's be off. There's another day of it tomorrow. Who knows what we'll kick over...and besides, I want to hurry and get to sleep so I can see you even more quickly."

Magda Reisner smiled, her brilliant blue eyes becoming even more radiant, even in the dark of night.

19 August
0630 hours
Haifa

The eastern sun arose upon an already bustling Haifa. Ships and men were busy unloading as Colin Blackford studied the port's activities, his foam coffee cup safely in hand. The morning's schedule promised a look around the ship's hold of a freighter in from Brazil. "The manifest says fruit," noted one uniformed patrolman in fair English, "But I suspect cannabis!"

Blackford nodded to his companion-for-the-day and took a swig of the strongest coffee he'd ever tasted.

Magda Reisner was tied up with administrative duties, or so she had told her new English friend as their morning shift began. "Besides," she teased, "we both have work to do. After last night, perhaps it's best we do it separately."

Blackford hadn't protested, but had extracted a promise for dinner later that evening at her apartment. Blackford's offer to cook for her had intrigued Reisner, especially when he shamelessly embellished his culinary skills. "Well, maybe we won't get as far as dinner," Colin hoped to himself. "If she asks me to do more than boil water, I'm sunk!"

Opening the car door for his British ride-along, the uniformed patrolman chortled, "Captain Reisner told me that under no circumstances are you to drive."

"Why, that little...I'll have you know I handled things quite well yesterday in her car," Blackford said smugly. And, entering the marked vehicle, he pulled the safety harness about his chest and mid-section and then said, "Right then. We're off! Now, what about this load of Brazilian bananas?"

19 August
1830 hours
Six kilometers east of Kibbutz Gilead

The first stars of the summer's night rose behind them in a clear, deepening azure sky. It was just dark enough to warrant the use of the night vision monoscope provided them by contacts in southern Syria. Hassan Merzhed closed his left eye and peered with his right into the green light of the so-phisticated device. The lights from the kibbutz appeared as bright, white pinpoints against the shadowy outlines of buildings and moving figures.

"We are too far away to see much in detail," Merzhed complained.

"We'll move closer later. For now, just look at the buildings, the towers. Get an understanding of the Jew's defenses," Issam Banazir responded. "All will be as Sheik Quomuz has instructed. He is a careful man."

Merzhed continued his surveillance. "It appears just as in the drawings; the number of buildings is the same. There is the communications building and a radio tower. They make the mistake of showing us where it is. I can see the lights from here. There is the wire fence and towers. It looks like a prison, yes? It will be a slaughter pen for the Zionist pigs!"

Mohammed smiled at Merzhed. "Now, my friend, as the sheik has planned, this attack will be different from other raids. This time, we will use the special weapons. The sheik's tactics at the American base in Britain was a test...and it worked! The political response was exactly what he had hoped for! The English and the Americans are at each other's throats!"

"Indeed," Banazir responded. "It is now time to demonstrate the true terror value of the weapons we have acquired. As we make our retreat, Mohammed will fire the chemical warheads in the mortar rounds. This time, the effect will be more than political, it will be physical. The Jew dogs will not be prepared for such an attack. These blister agents will sicken and kill them horribly and then they will fear us!! When we have moved the entire store to Africa, we will be free to use them whenever we wish!"

The compatriots smiled and nodded toward one another.

"It will be difficult for them to run away," Hassan Merzhed laughed. "Do you see the large building near the main entry? That is our target. Fools! They placed it so near for us to reach. You and I will work in close, kill as many as possible and retreat. Remember, stealth, speed and surprise are essential. Once we begin to withdraw, Mohammed will keep them occupied with the mortar."

Merzhed laid the monoscope aside, and squatting, sighed. "It will be fully dark soon. Then we can get closer for a look at our target. We have some time now to fortify ourselves."

Banazir agreed and began to rummage through the vehicle for a canteen and some food.

19 August
1845 hours
Kibbutz Gilead

The bright halogen flood lamps had just come on, bathing the entire complex in a silvery luster. From the dining hall, tape-recorded music began to play -- some jazz from America -- and two children ran to ring the big brass bell outside to call the others to the evening meal fifteen minutes hence. It had been another hard day of work at the farm, and, by twos and threes, the workers and their families began to file toward their daily gathering place.

JONATHAN BRUCE

Outside the main wire, five hundred meters distant, two of the camp's young militiamen strolled along a farm road, their automatic rifles slung inverted from their shoulders. "Gilead, this is patrol four. All is quiet here. We're moving toward the pumping station for a look. What's for dinner, Gilead? We're hungry." His companion smiled as the radio responded, "You don't need to eat, Four. You're already too fat!"

"She has you there, Eli!" The other young man spoke, gently fisting his companion in the ribs.

Approaching the pumping station, both men could hear the whirling of electric motors and the whoosh of water through the two-foot-diameter pipe. One of the men gazed up at the growing darkness and another felt his belt for a flashlight. "Just a quick look around...then dinner!"

Neither man felt the thuds of the copper-jacketed lead slugs slamming into their skulls and chests as Hassan Merzhed sprayed them with silenced submachine gun fire. The three-dozen empty brass cartridge casings bounced off the hard concrete floor with a sharp metallic jingle.

"Quickly!" Merzhed commanded. "The compound will call for them shortly. We begin now!"

Mohammed Qadir had almost finished assembling the mortar as one of the young guardsmen twitched in the final throes of death. His involuntary spasms subsided as his life ebbed away. Blood flowed quickly along the uneven concrete pad to which the irrigation pump was bolted. Tightening

~ 402 ~

the last thumbscrew on the mortar's azimuth lever, Issam Banazir looked toward Mohammed, who nodded. "All right. You wait ten minutes for us to approach the compound. Then begin your fire with the conventional explosives. Keep firing for three minutes steadily. Then wait ten minutes. Hassan and I will enter and kill as many of them as we can. I will call you and tell you when we have begun our escape. Then, after five minutes, resume the attack for three more minutes with the chemical warheads. If we have not returned, make your escape without us. We will already be with Allah."

Merzhed quickly lifted his dirty right hand and stroked the cheek of his young compatriot. And just as quickly, he spun on his booted heel and began a dead sprint along the rows of cotton and soybean plants toward a spot near the main gate.

Exactly ten minutes later, Mohammed Qadir released the safety on the nose of the first mortar shell. Its fuse was now activated, and the young Palestinian lowered the missile into the mortar tube, fins first, and released his grip.

The first volley shot from the steel cylinder with a soft, dull thud. Four seconds later, its deadly payload exploded into the earth, near the middle of the kibbutz compound. The sudden bright flash of heat spewed dirt and rocks high into the night air -- and two men standing near a building forty yards from the blast fell to the ground, their knees weakened by the concussion from the blast. Just as suddenly, another impact, then another and another. Rock and brick and pieces of steel exploded above and along the ground.

In the security building near the west side of the camp, a frightened hand pressed a large red button, and the wail of an attack siren mixed with the mind-numbing confusion from the mortar blasts. Finding an emergency frequency, the young voice trembled into the microphone, "Israeli Army, this is Kibbutz Gilead. We are under attack...we are under attack. Repeat..."

But the words fell silent as another mortar round sheared the radio transmitter tower from its footings and the steel lacework fell into a heap of twisted metal struts and wires. A woman and her young child, caught in the open by the explosion, fell dead, crushed beneath the wreckage.

The blasts seemed to be coming from every-where at once; a camp worker screamed to no one in particular, as Qadir's hands worked quickly to trigger and release a new crate of deadly rounds. In his haste, he inadvertently placed a bare hand on the mortar's tube, burning his palm and fingers. His hand jerked away and he swore -- only momentarily -- for there was yet more deadly work to be accomplished.

As the Palestinian's lethal rain continued inside the compound, the bodies of eight men, women and children lay motionless near the craters of the blasts that killed them. Three young kibbutz guards raced toward the main gate to close the wire structure against possible invaders -- but as they ran to the mesh-steel doors, rapid AK-47 fire from Banazir and Merzhed stopped them in their tracks and left them, mortally wounded, near the opening in the fence.

Two more rapid explosions from Qadir's mortar, and the attack entered its second phase. "It's time!" Merzhed yelled to his partner, as he sprang to his feet again and began his run for the compound entry. "The dining hall door is open! Run for that building!"

As the pair sprinted into the compound, a silhouette appeared in the brightly lit doorway. It was a man with an Uzi -- Merzhed could see fire spit from its muzzle and instantly, he heard the unmistakable humming whiz of nine-millimeter bullets passing near his head. Merzhed jumped to the ground, and, leveling his sights upon the doorway, dispatched the shooter with a quick pull on the trigger of his AK-47.

The alarm continued its shriek as a dozen kibbutz members scurried to preassigned bunkers and shelters to arm themselves and secure the children.

Merzhed looked sharply to his left to see a procession running into a concrete revetment, and he unleashed a short burst toward the lead runner. The burst ripped sharply into the seventeen-year-old's side. The youth's body shook from the blast and he fell to the ground in a grotesque lump near the giant tractor. An older woman behind a twelve-bottom plow was next. Her arms flailed in wild, involuntary spasms as her torso suffered hit after repeated hit by fire from the unseen Palestinian attacker.

The camp was drowning in a sea of fire, horror and blood. Banazir proudly smiled to his fellow gunman.

Fifty kilometers distant, an Israeli Army sergeant pressed her headphones hard against her ears. Two officers gathered close for a report from the radio operator.

"Nothing else, sir," the radio operator reported. "Just that it was Kibbutz Gilead and they're under attack; then the transmission stopped."

"Very well, Sergeant," came the officer's reply. "Activate the alert network." With a quick turn of dials, the communications specialist gained instant radio contact with every major Israeli defense installation in the country. Even Army Headquarters in Tel Aviv was included.

"Flash Priority. Repeat, Flash Priority. This is Army Command, Northern Group. Kibbutz Gilead is under attack. Repeat; Kibbutz Gilead is under attack."

As the technician completed her notification duties, a red telephone rang loudly in the Northern Group Command headquarters operations room.

A lieutenant colonel answered. It was Tel Aviv calling.

Across the room, an Army general hurriedly entered the scene.

"Lieutenant Colonel Stine, what's the situation?"

"Unknown, sir. We received a message that Kibbutz Gilead was under attack, and then their radio transmission ceased."

"Very well," the general noted and, turning to a wall-sized situation map, noted the presence of a tank battalion in the vicinity of the kibbutz compound and ordered its men to respond.

"General, Air Force Command for you..." an aide handed the senior officer a telephone.

"Colonel Blum, Tel Nof Air Base here, sir. Air intercept radar indicates possible intruders heading south from Syria. We have launched interceptors. Advise your situation and coordinate..."

The general lowered the phone and swore silently to himself. "Dear God, the Syrians. We are under attack..."

19 August
1930 hours
Tel Nof Air Base
West Central Israel

"Talon flight, 4 and 7 away..." ground control called as the warning klaxon shrieked its ear-splitting wail.

Overhead, a pair of single-seat Israeli F-15s from 33 Squadron raced northward into a blue-black night sky, trailing two moonlit, ice-white contrail streaks hot behind. As the interceptors reached an altitude two kilometers above their home base, flight lead Major Ben Avner shot a hurried glance back at his wingman, Captain Ronen Weizmann, who had pulled into echelon formation just below and left of his flight leader. The full moon shone brightly against Avner's helmet.

It had taken less than two minutes for the alert jets to load and launch toward the danger, near the oft-disputed Golan Heights. Avner's hands busied themselves with a hundred tasks at once, and his eyes quickly scanned the heads-up display without stopping to ponder the unnatural speed at which he hurtled. The Israeli pilot mentally recorded his heading, air speed and altitude as those numbers appeared on the transparent glass before him. Outside the safety of his canopy, visibility was perfect and unlimited; the air was crisp and clear.

Somewhere below laid the rocky and arid landscape of Avner's home. This was the land of his father and of history itself. It was, at times like this, a most inhospitable place. But it was the only place Avner and his people could ever truly call home. And it was a home, Avner believed to the depth of his thirty-four- year-old soul, "a home that was truly worth dying for."

"Pulling through 3,000 at 450 knots..." Avner called into his microphone and to his wingman.

"Closer, Ronen," the major mentally urged.

"That's it," Avner noted coolly to himself, as his wingman crawled to within a few meters. "Good."

The American built F-15 "B" models screamed hard in afterburner as the pair raced to twenty thousand feet at over five hundred knots.

"Level at 20-zed, holding at 500 knots," the major called as the distant horizon neatly dissected his canopy.

Captain Weizmann answered with a pair of clicks on the mike button on the column of his flight control, and then looked at his radar to scan for intruders. Israel was a small country and an enemy jet, flying at attack speed, could cross into protected airspace and be over almost any target -- virtually with no warning. That's why Israeli ground and airborne radar constantly scanned its neighbor's skies, ever on the lookout for an adversary bent on the destruction of Israel's people.

"No bandits," Ronen Weizmann called to his superior.

"Talon flight to Sword," Avner called to his mother ship, an AWACS hovering safely over the Mediterranean, out of the range of potential enemy fire. "Vectors, please!"

"Roger, Talon," the AWACS called. "Flight of three. I say again, indicating three tacticals launched and heading south from Damascus. Intersect border in five minutes. Your heading 025 degrees at 20-zed. Bandits 180 degrees at 35-zed and descending."

"Roger, Sword," called flight leader Avner, as he made a mental image of three Syrian MiG-29 jets streaking toward the Israeli border. "Talon flight climbing now to 40-zed."

Altitude was one of a fighter pilot's better friends in a fight. It was always better to dive on one's enemy when attacking. Avner believed in the power of gravity.

"Roger Talon," replied the AWACS.

"OK, Ronen. On me," the major called, rotating the nose of the fighter up as the pair rocketed skyward to a rendezvous with an uncertain, but very real, danger.

"What's the situation on the ground?" Avner inquired of the AWACS controller.

"Unchanged, Talon. Sword Silver directs you to intercept all unfriendly aircraft in our airspace. Possible invasion in progress. You are cleared to fire at will. Say again. Cleared to fire."

"Roger, Sword," Avner answered. He understood that the reference to Sword Silver meant that the Israeli General Command Battle Staff regarded the attack at Kibbutz Gilead to mean Syria had finally launched a much-feared and oft-predicted attack. Certainly, Avner quickly reasoned, the flight of three jets heading south from Damascus affirmed the fears of the General Staff.

"Talon 4 to 7," Avner called. "Arm and release safety."

Weizmann, abreast in Talon 7, complied at once. The younger pilot quickly took his eyes from his HUD and scanned the complex console of the jet. With his left hand, he electronically armed the store of four AIM-9 *Sidewinder* missiles. With the safety mechanisms removed, the AIM-9s could prove a lethal weapon in a dogfight. With an effective range of over twenty-five thousand feet, and guided as they were with infrared sensors, the *Side-*

winder's ultra-sensitive homing mechanism looked for and locked onto the "hot spots" on an enemy aircraft. Because the Sidewinder could "smell" heat, Weizmann and Avner would look for opportunities to shoot at an enemy from behind, because that's where an enemy's heat signature was brightest -- his engines.

But now, because Weizmann and Avner were facing a potential head-on attack from the Syrians, the major had opted for a shot from above the intruders. "Too bad it's not daylight," Avner considered. "In daylight the top side of a jet is hot from the sun." Dogfight wisdom dictated that a pilot uses every tactical advantage at his disposal. Weizmann's flight-school instructors had explained, "If you can't get him from behind, get him from above."

"Talon 7 armed and ready," the young captain called to Avner.

And not a moment too soon. For just as Weizmann radioed his signal, three small white boxes -- each indicating a potential adversary -- appeared on Avner's radar screen.

"Check HUD!" the major ordered. "Three bandits, heading now 190 degrees and 20 kilometers out...still on the Syrian side." Avner knew the rules of engagement. He couldn't fire into Syrian airspace unless an unfriendly aircraft had radar lock on him first. Firing without provocation would be deemed an act of war. "Maybe that's what these fellows want..." Avner pondered.

Weizmann's eyes caught the intruders, or at least their electronic images, in the same instant on his electronic display. Instinctively, the young pilot swept his head back to the left and then to the right, scanning the sky above him for a possible enemy. No matter that either his radar or the friendly AWACS could have "seen" an attacker long before Weizmann's sharp eyes could ever have hoped to catch a glimpse, but still, a successful fighter pilot needed to assure himself of his tactical situation, sometimes without resort to instruments.

"Talon 4, Talon 4, they're breaking," Weizmann advised his flight leader.

"I've got 'em 7," Avner replied calmly.

"Two left, one right," Avner called. "We'll go with the pair. Sword, vectors?"

"Two bandits now heading 145, descending through 10-zed. One bandit heading 220, climbing through 35-zed. Fifteen kilometers. I've got a fix," Avner replied.

A sudden calmness overcame Avner as he scanned the tactical display on his radar screen, and almost without thinking, silently recited from the Scriptures: *"He has bent and strung His bow; He has prepared His deadly weapons, making His arrows fiery shafts."*

Avner raised his eyes toward the horizon and readied himself for combat. As the opposing fighters prepared to duel in the sky above, a brutal battle scenario played out on the rugged ground below.

The kibbutz, now aglow in flames and smoke,

still rocked from sporadic automatic gunfire. Chunks of concrete and wood splintered into the air from simultaneous blasts.

Banazir and Merzhed stood back to back in the entryway to the dining hall and fired their guns at anything that moved. Two older women who'd risked a peek over the top of the butcher's block were quickly hit; their heads exploding in a grizzly display of blood and brain. The death count rose even higher.

No one, it seemed to the living caught inside, could help now. In an adjacent storage room, Miriam Glodz felt strangely calm as she huddled herself around a small boy beneath a steel table. Her soft and gentle hands pressed firmly over the child's ears, in a vain effort to save him the horror of the deadly noise coming from the main dining hall. She could feel the boy's heart race as his frightened body quivered in fear.

Outside, a small platoon of armed kibbutzniks formed in a far corner of the compound, nearest the machine shop, and began to advance toward the main gate and dining hall.

As the first team of six approached the side of the hall, Yoni, a twenty-one year old soldier-farmer glanced in an open window to see Merzhed firing his weapon at the half-hidden figures of the trapped commune workers. On instinct sharpened by mandatory military training, he raised the Uzi from his hip and prepared to fire.

Suddenly, a stream of fire from Banazir's AK-47 exploded rapidly into the small patrol of rescuers who had massed near the wall. Four men fell dead instantly, and Yoni slammed hard into the concrete wall, dazed, cut, and wounded, but still alive. Unable to move, due to his serious leg wounds, he could only sit in a defensive position, cradling his Uzi close by, as he attempted to stop his own bleeding.

Then, with a fast right hand, Merzhed spun Banazir and screamed an order to run for the gate as a fresh mortar barrage rocked the camp. Merzhed knew the cover fire would only last long enough to facilitate his escape. The lead terrorist was second behind his lieutenant out the dining hall door in a dead run. But the pair hadn't cleared the building by five yards when they were met with fire from a nearby bunker.

Three riflemen from the kibbutz aimed and fired again. Five quick rounds slammed Banazir full in the chest and the young Palestinian fell forward atop his own rifle, face down in the gravel. Death's groan escaped his chest and his eyes hung half-closed.

Merzhed didn't take time to notice the loss of his compatriot, nor would he have cared, for the stream of fire from the bunker cut off his escape. He dove behind the wall of an unfinished outbuilding. But his ears rang at another crash of mortar fire. The shell landed near Banazir's body, catapulting his corpse atop a nearby planting machine. Another blast found the power generating station, and suddenly, the complex was enveloped in darkness.

A moment of shocked silence was interrupted by the frenzied shouts of the farmer-militiamen. "Where is he? Where is the other one?"

"Quiet, damn you!" returned a commanding shout. "Josh, take three men and go around to the back. He's alive somewhere. Someone get me a radio..."

High above, Talon flight held level at forty thousand feet.

"Talon 4, I have lock on intruder at 35-zed, 13 kilometers and closing. I have a tone..." the younger pilot called into his microphone, his thumb ready against the fire control button on the F-15's stick. "He's still in Syrian airspace."

Avner, too, was ready to shoot, when he noticed his tracking radar...."What the hell...Hold 7! Repeat. Hold!" Major Avner called to his wingman. Avner again focused on the long-range radar display inside his cockpit. The intruders had changed course, and were flying parallel to the Syrian-Israeli border, just inside their own airspace.

Inside Talon 7, the captain's radar picked up the change of course. "Talon 4...Talon 4, these guys are breaking and splitting..."

"Quiet, 7!" Avner ordered, but the Syrian maneuver was, indeed, a strange one. Avner held his finger close to the fire button. "Come on, you bastards..." he urged.

"Talon 4, I have no lock," the wingman called to his leader, "Repeat, no lock from the bandits. They aren't acquiring or locking on."

As Avner scanned the three blips on his radar, the Syrian MIGs suddenly rejoined and set a new course, north toward Damascus.

"Roger, 7," Avner answered, noticing that he was flying within a few kilometers of the Syrian border. "Break, break, 7!" he shouted, heart racing. "Do not cross into Syrian airspace. Do NOT pursue. I say again...do NOT pursue!"

As the pair of Israeli defenders broke off the pursuit, the headset in Avner's helmet buzzed.

"Talon flight, Sword. Your bandits have cleared. Do not pursue. Repeat, do not pursue. Come to heading 120 degrees and hold. Vectoring Talon Alert 9, 11 and 12 to you. Hold at 40-zed."

"Roger," Major Avner acknowledged to the AWACS on a frequency his wingman would hear. But to himself, he swore, "Syrian bastards; they're trying to provoke us. Damn! What's their game?"

Suddenly, the border airspace was void, save Talon Flight 4 and 7 and a flight of three more Israeli defenders approaching from below and behind, as the flight of Syrian MIGs turned north for home.

In another corner of the kibbutz compound, a pair of members struggled to generate emergency lighting.

In the blackness, voices wailed. Some cried from their wounds and several more out of fear. The moon's glow gave a surreal quality to the unfinished drama.

"Someone turn off that damned siren!" a squad leader called out. "Is communications active? Can we make radio contact with the Army?"

A woman's voice called out, "We're going there now. Don't worry, we have weapons."

Merzhed was panting hard as he tried to focus on his tactical situation. In the darkness, he could hear the moans of the wounded and the crying of children. He sank low against a wall, behind a turned-over table. He would formulate a fast plan of action, lest the Jews recover and capture him. Outside he heard feet pounding against the camp's gravel yard and the shouts of armed men, organizing themselves against an unknown enemy.

19 August
2000 hours
General Staff HQ, Israeli Defense Command
Tel Aviv

Two dozen voices came to an abrupt stop as the Army Chief of Staff cleared his throat.

"The Prime Minister and the Knesset want an update in ten minutes," the General Bober announced to his emergency battle staff. "What is the precise location of our nearest armored unit in the vicinity?"

"The two units that should have responded to Gilead immediately were taken from their usual positions a couple of days ago and stationed along the Gaza strip. Elements of the 9th Armored Division have been on an exercise near the Golan. The lead battalion is under the command of Lieutenant Colonel Orr Bauer. He reports that one of his four companies was down for scheduled field maintenance. But his other three are operable and fueled. They are en route with M-1 tanks. Colonel Bauer is supported by helicopters, also en route."

"What is his estimated arrival?"

"The colonel reports twenty minutes, maximum, sir."

A ranking general nodded in approval. "We can't ask better than that. Tell him he has authority to fire at his discretion. He has my personal backing."

"Very well, sir!" a brigadier general responded.

"What of the Air Force?" The general asked, "Sword Command reported intruders..."

An Air Force staff officer answered. "Turned back, apparently, sir. Either they had planned a surprise or they were trying to provoke us into shooting. Either way, we have a flight of five F-15s in the area."

"Very well. Any word on casualties?"

"None at all, sir. No radio contact since the initial call for help."

Turning to walk upstairs to a briefing room and a meeting with the nation's political leaders, the general noted tersely, "Inform me of any...I mean ANY developments."

19 August
2015 hours
Kibbutz Gilead

Two kibbutz electricians ran to the camp's leader to report on the electrical system. "Completely destroyed. It took a direct hit."

"Can we use the alternate generators for emergency power?"

"We only have one operable, and we've connected

it to the infirmary. There were two babies in there."

"Damn!" the camp leader exclaimed. "We must make radio or telephone contact with the Army. Where is Hanni? Is she back from communications?"

"Here we are," the woman shouted, out of breath from the run across the dark compound.

"Status?"

"Completely dead. The transmitter tower was hit and the landline telephones are out. Maybe one of the blasts cut the wires. I have already assigned teams to look for breaks and repair them."

"OK," the kibbutz leader said, reaching for a satellite telephone and gathering a breath. "Some of the terrorists may be in the compound. We killed one -- he's over there."

The group paused to survey the dead Palestinian, illuminated by flashlight.

"I saw at least one other...but maybe he escaped..."

Inside the kitchen, Miriam Glodz huddled in the dark, unnerving silence, wondering if it was safe to crawl from beneath her hiding place. Only five minutes had passed since the last mortar round exploded in the commune, and there were no friendly voices to be heard.

"Grandmother Miriam..." her tiny charge began to cry, clinging to the older woman's neck. "Are they going to hurt us?"

"Quiet, child," Glodz said, brushing the boy's hair with her fingers. "I don't know, but we must keep very quiet while Grandmother thinks."

Suddenly, out of the darkness, a rapid-fire burst from Merzhed's assault rifle shattered the silence.

"Do you hear me, Jew?" Merzhed cried through a window in broken Hebrew.

"Do you Zionist pigs hear me? Do you?" he demanded to an empty room.

The camp leader was caught off guard by the terrorist's brazen call.

"You fucking pigs! I have your women and children as prisoners."

"Dear God!" a farmer called softly to his comrades nearby. "He's in the dining hall. He has prisoners."

No one in the group could think how to answer the terrorist. What did one say?

19 August
2030 hours
Port of Haifa Police District

Word of the kibbutz attack had not yet been heard. The mood was relaxed in the port police headquarters. Shift change, too, was uneventful -- save an impromptu birthday celebration for a junior officer at evening roll call.

"Police departments the world over must be the same," Colin Blackford mused. "The same personalities, the same banter, the same jobs." Blackford felt at home here, in a foreign city among these people. Even though he was a professional soldier, he felt at ease in the company of these professionals. He couldn't recall when he'd been as happy. Of course, meeting Magda Reisner hadn't hurt matters.

Waiting for Magda in the briefing room, Blackford took the opportunity to loiter after his uniformed partner had said good-bye for the evening and gone home.

Blackford sat as the evening roll call progressed and the sergeants made notes of people and events to watch for in and about the harbor that night. It surprised Blackford when the briefing sergeants spoke both in English and in Hebrew, but he later learned that many on the force were not native Israelis. One uniformed officer, Blackford found out, was born in Atlanta, in America.

As roll call finished and the patrol pairs headed for their cars, Magda Reisner walked purposefully into the room. Her head darted quickly about, and, finding Blackford, pointed to him and called him sharply. Her mood was anything but relaxed.

"Colin, come with me. It's on television."

Before Blackford could respond with a question, Reisner spun out of the door with the Englishman in hot pursuit.

"In here, quickly...." Reisner motioned, indicating a small office just off the hallway.

It was CNN, broadcasting from Tel Aviv. A kibbutz in northern Israel was under siege, and "damage estimates and casualty reports had not been made available by the Israeli government."

"Damn," Blackford swore aloud. "Quomuz...." Reisner's head turned sharply at the suggestion.

She had been thinking exactly the same thing.

As the correspondent engaged in feedback with the anchorwoman, the network ran file video pictures of a similar kibbutz in the Jordan Valley. The anchorwoman asked the correspondent to speculate whether this was "the long-feared invasion of the Syrian Army in an effort to recapture the Golan Heights, or whether these settlers were of the militant faction who had occupied Arab lands without permission of the Israeli government?"

"It's much too early to tell, Dena," Helene Rogers-Moore, the CNN bureau chief answered. "But CNN is en route to the Kibbutz Gilead and will report -- live -- on that situation as it develops."

Blackford looked back over his shoulder at a gaggle of some twenty officers and civilian personnel who had gathered to hear and see the television report. No one spoke. No one uttered a sound. Everyone was hanging on every word from the television, wondering if a relative, a friend, might be in peril. It was a small country and it seemed, at times, that everyone Might be related to everyone else. In Israel, Blackford knew instinctively, it was never "the other bloke's problem."

In Israel, people took such news personally.

Ten kilometers southwest of Kibbutz Gilead, the spinning treads of Lieutenant Colonel Bauer's lead M1 tank spewed dirt high into the air as the forward element of the 9th Armored Division raced toward an uncertain rendezvous. Inside, Bauer had established the needed radio uplink with the General Staff in Tel Aviv.

"Our ETA is about eight minutes. General...any word on fighting or enemy strength?" Bauer asked, as his tank ran over the desert floor in excess of ninety kilometers per hour.

"Negative, colonel," came the quick reply, "No additional information. But be prepared for full tactical maneuvering."

"Understood," came the calm reply.

"What about your air support, any word back from..."

"Not yet, general. The helicopters should be on-scene about now."

19 August
2040 hours
Kibbutz Gilead

Orr Bauer's calculation was impeccable.

Just as the kibbutz militia secured the main gate and had completed its first sweep of the compound, the frightening rush and roar of rotor blades from a flight of three Israeli Army Apache attack helicopters roared overhead. In an instant, a bright beam of light shot from beneath each of the helicopters, momentarily blinding those below.

The camp leader, knowing that the craft were friendly, raised his hands and waved to the nearest Apache.

Inside the dining hall, beams of light splayed through the broken windows and partially illuminated the terrorist's position. The light showed the renegade Palestinian his handiwork, at least ten dead, maybe more. Only six feet away, a group of three -- members of the Sagie family -- huddled between two tables. A child's gasp, occasioned by the sudden burst of light, caught Merzhed's attention and the terrorist shrieked at the trio in halting Hebrew. A live hostage would prove more advantageous than another dead Zionist martyr, Merzhed calculated.

"You...YOU, come here!" He demanded, this time in English.

"You come now, or I will kill one of you," Merzhed motioned with his arm.

Just overhead, above the dining hall, the roar of helicopter engines sounded once more. Quomuz could feel the static in the air caused by the spinning blades hovering only feet above the single story building.

Hassan Merzhed screamed again at the frightened prisoners.

The Sagies, dazed and confused, did not understand, nor did they comply. Enraged, Merzhed raised his rifle, and let fly a burst over their heads. Their eyes wide from terror, the Sagies sat motionless, frozen.

Hassan Merzhed again gestured with frantic, arm gestures and ordered, this time in broken Hebrew, "Now, you Jew pigs. Come now!"

Outside the kibbutz compound, an Israeli helicopter pilot radioed Colonel Bauer, "No, I don't think it is an invasion. It may be a terror attack. The camp leader says there is one of them still inside the dining hall. He has prisoners. There may be more than one of them. There was shelling, but it has stopped."

The Gilead secretary pointed to a pair of tangled corpses, who had fallen nearby.

Keying the tactical frequency, the Army helicopter commander continued his radio message to the onrushing tank platoon.

"There is no firefight here, sir. Many casualties. At least one terrorist dead; another with hostages inside a building. If he had help, they'll be outside the wire. Two of my helicopters are searching the fields with floodlights. Instructions?"

"No, Lieutenant," came Bauer's reply. "Proceed as you are. I'll be at your position...wait; I can see your helicopters now. I'll be on station in two minutes. Stand by while I upchannel. Bauer out."

The tank commander relayed the information to a tense General Staff Headquarters, which, in turn, dispatched the report to the Prime Minister and the Knesset.

19 August
2055 hours
Haifa Police Headquarters

"Major Blackford...Major Colin Blackford..." came the inquiry from a young civilian police employee to the group crowded around the television.

"There's an urgent telephone call for you in the dispatch warden's office."

"Yes, he's here! Thank you," called out Magda Reisner, tugging on Blackford's arm.

"Come on, you can take the call in dispatch," Reisner instructed. "I wonder who wants you right now?"

Blackford's confusion lasted only a moment, for upon his entry into the dispatch central office, a uniformed officer handed him a telephone. It was Chaim Aran on the line.

"Major Blackford? This is Chaim Aran. I know this is an awkward time, but there is a situation developing near Safad...it's in the north, Major Blackford."

"Yes, go on, I've been watching the television," Blackford answered hurriedly.

"Then you know we've a hostage situation, Major Blackford. It appears terrorists have taken some hostages at a kibbutz. I told you that you wouldn't have to wait for even a year! There are casualties but right now the Army is not in a position to deal with the gunmen. We've got hostage negotiation teams en route...would you be interested in joining them?"

Blackford didn't have to be asked twice.

"I'm ready, now, sir."

Aran was not surprised at the young Englishman's answer. "That's what Harold MacHugh told me you'd say! Talked to him just moments ago. Gives you the green light, as they say."

Blackford, impressed by the rapidity of events, responded with a quick "Yes, sir."

"Very well, then," Aran instructed. "An army helicopter will arrive at your location within minutes. Less than an hour's flight time for you."

Not wanting to delay events, Blackford didn't bother to mention he was dressed in street clothes. "Hardly the right attire for combat," he said to Reisner, as he hung up the phone.

"Listen, Magda, I'm off...looks like that spot of trouble at the, what did the TV call it, Kibbutz Gilead?"

The Shabak captain understood instantly and fully. There would be no emotional parting. There wasn't time for sentiment; both were professionals who knew their duties when called upon to perform them. Captain Magda Reisner would have her own hands full. When any section of the nation went on alert, it meant that the entire nation went on alert.

"We'll have to put dinner off, I'm afraid," Blackford offered, as he headed out the dispatch room door and toward the heli-pad atop the building where he stood.

Reisner caught him for a moment, and, placing her slender hand on his shoulder, only smiled. She closed her eyes and stood closer so that he might kiss her. Blackford embraced her gently, kissed her lips lightly, and turned toward the staircase and the beckoning police lieutenant. As the Englishman disappeared up the stairs, Reisner lifted the telephone and placed a call to Chaim Aran's private line. She would have to work quickly...

19 August
2230 hours
Kibbutz Gilead

Hassan Merzhed had formulated his escape plan. "With Allah's blessing," he considered, "I might escape to fight again. At least, I will have died well."

The plan was simple. He would demand a jeep, and, using a hostage as cover, he would drive himself back into Syria where the Israelis dared not tread. "Not that the Jew didn't want such a fight," he weighed, "but he will not fight it unless he has planned the conflict, on his own terms. He is smart, the Jew. He will not risk a conflict until there is much to gain."

By now, the dining hall was ablaze in artificial light, brought forward by the recently arrived armored corps. Overhead, the three Army helicopters made repeated passes over the compound, their search lamps criss-crossing the kibbutz searching for Merzhed's confederates. Outside the camp's gates, tanks and armored vehicles surrounded the wire fences and military medical personnel scurried about, tending to the wounded and the dying.

"I want my men at each door and window of the dining hall. No one enters or leaves without my personal direction!" Orr Bauer demanded to his staff. "There are live people in there! And they will come out still alive, is that clear?" No one answered the colonel. He hadn't really asked a question.

From the center of the kibbutz, an ambulance

helicopter lifted off, carrying two wounded women and children, early victims of the rocket attack. "That little girl will lose her leg," one medic had pointed out to a tank soldier nearby. Orr Bauer deployed his combat engineering team to the communications center and the power generation stations. "Reestablishing electricity and radio/telephone contact are our priorities -- after the victims, that is," Bauer had directed.

"There are many dead and more wounded," Bauer had reported via radio to his headquarters. "Many direct rocket hits. Those who are not wounded are in shock. The element of surprise was complete. Whoever did this," Bauer concluded, "surely knew what he was doing. This enemy was a trained killer."

Bauer knew they would have to take careful steps if they were to free the hostages.

Despite the power of the floodlights outside, it was still dark in the dining hall. "The darkness is my ally," the terrorist knew, as he prepared to deliver his demands.

"Jew! Can you hear me, Jew?" he attempted in English.

Bauer waived his arms above his head to silence those around him.

"I can hear you. This is Lieutenant Colonel Orr Bauer of the Israeli Army. You know, don't you, that you are surrounded?"

"It makes no difference to me, Jew. We are well armed in here, as your pitiful people will tell you!

Do you hear me, Jew? We will kill them all if it must be so. It would be a martyr's death for me and Hell for them!"

"Is it negotiation you want?" Bauer responded, playing for time as the civilian hostage negotiation team neared by helicopter. "What is your name? It is hard to negotiate with men you do not know!"

"Forgive me if I do not play your games, Colonel," Merzhed smiled. "There will be no negotiation. You will simply withdraw your forces and provide me with a jeep -- else I shall slaughter your women and children."

Bauer delayed his answer, allowing carefully calculated seconds to pass. "This is not what I was trained to do! I haven't the men or the equipment for this!" Bauer thought quietly to himself. Cupping his hands around his mouth to fashion a megaphone, the Army officer called out, "I haven't that authority..." Bauer then said, stalling again, "My orders are to take the building and kill you, no matter what the cost."

The Palestinian knew it was a bluff. "Then proceed, colonel. Come take your building. I will die a martyr's death anyway."

Minutes crawled slowly by. Neither word nor action from Bauer's forces broke the silence.

Sensing an advantage, Merzhed called out.

"Well, Colonel -- it seems you are not prepared to murder your own people. That is very smart of you," he taunted. "Now, deliver a vehicle and call for your men to retreat. Now!" Merzhed shouted the last word harder than those before.

Just as Orr Bauer began to feel that the fate of the families inside was sealed, the roar of a low-flying jet-helicopter broke the quiet. It circled the compound, and, hovering just above the main gate, positioned itself for a landing.

Hassan Merzhed tried to shout to the colonel outside, but the helicopter drowned out his words. Frustrated, he reached across the bloodied floor and caught a woman by her hair. The child struggled, and pulled against her mother's leg. But, the terrorist was too strong. "Stop struggling!" an agitated Merzhed screamed.

Outside, the team of police hostage specialists who had just arrived in the helicopter, stood in a tight circle around Lieutenant Colonel Bauer. Each man dropped at his side a satchel full of weapons and equipment. Meanwhile, Colin Blackford, who had arrived with the group, stood just outside the circle, waiting for instructions from the team leader, Eli Ben-Aaron. Blackford could not hear their conversation over the roar of the helicopter engine, but saw Eli Ben-Aaron and Bauer gesturing toward the mess hall. After the brief conference ended, Ben-Aaron turned to Blackford.

"We're glad you're here, Mr. Blackford," Ben-Aaron shouted over the engine noise that filled the compound. "You'll excuse the engine noise. It helps confuse the enemy inside."

Blackford nodded his understanding.

"Your experience with the terrorists may be

helpful to us. We're not accustomed to negotiating. But the new political pressures from the west dictate we try new avenues...but please, remember that you are an observer here. Do not intervene directly."

Blackford, who'd protected his ears with spongy-yellow earplugs during the flight, caught enough of Ben-Aaron's words to understand.

"I won't get underfoot!" Blackford returned the shout.

"Very well, sir. Here's the situation." Ben-Aaron displayed a hand-drawn map the camp director had given Colonel Bauer. "There may be one or two terrorists inside this building. We must assume there are two. This building serves as the camp's mess hall. The colonel tells me he has learned there are several large rooms inside, plus two kitchens and smaller side rooms. There is some storage space in the attic and there is a partial basement which serves as a bomb shelter." Ben-Aaron continued, "Both terrorists are well armed and may have anti-personnel grenades or explosives. At least one has an automatic rifle -- and from the looks of things -- he's a crack shot. He's demanded a vehicle and that our soldiers pull back."

"So, what's the plan, then?" Blackford asked.

"We don't negotiate with terrorists, Major Blackford." Ben-Aaron answered flatly. "Every Israeli knows the price of appeasement. We are never prepared to negotiate with the devil."

Blackford look puzzled. Hadn't Chaim Aran said Blackford was to join a hostage negotiation team? "Why didn't the Army just go in, then?" Blackford asked.

"We're used to fighting in tight spaces. We've been trained for this kind of warfare. The army is too big and clumsy for such fighting. We want to save our people, but killing the terrorist is our main objective. Every terrorist must know he will fail in his efforts. It is crucial the world understands that." And, pausing to reflect on Blackford's reaction, Ben-Aaron finished, "This is a different kind of war here, Mister Blackford."

Blackford nodded his head in understanding.

Ben-Aaron nodded back and patted his British colleague on the arm as another helicopter descended into the compound. Ben-Aaron reached into a hard-sided brief case, produced a German-made nine millimeter pistol and handed it to Blackford. The police team leader leaned close to Blackford. "I presume you know how to use this...it's fully loaded; eight hollow-points in the magazine plus one in the chamber," the Israeli said.

Blackford, thankful to have a sidearm, turned the gun in his hand to ensure the safety was on, as Ben-Aaron checked with one of his team, a camera operator. "The modern warrior brings his DVD-cam to the fight, eh?" Blackford observed to himself.

Ben-Aaron was off and running with his team. "We're going in!" he yelled to Bauer, who could not hear the policeman. And, with a wide sweep of his arm, Eli Ben-Aaron deployed his "negotiators" around the building. But, before he had run ten feet, he turned to Blackford and yelled, "You will watch the front door for us, won't you?" Ben-Aaron didn't wait for a reply.

Four sets of rotary blades beat hard against the night air. Even with his earplugs intact, Blackford's head hurt from the deafening, sucking whine of the turbojets mounted atop the helicopters poised on each side of the dining hall. The glare of floodlights aimed against the building's whitewashed exterior added to the spectacle. Men brandishing arms ran quickly into tactical positions and orders were communicated among the men by hand and arm. The noise and the light were part of the Israeli tactic: "Keep the terrorist off balance at all times. Confuse him. Regain the initiative." That was basic to anti-terrorist training, Blackford knew.

Inside, the sights and sounds had their effect upon the living. The combination of dark shadows and bright bursts of light, together with the incessant helicopter noise, put Merzhed even further on edge. Merzhed was momentarily thrown, even forgetting for a moment his sworn plan to eradicate those cowering around him and wondering what move the Israeli would make next.

But Merzhed was stoic enough not to lose control. He had been trained well. If one maintained focus, he believed, one could survive. His options were few and his time was growing short. Most certainly, the terrorist knew, the Israelis would have snipers positioned in such a way that he would die the moment he left the dining hall. His only answer would be to call their bluff. He would need a shield; a human shield.

He'd held the kibbutz member by her hair for a full five minutes, and her daughter still sobbed from the terror that surrounded them all. With his free hand he swung the barrel of his Kalashnikov hard into the throat of the woman and coarsely ordered her to stand. The force of the gunpoint against the woman's throat gagged her and she began to choke as she tried to stand. Her seven-year-old daughter, tried to stand too, but a kick from Merzhed's boot knocked the child into a crying heap.

When the frightened mother stood half-erect, Merzhed wrestled her around so that her back was full against his chest. He dug the muzzle even deeper into her throat.

"Don't move!" he commanded.

The trembling woman's bladder evacuated, soaking her trousers. His prey now all but immobilized, Merzhed reached to the floor and yanked the child up by the hair. The child began to cry jaggedly in terror as the Palestinian secured her over his shoulder and back.

"WALK!" Merzhed commanded the mother, knifing the gun into her ribs.

Outside, Colin Blackford and the Israeli army kept a sharp eye on the doors and windows, waiting for the command to pounce on the terrorists inside. Their wait was a short one, for, in the harsh glare of the floodlights, the main door opened and the figure of a brutalized woman appeared. As she walked fully into the light, she raised an arm to protect her eyes, which had acclimated themselves to the darkness of the dining hall.

"Don't shoot..." The woman cried in Hebrew. "Don't shoot, he has my daughter! For the sake of God...PLEASE!" she screamed. "He'll kill her."

"God damn it!" Blackford swore to himself. "Damn him!"

Nearby, Eli Ben-Aaron rose to his feet; his pistol was aimed squarely at the terrorist's head.

"No clean shot...the child!" Ben-Aaron swore to himself.

Slowly, the terrorist moved his human procession by inches along the wall of the dining compound, so that he was shielded from the rear by concrete, from the front by the woman and from one side by the now-still child.

"Turn off the engines! NOW!" Merzhed demanded in English.

Above the din, Eli Ben-Aaron barely understood the terrorist's words. He knew what Merzhed wanted, time. Negotiation equated to time, and time was Merzhed's ally here. Ben-Aaron shook his head in response to a questioning look from one of his subordinates, a lieutenant. The junior officer knew Ben-Aaron's edict: there is no appeasing the devil. The engines would stay on, as would the lights.

Ben-Aaron knew it was a gamble, but he wanted to force the terrorist to make a mistake. Ben-Aaron would concede nothing to Merzhed.

Merzhed repeated the demand.

Ben-Aaron's reply was an intentional silence.

For a slight moment, Merzhed was unsure of his next move. Then, with few options left, he began to move toward a land rover parked nearby. It had not been damaged in the attack, and there was a chance Merzhed might make his way to the vehicle with his human shield intact.

The Palestinian had made his way only a few feet from the wall when Ben-Aaron, Blackford and the other soldiers recognized the goal. Merzhed was ten yards away from the vehicle as five counter-terrorist soldiers moved to ring the vehicle on Ben-Aaron's order.

Merzhed moved closer still, the woman in front of him all but paralyzed from fear.

The terrorist moved another five yards toward the vehicle when Blackford, on instinct, bolted from his position directly in front of the dining hall entrance to a point just behind the terrorist. Blackford, now too was fully bathed in light as he turned to raise his pistol at the terrorist's head.

"BACK!" Merzhed screamed, again in English. "Stay BACK! I will kill this woman!"

Eli Ben-Aaron was not prepared to permit Merzhed to escape, for the terrorist's plan was obvious, and Ben-Aaron was not going to allow a hostage to be taken. Experience taught that if one allowed a hostage to be taken, the resolution was always in favor of the hostage taker. There was never a benefit to be gained by acceding to the demands of a kidnapper.

Neither was Eli Ben-Aaron prepared to witness the murder of a mother and her child in this deadly game of terrorism. Ben-Aaron knew full well that his enemy would make good on his threat, because his enemy had no fear of death.

Ben-Aaron stared intently as the terrorist inched toward the circle of men protecting the escape vehicle. Out of the corner of his eye, Ben-Aaron suddenly noticed the crouching figure of Colin Blackford stalking the terrorist. Ben-Aaron knew instinctively Blackford would try a headshot if he could get clear, but the motionless child draped across Merzhed's shoulders made such a shot impossible. In frustration, Ben-Aaron waved Blackford off.

Blackford held fast, swearing to himself.

Merzhed was now only inches from one of Ben-Aaron's men, with his hateful glare fixed on the Israeli. He spoke not a word, but his message was clear. "Move out of my way or I kill the woman and the same bullet kills you."

Outside the compound, Colonel Bauer's armored troops fanned out in all directions, sweeping the rugged countryside for signs of other terrorists. The radio traffic was abuzz with a dozen sharply given orders and coordinates as each team was dispatched into the darkness. Bauer, in the lead tank, monitored all communications between his men. He was well within eyesight of the drama unfolding within the compound near the dining hall. In his right hand, he held a cell phone, a constant link to Army command headquarters and the Knesset.

He reported the scene between Merzhed and Ben-Aaron to the national command center with an accurate, almost dispassionate detail.

In the kibbutz, the parties to the standoff held motionless.

It was Merzhed's move.

Suddenly, in a blaze of noise and light, a small boy burst from the front door of the dining hall, screaming at the top of his lungs, with Grandmother Miriam in full pursuit, her instinct to save the child. She lunged for him, both falling to the ground. As the child writhed, Miriam Glodz encircled the boy in her arms and covered his tiny body with hers.

In an instant, the soldier closest to Merzhed turned his attention from the terrorist and toward the boy. That was all the time the Palestinian needed, for in a flash he shoved the woman to the ground and quickly seized the soldier from behind, rifle point jammed hard into the man's side. In the exchange, Merzhed had now positioned himself to easily slip into the open vehicle and behind the wheel, cracking the little girl's skull against the side of the vehicle in the process. Still his grasp remained firm and the child now hung limp against Merzhed's chest.

With his left hand on the trigger and his right on the ignition, Merzhed turned the keys and the Land Rover roared to life. Merzhed quickly grasped the gearshift, and in the next instant, squeezed a burst of fire into the solder's back. At the same moment, Merzhed flung the little girl to the passenger side floor of the jeep. She collapsed in an almost lifeless heap.

The blast from Merzhed's gun killed the young officer instantly. Merzhed jammed the accelerator down and careened toward the now-closed camp gate. Wire, wood and metal splintered when the hurtling vehicle crashed through to open country. Only an Israeli M-1 tank and a few soldiers barred his path.

On instinct, both Bauer and Eli Ben-Aaron ordered their charges to open fire. Not that either wasn't fully aware they had ordered the death of the young girl they were trying to save -- but this terrorist had to be stopped!

A volley of gunfire arose from in and around the camp compound. Thousands of rounds peppered the sand and dirt as Merzhed raced wildly, bounding across the farm fields and toward the Syrian border and a rendezvous with Mohammed Qadir, the mortar man who had rained death down on the compound at the onset of Merzhed's attack.

Merzhed's quickness had caught the Israelis off guard. He'd cleared both the compound and the encirclement of armor and was en route to a safe escape. Bauer responded, immediately ordering his "eyes" back into the air. In a moment, three helicopter gunships roared to takeoff speed and their crews lifted into the night sky. Meantime, Bauer's tanks joined in echelon formation, their high-intensity halogen beams united to sweep the blackened countryside for the escapee and his helpless prisoner.

Remembering the details of his escape plan, Merzhed reached inside his trousers for the radio.

"Mohammed! Launch the next round! Fire the chemical weapons! Do it now! Do not wait, do not wait!!"

At the pump station, the younger terrorist opened a cache of chemical-laden mortar rounds and, quickly prying the safety pin from the detonator, he hefted the nearly eight-pound round atop the mortar's barrel, then let fly.

The weapon let loose a loud "whoosh" as the first missile, bearing skin-blistering chemical agents, arced through the night and toward the confusion at the kibbutz compound. No sooner had the first rocket sped away, than did Mohammed launch a second, and a third and a fourth until the entire case of twenty was depleted.

In the near distance, Mohammed Qadir could hear the series of explosions from the shells. But he had little time to survey his work.

Suddenly the countryside was ablaze in light, noise and rapid movement. Red, green and white phosphorous flares shot into the sky, then were held almost motionless in their parachute-aided descent. The pursuit was so wild that it impeded itself, allowing Merzhed the advantage of stealth.

In only a moment, Merzhed was near the pump station where Qadir crouched in the darkness, automatic rifle at the ready. Merzhed screamed, "Mohammed! Mohammed! Quickly, we must run!"

Out of the darkness, the younger man emerged, his nostrils flared and wild-eyed in fear and excitement. Without fully stopping, Merzhed reached a hand to accept his compatriot's gun and, in the next instant, the younger Palestinian dove headlong into the open sided jeep, his feet tangling with the motionless body of the young girl on the floorboard below.

Not a mile behind, Merzhed could see the piercing fingers of light painting the ground below, in a vain search for the escapees. He knew it would be a race to the Syrian border. He hoped the Israelis would withdraw from the pursuit just west of the line. On signal, Qadir keyed the microphone of the portable two-way radio, set on a Syrian defense frequency, and began to call out a coded message to Mustafa Quomuz...help was on the way, but the Syrians, too, dared not cross into Israel. The Israelis were too potent a force to be dealt with. Their air force was renowned for its lethal tenacity in combat. Still, the Syrians could be of some assistance, and Merzhed swore aloud that his friends in Damascus had better honor their promise of support in his escape.

Colin Blackford gripped a side rail on the hurtling vehicle and reached a sleeve to his face to wipe the sand from his eyes, hoping to spot the fleeing Palestinian. The blackness of the night allied itself with the raiders, and all the Israelis could do was sweep the landscape with night vision optics and searchlights; the lights, in fact, all but negated the effectiveness of the night-vision goggles. But luck once again was with the daring Palestinian, and Blackford knew the search would most likely turn up nothing. Still, the enemy might make a mistake, and one could not catch a criminal unless one looked, Blackford reminded himself.

Only feet ahead on the ground lay two kibbutz guards, the first casualties of the murderous attack. The Israeli officer in the half-track ordered three of his men down to attend the bodies. The truck and its remaining occupants would continue the search.

Accompanied by an Israeli helicopter, the half-track resumed its thundering pursuit, and Blackford held tight to his pistol, trigger at the ready, hoping upon hope that a movement in the shrubs beyond would reveal his quarry. But with each passing moment, Blackford resigned himself to the fact that Merzhed had taken yet another round. An infuriating sense of helplessness overcame him and he cursed the sky above him.

Not a half-mile distant, the Israeli attack helicopter criss-crossed the region, searching in vain for the Palestinians, who were now less than a kilometer from the Syrian border. Mohammed Qadir, glancing down by his feet at the tiny human form which lay limp against the Land Rover's floor, asked: "Shall we kill her and throw her to the dogs? Is she to be atonement for my brother's death?"

"No, my friend," Merzhed responded, "Your brother tonight rejoices with Allah. For now, she serves us better alive than dead. Perhaps she can be used for barter...and if not, then, to Hell with her."

Overhead and unseen, seventy-five kilometers

distant and thirteen thousand meters above, a new flight of five Syrian MiGs formed up for another run toward the Israeli border. Obeying an earlier request from Quomuz, the Syrian government made good on its promise to conduct "regularly-scheduled training exercises" near Israeli airspace.

"Talon 4, this is Sword. Talon 4, this is Sword. Reply..."

Major Ben Avner, who had held in a wide circle twenty kilometers south, southwest of Kibbutz Gilead, responded to the call from the AWACS controller. "Bastards!" He swore to himself. "Not again."

"Sword, this is Talon lead. Over."

"Talon, we have three...make that five intruders, at 34-zed, bearing 150 degrees. Repeat, five intruders at 34-zed, bearing 150 degrees. You are cleared to intercept and engage...."

Avner switched to his tactical frequency and called to the other four aircraft in the patrol.

"Talon flight -- Talon flight. Intruders at 34-zed and descending. 7 on my wing. Nine, 11, and 12 break right. Attack formation Sierra. Repeat, attack formation Sierra. Climb to 46-zed and hold. Engage our airspace only. Repeat, our airspace only, unless you have been acquired...Talon lead out."

In quick succession, the five Israeli F-15's broke into flights of two and three, echelon left. As pre-briefed, the two flights would separate and attempt to pincer the opposing aircraft into a crossfire...if they crossed into Israeli airspace.

Just as the formation split, Avner called for afterburner so that his flight would arrive on station near the Syrian border before the approaching bandits.

On the desert floor below, as his tank bounced through the night, Colonel Bauer cupped both hands hard over his earphones to receive the tac-com downlink communication from the AWACS battle control center.

"Talon flight in pursuit. We have five intruders vectored toward your position, ground. Anticipate incoming."

"Roger," Bauer answered. "Possible air attack."

"Any intel on ground forces?" Bauer asked the AWACS controller. Surely a satellite or recon flights would have picked up significant troop movements, the tank commander knew.

"Negative ground forces arrayed your area."

Switching radio frequencies, Bauer quickly called his column and warned that the Syrians might provide cover fire from the air to aid the terrorist escape. Even if there were no photos of troop convoys or tank columns, there might be small squads of enemy forces armed with anti-tank weapons like the TOW Missiles Bauer's own forces carried.

"This rugged country can hide a thousand men unseen from the air, especially if they move quickly, in the dark. We could be heading into a trap..." Bauer reasoned correctly.

"Can they really be that foolish?" Bauer asked of himself. "Risk whole-scale war for a harassment or reprisal raid?" It made no sense, especially since some portions of the occupied territories were recently returned to the Palestinian Authority. "Such an attack seems so illogical...."

The colonel was not prepared to defend against a full air-ground attack. As effective as the F-15's and the Israeli air-defense network were, one could not assume all the Syrian fighters would be stopped. He knew that the Russian-built MiGs had proven effective in combat. Even one enemy aircraft, laden with canisters of cluster bomblets or napalm, could decimate his small force.

Politically, the use of such aerial force made no sense to Bauer.

But the Army commander had no time to ponder the wisdom of his enemy's actions. It would be for the journalists and the politicians to make sense of it all. Bauer, it appeared, had a fight on his hands and he hadn't many forces to commit to battle. He worried that he and his men were about to fire the first shots in a conflict that might grow into a very large war.

Suddenly, the capture of the terrorist became irrelevant. If the information provided by the AWACS crew was correct, the first wave of the attack, led by Syrian fighter-bombers, would be overhead in minutes. "May the devil take the terrorists," Bauer cursed.

He quickly called for a redeployment of his forces. He ordered his two M-1 tanks to either flank and the TOW Missile ATV's to the center of the formation, flanked by his small band of motorized assault troops, numbering no more than a hundred men, on either side of the missile-laden vehicles.

"And get Sergeant Kadec and his squad forward," Bauer called to his lieutenant. "Let's see if we can hit anything with those damn Stingers. We've only one chance against a low-level attack...and Kadec is it!"

"Radio, get Sword Silver Command. Urgent priority!" Bauer called to his tank's radioman. If Bauer was going to start a war, he wanted the blessing of the high brass in Tel Aviv.

Talons 4 and 7 broke into a high climbing turn to the north, as their radar focused on the five Syrian jets streaking once again for the Israeli border.

Major Ben Avner studied his heads-up display with a keen intensity, wanting not to be fooled by yet another Syrian feint like the one only hours before.

"They were trying to lure us into a fight," Avner reasoned. "That way they could justify the attack on the kibbutz as a reprisal for our aggression. Perhaps that was their plan...."

"Seven, hold at 46-zed," Avner coolly commanded his young wingman. Then, ensuring that his other charges were properly aligned for combat, the Talon flight lead called:

"Nine, are you in position?"

"Roger 4," came the terse reply.

Avner's eyes remained fixed on his radar return. A maze of triangles, circles and rectangles danced on his screen, each representing aircraft, friend and foe, in their deadly arabesque fifteen thousand meters above the earth.

AWACS control relayed Talon flight's tactical information to Colonel Bauer on the ground below and to the Israeli General Staff, which, in turn, relayed a hundred orders to the nation's military which had been on high alert since the first distress calls rang from Gilead.

Meanwhile, inside the kibbutz compound, the second wave of explosions had just subsided. As the members and soldiers uncovered themselves from their defensive positions, they winced at an odor, akin to burned garlic, and a light brown mist that began to fall in their eyes and mouths…small droplets of chemical gathered on metallic surfaces and splashed against the sides of buildings.

"God above!" one of the Israeli officers cried aloud to those in his command. "Chemicals! Get your masks on! Mask up!"

But it was too late for those in the compound. The entire area had already been saturated, and only a few of the soldiers could don their masks in a hurry. The civilians had no such protection. Miriam Glodz, standing amidst a gathering of women and children, began to rub her stinging eyes and mouth. The pain was unbearable.

Likewise, the others in the compound started to choke and spit as the chemicals began their horrid work on the mucous membranes of those in the blast zone.

One man tore at his eyes as he raged blindly in pain. Another man fell into the side of a truck, choking from the chemical burns in his throat and eyes. Still another young woman fell to her knees, her stomach heaving violently, and crying aloud for someone to come to her aid. The nightmarish scenes were repeated throughout the entire camp.

Outside the kibbutz and away from the chemical blasts, Ben-Aaron keyed the microphone on his satellite radio and uttered the words no one wanted to hear: "We've been attacked with chemical weapons! Send an army decontamination unit immediately, and blockade all roads leading to the kibbutz!"

In Tel Aviv, the officers of the general staff gasped collectively, as they sprang to renewed action at the new revelation. This was a horror long feared, but never before realized.

Far to the north, Merzhed crossed into Syria and slammed hard on the brakes. A swirl of dust and rock spewed into the night air. He looked hard over his left shoulder to see if his would-be captors were close behind.

No Israelis were in sight, and the plan had worked well, but there was still this was no time to relax. Even if the Israeli Army had relented, the Mossad or a team of commandos might be near and he had risked too much tonight to die stupidly.

"Mohammed, wake the child. Is she alive?" Merzhed asked. "Our mission is only half complete if we did not retrieve a hostage."

The younger Palestinian reached to the floor of the Rover and, shining a flashlight in the child's eyes, forced a pitiful groan from the girl.

"She's alive. What do we do with her?"

"We'll do nothing. Just keep her alive until she

can be delivered to our friends," Merzhed smiled. "Quickly! There are many more miles to cross before we can sleep."

Qadir nodded, then turned to rummage through a satchel containing a jar of tea and a loaf of bread, as Merzhed spoke a coded message to an unseen listening post, not fifteen kilometers away.

"Issam died well. He rejoices with Allah," Merzhed said, almost casually, to his cohort, who replied, after considering what his leader's words. "He is a martyr, then, like my brother. God is great."

"Talon flight; Sword, over."

"Go ahead, Sword," Avner answered.

"We read your flight of five no longer inbound. They've turned ninety degrees and are now headed along a parallel course, five kilometers north of the border. I repeat. Your intruders have not crossed into our airspace. Can you confirm?"

Avner had seen the shift in the Syrian flight path.

"Not again, this cat and mouse...." the major said to himself, tightening his jaw firm inside his oxygen mask. Just make one mistake, Arab. One of you, please. If there is a God, then make just one mistake. I shall be waiting for you..."

Avner called, "Talon flight, reform. Come left to 265 degrees and hold."

"Roger 4," Talon 12 responded, "No intruders. Will we shadow them, sir?"

"Roger that," Avner said, knowing all four of his flight members had sensed the Syrian gambit.

"AWACS control, we are static at 46-zed, parallel.

Inform Silver. Request guidance, over."

It wasn't more than a minute after Ben Avner had changed course that orders to assume a defensive posture passed through Colonel Bauer's earphones.

"What? Withdraw from the search?" came the colonel's angry and confused query. "Why?"

"General Staff has ordered us to hold, sir," the tank's radioman explained to his commander. "I guess they don't want a war right now, sir."

Bauer slammed his fist against the warm steel surface of his tank in total disgust.

20 August
0115 hours
Five kilometers south of Kibbutz Gilead

CNN's portable camera lights pierced the cool night sky. A fresh wind from the south helped prevent the spread of any airborne chemicals toward the hastily-convened press area.

"Dena, the Israeli security forces are keeping us a full five miles from the kibbutz." Helene Rogers-Moore reported, somewhat breathlessly. She had just landed in the Eurocopter she'd hired immediately after she'd gotten word of the attack. Rogers-Moore and a crew of three video technicians had scrambled quickly to get to Gilead. But that was CNN's reputation, and even though the television crews were generally regarded as a nuisance by the military worldwide, the organization had a hard-earned reputation for instant accuracy. Even the military itself had often relied on CNN for intelligence information in hot spots around the globe.

Rogers-Moore, too, was well known and respected by the Israeli officers she'd met in her four years in country. She'd been there the nights of the Scud terror in Jerusalem and Tel Aviv. And even though she'd earned the wrath of several well-placed Israelis for her refusal to don a gas mask and chemical warfare protection during the Scud explosions, she'd stayed on the air and reported the news quickly, fairly and without undue emotion.

"Dena, you're seeing Kibbutz Gilead illuminated in the distance. From here, we can see men and tanks and trucks moving about down there. There's lots of activity...lights seem to be everywhere!"

"Is there any word on casualties or hostages, Helene?"

"Chemical weapons! That's the unconfirmed word from inside the compound, Dena! The long-feared use of chemical weapons may have been realized in this attack. We've learned from troops going into the area that there's a chance of several...maybe many, wounded and dead. Details are scarce right now, but the Israeli command believes this was a terrorist raid and not an attack by regulars from any of the neighboring Arab nations. It's just too early to tell."

"And hostages...any word on hostages?"

"No word at all on that score, but hostage-taking hasn't been the usual plan of attack in these cross-border raids between Arab and Jew. It's unlikely if not totally improbable, Dena. This raid was more than likely a warning to future, would-be settlers in the West Bank or in areas disputed by Syria. But if one side actually used WMD, then this incident will have far-reaching effects."

A buzz in the correspondent's earpiece from her producer told Rogers-Moore it was time for a commercial break in Atlanta.

"That's the situation on the ground at Kibbutz Gilead. Reporting live, this is Helene Rogers-Moore, CNN, Northern Israel."

In Damascus, Mustafa Quomuz watched the broadcast and nodded with satisfaction.

An Apache attack helicopter, its searchlight so brilliantly ablaze that it blinded Eli Ben-Aaron, flew in low over the compound and, turning sharply to the left, raced toward the Syrian border.

Ben-Aaron jammed his finger into his ear, trying to hear the Israeli defense command on the other end of the line.

"That's right, Silver, chemical weapons. I repeat: CHEMICAL WEAPONS. And they've taken one hostage, confirmed. A little girl; seven years old, named Sara...Sara Sagie. Her family was in the dining hall and the one who escaped had the mother until she was able to free herself," Ben-Aaron reported via the secure-voice satellite uplink.

"She's in hysterics, poor woman."

"Who is responsible, Ben-Aaron? Any signs...."

"It was Jihad...I'd stake my reputation on it. Probably one of Quomuz's people. It's been years since we've had a clean photo of any of them. This man was ruthless. Utterly fearless...well trained. But the use of chemicals...well, this opens an entirely new front!"

"You know this was motivated by our recent crackdown on Palestine, don't you? Perhaps bin Laden's people, at least some of them."

"That would be a fair statement, sir."

"Then you understand the significance of this?"

"I do. The government and the Americans have been secretly trying to work out a settlement with Hamas. But other extremist Islamic groups in Palestine despise the idea."

"You understand, then. We cannot allow this attack to jeopardize the process. The Americans are putting such pressure on us. Even though we have always reserved the right to use tactical strategic munitions in response to a chemical attack...we simply do not presently know who did this. Hence, such a response would be inappropriate at this time."

Ben-Aaron, slightly exasperated at his superior's suggestion that he, Eli Ben-Aaron, might be singularly responsible for the diplomatic consequences of the attack, answered only, "Yes sir."

"Did you take any prisoners?" a familiar voice, that of an army general officer on the line interrupted.

"None, sir," Ben-Aaron replied. "But we have one dead terrorist. As soon as we've decontaminated the area, we'll be taking photos and finger-prints. The moment we have that information, we'll e-mail the file on the secure uplink right away."

"We want the body, Ben-Aaron, in Tel Aviv to-night. Do you hear me? I want the body!!"

"Sir!"

"And Ben-Aaron, make sure the child's family is brought here straight away...or at least those that are still alive. I can't have them talking to the press. Of course, we'll take care of them here."

"Very well..."

"And Eli, not a word to the press about either the chemicals or the hostage. One of the networks has been reporting about the chemicals, but we're saying nothing. Understood? That comes from the Prime Minister's office and the select defense committee of the Knesset."

"Not a word, Sir."

The line from Tel Aviv and Jerusalem went dead.

20 August
0535 hours
Kibbutz Gilead

As daylight crept from the east, Colin Blackford sat alone near the entrance to a makeshift morgue outside the far western gate to the kibbutz, ex-hausted from the night's chase across the rough border terrain. At least fifteen people with red and blistered skin lay on cots and another dozen or so wore oxygen masks to aid their breathing, their lungs seared by the chemical bombs launched by Quomuz's men. Inside the camp, a team of physicians worked frantically to stabilize the chemical wounds, frustrated by the knowledge they had never treated such victims before and unsure how many of the wounded would survive these horrible toxic injuries. Blackford guessed that the enemy had launched the chemicals from a mortar, not more than a kilometer distant. The munitions had exploded and spread poisonous droplets about the camp. There was no evidence of a mortar hit outside of the fences, so Blackford felt reasonably certain he was safe where he sat. At least, that's what the medics had told him as they set up the morgue near an area that had been spared any mortar blasts.

Teams of medics, decontamination technicians and kibbutz members volunteering for emergency duty scurried back and forth carrying litters, upon which lay the remains of the dying and the dead. According to the informal reckoning of the kibbutz secretary, there were at least thirty dead and at least half again as many seriously wounded.

Inside the camp, teams of workers clad in blue plastic decontamination suits wielded large soap-filled mops as they scrubbed the buildings and vehicles. Two large streams of water gushed from a pair of fire hoses as the decontamination teams attempted to dilute and flush the deadly chemical agents into a trio of hastily-dug ten-foot-deep pits. Another team of bulldozer drivers and heavy equipment operators prepared to cover the toxic runoff with tons of earth as the water flowed into the ditches.

Just outside the compound's main gates, one helicopter landed as another lifted into the morning sky bearing the last of the wounded to nearby hospitals. Blood was in short supply at the camp and medical personnel adjusted I.V. lines as the choppers raced away.

"Odd," Blackford thought, as the kibbutz and emergency workers went about their business of caring for the bleeding and dying. "These Israelis seem so calm, so businesslike. Perhaps they are better prepared for such things...or just accustomed to it."

Blackford had seen enough action in his career not to be sickened by bloodshed. Nonetheless, he still could not overcome the terrible sense of waste and frustration at the deaths of so many, so young. It reminded him of a day, not so long ago, on a bus in a clearing in his native countryside, when another terrorist had taken the lives of school children. But this time, the enemy had apparently used a larger quantity of chemical munitions. "There will be bloody damned hell to pay for this one," Blackford assured himself. "The bastard is getting bolder with each attack."

Blackford instinctively patted his pocket in search of a cigarette. He'd not smoked one in months.

"Why did it have to be children? Always the children..."

"MISTER BLACKFORD! A word please," shouted Ben-Aaron shouted from his makeshift communications center between two parked army vehicles.

Colin Blackford lifted himself from the ground and quickly dodged a pair of stretcher-bearers headed for the next hospital flight.

"Sir!" Blackford greeted Ben-Aaron solemnly.

"So, how do you like our country, Mr. Blackford?" Ben-Aaron asked, with more than a touch of irony in his voice.

Before Blackford could answer, Ben-Aaron communicated a message.

"Chaim Aran wants me to send you back to him quickly. I'm sending the video with you. The computer people want to get a look at the evidence. Perhaps we can find some clues about our attackers...By the way, it seems that Chaim Aran has been talking to your Sir Harold MacHugh. I've never met him, but if he's involved, you can suppose it's important. Do you know this Sir Harold MacHugh?"

"Oh.... we've met," Blackford offered, in an understatement uncommon to the Blackford of old.

"Yes, we've met...."

An hour later, the young SAS officer found himself in the center jump seat of the French-built medical helicopter, bound for Tel Aviv.

Sir Harold MacHugh and Chaim Aran had a new, urgent tasking for Colin Blackford.

SEVENTH PSALM

21 August
0115 hours
Washington, DC.

Eldon Klein had been awake for hours when he sat at the secured telephone to place a call to his counterpart, the Israeli Minister of Defense. The call would test Klein's ability as a negotiator.

After brief pleasantries had been exchanged, Klein began in earnest. "I'll be brief. The President asks me to convey to you, and your government, our deepest sympathies. He has conferred with the British government and we both wish to communicate our appreciation of the impact that the recent chemical weapons attack has had on the people of Israel."

The Israeli said nothing in response. He already knew Washington's position.

"But we respectfully ask you to forbear any retaliation."

The Israeli responded, tersely but politely to Klein in the formal language of diplomacy. "In this instance, we respectfully acknowledge the position taken by London and Washington. However, we reserve the right to act in our own time and in the manner of our choice, including the use of high-yield tactical munitions."

"I am told," Klein responded carefully, "that the British are prepared to take immediate, covert action in pursuit of the perpetrator. I understand your Shabak may have a lead and that the SAS has an operative in place to respond.

"As I said, Mr. Secretary, all options are available to us. You must certainly recognize the unique repugnance that a chemical weapons attack holds for our people."

"I fully appreciate that, Minister. I might only remind you of the delicate situations in Iraq and Iran. A disproportional response from your government might trigger a larger confrontation that we are not equipped to fight. Do I make myself clear, Minister?"

"You do, Mr. Secretary. And, likewise, is our position ambiguous to you?"

"No, Minister, it is not. All I can ask is for time to respond, quietly and effectively."

"Then we shall carefully monitor your progress, Eldon. But know this: Even our most reluctant citizens will demand a response to our enemy's use of chemical or gas weapons. Thus, time is short. ...Please give the President our respects."

21 August
0700 hours
Tel Aviv

Magda Reisner stood alone in the growing light at the end of the helipad. Her hair streamed back as the wash whipped at her face and eyes. The aircraft had barely touched down at the Central Police District headquarters, when Colin Blackford jumped from the open door and onto the hard concrete. He hadn't expected a friendly greeting, but his tired face brightened at Magda's approach.

"I watched it on CNN. I was in the control center. Deputy Director Aran saw it, too," she reported, slipping her arm around Blackford's waist.

Blackford managed a tired smile.

"Tell me you weren't exposed to the chemicals! You haven't eaten, I suppose?"

"No, I wasn't, and actually, I'm starving. Isn't that odd?" Blackford shook his head at himself, thinking himself selfish for his hunger after failing in the bad night's drama.

"I thought as much," Captain Reisner smiled. "I haven't eaten either. So, we're away--OK?"

"I'm keen for it. But I'll have to drop this off first." Blackford raised the DVD he'd been given by Eli Ben-Aaron. After leaving the DVD with one of Aran's aides, they set off for Magda Reisner's flat. Blackford had dozed off on the way; he was too tired to ponder the prospects of romance. All he wanted was a shower, a good meal and a bed.

Chaim Aran hadn't put the telephone down in hours.

He'd been in constant communication with the Minister of Defense, Director of State Security, and the military intelligence services throughout the night. Now, he and everyone else knew, it was vital that the identity of the raiders be exposed. The Israeli Prime Minister was insistent on quick resolution. After all, his political future was inextricably linked to the success of the peace talks he'd been conducting publicly and in secret with representatives of Hamas, the new political authority in Palestine.

The DVD was quickly reviewed, copied and distributed to a variety of security and intelligence agencies. Each organization, in turn, sought information regarding a key aspect of the attack and the Israeli response. But no question burned more brightly than the one that sought the exact identification of the raiders. That's why the body of the dead Palestinian had also been quickly flown to the forensics lab at Abu Kabir in south Tel Aviv for fingerprinting, photographing and DNA testing. If there was any record of the dead man on file, anywhere, the man would soon be identified.

So very much was riding on the answer.

Chaim Aran would not leave his headquarters, surrounded by television monitors, fax machines, radios and wall maps for hours, perhaps even days.

Colin Blackford was almost asleep, standing slouched against the corner of the shower in Magda's apartment. The hot water streaming over his head and shoulders carried away the dust and pain. His muscles, aching from the tension of the Gilead tragedy, slowly unwound and eased as the water performed its soothing magic.

He smiled, not quite recalling how he'd come to lose his trousers or who had turned on the water. Perhaps he had. Then again, perhaps not. The prospect of the latter roused the Englishman and he reached for a bar of soap.

"Pink soap?" Blackford sniffed at his hand. "Smells like her, anyway."

Blackford surveyed the contents of the woman's

shower. The wire rack before him contained what seemed an endless assortment of plastic bottles, tubes and elixirs, all inscribed in Hebrew.

"Christ!" Blackford laughed, "All I need is the shampoo. God knows what this lot contains." Grinning he yelled, "Magda! What on earth do you use for shampoo?"

Magda Reisner made no reply.

"Magda!" Blackford tried again.

Again, no answer.

"Hell, perhaps I'll use this stuff...." Blackford began to lather the pink soap between his hands and rub the foam into his scalp.

"Here," came a voice from behind. "That's not for your hair. Let me help."

Blackford turned quickly, to find her standing behind him, naked. He reached to embrace her slender athletic form, but a stream of soap ran into his eyes. "Arrgh! That stings..." he laughed, as Magda's slender fingers gently wiped the soap from his brow. He blinked the water from his eyes and looked at her smiling face. She kissed him lightly as a trickle of water ran from her pert nose onto his face. "I'm proud of you," she whispered with a smile, slipping her arms over his muscular shoulders.

"Proud? Why? I didn't do anything. I just watched."

"It's not everyone who will put himself in the line of fire for us! You didn't have to take this assignment..."

"Well, actually I wasn't...." Blackford

started to protest, but he lost his train of thought as Magda pressed her open mouth and tongue against his.

"You were saying?" Magda teased, cupping her hands around Blackford's firm jaw, and, before he could answer, again pressed her mouth upon his. Blackford's muscular arms wrapped themselves around the woman's waist, and he pulled her closer. The water played an enticing rhythm on the couple's warmly entwined skin and enhanced their excitement at each new touch and sensation. Soon, the pure joy of anticipation and exploration gave way to a consuming passion. Magda's nimble athleticism matched her lover's strength and visceral power, and soon, she flexed her well-toned legs and hips around him and engulfed him entirely.

"You're gorgeous!" Blackford whispered seductively to the woman, amazed at how willing he was to emotionally surrender to her.

In one another's embrace, each found fulfillment beyond expectation, and for the moment, Colin Blackford forgot that he was exhausted.

21 August
0730 hrs
London

"Sir Harold, I've got Major Blackford on the line," MacHugh's private secretary buzzed on the intercom.

"Colin? MacHugh here."

The Englishman squinted at his watch to find the time as he held the telephone in one hand and Magda Reisner in the other.

"Sir...uh, what time is it?"

"Late, Colin, later than we'd like," MacHugh answered gravely.

"Sir?"

"Good work last night, Colin. We know you did all you could. But you've got to get back here straight away. There's nothing you can do there now. Developments warrant an immediate change of plans. I've already arranged it with Deputy Director Aran."

"All right, sir. But may I..."

"You witnessed his mayhem last night, didn't you?"

"Who?" Blackford answered slowly, still groggy.

MacHugh answered quickly, sounding somewhat exasperated. "Quomuz, damn it! Who did I send you there to find?"

Blackford quickly sat upright, reaching for the light, as if that would somehow aid his understanding. Magda rose beside him and nestled her ear close to the phone, her breast pressed close to Colin's chest. Blackford instinctively reached to stroke her hair and skin.

The Scotsman, mildly aggravated, continued. "Damn it, Colin! That attack was Quomuz's handiwork. That's right. Shabak and our own intelligence confirm it from the video pictures. It was one of Mustafa Quomuz's first cousins and a trusted cadre member, Hassan Merzhed. He's the man you nearly shot. This means that Quomuz must have been nearby!" Blackford, now fully awake, was stunned by both the exactness of MacHugh's information and the speed with which it was apparently gathered and transmitted to England.

"Yes, sir, I might have taken a shot."

"Not for a moment, Colin. You might have killed the girl. I talked with both Aran and Eli Ben-Aaron. They were damn lucky to have you. But none of you could have safely gotten a shot off."

"So what's our next move?"

"You...You're our next move. You leave Tel Aviv for London at noon, so get cracking."

The line from London fell silent.

"The old bastard, how did he know where I was...?" Blackford turned toward the woman.

"Because, darling..." Reisner said, stretching her fully naked form on top of him, "...last night I told the Command Center you'd be here with me after your return from the kibbutz. I had a day off coming, so...."

Blackford smiled. "So, last night you knew I'd be here this morning. Pretty confident, weren't you?" Blackford teased.

"Indeed I am," Magda answered. "Wouldn't you say I have reason to be?"

Blackford didn't answer, but instead quickly reversed their positions and, gently tossing her onto her back, kissed her open mouth.

The flight from Tel Aviv was uneventful. So much had transpired in the past 48 hours, Blackford had hardly taken time to anticipate Quomuz's next move. But MacHugh's tone had been urgent, and Blackford guessed something big had transpired to warrant his quick return to England. After all, Blackford recalled, the "plan" was for Blackford to stay in Israel to help the Israelis track Quomuz.

A uniformed Metropolitan Police officer met Blackford in customs and walked him through the process quickly via the side door. No more than ten minutes after landing, Colin Blackford found himself in the front seat of a marked police car, speeding toward New Scotland Yard and a meeting with Sir Harold.

There was hardly time to even remember Magda, and it pained him to think he might not see her for a very long time.

21 August
1440 hours
Damascus

Mustafa Khalil Quomuz spoke quietly but quickly into the satellite telephone, telling his listener that the mission had gone as well as planned. "We have achieved far more than I could have wished," he explained. "They deployed as we hoped they would, and they are as lethal as our advisors predicted. We are ready to begin plans for the operations in Europe."

"You have done well," the voice responded. "Allah has blessed us. Now we await the Zionist's futile response. The Americans and British are occupied in Iraq and cannot fight us with their hands tied."

"Agreed, my sheik," Quomuz answered. "I will contact you when I am next in Africa."

22 August
1122 hours
New Scotland Yard

"There you are Blackford!" MacHugh boomed as the young man entered the Chief's chambers. Blackford felt uneasy. The normally jovial Harold MacHugh seemed one-off today, something Blackford had never before noticed in his superior.

Perhaps the situation at hand had worsened more than Blackford had imagined.

"I have the news you've been hoping for; you're going back to the SAS for training! Your job right now is to report to Credenhill and get fit. You know, all the usual fare: parachuting, explosives, night vision gear, special tactics, the lot. Then it's back here. By the time you return, we're hoping that Quomuz will have resurfaced."

Colin Blackford perked up quickly at the news. "Damn!" He swore not inaudibly under his breath.

"Damn, indeed," MacHugh rejoined. "It's likely

to be stickier than you may think. We can't anticipate what our man will do. He will certainly rees-
tablish his base. He may try to lose himself in Jordan or Syria."

MacHugh's voice trailed off momentarily, as his
mind imagined the terrorist materializing at every
possible rendezvous in his old Middle Eastern
haunts. Harold MacHugh's eyes suddenly filled
with fire. "But my instincts tell me he'll head
straight for the African continent. There's much
afoot there, funded by al Qaeda. That may be where
he's stockpiling his chemicals, and now he's proven
a willingness to use them. This most recent attack
changes everything...and changes nothing! Iraq
used blister agents on the Kurds twenty years ago.
My money says this was the same lot! Clearly, our
man Quomuz has the stuff and now he's upped the
ante! Even the opposition in Parliament has gone
quiet on the war effort. Look here, bin Laden has
been his benefactor before. My experience of his
methods makes me think he'll be looking for a
high-profile assignment. Perhaps chemical weapons
on a massive scale?"

"Getting me into an Arab country won't be easy,
sir," Blackford cautioned. "If that's where I'm going..."

"It's already been arranged. Suddenly, what
with the chemical attack, the PM is on our side
again." MacHugh looked stern. "Your experience in
Afghanistan will serve you well. "

Before Blackford could respond, MacHugh
stood and offered his hand. "Your training schedule

begins in two days, so you've not much time. I'm sorry to lose you. So, your job is to get fit, get fine-tuned by the SAS, and then find Quomuz and bring him back. It's that simple. Remember, lad. I'm in your corner should you need anything. All you ever need to do is ask." With that, the two men shook hands and Blackford turned away.

"Simple, hell!" Blackford grimaced to himself as he left MacHugh standing before the mammoth wooden doors.

SEPTEMBER

1 September
0430 hours
Colchester Barracks

Petra Voss sat alone in her cold, dark cell. As she had done so many nights before, she sought refuge from within, replaying invented memories of a life long gone these past twenty-five years and of the mother she had never really known.

"Irmgaard" was the woman she had created in her mind, a gentle woman with long auburn hair and piercing green eyes. A mother, who would hold young Petra and brush her hair and sing her folk songs, a mother who fed her and bathed her and who would tuck her into bed every night, a mother who had loved her. A woman who stood in marked contrast to the few truths Voss had learned about the woman she called "Muti."

The darker passages of her memory recalled vividly a mother who had been taken from her in the night by the hated authorities and a mother who was later murdered in prison. At least, that was what Voss had been told by her uncles in Hamburg whose families had taken her in after her mother's disappearance.

"Damn the Polizei for murdering her! Damn all of them!" Voss would fume.

Now, as she sat on the Spartan steel cot, Voss closed her eyes tightly and covered her ears with her cold palms, mixing distant facts with a self-created fiction, to reconstruct vague images of the mother who had departed her life more than twenty-five years earlier. There were old newspaper accusations that her mother had been radically involved with the Bader-Meinhof Gang and how the group had been accused of several lethal attacks on embassies and military bases. And she recalled nights when her mother would return late and in a panic, her clothes smelling of smoke and her face marred by dirt and blood. And she remembered the night when the Polizei had taken her "Muti" away in chains and how she had never seen her again. Not even at her mother's funeral.

As she grew, her uncles told her to forget "Irmgaard" and "Muti" and discouraged Voss from speaking the woman's name in their presence. Her relatives, devout socialists and sympathizers with the "causes" for which the Bader-Meinhof revolutionaries had fought, were driven underground and seldom spoke with outsiders.

Even as she rubbed her tired, dry eyes against her hands, Petra Voss did not regret the path she had chosen in her teens, which led her to the cold isolation of Colchester. After all, "they" deserved her wrath. "They" had murdered her mother; the police, the German state, the Americans who infested her homeland and the Jews, who had financed them all.

It was in the fertile ground of Petra Voss's young mind that the first words of revolution spoken by secret friends of her late mother had taken root. It was that evening in Hamburg, years ago, when she'd first met the olive-skinned student with the gentle hands, who was some years her senior. He'd spoken so eloquently and passionately about his hatred for the Jews who infested his Palestinian homeland. He'd orated passionately about how the German government--the same German government that had murdered her mother--had financed and supported the Jews in their evil, colonialist schemes!

She recalled how she had trained and become skilled as a fighter at Quomuz's behest and how she had served on many dangerous and bloody missions he had given her over their years together. She hated the fact that somewhere along the past quarter century, she had lost herself in his identity and had given herself so completely to her hatred and to his service.

And now, despite her circumstances and an almost certain lifetime of incarceration in a British prison, Petra Voss swore a new and bitter allegiance to a deeper cause: the death of Quomuz! He who left her to die would himself, somehow, some day, perish at her hands.

DECEMBER

2 December
2000 hours
Hamburg, Germany

The Fokker 70 jet dipped her ninety-foot wing-
span gracefully through a layer of early winter
drizzle over the Elbe River and turned slightly to the
southeast. The Euro-Petro logo served as cover for the
fact that the commercial aircraft, registered in Malta,
was secretly owned by the Israeli government. Minutes
later came the call from the craft's left seat.

"Hamburg approach, Fokker seven zed request
precision approach."

"Roger, Fokker seven zed. Descend and maintain six thousand. Contact approach one-one-niner
point four."

"Six thousand, roger, Hamburg approach, contact approach one-one-niner point four," came the response in excellent English from the Fokker cockpit.

Air traffic was light this evening, the pilot noted aloud to his crewmate. "But then, at this hour, why shouldn't it be!" his copilot said. As the craft descended, twin rows of landing lights glinted through the misty evening sky. A few minutes later, the plane lowered its gear, and then gently kissed the wet, black tarmac.

Although the landing was smooth, Magda Reisner frowned when she noticed she had forgotten to buckle herself in. As was planned, Hamburg Ground Control directed the jet to the far end of Terminal 4, a massive structure bathed in halogen light, which stood nearest the parking garage where two nondescript Mercedes-Benz sedans waited, with their engines running.

The jet engines whirled to a standstill as Reisner and her team quickly made their way down the gangway, through an open door beneath the civilian passenger area of Terminal 4, down a deserted walkway and into the waiting vehicles. Five identical canvas bags landed in the trunk of each automobile with a distinctive metallic "thunk" as the team settled themselves in behind the smoked glass windows and felt for their respective seatbelts.

Reisner checked her watch. "Right on time," she smiled as she buttoned the top of her dark blue jacket as the sedans sped away into the rainy urban night.

"We were lucky that German intelligence spotted the safe house," Reisner admitted to the members of her team as they rode through the night. "It was actually an accident, you know. The local Polizei thought there was a hashish sale going on. But the intelligence service caught wind of it and stopped the operation before an arrest could be made. But if this really IS Quomuz, what the devil has he got planned NOW? Our analysts predicted he'd avoid Germany. His money is drying up and his comrades seem focused on disrupting the Americans in Iraq."

A senior male operative answered. "Yes. But there is a large Arab community here. Mostly Turks, but many other Muslims who will harbor him. He has roots here; my dossier file indicates he was a student here many years ago. Perhaps he's organizing old friends, no?"

"But to what end?" Reisner puzzled. "He isn't here for the schnitzel. He's here for a purpose."

"And we've not actually seen him here, correct?" the male asked team-leader Reisner.

"No. The Germans correctly decided to pull back and notify us. Their government doesn't want an arrest and incarceration. They've too many Jihadists here as it is. They are all too happy to look the other way while we settle an old score."

"Well, it's the least they can do for us," the older Israeli assured himself.

4 December
1320 hours
No. 28 Markt Strasse
Hamburg, Germany

Hamid Omar dropped the last box near the small bathroom. The swarthy little man with the pock-marked face and gaunt appearance cleared his throat. His diminutive stature and humble demeanor masked the fact that he was one of the most callous terror operatives in the world. Hamid had personally engineered six successful attacks against Israeli and American targets within the last eighteen months. He had also personally executed two members of his own organization who had been suspected of disloyalty. Omar was not a man to take unnecessary risks. He was deeply honored to welcome Quomuz to Hamburg, and to provide him with logistical support for the next operation. He had respectfully welcomed the sheik upon his secret arrival. "My brother, please accept my apologies for your travel through the sewers beneath this infested hole. But here is where you will be safe, Allah willing, until we can make additional travel arrangements for you."

His cohort, Akhmed Zamen, grunted a nonverbal agreement, as he was incapable of speaking.

"It is good to see my old comrades again," Quomuz said, embracing the pair. "You especially, my brother, Zamen. You look well for a man who has faced the Great Satan!"

Some years earlier, Zamen's face had been disfigured by a burst of submachine gun fire during a desperate firefight with Israeli security forces in the West Bank. The terrorist had barely escaped with his life. He spent nine months recuperating in a Syrian military hospital. Surgeons had saved his life, but his tongue, several teeth, and much of his jaw were gone. Akhmed held a large brown envelope in his strong and meaty hands. The same hands had more than once bloodied Israeli counter-intelligence operatives who had made the mistake of trusting him.

"But I have been here too long. We risk much by our presence. My old friend Allmenroder cannot protect us against the prying eyes of every infidel," Quomuz said.

Akhmed passed an oversized envelope to Quomuz.

Glancing at the contents, Quomuz noticed several thousand euros, maps, keys, two forged passports, and ancillary documents. Quomuz thanked both of them for their assistance. Without acknowledging Quomuz's gratitude, Hamid continued. "Until it is time, you must remain close to this apartment at all times, Quomuz, my brother. Understand? As you have taught us, we never come or go at set times," he admonished. "There are final plans to be made. I must pay our friends to secure your passage. I will return this evening." With that, Hamid swiftly departed.

However, none of the three suspected that Shabak operatives had had Hamid and Akhmed under surveillance for over six weeks. Their so-called safe house was anything but.

As the pair departed, Quomuz surveyed his surroundings. Layers of grime on the few uncracked windows filtered out the bright midday sunlight. The paper-thin walls did little to block out the annoying techno music, which seemed to flood Quomuz's ears.

Turning to Zamen, Quomuz explained, "I must be quick in my departure. Allah has generously provided us with the money to purchase the equipment we need to perfect our chemical weapons currently stored in Africa. The German weapons-makers appreciated our cash. Their corporations have complained to their government that they can no longer maintain their international obligations under the current and projected defense budgets," Quomuz laughed. "So, they looked under the table for us, their sworn enemies. I have told you, my brother, Allah will strike the infidels down from within. Soon our enemies will be no more."

"Before I go," Quomuz thought to himself, "I need a long, hot shower and some food and sleep."

4 December
1330 hours
Feld Strasse
Hamburg, Germany

Magda Reisner keyed the microphone on her coded radio, as she pulled her scarf close to her neck to keep out the winter breeze. "Team three,"

Magda inquired, "Any movement?" One block away, two of Reisner's subordinates kept watch from a park bench. "No change, one," the woman reported. "Not a sound. Not a movement out of the house. And this concrete bench is getting awfully uncomfortable."

"We cannot strike until we are certain of his movements," Reisner said, reminding her team that their quarry, Quomuz, was the entire reason for the operation. He had to be taken.

"Very well, three," Magda ordered. "Take another stroll down the block; just keep the house in view." "Affirmative," the woman on team three acknowledged.

"Come on then, let's stretch our legs," she said to her male surveillance partner. With that, the woman took the man's arm as the pair strolled east along Markt Strasse toward its intersection with the Karolinen Strasse park boundary, keeping their eyes on the Palestinian safe house.

Reisner then called the second surveillance team position on the roof of a nearby store. "Team two. Eyes up."

From beneath a black tarp stretched over a metalwork frame, which gave the appearance of a repair crew, team two trained its high-resolution binoculars on the windows and back door of the safe house.

Ten minutes later, team two radioed in. "We've got movement here."

A tall, slender man with black hair and dark

brown complexion opened the back door of the safe house and walked quickly through an alleyway. His features were barely distinguishable beneath the scarf he wore around his neck and mouth. Team two shot a half-dozen digital photographs of the man and quickly sent the pictures, electronically, to a Shabak operative in the Israeli consulate building some kilometers distant. It would be at least an hour before the pictures were analyzed and the results re-layed to Magda Reisner.

"Alpha of team two in pursuit," Reisner heard in her earpiece.

4 December
1400 hours
RAF Brize Norton, England

Colin Blackford double-checked his gear bag. One 9-mm submachine gun with collapsible stock, two Glock nine millimeter pistols, and five hundred rounds of ammunition. Plus, a Nikon camera, field glasses, survival knife, maps, and the cash; lots of cash. Colin had just signed chits for three thousand pounds sterling, ten thousand American dollars, and over fifty thousand euros; all secured in two nylon money belts he wore around his waist. Sir Harold couldn't refrain from a jest. "Well, my boy," Ma-cHugh began, "At least if you buy it on this mission, you'll die a wealthy man. The ruddy beggars who strip your body will be bloody surprised."

"Thanks, sir, I'd never considered that eventuality," Colin retorted.

"OK, Colin, here it is once more," Sir Harold continued. "You land at Ben Gurion Airport, but someone from Director Aran's office will pick you up and get you through Customs.

"After Aran's team has briefed you," MacHugh continued, "at the right moment, the RAF will arrange airlift for you."

"Right then, got it? Any questions, man?"

Blackford drew a breath and asked, "What if he crosses my path, sir?" Sir Harold cleared his throat and paused as he asked the other police officers to leave them alone for a few minutes. He sat down next to Colin and faced him directly. "Colin, this comes from the highest levels of Her Majesty's government; straight from Number Ten Downing. Mister Quomuz is ultimately not to be extradited to the U.K. in custody, do you understand?"

Colin understood perfectly well, but asked for confirmation anyway. "Do you mean that I am to kill him, once this is all finished?" He stared directly into the eyes of his mentor and superior.

"Understand something, Colin," Sir Harold continued. "If we bring him back here for trial, al Qaeda may attempt a rescue mission or terror attacks in revenge. Under our system of justice, the most he faces is an indeterminate life prison sentence. We don't have the death penalty anymore, Colin. Not officially, of course."

Colin did not miss the significance of Sir

Hugh's emphasis on the word "officially."

Sir Harold continued, "Colin, when it gets down to brass tacks, think of the Crown and think of those children. Then pull the trigger. Have a safe trip, my good man."

"And by the way, for what it's worth, my old chum the Brigadier reports that you performed brilliantly during your SAS refresher training at Credenhill. It seems you set some physical endurance records that will likely stand for years to come. I'm proud of you, my boy!"

MacHugh then grasped Colin's hand firmly. Without further words, the Scot spun around and departed the security office.

5 December
1230 hours
Feld Strasse
Hamburg, Germany

Mustafa Quomuz hadn't seen daylight in the few days he'd remained hidden in the safe house. He was anxious to move the equipment he had obtained, through intermediaries, to the docks and all the way to Africa. He'd surveyed the barren walls of the house and read the few newspapers and magazines Hamid had provided. He had not sensed the presence of police or foreign agents, but neither had he risked discovery. He had been careful to avoid walking near, or even standing by, the carefully shuttered windows.

Outside and a block away, Magda Reisner and her team members maintained their vigil.

"I don't like the look of this," she confided to her subordinates. "Just the one man coming and going these past few days. The photos revealed nothing and our scanners haven't picked up any cellular communication," she admitted. "And I don't want to chance an encounter by placing electronic surveillance. We'll simply have to use intuition and choose a time to make our move. But I wish we had confirmation Quomuz was in there."

6 December
0600 hours
Ben Gurion Airport, Tel Aviv

The unmarked Royal Air Force BAE 146 made a perfect landing and gently rolled to a slow stop. Blackford was slightly irritated the craft had made two earlier stops to pick up diplomatic personnel enroute to Israel. Upon deplaning, however, Colin was surprised to be met by Deputy Director Aran who personally ensured Blackford's speedy passage through Israeli customs.

Colin thanked Aran as they settled into the latter's staff car, "Deputy Director, Sir Harold sends his warmest regards, and a small remembrance." With that, Colin presented Aran with a bottle of the fine single-malt whisky that was Sir Harold's favorite. "Well, you know," the Deputy Director began, "I think this could have some medicinal value; my thanks to you and Harold." After a brief ride to Blackford's hotel, Aran extended his hand saying, "Please drop by my office tomorrow morning at 0900, Major, I have some information you will surely find useful." With that, Colin climbed out of the car and the Deputy Director's car sped off.

8 December
0300 hours
Hamburg, Germany

The two Mercedes cut through the thick layer of mid-winter drizzle over the Elbe River and turned slightly to the southeast. Traffic was light at this hour. Minutes later came a call from the mission commander, Magda Reisner, in the lead vehicle. "We'll hold one block away until I give the order to move in." There was no sense arousing the terrorists' suspicions with a strange car parked in front of the building.

Reisner and her team soon neared the safe house and turned into an alley, taking up a ready position. As the cars coasted to a stop, and the drivers silenced the engines, the captain checked her watch. "Right on time," she said, unbuttoning the top of her dark blue jacket. Her team disembarked, and assembled near the trunk. The four black nylon gym bags were quickly unloaded and the Israeli operatives proceeded quietly into the chilly mist.

Two agents crept around the back of the apartment building, in search of the fire escape door that led to a bedroom window. Magda and the other team members ascended the front steps, eased past the mail boxes, and paused near the apartment door. The seasoned agents had practiced these tactics countless times. Magda's footfalls had been silent, and the two teams paused in place, awaiting Reisner's signal that would prompt them to action.

A moment later, the aged double-locked wooden door blew open and crashed to the floor. The agents lobbed stun grenades into the small flat, and then following the loud concussions, Magda and her three operatives rushed in, with weapons at the ready. The sleeping men inside were caught completely off guard by the simultaneous blasts.

Before either terrorist could react, their flat was filled with eight heavily-armed Israeli agents, intent upon killing or capturing everyone inside.

Reisner focused a red-laser dot quickly on Zamen's sternum as she shouted, "Freeze!" Still, he dove for a nearby pistol but not before his chest exploded from the force of three silenced nine millimeter rounds. His fellow terrorist, by contrast, tried to stand, but was quickly felled by a blow from the butt of an assault rifle. Dazed, he fell naked to the floor, as three of Reisner's team proceeded to shackle the terrorist's hands and feet, and covered his mouth with silver duct tape. Magda pressed the cold steel barrel of her Glock into the man's throat so hard that he gagged.

"Give it up," Magda said through her teeth, as she snarled into the terrorist's face. "Now, let's all take a ride, shall we, Mr. Quomuz?"

Before departing, Reisner confirmed that the first man was actually dead. Then she quickly sent a coded verbal radio message to an operative at the Israeli Embassy, who, in turn, notified Jerusalem.

"Touch nothing," Captain Reisner reminded her team. "We're sending a message here. We want the al Qaeda to find this one...just the way he lies. As for Mister Quomuz, let's get him in the car promptly." After a quick jab from a needle wielded by one of Magda's team, the prisoner began to fade into a dream-like state.

"This isn't Quomuz!" one of Reisner's team shouted. "It's the other bastard!" The words stunned Magda. Silence filled the air for several agonizing seconds. Reisner felt deeply angry at Quomuz for once again slipping through their dragnet, but there would be time to figure it out later. She barked, "Let's get the hell out of here! Bag this one and let's go."

Within a minute, Magda Reisner, her team and their prisoner were in the vehicles and on their way to Hamburg Airport. There, the Fokker waited near the north end of the cargo terminal ready for immediate take off. Ten minutes after boarding, the team and its prize were airborne over the North Sea, headed for Jerusalem.

Magda Reisner, still furious at having missed Quomuz, tried to find solace in the fact that at least none of her team was injured or killed.

10 December
0900 hours
Shabak Headquarters
Tel Aviv

Hamid Omar slept off the effects of the sedatives that had kept him docile for the last forty-eight hours. Team members had kept a twenty-four hour gunpoint vigil over the prisoner, still unconscious from the heavy doses of sedatives injected after his capture. Fingerprint and DNA samples had confirmed the man's identity as well as the identity of the slain man, Zamen, left behind in Hamburg after the raid.

"He's coming around, Magda," a woman agent noticed as Magda Reisner downed the last of her third cup of strong coffee.

"Hamid...Hamid...can you hear me?" Magda called out in a perfect Palestinian-Arab dialect. Hers was an unexpectedly soft voice, given her disdain for the prisoner and the terror he had wrought. The prisoner's head rolled back and forth, trying to shake off the effects of the drug. His half-open eyes squinted and teared at the bright light shining down on the cot where he lay.

Some mumbled Arabic was all the restrained man could manage, still unable to focus on his captors.

Magda stood over the prostrate captive and noted to herself the irony that found him now completely at the mercy of a woman. Reisner reveled in the blow to his Arab male ego.

"Hamid...Hamid, you are in the custody of the Israeli government. The government I work for. Can you hear me?" Magda called out.

Hamid shook his head again, trying to surface from the grogginess. His brain only half understood the agent's words. But he sensed enough to try and gather his wits against the Zionist enemy. Another woman agent, sitting in a chair on the other side of the cot, checked the safety on her short-barreled M-16 and laid it across her lap, finger at the ready.

"Hamid...wake up," Reisner called again. "Can you hear me?"

As his head began to clear, Hamid rubbed his eyes, sat upright and noticed that his right hand had been shackled to the floor. He stared momentarily at the two female agents and the weapon wielded by one of them.

"I imagine you are surprised to see us, eh?" Magda offered with a slight air of superiority.

"Who are you?" Hamid demanded, in English. "What do you want with me?"

"First, do you want some coffee?" Magda asked, deflecting her captive's outburst.

Hamid, taking measure of his surroundings, half closed his eyes and said nothing in response to Magda's question.

"Suit yourself," Magda continued, half-smiling. "I'm good for another cup. Ruttie? Oh, and you can take the gun. I think our guest will be interested in what we have to say. I don't think he's dangerous, at least for the moment."

The woman agent rose without looking at Hamid and walked out of the interrogation chamber in search of the coffee.

"You haven't told me who you are and what you want," Hamid demanded, his head aching from the effects of the sedatives.

"I should have thought you would have pieced that together by now…You know you are our prisoner and you know full well we'll never let you go. To the rest of the world, you are already dead."

"Fucking Israelis…"

"Ah, there's a good man, getting your spirit back!" Magda responded. "So let me try again. First, you need to know that your al Qaeda cohort, Mister Zamen, is dead. He took several bullets through the chest. Right now, he's probably enjoying all those virgins that were promised him." She paused to let her sarcastic comment resonate. "Second, your, uh, well…what shall we call it; your cell?" The captain continued. "We captured a treasure trove of valuable intelligence in that flat. The operatives you were training in Hamburg are being rounded up and most are already in the custody of the Bundes Polizei. And I shouldn't think they'll be doing much sightseeing any time soon. When the Germans are done extracting information from them, the Americans have accommodations waiting for them at Guantanamo."

Hamid Omar began to wonder how his confederates had been taken so easily, but he kept his facial expressions in check, lest they belie his fears that all means of escape had been eliminated.

Magda continued, bluffing slightly. "I see that you appreciate our thoroughness..." Magda let the comment hang momentarily before continuing. "So, why, you may be asking, are you still alive...and why are you here, of all places, instead of a German prison?"

Hamid paused before answering. He had few tools available to him, save his well-practiced guile. "Go on...why am I here?"

His female captor continued. "I shall be direct...I have plenty of reasons to kill you. Personal reasons...and no one in my government would mourn your loss. But..." Magda paused again, stood over him, and pointed a finger directly into his eyes. "I want Mustafa Quomuz, and you're going to give him to me."

In an unguarded moment, Hamid reacted visibly; his eyes flashing, he spat at the woman, saying "Israeli bitch, I will never betray my brother!"

Magda didn't flinch but pressed on with her well-orchestrated ruse. "What I can't understand is how you managed to trust Quomuz, especially since he's the one who gave you up. Our embassy in Berlin received a phone call from someone identifying himself as Quomuz. He provided the address of your flat, and he said we might be very interested in what was inside. How else did we find you so easily?"

Reisner sensed that the terrorist Hamid was listening, but the man remained stoic and silent.

"I'll give you one chance to talk. You should tell me now, because, as you know, we do not ask a second time."

Hamid stared at the woman for an angry second before again spitting in her face.

"Whore!" Hamid screamed.

"You've made your choice, Terrorist! We shall resort to other means."

11 December
1630 hours
U.N. Food Distribution Center
Diri, Western Sudan

Sister Anne-Marie Rittenhaus, a fifty-seven-year old diminutive Belgian nun, wiped her brow and studied the northeastern sky in vain. The long-awaited supply plane was either overdue or missing altogether. "That makes two days in a row," she sighed. A food drop had been promised for 1500 hours the day before, but it, too, had failed to materialize. Threats of insurgent ground fire, the Sister had been told. Such was the nature of the U.N. supply operations in this barren corner of Darfur Province.

Promises made. Promises unfulfilled.

The Diri feeding center was rapidly exhausting its stocks of corn meal, powdered infant formula, and dried beans. As distasteful as it was to do so, the nun had just ordered the daily food ration reduced to "emergency" status: one and a half cups of rice or flour, a tablespoon of beans or lentils, a spoonful of oil and a pinch of salt. Emergency measures would remain at this level until the next food drop materialized, all the U.N. field workers agreed. And that was if no more raiders appeared to threaten their efforts.

The cantonment area that had been hastily constructed by Dutch military engineers provided only a minimal security barrier for the food supplies contained within. The U.N. engineers had also sunk a deep-water well that produced over fifteen liters per minute. The well was the only bit of good luck the camp seemed to enjoy at the moment.

An officer in the Royal Dutch Marines, Major Jan Loos, commanded the thirty military engineers and twenty-two infantry soldiers who kept a tenuous peace at the Diri site. He knew he didn't have enough men or weapons to offer a meaningful resistance if the camp came under an organized attack. "Why don't I have more men and guns?" Loos asked himself secretly, not wanting to divert the care giver's attention from their relief mission.

Mother Superior Anne-Marie and her six Sisters of Medical Mercy, all trained as nurses in their native lands, had served in this westernmost province of Sudan for over two months, laboring day and night to attend to the needs of the more than nine hundred Nuba people who found themselves refugees in their own country. The tears she cried silently were neither for herself nor the empty rumbling she felt in her own belly. They were for the three-year old child, Lanni, who had died in the elderly nun's arms not an hour earlier.

There would be many more such deaths, Mother Superior knew. It tore at the humble woman's heart to hear the starving children asking, daily, "Mother Anne-Marie, will we eat today, maybe?"

The Westerners who toiled the few kilometers outside of the nearest town knew it as the Diri Center, little more than a squalid collection of three-dozen rag and stick huts, with plastic sheeting for roofs, surrounded by an equal number of cattle pens. The arid plain no longer sustained plant life, and the diminished rainfall had taken its toll on livestock as well. But the care givers did the best they could with the meager resources at their disposal.

The Mother Superior and her Belgian nursing sisters were aided by a small medical team from Doctors Without Borders. The chief physician, Dr. Guy LeClerc, was normally a robust and friendly Luxembourgian. But this afternoon found Dr. LeClerc crestfallen.

"Sister," the physician began, "I fear we have another outbreak of diarrhea among the refugees. Unless I can get it under control, I know that many of the children will die."

"But Doctor LeClerc," Sister Anne-Marie offered, "Just tell us what to administer, and my sisters will begin at once. We will work throughout the night, if necessary."

"Dear Sister Anne-Marie, I am afraid it is not so simple. Our stocks of antidiarrheals are exhausted. Acute malnutrition is the enemy. The children are, quite literally and sadly, 'wasting.' The inability of their immune systems to ward off disease and infection is taking its toll. This also means that their vital organs stop working. I'm afraid there is nothing we can do. I feel as though I have failed them!"

As the physician and the nurse stood silently, Major Loos approached. "Doctor, Sister, good afternoon to you both," he began. "I must ask you to keep your staff members close to the center of camp tonight and in the near future. Please don't let them stray very far. I have received some unsettling reports."

"What's in the offing, Major?" Doctor LeClerc queried. "My physicians must make their rounds to the outlying villages."

"I have received a dispatch from my higher headquarters in Kigali. Rebel militiamen are getting bolder. Yesterday they raided a region not fifty kilometers from here, sacking three villages and killing more than two hundred, including three Irish relief workers. They stole U.N. food supplies, as well as all livestock," the major reported. "I've been ordered to shrink our defensive perimeter, and to restrict all unnecessary outside travel."

The doctor shook his head in disbelief.

"But there's more," the Dutch officer reported. "My men found this; a pamphlet....it is from a group of marauders who call themselves 'The Islamic Blood Brigade.' Let me read it to you."

"We shall not be satisfied by anything less than the deaths of these wicked infidels, even if they repent or offer an apology for their trespass. Apology is worthless for the respected Prophet Mohammed; peace be upon Him and by God, even His hand will not heal our wounds."

"But, Major," the good doctor pleaded. "Certainly your soldiers present a significant deterrence to this local militia?"

"I'm afraid not, sir," came the major's terse reply. "We're out-manned and out-gunned. The heaviest weapon at my disposal is one sniper rifle, on loan from the American Army. My engineers carry only their side arms, and my other soldiers have only their infantry rifles," the major recounted.

"But, Major, certainly you're not contemplating killing these tribal militiamen, are you?" Sister Anne-Marie asked. "Surely the mere presence of a well-armed Western force such as yours would be enough to deter them?"

"Dear Sister," Major Loos continued, "These Janjaweed militiamen are cutthroats who fear nothing. They would rather die today with a full belly, than live until tomorrow with an empty one. They have no regard for human life, nor would they think twice before killing any of us Westerners."

"My dear Major," the doctor interjected. "You

forget that Sister Anne-Marie and I wear the Red Cross armband. We're medical personnel, and therefore noncombatants. We are afforded protection under international law." Sister Anne-Marie nodded in agreement.

"Idealists!" Major Loos thought to himself. But before he spoke, he composed himself as a gentleman, and concluded the conversation succinctly. "The only 'law' these tribal militia understand is the muzzle end of an assault rifle. Sadly, they hate you for the work that you do. It makes no sense, Doctor, but so little makes sense in this land. Good day, now." With that, he spun around, and resumed his inspection of the few defenses available to him and his men.

Doctor LeClerc shook his head in muted disbelief, as he watched the major saunter away. "Groups of angry men with guns; how horrid! Pray for us, Sister," the doctor implored the woman. "Pray for all of us. Now, come. We must attend to those we can help."

The noble physician then turned and surveyed the seemingly endless line of women, oddly, he thought, that were dressed in bright colors. The irony did not escape the caregiver's eyes; a throng of starving, homeless women dressed as if for a festival in hues of green and yellow; blue and red. Many of the women, clutching infants, shielded their children's faces with the scarves that covered their own heads. The gaunt faces of the desperate turned, embarrassed, away from the doctor, who motioned for an assistant to join him near the table where the scant medical supplies lay arranged for LeClerc's access.

The physician noted that there were virtually no men in the long line. "Either dead or conscripted to fight," he reasoned.

One woman, who could not have been more than thirty years old, trudged slowly to the doctor's table and held her infant up for medical inspection. LeClerc swatted away a horde of disgusting flies from an open wound on the child's leg.

"Ask her name and how this happened," Le-Clerc instructed his interpreter.

The woman spoke haltingly, exhausted from her endless ordeal as an "internally displaced person" in her native land.

"Her name is Gadah and this is the youngest of her five children," the interpreter said. "She said her husband was killed by the Janjaweed militia two months ago, and she and her children have been running and hiding ever since. The child was injured when a mine exploded. The shrapnel cut his leg. She has had no bandages or medicine and the child has a fever."

LeClerc reached for one of the remaining syringes in a cardboard box and withdrew an antibiotic from a glass vial.

"Tell her to hold the child's bottom for me while I give him a shot."

The child, weak from fear and hunger, made no sound as the doctor punctured his skin and administered the medicine.

"Where will she go now?" LeClerc asked the Interpreter.

"She will stay here in the shelters until they must leave again. She says she will go back into hiding in the mountains. She thinks she will be safer there from further attack. But there is no food in the mountains. Starvation and thirst forced her to leave the cave she had shared with many others. That's why she came here, seeking refuge for her children. She is fearful of more violence."

"Tell her to go over by the water barrels and to wash the wound thoroughly. Tell her to keep the flies out of the boy's flesh and have her come back here tomorrow. Perhaps we'll have some new bandages by then...We have enough clean water. For now, at least...."

LeClerc looked back along the line of refugees, moving past the water hawsers in a silent, ghostlike procession, and sighed to his aide. "We offer very little safety here, if the Dutch major is correct. The Janjaweed is still nearby..."

In the distance, the three sisters worked to build another makeshift shelter of sticks and rags and cardboard boxes. Apart from the meager defenses offered by the Dutch Marines, it was all the shelter that would protect the hungry masses. The sisters did so, secure in the knowledge that their very presence in this unholiest of places would offer some much-needed help. They were also vaguely aware that their actions enraged the Islamic militiamen who, no doubt, watched their every move, waiting for a chance to strike.

As Gadah nodded and smiled faintly, another woman with sunken eyes bowed her head and offered the physician another child whose future was uncertain.

12 December
1300 hours
Shabak Headquarters
Tel Aviv

"This is not a 'truth serum,' despite what the common understanding would tell you," the Shabak physician explained to Magda Reisner, preparing to draw a syringe full of thiopentathol from the cold glass vial.

Four well-muscled male agents carried the heavily-shackled and blindfolded Hamid into a cold, cinder-block interrogation room and laid him on the waiting steel table. Holding his arms at his side and restraining his thrashing feet, the men took care to avoid injuring the terrorist's head.

Reisner and the physician conferred in an anteroom while the security personnel ensured that the terrorist was safely secured to the examination table. Reisner knew this man would be tough to break. The usual means of persuasion had proven ineffective.

The physician continued, "It's really a barbiturate; a powerful anesthetic. It works on the receptors in the brain and spinal cord. So we must be careful; any head injury might prevent its use," the doctor warned. "This stuff is tricky enough, so be careful with him."

"He's no use to us dead," Reisner added.

"Now, there's no guarantee what he tells you is reliable," the doctor cautioned before the interrogation began. "The drug produces a dream-like state. It interferes with judgment and his higher cognitive function, but the subject may mix fact and fantasy. There's simply no guarantee he'll tell you anything truthful. Even in a stupor, he'll know he's being drugged. In fact," the doctor paused, "you should tell him we're using a 'truth serum,' because we'll be relying on his believing that he cannot tell a lie while he's under the influence."

As soon as the terrorist was strapped firmly to the table, Reisner entered the room and leaned close to his blindfolded face.

"I told you that we would resort to other means, Hamid! The needle we're about to put in your arm will make you talk. You know we've used these drugs on others in the past, and you know we've ALWAYS gotten results."

The terrorist shrieked anger and hatred through the black cotton mask.

"Go ahead, doctor. Prepare the needle!" The captain was careful to emphasize the latter. Hamid felt the sharp sting of the injection as the physician slid the needle deep into the inside of his right forearm.

"This should only take a few moments," the doctor explained, removing the needle from the man's arm.

The terrorist's head began to spin and his stomach was quickly filled with nausea. It took only a few moments for the man's thrashings to subside, as Magda Reisner directed that the lights be dimmed and the mask removed.

22 December
1730 hours
Port Sudan

A freshly shaved and shorn Mustafa Quomuz leaned against the port gunwale and watched with eager anticipation as the rusting freighter eased into its berth. The dockworkers tied off the hawsers and made the ship fast to the pier. Hatch covers were loosened and the creaking derricks swung into position, ready to begin the ancient ritual of off-loading. The SS *Aden Trader* was ready to disgorge her cargo of oilfield machinery, agricultural fertilizer, and hospital equipment, and Quomuz was eager to disembark and be on his way to safety in the west. "Too many prying eyes in this port; perhaps the CIA or the Mossad," Quomuz feared.

The journey from Hamburg to Syria was still easy. Despite the many precautions taken by the world's police forces, clandestine travel was still easily facilitated. Ample cash placed in the right hands did more to ease transit than all the passports ever printed. Safe houses manned by sleeper cells of other true believers helped cover his trail. Quomuz knew the West would never unearth all his allies.

Likewise, the sea voyage from Syria to Sudan had been slow and uneventful. Before embarking, Quomuz had, like other times in the past, disappeared into the community of Syrian Alawites, by day, praying frequently in mosques and sequestering himself with friendly radical clergy; by night, though, he frequented the waterfront haunts of Latakia where merchant seamen would congregate. He befriended Arab sailors, and eventually booked his passage on a tramp steamer with a captain whose discretion could be purchased easily with fresh American dollars.

As the crewmen lowered the gangplank, dockworkers activated a giant crane from the pier and began to lower its grapple into the amidships hold of the aging hulk. Quomuz edged forward and pressed an American hundred-dollar bill into the palm of the ship's second officer. This guaranteed that Quomuz's cargo would be offloaded first. His shipboard business concluded, Quomuz disembarked and sought out his favorite hotel.

This portion of his mission having been successfully completed, Quomuz decided that he needed some rest and relaxation. The Abebi Hotel was an al Qaeda front heavily involved in the slave trade. Young girls from Africa, Thailand and the Middle East were known to be kept there for purposes of prostitution. Quomuz rationalized that the Jihad owed him some small reward for the safe landing of the special cargo onto Sudanese soil. Today, he rather fancied a thirteen or fourteen-year-old tribal girl from one of the Darfur tribes.

A quick phone call to the front desk, and a promise of fifty American dollars, produced the desired results. Within ten minutes, a male appeared, with a young girl in tow. Upon receipt of the promised currency, the young man departed, and Quomuz locked the door.

The child did not appear to be frightened, yet she seemed slightly apprehensive. Her outward manifestations of calm belied her inner terror. Although only fourteen years old, she had been a sex slave since the age of eleven. She had not yet hardened to the horror of being used by savage men. She had been captured when her Nuba village was raided by armed horsemen who had burned everything and taken many of the women and girls into bondage. Like so many of the women in her village, she had been bartered among various tribal chieftains until the local al Qaeda operative had purchased her eight months earlier. She had been used primarily in the hotel's kitchen as a dishwasher, but three or four times weekly she was taken to the rooms of visiting foreigners.

Quomuz was momentarily taken with her soft brown eyes, and the apparent firmness of her budding breasts. "Remove your clothes, at once!" he ordered in Arabic, and she reluctantly began to comply. Unsatisfied with the pace of her disrobing, Quomuz removed his heavy leather belt and began flailing it without mercy against the helpless child. In a psychotic and self-sustaining frenzy of perversion, Quomuz actually enjoyed hearing his young victim's screams. Her terrified shrieks only exacerbated the pace and intensity of her tormentor's strokes. After fulfilling his sadistic proclivities, Quomuz inflicted upon the girl sexual savagery of an intensity even he had seldom experienced. After satisfying his depraved lust, and without a single word to his victim, he ejected the crying girl, bleeding, from his room, and locked the door.

Quomuz slept contentedly for the next eight hours without interruption. He needed his rest, for the upcoming journey would take him into the most dangerous part of the Sudan. Not even he would be safe without the purchased loyalty of several dozen tribal militiamen.

By the next morning, Quomuz's cargo had been transferred to the Port Sudan railway station and loaded onto four flatbed cars, and the train was scheduled for departure at 9:30 am. Even the blazing mid-morning sun could not abate Quomuz's enthusiasm, as he settled into his seat in the open-air passenger car.

The train slowly lurched from the station, and then proceeded gradually, steadily, toward Gedaref in the southwest. The locomotive's speed along the aging track was agonizingly slow, Quomuz knew well, for he had made this special journey many times on behalf of his al Qaeda benefactors and his suppliers in Syria and Iraq.

The aging engine and its skein of passenger, box and flat cars bumped along over uneven tracks and ties, laid down more than a hundred years earlier by European engineers. The Sudan Railway was in a hopeless state of disrepair, and Quomuz began to curse his decision to transport the cargo by rail. "But there was really no other option, to carry this much special cargo," Quomuz satisfied himself.

To be certain, airlift would have been faster and easier, and for al Qaeda, money was no object. But such an airlift would have aroused unwelcome suspicion from aviation authorities and there were no suitable runways in the west of Sudan to accommodate an aircraft large enough to carry these chemicals. For that matter, neither al Qaeda nor the jihad itself had access to the massive airlift craft owned by the hated Americans. "Better to use the tried and true railroad," the terrorist resolved to himself. "Slow, but reliable."

His masters had provided Quomuz unlimited funding for this operation. Their coffers were full, thanks to their many Islamic charities throughout the West, often funded, inadvertently, by people who claimed to despise violence.

The drudgery of the journey allowed Quomuz time to reflect on the uninviting scenery displayed before him. The poor farmers and herdsmen who waved toward the train reminded him of his own ties to the land. But for the Israeli interlopers, he would have inherited his father's shop, and he might have been content to live peacefully as a merchant. But the Zionist cur had left him no choice. In the empty faces of Sudanese peasants, Quomuz saw himself and every other displaced Palestinian. He resolved to continue the struggle for his own people, as well as for all of those dispossessed by foreign greed worldwide.

After passing through the arid landscape around Gedaref, the train pressed on through an area of fertile valleys and fields, adjacent to the venerable Blue Nile. Here, the life-giving waters had sustained crops of cotton, tobacco, and vegetables, as well as thriving herds of livestock, for the children of Islam for centuries. During a stop in Singa, the regional capital, Quomuz noticed a certain measure of prosperity among the local people. They exuded a more healthy appearance than their fellow countrymen further to the east.

It was in Singa that Quomuz had to provide additional incentive to the train's crew members. When the engineer suggested he was in need of rest for the night, Quomuz and three hundred American dollars persuaded the man to continue the journey throughout the night until the train reached Kosti, along the White Nile.

Early the next morning, the locomotive's steam whistle awakened the terrorist from his slumber. The train was on the bridge over the White Nile, and Kosti lay less than a mile ahead. Fortunately, a relief engineer was waiting and the stop would be minimal. Within fifteen minutes of entering Kosti, the train, with its fresh crew, was trudging westward through the Nuba Mountains and along the Kordofan Plain. At least the Nuba offered Quomuz a much-welcome view, as compared to the seemingly endless monotony of the flat plains through which he had just passed.

Leaving the Nuba behind, the train began to parallel the Abu Habl River, with its diminished water level. The farmers and herdsmen became fewer and fewer, as the landscape took on a desperate arid quality. Soon, the water level dropped off totally, and most signs of life disappeared altogether. Quomuz was a frequent visitor to this land and he was well aware of the civil war that had wracked the western Sudan for the last twenty years. But even he had never imagined it could look this bad.

He suddenly began to wish that this mission could be concluded quickly, so that he might return to a more hospitable environment.

Departing the Kordofan Plain, the ungainly train entered the southern tip of Darfur Province. Quomuz squirmed slightly in his seat and his throat tightened. This was the most desolate and brutal territory in all of Africa. Although eight of Quomuz's men rode with and near their lethal cargo, Christian tribal militias and paramilitary men financed by the West had been known to attack these trains, and to rob and even kill the passengers. Quomuz would feel more secure when the train reached Nyala, and his Islamic contacts would meet him. As a precautionary measure, he instinctively reached for his Glock, and chambered a round before returning the pistol to a holster beneath his robes.

The final hundred and sixty kilometers into Nyala passed without interruption. Other than the train striking and killing a few stray goats near Umm Boim, nothing noteworthy occurred. The lumbering iron behemoth groaned and creaked as it coasted into the Nyala station. Quomuz silently thanked Allah for granting him safe passage through an inhospitable land. He eagerly scanned the awaiting crowd for signs of his contacts and the trucks necessary to complete the journey to the mountains beyond.

He didn't have long to wait.

28 December
1830 hours
Kansas City

Jared Hurst loosened his tie and, placing both hands against his twenty-fifth floor window, surveyed the Kansas City skyline. The sun was disappearing into the snow-frosted fields of Kansas as the new litigation associate at Archer and Owens turned and made his way to the door. He'd had a surprising telephone call earlier in the day from an old client, who had invited him for a cold beer and conversation at Kelly's in trendy Westport.

"Hey, Jared….it's Zach Pollard," the caller had said, slowly, as if he were apologetic for something. "I'm in town, you got some time, I mean…if you're not busy. Maybe get together for that beer?"

It had been a long day of depositions, no lunch, and an inbox full of correspondence; a cold beer sounded like heaven. After forty minutes of traffic, the former Air Force attorney found a parking place and headed for one of his favorite haunts, Kelly's, a Kansas City landmark.

As he entered the bar, Jared removed his overcoat and wove his way past gaggles of well-heeled twenty and thirty-something holiday revelers. Hurst felt oddly out of place. He was beset by a recollection of recent history that he had hoped to forget. "One might leave the military," he thought, "but the military never leaves you!"

Hurst spied his former client in a corner booth. As he approached, Pollard stood, then lowered his eyes and extended his hand to the former captain who had saved him from prosecution. Hurst sensed great sadness in his former client, but he offered Pollard a sincere smile and drew a deep breath as he returned the man's grasp. Clearly, the attorney knew, Zach Pollard still bore wounds from the events of more than eight months earlier.

A saucy, long-haired waitress stopped at the booth to take their orders, two on tap, and quickly returned with the frosted mugs. "So, um, Zach," Hurst began, smiling nervously, not quite sure how to begin the conversation. "What the hell brings you to town?"

Pollard took a pull from his beer, and, slouching back against the wall, said, "Well, I'm looking for a flying job. I'm on my way down to an interview in Wichita with Cessna. Doesn't pay much, but it might keep me flying," Pollard smiled.

"Hey, maybe you can give me lessons some day; I've always wanted to learn!" Hurst said, looking down at his glass.

"Yeah, who knows?" Pollard smiled. "But, uh, I called around and I heard you were here. I owed you a beer and I just wanted to say 'thank you' for all that you did. I kind of lost track of you after the Air Force decided not to prosecute. They let me out of pretrial confinement about a month after you were sent back stateside, and then they kept me restricted to the base at Lakenheath for an additional two and a half months, and well, my career just sort of ended there."

Jared Hurst took a long swallow of beer, and then asked, "So, tell me, what happened?"

Pollard half smiled. "Well, it was like you said back then. They had no case against me. But they had to make it look like they were doing something, you know, for the politicians and the press. So, they kept me confined to the base for those months."

Hurst winced and shook his head.

"It wasn't really all that bad, I guess. It wasn't like they had an armed guard on me, or anything. But I didn't have anything meaningful to do. They detailed me to the Base Education Center, where I simply handed out tuition assistance forms to airmen all day long. They wouldn't let me fly, and they never restored my security clearance. They yanked my flight line badge, and Riordan personally ordered me never to set foot at the squadron again, under penalty of court-martial. Most of the guys stopped coming around. I guess I was kind of an embarrassment. Even Mercer, well, I mean, he stopped by just before they shipped him back to Eglin to attend flight test school. Besides, he wants to be a general someday. Guess he couldn't afford to be associated with a terrorist," Pollard added, sadly.

"So, when did they finally let you go?" Hurst asked.

"After they promised you there would be no court-martial, and then you left, I kept asking them when they'd release me. No one ever answered me. They gave me a new defense counsel, but he wasn't really interested. General Kilrain, I guess, got in all sorts of trouble, too. They tried to blame him for the attack, which was bullshit. Prior to the terrorist attack, the word was that he was a lock for his second star."

"Yeah, I saw some of that on the news," Hurst recalled, taking note of a shapely woman who stood at an inviting angle near the bar. "They needed a sacrificial lamb. They'd do anything to save the goddamn Next-Gen stealth fighter. The Chief of Staff didn't want any stink from the Lakenheath attack on him, so the Pentagon JAGs recommended throwing Kilrain to the wolves. Too bad, he was a good guy."

"Yeah, well," Pollard continued, looking into the distance. "So, finally, after about a dozen phone calls and e-mails to my congressman, they let me go. Like you said, General Kilrain couldn't help. I never talked to him. They made Riordan the interim Wing Commander and he signed the orders."

"So, I guess it's safe to say they never promoted you?" the attorney said, knowing well the answer before he asked the question.

"No…you know how it is in the Air Force. Somebody gets the idea that you are a liability to his career, and you cease to exist. No. I didn't get promoted, and when I asked about another flying assignment, well, all I ever got was silence. I didn't even get the medal that the other guys who flew to Syria got. All I got was an honorable discharge two months later. The end!"

Hurst could only shake his head.

Zach Pollard drank deeply from his beer, and continued. "But here's the lowest blow. They spiked any chance I may have had to fly in the Air National Guard or the Reserves!" Hurst thought he saw a small tear welling up in Pollard's right eye. "Riordan never completed my final Officer Performance Report, so now I have a gap in my official record. He even notified the FAA that my authorization to fly government aircraft was suspended due to concerns about my mental health," Zach Pollard continued, staring into blank space. "The Defense Criminal Investigations Index shows that I was placed in pretrial confinement awaiting court–martial for treason and abetting terrorist activities. Do you think that anyone in the Guard or Reserve would take a chance on a guy like me? It's gonna be tight even getting a civilian job with that hanging over my head."

"I guess we all got some battle damage after the attack," Hurst said.

"Huh?" Pollard responded; he was genuinely surprised.

"I'm afraid I did too good of a job for you, Zach," Hurst laughed, sarcastically. "It seems that my JAG superiors didn't like the fact that I had defended someone accused of terrorism. My Air Force chain of command disowned me, too. Just like you, I ceased to exist. A Staff Judge Advocate assignment they had promised me just vanished, and then they asked me if I wanted an early out…and I took it. Besides, the money's better out here."

"Shit, I guess I cost you your career. I'm sorry, man," Pollard apologized.

"Forget it. I made a choice. It was either do my best for people like you…or cover my own ass and get promoted. I always knew the Air Force wasn't REALLY interested in having good defense lawyers. Doing too good a job defending people has always been the kiss of death in the service, like some of those guys who defended those who refused to take the anthrax vaccinations. All of those lawyers got quietly invited to leave the service, too. Truth is, most of the JAG Corps senior leaders long

ago surrendered their legal ethics in favor of protecting their careers."

"Jesus," Pollard said slowly.

"Enough of that," the lawyer said, taking a long
pull on the last of his beer. "So, what about you,
your family and stuff?"

"You know, it's the damndest thing, Counselor," Pollard smiled.

"What's that?"

"I still think about 'her;' Tracie, I mean. I know
all that stuff they said she did. But I miss her. It was
odd. I guess I really never knew her. We were only
together a few times, but, it's like, well, I guess I
really loved her," Pollard murmured sadly. "Helluva
thing, huh?" Pollard opined.

"Yes, a helluva thing." Hurst answered softly,
and, rising, walked toward the bar and raised two
fingers to buy another round.

FEBRUARY

2 February
1000 hours
Deputy Director Aran's Office
Tel Aviv

"Major Blackford, welcome again," the Deputy Director offered. "I trust your time at Tel Nof Air Base was well spent? We're very proud of the special operations and our combat search and rescue teams there."

"Exceedingly useful and illuminating, sir," Colin replied.

"Good to hear, my friend," Aran retorted. "Now the time is at hand for you to leave us. Your RAF friends will fly you to an American air base in the Horn of Africa, where you'll pick up supplies and final instructions. Then the RAF will take you the rest of the way to the Sudan."

"I shall be saddened to leave your lovely country, sir," Colin said, thinking of Magda. "But it will be good to get back into action, wherever that may be."

Deputy Director Aran did not miss Colin's query. "Indeed, my friend that is why we have one final briefing for your consideration." Reaching for the intercom button on his phone, he simply said, "Send in the captain."

Colin was both delighted and puzzled to see Magda Reisner enter the room, followed by three noncommissioned officers. Last he'd been told she was off to America for two weeks of training with the Defense Intelligence Agency.

Since neither of the pair spoke immediately, Aran broke the silence. "I believe you two remember each other?"

"Indeed," Colin replied, smiling.

"Thank you, Major. My recent weeks were spent productively," she replied, with a profound sense of understatement. "Shall I begin, then?"

"Let's start with a video tape." Reisner set the scene, as the lights dimmed and two computer screens flickered to life. "We've come into possession of a certain member of Quomuz's team." She conveniently failed to explain either how the Israeli intelligence service had captured this particular conspirator or to disclose the methods used to take down the Hamburg cell.

"This is a man named Hamid Omar." Blackford leaned toward the nearest screen for a better look. "He was subjected to several sessions of psychological interrogation, but to no avail. That's when we changed tactics. He was not allergic to Pentathol, but even under the influence of the drug, he was initially resistant to our questioning. The tape you're looking at was made during the sixth session. We had to space the interrogations apart to allow him time to recover from the drug's effects. It also gave us time to verify some of the bits of information he shared and to create new prompts to make him speak. The sixth session, as you're about to see, was the most productive."

The video camera had been placed on the ceiling directly above the manacled terrorist's face. His interrogator was a woman Blackford had never seen, but he presumed her to be another Shabak operative.

As the video continued, Blackford noticed the interrogator walk near the man, his eyes half opened and his mouth fully agape.

"Hamid, it is Petra. Petra Voss," the interrogator began in Arabic. A translator repeated the conversation in English on the tape.

"What is my mission, Hamid? Those two, Zamen and Quomuz…they could not tell me. What is my mission? They had a different mission than mine…"

A strong dose of the bbarbiturate began its work quickly.

Hamid began to answer haltingly, deliberately,

his head clearly reeling in confusion. "I was responsible....the equipment. From the Germans. Injectors, mixers, shells."

"But what of Quomuz?" the woman asked softly in Arabic.

"Quomuz left....through the sewers....around midnight. He had...a secret contact. And two bags … had cash...lots of cash."

"Where did he go? Where did Quomuz go, Hamid?"

"The docks, on a ship....back before morning...but we heard no more from him. The sheik didn't return. I don't know … I don't know. The crates."

Aran, Reisner and Blackford listened carefully as the sedated man continued.

"The ships. Find men. The ships." The interrogator prompted. "You are the supplier, Hamid. Who will help us?" she asked.

"The faithful sailors at the docks. Red Sea."

"What sailors? What sailors?" the agent pressed, but the terrorist began to slip into a deeper sleep.

Hamid began to drift into darkness, mumbling, his head turned to the left and his eyes closed fully.

"What did he just say?" Aran demanded.

That's when Reisner announced. "Sir, we've played this over and over, our forensics people even scrubbed it through their stabilizers. Our best guess is that he said 'Darfur. The caves. The sheik must...' After that, it's completely unintelligible."

The tape continued and the woman interrogator

then appeared to raise her hand to slap the terrorist into consciousness, but the doctor intervened. Placing his stethoscope against the man's chest, the physician looked at the female agent. "That's not how it works, Lieutenant. He's fully under, and he won't come back for several hours."

As the tape ran to black, Captain Magda Reisner found herself amidst a pile of photographs, tactical maps and intelligence assessments that Aran had unfolded. Colin Blackford scooted his chair near Reisner and began to gaze at the information.

"I missed him by hours. Damn him. Damn our luck. Had I only moved earlier!"

Aran cut his subordinate short. "Another day, Magda; another day. So, where's our Quomuz now?"

"The Sudan," she pronounced confidently to her superior, pointing to a spot on one of the maps. "Quomuz is headed for the mountain caves there, hundreds of them. I can feel it. I know this to be true. Islamic militia, ties to the al Qaeda. Right here," she emphasized, pointing, "the western part of Darfur. God himself knows that place is hell on earth. If he has the chemicals and the means to use them now…"

"Then we haven't a moment to lose," Aran answered. Picking up a secure telephone line, he placed a call to Sir Harold MacHugh in London.

Reisner continued, explaining that Israeli intelligence had earlier confirmed that Quomuz had been spotted on the Hamburg docks. But then he seemed to have vanished, literally overnight, without a trace. She related that, on a hunch, all ship departures were checked with the Hamburg Harbor Master's office. Only one ship had departed on the day of Quomuz's disappearance, and that was bound for Beirut. The chances were very good that Quomuz had been smuggled aboard.

"American satellites tracked the SS *Aden Trader* around the clock until she docked in Latakia, Syria, three weeks ago," Magda advised. "Any questions so far?"

Colin couldn't resist asking, "Why didn't your government ask either an American or a British warship to board the freighter and search for Quomuz, based on the existing international arrest warrant?

"Good question, Major," Magda replied. "We discussed that scenario with our Diplomatic Corps, and they were opposed to it. It seems that the freighter is registered in Turkey, and we didn't want to risk irritating a country that is not openly hostile toward us. Besides, there are a million places for one man to hide aboard a ship that size."

Pausing only briefly, she pressed on, "Once it docked in Syria, our operatives watched it day and night. The Captain filed papers showing that the ship's destination was to be Port Sudan, on the Red Sea. It was unloaded in record time. It seems that dock workers were offered bonuses, in American dollars, in return for working overtime."

"Our Mister Quomuz, flush with al Qaeda

cash?" Colin opined.

"No doubt," Magda agreed. "Now here's the strange part. The ship was immediately reloaded with its waiting cargo, but at a slower than normal pace. Any thoughts as to why?"

"Exceedingly odd development, if you ask me," the Director chimed in. "Were they waiting for someone...or something?"

"Right, sir," Magda stated. "They took on several hundred crates marked 'oilfield equipment' and 'medical equipment,' plus hundreds of pallets marked 'agricultural chemicals.' Then the ship sat idle for more than two days, before quickly loading over a thousand steel drums marked 'lubricating oil.' Again, any thoughts?"

Colin couldn't resist speculating. "Here's what's odd," he began. "The Sudan actually has a respectable petroleum production infrastructure, including at least two refineries." Then he posited, "So why would they need to import a thousand drums of lubricating oil?" After only a moment's hesitation, he continued. "Likewise, they produce almost all the petrochemicals required for domestic agricultural fertilizers. Again, why the need to import any at all? Unless..."

Aran cut him off in mid-sentence. "Unless all the cargo was intentionally mislabeled, to allay any international suspicions?"

"Exactly! Our analysts concur," Magda answered. "One of our dockside operatives was able to swab a few of the drums with chemically sensitive detection paper. The swabs reacted positively for the presence of biochemical agents, as well as the precursors to manufacture more."

"Makes complete sense," Blackford reasoned. "I've got a wager that he's hiding anthrax, Soman, VX…what have you…in those caves. And what better camouflage! The Sudan has been a bloody awful mess for years; war, disease, famine. No one in the West really noticed, cared or had the political capital to invade. Quomuz has loads of good will there. And he was willing to take Mr. Hussein's weapons program, free of charge, of course. One can only imagine the consequences! Then, that's it!" Colin shouted. "The bloody goddamn WMD that my government and the Americans have been so feverishly seeking in Iraq…well, they weren't in Iraq."

"It appears that way, major," Magda confirmed. "We've lost the high ground."

Aran changed the subject. "On to other matters, and a word about the locals in Darfur. The Janjaweed. Islamic militia, psychotic killers, they are!" Aran said firmly. "Take a look at these pictures," turning his computer monitor toward the Briton. "These were taken by an American spy satellite, a day after a murderous assault." Blackford could see the tell-tale remnants of the battle, still smoldering when the photos where shot.

Aran continued. "Last month alone, more than four hundred of them, on horseback, and armed to the teeth, attacked the village of Donki Dereisa. Don't laugh about the horses, because the assault was supported by at least one fixed-wing aircraft and mechanized Sudanese infantry. The plane dropped several bombs on the village killing more than two hundred people, including a dozen children who were taken prisoner and burned alive later that day! A tribesman who tried to save them was himself beheaded and dismembered. And," Aran grimaced with irony, "of course, they steal all the cattle and goats. The countryside is littered with the remains of these devastated villages; hundreds of them!"

Blackford raised an eyebrow.

"Thus, Major, there will be no quarter given to, nor expected from, these madmen. They are brutal and have absolutely no regard for human life."

"I shall keep that uppermost in mind, Director!" Blackford responded.

"Well, my young friend," Aran said as he pushed back from his desk. "Enough of this business for the moment. I'm afraid this is where the good Captain Reisner leaves us," the Deputy Director related. "She has been promoted and tomorrow begins new duties. I am saddened to lose her."

Ironically, Colin had the same thought, but offered, "Congratulations, Major. You've earned your new position. Is there any chance of my buying you dinner tonight, to celebrate?"

"Why, Major Blackford," she replied coyly. "In Israel, there is always a chance!" With that, she spun and departed Aran's office.

Aran did not fail to notice the chemistry between the pair, but he had no time to dwell on the purely personal matters of his subordinates. He pumped Colin's hand vigorously and simply stated, "One of our men will meet you in Cairo and will provide final instructions that will include all your travel arrangements. Good luck, Major!" Colin could only muster a hearty "Thank you, sir," as he exited the Director's office suite.

Immediately after Major Blackford had departed his office, Aran pushed a button recessed on the top of his desk, and his computer monitor flashed to life. A moment later, the encrypted video "red line" connected to the face of a military officer, who, looking into the camera, answered with a crisp "Prime Minister's Office." Without hesitation, Aran stated, "Chaim Aran here. Is he available; it's highest priority?" Within ten seconds Chaim Aran was speaking face-to-face with the Israeli Prime Minister.

"I was anticipating your call, Aran. Do our British friends concur in our plan of action?" the Prime Minister asked.

"Yes, Prime Minister, the briefing went off flawlessly. Our British bloodhound has been given the scent and he's on the trail of Mister Quomuz. And as you directed, sir, Major Reisner has been dispatched."

"That sounds well and good, Director," the pensive Prime Minister replied. "But how do you plan to monitor one man on the ground in that God-forsaken wilderness?"

Aran drew a measured breath before continuing. "Prime Minister," he began slowly. "Perhaps you recall an appropriation bill the Knesset passed six years ago to support our emerging national minerals industries? The money is supposed to support mineral exploration initiatives in some of our remotest regions."

"Indeed, I do recall that bill," the Prime Minister responded. "It is one of our stated national goals to make Israel more self-sufficient in the areas of strategic metals such as copper, tin, iron and lead. But what on earth does this have to do with finding Quomuz?"

Aran drew two deep breaths before responding. "Sir, as you know, most of those funds were used to charter and capitalize "P.A.M.G.," the Pan-African Minerals Group, Limited. As you might recall, Prime Minister, P.A.M.G. was chartered in Nairobi, sir, under Kenyan law."

"Yes. I recall. The venture has shown some promise, has it not?"

Aran continued. "It has, sir. And the fact that P.A.M.G. Corporation has no direct link to our government has proven beneficial to this operation."

"Indeed?" the Prime Minister, smiling, bade Aran to continue.

Aran had anticipated his superior. "Prime Minister," he said, "We needed a secure location near Western Darfur from which to operate our new *Heron* drones. As you know, sir, the new *Heron*, IDF designation "Machatz-1," the latest unmanned aerial vehicles, or UAVs, can remain aloft for more than forty-eight hours with a maximum altitude of ninety to one hundred meters. She's controlled remotely by some highly experienced personnel, has an all-weather, high-gain video camera equipped with night vision capability, and can carry two *Hellfire* missiles."

Aran continued, "These are the same drones we just agreed to sell to India. The Americans weren't very happy about that, you know!

Yes, I know. I spoke with the President; he was hoping to sell them the *Predator*."

"Correct, sir," Aran replied, recalling that the Prime Minister had lobbied hard in support of the Israeli Air Industries recent sale of fifty *Heron* drones to India. "With your permission, sir." Aran went on. "Among our current mining concessions are operations in Chad, the Central African Republic, Nigeria, and Kenya. These four are ongoing diamond, copper and gold mining ventures. To be certain, the long-range economic implications are respectable. But, in the matter before us, we are going to exploit the tactical value of our presence in the region."

Aran continued: "At each mining site, we've built a two-kilometer compressed-earth airstrip to accommodate our Fokker F-50 supply aircraft. Two or three times daily, our engineers receive 'supplies' from the home office. Never have local authorities bothered to inspect these aircraft or their cargo."

"So far this all seems rather mundane, not

unlike operations at similar locations around the globe," opined the PM.

And that is precisely our point, sir," Aran continued. "To the locals, we look just like any other mineral prospectors, but, with one big difference. We own the night."

The Prime Minister smiled.

"Again, sir, things are not as they appear. At night, our teams of 'engineers' launch and recover their drones. At any given moment, around the clock, we have Herons aloft in twelve foreign countries. We are monitoring al Qaeda and Islamic Jihad and countless other malcontents, quite literally, in their own back yards. None of them has a clue as to what we're actually getting at."

"Very well, Aran. Do keep me posted on developments."

"Yes, sir; at a moment's notice."

3 February
0930 hours
Quomuz's Camp
Western Sudan

"Tariq," Quomuz ordered, "Fix the two 12.7 millimeter machine guns on each of the trucks. And place one on the cab of mine." Gesturing and pointing, Quomuz directed that the Chinese-built ZSU-23 anti-aircraft guns be placed atop a small ridge overlooking the camp. Once, there had been hundreds of similar weapons in the Taliban inventory, most of which were left over from the Russian occupation of Afghanistan. In the years before the Americans had routed the Taliban, a steady flow of armaments had wended their way on tramp steamers and lonely rail cars to these inhospitable mountains of western Sudan. Quomuz had more than a dozen in his camp at that very moment. Quomuz favored these three-barreled guns, because, on occasion, it allowed his forces to fight a more powerful enemy with overwhelming power. When deployed into groups of two or three, the armor-piercing bite of their phalanx effect was lethal, Quomuz knew. With a range of nearly four thousand meters, no infantry or light vehicle could survive long enough to mount an effective counter-attack. Hence, the carnage inflicted upon the non-Muslim forces in the south in the never-ending Sudanese civil war.

The teaching cadre at Abu Du'an had trained Quomuz's men and machine gun crews in assault tactics. He planned to have his fighters conduct a frontal assault on the U.N. airfield at Diri, backed up by no fewer than six ZSU-23 crews strategically deployed in a crossfire formation. He wasn't taking any chances. The destruction of the U.N. presence must be complete.

He planned to launch the assault at 1700 hours, just as the United Nations garrison prepared for its evening meal. "Westerners are so predictable," he reminded himself. "They plan their schedules to accommodate their stomachs." He recalled reading once that the Japanese had planned their attack on Pearl Harbor to coincide with the U.S. Navy's breakfast schedule.

But his thoughts were soon interrupted.

"Sheik Quomuz," Daoud screamed excitedly, "Mullah Akhund approaches. He has a great honor for you!" Daoud Nabilla, a twenty-six-year-old Egyptian, served as one of Quomuz's trusted aides.

Mullah Akhund was the revolutionary spiritual advisor at the Nyala mosque and a man known to Quomuz as a powerful leader of the faithful, especially the young men in the madras, who, like others before them, had been indoctrinated into fundamentalism and enlisted to join Quomuz's cause.

So well regarded was one by the other, that each man felt free to ask the other for special favors. Never had either one refused. So on this morning, Quomuz's curiosity was more than piqued when the white-robed mullah approached from the south. "This must be very important, for Akhund to leave the mosque and travel to my camp," Quomuz pondered. As Akhund came near, Quomuz could only anticipate that his friend had a special tasking for him.

The mullah's entourage approached on foot, along the main highway from Nyala. Mullah Akhund was in the lead, elegant in his finest celebratory attire. The other holy men followed in close succession, on either side of their leader, and a small crowd of about fifty faithful, many of whom carried canes and whips, succeeded them. In the midst of this throng, there was a diminutive figure, covered head to toe in a pale green burqa. At random intervals, Quomuz could hear various men in the group taunt this unfortunate soul with insults and strokes from their sticks.

Finally Mullah Akhund was close enough for Quomuz to hail, "Allah is great, for He brings my good friend Mullah Akhund to my humble command! As you can see, I prepare my men for battle. Our preparations are yet incomplete." The mullah smiled and loudly replied, "Quomuz, my faithful friend, let us talk this day only of Allah and His divine law; for I have a special request to ask of you in His name."

The two men withdrew from public view, and took tea in Quomuz's private tent near a French-built Gazelle helicopter. The mullah spoke first. "Quomuz, one of my faithful, Samiullah Nastif, has a wife who has dishonored him and Allah's holy word. Sharifa Nastif refuses to pray as required. She defiantly refuses to honor our tradition of *purdah*. She will not wear the burqa as Samiullah directs. She disobeys his every word," the aging cleric related. "As I have instructed, Samuillah has scourged his wife on each occasion, but it seems to do no good. Then, shame was visited upon his house when two days ago, he caught her in the act of adultery. The whore had adorned herself with the colors of a harlot on her face. Her lips were painted red and her eyes, the color of the night sky. The offending male escaped, and his face was unknown to Samiullah.

SEVENTH PSALM

Despite her husband's order and his many beatings, the wife will not reveal the name of her fellow adulterer."

Quomuz, imagining to himself the color of the woman's lips, admitted to the mullah that he was puzzled by this story. "Was this not a private matter to be settled as the husband decided, as was Samiullah's right, under the Sharia?" Quomuz asked the cleric.

But even the murderous Quomuz was taken slightly aback at the mullah's request. "Samuillah wishes to be rid of his wife for good. I have approached the Umma, seeking their guidance on this matter. They have unanimously approved a qasas. It is Allah's will that this harlot's throat be slit publicly." The mullah paused to sip the fine, strong tea his host had provided. Then he continued, "I ask that you honor me by performing the purification." Quomuz hesitated for only a moment before responding in the affirmative. "Bring her back to me in seventy-two hours. For on that day, in Allah's name, I will purify Nyala with the blood of this harlot."

As the mullah withdrew from the tent, he thanked Quomuz and walked quickly to the group of men to tell the aggrieved husband that Allah's justice would be certain.

Quomuz, however, turned and began to smile. Most of the prostitutes he had used in Amsterdam, Paris, and Hamburg had worn red lipstick; he preferred them that way. Although he swore his life to defending the faith of Islam and had fought alongside the most zealous of Taliban warriors, he was, nevertheless, especially thrilled by painted street-walkers as they plied their wicked trade. He justi-fied his patronage of prostitutes as a personal cru-sade to corrupt the Western kafir. And he had, on every occasion, rationalized his transgressions by telling himself that in debauching Western women, he was destroying the pillars beneath the insidious house of Satan.

The six ongoing murder investigations in Europe each involved a painted, dead prostitute with a grotesquely slit throat. None of the investiga-tors involved had any idea they sought the man named Quomuz.

4 February
1545 hours
West of Kulaykili
Southern Darfur Province, Sudan

The RAF *Hercules* lowered its gear over the drought-hardened lake bed that once had sustained life in these arid, high plains of the Darfur. The four Allison turboprops blew dirt and dead scrub branches into a small blizzard of choking dust. The men on the ground there to welcome the craft had to cover their faces against the blast of debris as the craft made its way to a landing on a makeshift air-strip where the men stood. A choking trail of dust rose from the ground as the aircraft touched down and coasted toward the runway's end. Despite the best efforts of the flight crew, the aircraft's rollout was jarring and bumpy, forcing Colin Blackford to grasp the sides of his webbed seat to keep his head from being tossed into the bulkhead of the large, drafty aircraft. The noisy aircraft slowed and began to turn and dust began to fill the cargo bay. A load-master began to lower the massive hydraulic tail ramp that would allow Blackford to quickly deplane with his transportation and gear. Blackford peered out the portholes of the C-130 and, through the whirling dust, saw a rank of men and several vehicles poised by the side of the makeshift runway.

Ten thousand pounds sterling, paid by the Foreign Office into William Deng's Swiss bank account, had assured the RAF's use of his private airstrip, as well as the protection of his mounted militia and a trusted guide. Deng would be among the men who had watched his landing, Blackford assured himself.

Quickly, the tan and brown camouflaged lifter rumbled to a creaking halt, and the Land Rover provided to Blackford for his mission strained hard against the several tie-down chains that restrained it in the Herc's cavernous belly. As the senior load-master finished lowering the aircraft's ramp, the enlisted crewmen released the restraining chains, and prepared the Rover for deplaning.

"End of the line, sir!" a young RAF airman shouted to Blackford over the din of the roaring engines. "End of the line and beginning of the hunt,"

Colin allowed himself silently, barely able to hear himself think, as he climbed into the Rover's cab. The Herc's pilots did not retard the engines any more than fifty percent, for their mission was complete and they dared not tarry on the ground any longer than was absolutely necessary.

"Thanks, mates," Colin barked to the crew, as he turned the ignition switch. The Rover's V-8 diesel roared to life and, dropping the shift into first gear and slowly releasing the clutch, Colin guided the rugged four-wheel-drive vehicle down the now fully-extended loading ramp. No sooner had the Rover cleared the aft end of the ramp, than the loadmaster began the retraction process. Blackford had barely cleared the ramp when the flight crew revved the engines to full power, and within a moment, the mighty plane completed a one-hundred-eighty-degree turn and immediately began its take-off roll. At full throttle, the crew adroitly lifted the *Herc's* nose gear, and then gently coaxed her main wheels from the dirt and rocks below. In a brief seventy seconds, the plane slipped free from the desert's grasp, and continued its climb out. Only three minutes later, it was a distant dot on the horizon.

Colin glanced toward the six militiamen to his left. Their apparent leader dismounted one of the trucks and slung an AK-47 over his left shoulder. The slender, dust-covered black man approached slowly. He finally opened the Rover's left-hand, passenger-side door, and took a seat. Unwrapping the tail of his turban from his face, the man spoke in surprisingly good English.

"Welcome to you, Major Blackford." The man spoke easily, with a broad smile. "I am Jonah Deng, son of William Deng of the Dinka people. We fight for the Sudan People's Liberation Army. My father has sent me to guide you through this territory. You are very welcome here."

Blackford had been briefed that Deng was a friend, a Christian, and that his "army" were mostly family and tribal members, veterans of the endless civil war that had torn Sudan for decades. In the Sudan, conflict had raged for years between north and south, Muslim and Christian, tribe and tribe. The dialects were many, the alliances too numerous; one simply never knew who was fighting whom in this Godforsaken land, Blackford knew. Although unwilling to lower his guard, the major was thankful for a friendly face in so inhospitable a land.

"It is too risky to travel the few roads we have," Deng advised. "I was told that you would go to Nyala, where the railroad ends, and then into the mountains. Is that still your mission, Major?"

"Indeed," Blackford answered, looking at Deng and then outside the Rover toward the tall men gathered about the trucks.

"Then we will drive toward the sun. We will proceed to the west by northwest to our camp. There will be food for you and a bed, such as we have."

Soon, the small procession of four vehicles advanced slowly over the hardpan, rocks and dry creek beds in the general direction of Nyala, one of the few outposts of civilization in south Darfur province. Blackford and Deng took the lead in the Rover, with Deng's men trailing behind in their makeshift assault vehicles: utility trucks with .50 caliber machine guns bolted to the floorboards of the cargo beds. After an hour of travel, the sun had nearly set, and Deng pointed to the lights of a small encampment near Marqubah, about two kilometers distant. "It will be good to get some food, eh?" Deng mused in Blackford's direction. "That is our home for the night. You are welcome to share it."

The camp was temporary refuge to about fifty militiamen, their women and children, and a smattering of livestock. The few cattle left to them were both a means of survival and the measure of the tribe's wealth and position. So revered were the animals, that Dinka men even took the names of their favorite animals as their own.

The headlights of Blackford's vehicle soon revealed tents of all colors and sizes in a half-circle cluster. A dozen fires of varying intensity illuminated the darkness. And as Blackford jumped down from the cab of his vehicle, he tried to pat the dust away from his desert camouflage uniform. He noticed the smell of food and cooking fires and odors from the tents and fires nearby. Regardless of its origin, a tired Blackford reasoned, any food would sit well with him now. He'd come a long way in the past two days and there would be many more tough miles ahead before he would rest easily again.

Blackford looked around and surveyed the scattered evening fires, where women and their daughters cooked a traditional evening meal of naan bread and rice mixed with mutton. He watched as a goatherd's wife busied herself nearby with her evening ritual, much as her mother and her ancestors had done for several hundred years before her. It mattered little to the withered, frail woman tending the fire that whirling clouds of dust fell like a scab upon the family's food, gurgling in the hot oil at the bottom of her ancient, blackened kettle. Blackford nearly lost his appetite for a hot meal, and instead turned and walked into the large brown tent that Deng and his men had provided near the center of the encampment. Blackford stowed his gear near a cot, then straightened himself and arched his back and felt his bones stretch and pop, as he tried to shake off the events of the past few days.

Deng and his men invited the British soldier to sit with them and share their supper, a traditional meal of a simple broth made from goat's meat and naan bread, covered in sticky sorghum. Blackford was careful to drink only the water he had packed in the back of the Rover. "No need fighting two enemies on this trip," Blackford reasoned to himself. The men spoke very few words to one another as they quickly devoured the meager offerings their cook fires had provided.

With his hunger at least temporarily assuaged, Blackford lay back against his rucksack and closed his eyes. He reflected on the last forty-eight hours, as well as the forty-eight yet to come. First, the RAF flight to Cairo, then a dusty ride in an embassy staff car to an old expeditionary air base. Then, after less than a full night on a cot in a tent, he'd begun the final leg of the journey aboard the noisy, yet rugged, Royal Air Force Hercules.

"So you've come to kill Muslims?" Deng asked, lightly punching the British officer on the arm.

Blackford opened his eyes and looked at Deng for a moment before answering.

"Well, not so much Muslims as one man. His name is Mustafa Quomuz."

Deng's quick reaction told Blackford all he needed to know.

"So, you've heard of Quomuz."

"I have. And if you do not kill this man first, Major, then I will!" Deng answered, his gaze now fully fixed on the Briton.

Blackford took a sip from a water bottle as the twenty-five-year-old Deng continued.

"He is a brutal killer, this Quomuz," Jonah Deng said. "He has been a friend to our enemies for years. And he kills not so much for his faith as he does for his own pleasure, I believe. He has friends in the north, many people in power, particularly the Umma Party. He is a hero to many there and his comings and goings are celebrated. It will not be hard to find him if he is here…."

"So you know his movements, his whereabouts?" Blackford asked.

"Generally, yes. I have cousins, many cousins,

who will get word to us."

"But if you know where Quomuz is, why haven't you killed him as you desire?"

"Ah, finding him is not the problem, Major. Killing him is. He is surrounded, day and night, by men loyal to him. The Janjaweed, an Islamic militia, are his faithful brothers. We do not have the weapons to kill him from a long distance. A rifle is not enough. You must either get close to him or you must kill him from a long distance. I can do neither, Major Blackford. Perhaps you can."

Blackford considered his guide's words carefully, as he let them sink in. Blackford sensed an opening, so he broached a subject he knew he had to handle with care.

"And what can you tell me of his other weapons?" Blackford paused, "Chemical weapons. Do you know about these?"

Deng smiled broadly, his wide smile flashed against the dim light of the tent. "Ah, the great 'secret' weapons! They are not such a secret here, Major Blackford! Our enemies have them and they have used them!" Deng paused. "But you look surprised!" Deng observed.

"Indeed I am. Please…continue, Mister Deng," Blackford asked, leaning forward.

"Our enemies in the north started buying them from the Ba'athists in Iraq nearly ten years ago. They arrive by ship in Port Sudan. But, of course, we do not control those regions. What I know is only from what our friends in the Beja Congress in the east have told us. We know that Quomuz, bin Laden and his Jihadists put the chemicals on rail cars and transport them far to West Darfur, in the Marrah Mountains. The trains are heavily guarded by the Islamic militias and the caves and valleys there make a very good hiding place."

"By God, man…you do seem very knowledgeable about all of this. Why do you seem to know so much while my government, the Americans, even the French, know so little?" Blackford demanded, sitting upright.

Deng smiled, thoughtfully, and continued. "I may not be a formally-educated man, Major, but my father taught me to read! I read many things. I have read enough to know that your government, the Americans, the rest of the world, cares very little about the Sudan. Since my father's birth, more than fifty years ago, my country has been at war almost every day. We have suffered drought, pestilence, and death. More than two million of my people have died and another five million are exiles in their own country. And only in the past few years has the world taken notice."

Deng's voice began to trail off.

"Go on," an eager Blackford urged.

"Yes, Quomuz and his men have the weapons. But they don't have the means to use them effectively. He has used them in mortar rounds and a few light artillery shells. But we also know that the chemicals have killed many of his fighters, because they do not have the protection, or the means to safely deliver the weapons in large quantities. I was told those five years ago, one barrel of the anthrax opened on board a train, somewhere in the Nuba Mountains. Maybe as many as one hundred people died, but no one knows. They just burned the bodies where they lay by the tracks. To you in the West, what difference would another dead Sudanese make?"

"Look, Deng, I haven neither the time nor the interest for politics," Blackford insisted. "I cannot answer for what my government has done...or failed to do."

"I'm not blaming you, Major. My country is a wasteland, the bodies of my people are countless, and the destruction of our villages in the south is nearly complete. Quomuz and the government in Khartoum have used the gases and the chemicals and he has killed our people. It is as simple as that. So if you are here to hunt this jackal, Quomuz, then I welcome you as a brother."

Blackford looked hard at the man as the fuel-oil lamp began to burn low. There was little else to say this night.

5 February
0600 hours
Northeast of Nyala
Darfur Province

The early morning sun illuminated the east face of the terrorist's camp with an azure hue. The sunlight glinted off the Plexiglas canopy of Quomuz's helicopter, two hundred meters from the operations tent. A dozen barrels of fuel, his total available supply, were stored nearby. The Janjaweed had promised several truckloads of fuel by week's end.

A munitions tent, some three hundred meters further west, housed the few remaining missiles, rockets, and artillery shells in his arsenal. The remaining chemical artillery and mortar shells were safely stored in the caves above. On the personal orders of Quomuz, the Red Crescent banner was prominently displayed atop the munitions and communications tents. Under international law, hospital tents, vehicles, and buildings properly marked with the Red Cross or Red Crescent were deemed "protected places" and were immune from enemy attack. As Quomuz had boasted to his men on many occasions, "The Western military powers have a fundamental weakness; they revere the law too much for their own good." Competing militias had siphoned off most of the stockpiled weapons from the caves during the civil war that had wracked Sudan for the last thirty-five years.

Seven Russian-built trucks were parked haphazardly along the gravel road leading from the hills toward Mazar-e Sharif to the west. Two barely roadworthy vehicles sat near the helicopter pad and a pair of motorcycles leaned against an earthen berm.

Diesel fuel, too, was a precious commodity; only about five hundred liters remained immediately available. However, another three thousand liters was cached in nearby caves, a few kilometers distant. The fuel tanks on the trucks were intentionally kept nearly empty. Quomuz did not want any of his fighters to consider fleeing if the tactical situation became too difficult.

Quomuz trusted no one, not even his al Qaeda protectors. And Quomuz was a man not reluctant to bite the hand that fed him. He'd notified his fighters that he would not order the assault on the U.N. Center at Diri until he had the right number of fighters at his immediate disposal. They were told that the necessary forces would be ready in another forty-eight hours.

"Time is on my side; praise be to Allah," the terrorist mused, as he sat back and enjoyed his morning tea.

Less than three hundred kilometers distant, Blackford rose early, just as the sun had begun its daily journey. He hadn't slept for more than a few minutes the night before. The flight had been a long one; security dictated that the Hercules fly south down the Red Sea, then south by southwest over Ethiopia and Kenya, then finally northwest over friendly southern Darfur. His present environs and the mission before him had likewise conspired to deny him sleep. "No matter," he thought, adjusting his field cap, as he walked outside the tent and into the Sudanese morning. His nostrils were immediately filled with the foul odor of raw human sewage pooled in the nearby ravine. Blackford winced at the odor, which, combined with an empty stomach, almost made him queasy. "Perhaps some water," Blackford said aloud to himself, reaching for his canteen.

As he drank, he made a slow, full circle to survey the situation. To the east, several hundred kilometers distant, lay the Nuba Mountains and the Kordofan Plateau, with its markets located in the ancient trading center of Malakal, which stood near the White Nile and its life sustaining waters. To the northeast, Blackford remembered, were the trade routes of the Nubian Valley, leading into southern Egypt. The Muslims and Arabs who controlled that valley held the jugular of Darfur's commerce with the north. Directly to the west lay the Marrah Mountains and his adversary, Mustafa Quomuz.

As he looked hard into the distant mountains, Blackford reminded himself why Quomuz had selected this region to cache Saddam Hussein's stores of anthrax and nerve gas, and the equipment to manufacture even more, if necessary. Hundreds of unmarked caves dotted the landscape. Quomuz could easily operate in these environs indefinitely, far from the prying eyes of satellites and reconnaissance aircraft. "Clever fellow, Quomuz. This isn't going to be easy," Blackford reminded himself. "Not one bit."

SEVENTH PSALM

5 February
1935 hours
P.A.M.G. Mining Corporation
Site #2
30 Kilometers North of Birao
Central African Republic

The dry mountain winds swept in from the peaks to the west, carrying dust and heated air, but precious little moisture. "A pleasant evening rain would be quite welcome right about now," Magda thought to herself. She glanced out the P.A.M.G. trailer window, as she pointed her night vision goggles skyward. Thankfully, she reasoned, the slim quarter moon offered little illumination that would cause the Heron drone to be silhouetted against the night sky. The drone was due back within the half-hour.

Reisner took another sip of the strong coffee that was grown locally, and which provided significant income to the nation's small farmers.

At the other end of the trailer, her teammate gazed at the video display before him. The controls in his hands resembled a video game so common to teens the world over. While the young lieutenant switched camera views in the nose of the thirty-foot-long craft, the onboard GPS sensors navigated the Machatz back to the safety of the "mining site," near Birao. Outside the trailer, three of Reisner's men patrolled with stealth, vigilant to any intrusion. The government of the Central African Republic had granted a six-year concession to P.A.M.G. for the purpose of developing a copper mining and processing operation in this poverty-stricken region. The government had enough trouble dealing with a stagnant economy and radical political opposition without the taint of an Israeli covert operation on its soil. Hence, certain Ministers in the C.A.R. government would be loathe to learn that the Shabak was using the site as a counter-terror command post.

Within the last week, however, P.A.M.G. engineers had straightened, lengthened and paved the gravel road. A few thousand euros had assured that the District Commissioner's signature properly appeared on the construction permit in record time.

Almost immediately thereafter, twin-engine Saab 340 cargo aircraft began arriving daily to offload new seismic measuring equipment and computers. Large wooden crates marked "engineering equipment" were unloaded and opened, and their contents were carefully tucked away in the maintenance sheds. A casual observer would be none the wiser for it.

But to the embedded team of Israeli technicians, the Birao site was now a fully operational tactical air base. The three Machatz-1 drones secreted nearby had all been assembled and test flown shortly after uncrating, and the ground crew settled into the nightly cycle of launching, flying, recovering and maintaining the unmanned aircraft. Technicians captured real-time images from the drone's cameras, and then forwarded the video, via satellite uplink, to the Intelligence Directorate in Jerusalem. At any given moment, the Birao "engineering trailer" served as command post to two airborne Machatz, while another was on standby, and a fourth was undergoing maintenance.

The requirement for secrecy necessitated that launch and recovery occur only at night. Hence, Major Magda Reisner and her team slept by day and worked by night.

6 February
0900 hours
Northeast of Nyala, Southern Darfur Province
Sudan

Quomuz fixed his white and gold ceremonial headdress snugly. It had been presented to him years earlier by Sheik Fathi al Biliwar of the al Qaeda movement in Kabul, as a reward for an especially difficult assassination mission. Quomuz prized the headdress above all of his worldly goods and wore it only on very special occasions.

Today's holy duties presented such a worthy opportunity.

As he approached the bound and kneeling woman before him, he held the sharpened dagger in his left hand. The woman's hair was pulled back behind her head and tied with a short length of white ribbon. Her face was plain and unadorned by makeup. As he gazed down at the sobbing, helpless figure before him, the terrorist commander's eyes met the mullah's for a moment.

"Damn! Why was this harlot not blindfolded?" Quomuz screamed. His lieutenant, Daoud Nabilla, sprang from the crowd of men and produced a swath of soiled cotton wrap. He quickly fashioned a make-shift blindfold, before scurrying back to the group of faithful.

The terrorist commander ordered most of his fighters to assemble to witness the *qasas*. This would be a useful object lesson for all concerned and his public stature would be enhanced by performing the grotesque but holy task. The men would see the swift, certain beauty of Islamic justice and each male witness would more clearly understand his individual authority as husband and master of his household. The few women present would be reminded of their centuries-old obedience and subservience. Not one would likely question her husband's authority in the future.

"Allahu Akbar!" Quomuz began. "This woman has defiled her marriage, and in so doing, has dishonored Allah. She has dishonored her husband and your people as well!" He paused to scan the crowd and was elated to notice a sea of smiling faces nodding approval of his words. Quomuz drew a deep breath before continuing. "Today, this harlot must pay with her life for her sins against the Koran. Her husband demands this, and the law permits this. Mullah Akhund has ordered it so." With that, Quomuz cast a glance toward the woman's husband, Samuillah Nastif. Their eyes locked for several long seconds and the husband's eyes were transfixed on Quomuz. The executioner smiled as Samuillah nodded ever so slightly, affirming his choice that his wife's life be forfeited for her wickedness.

Quomuz raised his left hand toward the heavens.

Then, in a sudden flashing arc, Quomuz's blade swept across the woman's neck and deeply into her throat. Her windpipe and carotid artery were severed in an instant, sending a wild spurt of crimson blood onto Quomuz's robe, hands, and forearm. The woman made no scream, but the gaping slash continued gurgling a hideous mixture of air and frothing red foam, as her life-blood oozed away from her nearly lifeless form. A few sickening moments later, her lungs involuntarily gasped a final breath, her heart collapsed, and the cold grip of death claimed her.

Quomuz stepped back, held his bloodied dagger toward heaven, and cried, "Allah's will has been done this day!" The crowd cheered its approval with wild enthusiasm. Several elders approached Samiullah, the husband, to offer congratulations. Others crept near the slain woman's body to gaze at the result of Allah's just punishment. Husbands of the few women present pushed their wives and daughters forward as a reminder of a husband's divine authority. The women, careful to hide their tears, lowered their eyes to the woman where she laid, her blood seeping into the sands below her.

Mullah Akhund approached Quomuz quickly and embraced his charge. "My son, you have pleased Allah this day and earned forgiveness for what few sins you may have committed," the cleric opined loudly. Quomuz reached down to wipe the bloody dagger clean on the dead woman's sleeve. He turned and, calling to Nabilla to gather his commanders, walked back to his tent.

6 February
1400 hours
West of Kulaykili, Darfur Province
Sudan

"How far from here to Nyala, Deng?" Blackford queried.

"Not more than fifty kilometers."

"Right, then," Blackford said to Deng. "We're off. The Rover still shows nearly full after the sixty or so kilometers we traveled last night. It should be enough to get us there and back. Regarding your vehicles; do have you enough petrol?"

"Your government's generosity has helped us secure the fuel... We stole it from a Janjaweed encampment. But fuel is precious. We have very few vehicles."

In addition to Blackford and Deng, there were twenty fighters, most of them were Deng's kinsmen, plus there were several from other regions in the south. Most were dark-skinned African men, but three had lighter skin, and fortunately, were fluent in Arabic. They had been helpful in translating communications intercepted from the allies of the hated Khartoum government.

The sun had been up for three-quarters of the day as the small caravan slowly wended its way across the hard-baked desert floor. Occasional stands of palms and scrub bushes dotted an otherwise bleak and barren landscape. Deng was careful to keep the vehicles far from any regularly traveled roads, lest they be spotted by forces aligned with Quomuz.

The drive was slow and monotonous, Deng taking care to keep the Rover's speed slow enough to minimize the inevitable dust trail that would be a giveaway to any unwanted onlookers.

"And how will you get word on Mister Quomuz's whereabouts, Deng?" Blackford inquired.

"I have arranged to meet a contact near Umm Sarir. A faithful cousin; he and his wife's kinsmen have been in Nyala and can report our man's movements if he has been there recently."

**7 February
0200 hours
P.A.M.G. Mining Corporation
Site #2
30 Kilometers North of Birao
Central African Republic**

"Got 'em, ma'am," the young lieutenant called to Magda Reisner, as he readjusted the focus on the infrared nose-camera of Drone #3. "Looks like they're on the move. Three trucks, maybe twenty men. Is our British officer among them?"

Reisner didn't answer, but smiled to herself, knowing Blackford was wholly unaware of the UAV's circling presence in the darkness above. "Smile at the birdie, Colin," she mused.

7 February
0600 hours
Southeast of Nyala, Darfur Province
Sudan

In the waning darkness, the drone above maintained a distance and altitude sufficient to prevent its accidental discovery. Below, Major Blackford fumbled with the map and swatted away the flies that had flown in through the dust-covered, half-opened window. A long pull of water from his canteen cut the dust from his throat. "Flies and dust, even before first light," the major thought. "What a dismal environment!"

"Near Umm Qullah," Deng said, pointing to the map. "It is mountainous country with many caves. He can hide and fight in there for a very long time. It will be very difficult to find him there."

"So, I make Umm Qullah about thirty kilometers from here, and he is near there, eh?" Blackford pondered the topographical map. "The terrain suits us. If he can hide, so can we. But we shan't be able to traverse those elevations in these," Blackford said, slapping his hand on the dust-covered dash. "Deng, can you find us a place to stash these vehicles about ten kilometers from Quomuz's camp?"

"I will certainly try," Deng smiled. "At the very least, my men can drive them to safety after we have arrived at the point you decide."

"And these men of yours. Can they fight if need be?"

"My men are loyal and they hate the Janjaweed. Every man with us has suffered some loss at the hands of the Islamic militias."

"That's all well and good, but this is NOT a reprisal raid. We are NOT going to attack Quomuz's encampment or provoke an engagement. First of all, we haven't enough men and equipment. Second, we shan't want to diminish our chances of killing Quomuz. That's why we're here; just for Quomuz."

"I fully understand, Major," Deng smiled. "Just know that these men are not afraid to fight and die, if that was what you were asking. And, your rifle, it is powerful enough to hit this man from a distance?"

Blackford grinned proudly. "This is the latest British weapon, the L-115A in .338 caliber; effective even at twelve hundred meters."

"Had only we armed ourselves with such weapons," Deng shook his head. "Perhaps the odds might have been more even when the militias attacked us."

The barren brown foothills of the Marrah range soon crept into view and Blackford eyed the terrain carefully, looking for any telltale information the terrain might yield.

As Deng surveyed the map, Blackford opined, "I rather suspect we shall want to approach him from the southwest, through the higher country. We shall have to keep low to the ground and invisible. Our foot travel must be at night, and we'll want to find high cover near his camp to give us a chance to survey him without being noticed."

"Turn back to the east, Major, and across that small stream. We must avoid Nyala; there are too many prying eyes there. That is where the train ends and that is where Quomuz has many friends."

Blackford glanced at his watch. It was nearly 0630, and the rocky terrain bounced the slow-moving vehicles as if they were toys upon a storm-tossed sea.

"My men are farmers and herders. These trucks are not usual for them. Were it not for the war, these men might never have ridden in a truck. We were herdsmen and proud to live as we always have. It was the men from the north that brought these mechanized weapons to our world."

After another two hours of bone-jarring travel, the rugged foothills rose before them, and the team made its way to a small boulder-strewn canyon. "Here is where we must leave the trucks. We are not more than ten kilometers from Quomuz's camp. As you say, Major Blackford, we must now travel on foot from here. We have seen no people for several kilometers. The trucks should be safe here for the night. I will post two of my men here. They will protect the vehicles."

Blackford surveyed Deng's men, attired in an odd assortment of desert robes, discarded camouflage jackets and pants, and old leather boots. Blackford could not distract himself with their appearance. His only concern was: could they, would they…fight?

"And have them cover as much of the trucks as they can with that brush over there. Throw dirt on the windscreens. Anything to prevent a reflection from the sun."

As Deng's men unloaded their weapons and personal effects, two others began the task of covering the vehicles as Blackford had directed.

"We're off then," Blackford soon commanded. Then he, Deng and sixteen of Deng's men began the trek upward into the rocky terrain. "We'll make for that field of boulders about two kilometers up the mountainside," Blackford directed. "We'll stay in the rocks and ravines. I don't want us to be seen. We're close enough to Quomuz's camp that he'll have patrols out looking for trouble."

"Ah, then we'll use those rocks for cover until darkness!" Deng said, anticipating Blackford's tactical plan.

"Right-o. We'll traverse this open area and up the hillside in teams of two. Tell your men to keep low and keep quiet. Quick's the word from here on out. Find the larger rocks and hide down behind them. Right, off with you!"

7 February
1220 hours
Near Nyala, Southern Darfur Province
Sudan

At about the same time, Quomuz called out to the devout Muslim warriors in the camp, "We muster our forces here to seize the United Nations food depot at Diri. There are hundreds of tons of fuel, food and medicine destined for the infidels."

"Let them starve!" one of Quomuz's captains muttered.

If taken, Quomuz explained, the seizure of the U.N. depot would serve two purposes. First, as a psychological ploy, Quomuz and his mercenaries would have defeated the well-equipped U.N. forces and taken the much-needed supplies of fuel and food. Second, an unmistakable message would be sent to the Western world: Stay away from Muslim nations. And, Quomuz assured himself, his personal stature as a great sheik would only grow among the faithful.

7 February
1300 hours
Near Kulaykili, Southern Darfur Province
Sudan

The brutal rays of the mid-day sun baked the weathered crags and peaks around them, and Blackford reached into his rucksack for another canteen.

After slaking his thirst, the major peered out from his crouching position behind the boulder that provided cover for Deng, another man, and himself. Blackford began a slow scan of the ridge line above him.

"No unfriendlies," he muttered to no one in particular as he slowly surveyed the barren rocks beyond. "Not a hint of movement, perhaps luck is with us. Let's have a go. Much ground to cover before sunset."

With a few quick words to his men, Deng arranged his followers in a single-file rank, each man trailing at a ten-pace interval behind the other. Deng and Blackford took in the lead.

"And pass the word, Deng. Not a sound from here on out."

"Never worry, friend. We may dress as herdsmen, but my men are fighters!" Deng's eyes shone from the darkness.

The platoon of men quietly made their way along a ridge line, working north by northeast, slowly and carefully in an effort to avoid detection.

After a silent hour over boulders, ravines and scrub vegetation, Blackford called a halt. His ears perked at the familiar noise of men in camp.

"Jonah, you and the men stay here. I'll go ahead, over that rise. I want to take a look."

As Deng's men crouched in the darkness, Colin Blackford fell to his belly and began a fifty-meter crawl to the top of a rock-strewn ridge line. With his Glock pistol in one hand, his binoculars secured to his back, his gloved hands and booted feet worked their way, crab-like, over jagged rocks; he was soon atop the hill.

Unstrapping his binoculars, Blackford took aim at the center of the camp. "Bull's eye!" he muttered. "Spot on where Deng's man said it was. Visibility couldn't be more perfect. There is ample daylight and the sun is to my back. Perhaps we've some luck on our side!"

Calming his nerves, Blackford began a measured assessment of the enemy encampment.

"Right then, I'm about two kilometers from him," Blackford spoke silently to himself. "He's camped at the base of a small horseshoe canyon. Stream running right down the middle. Two roads in and out to the south. Looks like fifty, maybe sixty, tents and a few very small buildings. Several trucks, one helicopter. No established sentry posts that I can see...."

As Blackford made careful mental notes of the crates, fuel drums, boxes and vehicles, he saw two or three muzzle flashes, and then heard the gunfire echo against the canyon walls and up to the stars.

"Bunch of louts!" Blackford muttered. "No military discipline whatsoever. Perhaps that will come in useful soon."

After nearly half an hour of mentally mapping the Quomuz camp, Blackford turned his attention to the slopes above. Dim lights flickered from the entrances to more than a dozen caves. "Bloody hell," Blackford swore. "That's where he's got the chemicals! Small wonder aerial recon can't find them! He's got them deep inside the rocks. We shall have to keep clear of that nasty stuff."

He then turned his vision to the terrain immediately below him. "There's a good spot, only three hundred meters down the slope." Not far below Blackford's vantage on the ridge line was a small plateau, covered with high boulders, and sheltering a small ravine against the mountainside. "That will do VERY nicely!"

Satisfied with the tactical layout, Blackford rolled over onto his back and snapped the cover over the lenses of the government-issue binoculars. Taking a last look around in the hot afternoon sun he began to slither his way back across the hill to Deng and his compatriots.

Blackford whispered aloud. "Deng, leave four of your best men on this side of the ridge, spread them out twenty-five meters apart and tell them to find cover. They're our backside protection. You bring the others and come with me."

Deng quickly disappeared into the rocks and whispered Blackford's instructions to his men.

As soon as the four sentries were posted, the remainder belly-crawled, silently, atop the ridge and began the slow, careful descent through the searing heat toward the plateau that Blackford had identified.

A hard hour later, Deng's men had joined Blackford behind a stand of boulders atop the plateau, halfway down the mountainside and only two kilometers from Quomuz.

Blackford, now nearly breathless from the downhill crawl, patted Deng's shoulders. "Well done! Not bad for a lot of cattle herders!"

Deng smiled in return. "We have had to become good fighters, I'm afraid," the tribesman whispered carefully. "I've sent two sentries in each direction to protect us here. There are good hiding places on either side. They will be able to warn us if trouble comes."

"Ah! Then tell the others to hide in the ravine and to eat and drink silently. In an hour we shall be very busy indeed."

The intense rays of orange sunlight scorched the western horizon over the plains of Kordofan. Activity in the Quomuz camp had begun to abate, as the day's tasks were nearing completion. Tomorrow would also be busy, in preparation for the sheik's planned assault on the U.N center at Diri.

"Everyone alert now!" Blackford whispered to Deng and his men.

Deng, translating the Briton's words, directed the squad to disperse in a picket line behind the rocks that shielded their position on the plateau from below.

"No one fires unless I give the command," Deng ordered in his native tongue. "The Englishman is here to take out their leader. We are NOT here to engage in a firefight. They are too many. He must make his kill and then we escape!"

As Deng finished placing his men in strategic positions, Blackford uncased his new sniper rifle and began to assemble it slowly and carefully, taking great care to ensure no grains of sand fouled the threads on either the barrel or on the ungainly silencer.

Two hawks circled overhead and a hot breeze blew down from the mountainside as Blackford secured the handgrip and stock.

"Right then, one in the chamber and five more in the mag," Blackford smiled. "I ought to be docked a month's salary if I need more than one." Blackford reasoned he'd likely get off no more than two shots. Even though the shots would be silenced, a miss would surely alert Quomuz, who, in turn, would mobilize his fighters to retaliate in every direction.

"This won't be pretty, regardless of outcome," Blackford knew. "For even if I take Quomuz out, surely his lieutenants will seek immediate revenge. And only God himself knows what will happen if I only wing him."

Giving the special sniper rifle one more thorough examination, Blackford rolled over on his belly and crawled out from behind the boulder that had shielded him from view. Taking great care not to raise any telltale dust, he writhed his way another ten meters behind some smaller boulders which afforded him an open view and a clear field of fire.

"Damn!" Blackford swore as he sighted the heavy gun toward Quomuz's camp. "I've misjudged the range. I'm at least eight hundred meters too far out. Damn! I misread the distance in the viewfinder."

Although the sun still sat high enough to provide adequate light, in another hour or two the shadows would soon overtake the canyon, and Blackford with it. There was no time to lose, Blackford knew.

"Deng, you and another man, you'll need to come with me," Blackford sang out low to his compatriot. "We've got to get in that small gully. You see it. Just below that stand of small trees."

This was a risky move and not one Blackford had counted on. Although the half mile between the plateau and the gully afforded a man ample cover, the risk of detection was great. It only took one accidental pair of eyes from the camp below for the game to be over!

"Damn my foolishness!" Blackford swore as he took off on a low trot, carefully wending his way from boulder to gully to brush, taking great care to step with his jump boots on flat surfaces only, thereby avoiding a rock or crevice that would send him spilling noisily to the ground.

It seemed an eternity for Blackford, Deng and the third man to reach the relative safety of the gully he had spied from the plateau. But, upon arriving face-first in the dirt of the small ravine, and after assuring himself that they had not been seen, Blackford rose up slightly to eye the camp and his potential target.

"This is a merry chase you're leading us on, Englishman!" Deng poked at Blackford.

"I'm a goddamn sod!" Blackford swore in a whisper, and returning to his surveillance, he was grateful that he'd seen no suspicious movement in the Quomuz camp, now only six hundred yards distant.

Deng quickly positioned himself behind a small pile of rocks, and the third man found a dug-out section of earth behind the two. Time now to sit, wait, and hope for a clean shot, Blackford considered, drawing a deep breath and hoping his heart would slow to a manageable pace. After a five-hour wait, Blackford mused that he had beaten the sun, but just barely. As he positioned himself within a rocky crevice, Blackford saw the bright yellow disk break the horizon and the first pink rays of the early evening sun fall silently on the hard sands of Darfur.

Mustafa Quomuz had work to do. Much preparation was needed before his cadre would be ready for the assault on the U.N. compound at Diri, some eighty kilometers to the west.

"Dauod!" Quomuz yelled through the flaps of his tent. "Ensure that Ahmet and his brother bring the ammunition down from the caves. And make sure there's enough for the .50 caliber big guns."

Quomuz's orders quickly brought the camp to life, and Blackford could hear the shouts of men in the near distance. Sounds carried well and reverberated off of the surrounding canyon walls. It sounded to Deng as if Quomuz and his men were much closer than their eyesight actually revealed.

As a trio of men scurried out of their tent and up the mountainside, Deng noticed another pair of men walk out from one of the many caves that dotted the mountainside about Quomuz's camp. "There, there!" Deng called quietly to Blackford. "He keeps his munitions and the chemicals in those caves. Hundreds of them…"

Shortly after the first three-man group ran up the mountainside, another squad of four men, leading horses, made their way up toward the caves.

"A busy lot!" Blackford thought to himself. "What they lack in military organization they make up for in enthusiasm."

"Now, you bastard, where have you buggered off to? Perhaps in one of those caves or away having a lovely shit. Just show your face, you bastard. Just show me your face!"

Blackford didn't have long to wait.

No sooner had Blackford made his wish than it was granted. For as he peered through the powerful range-finding scope affixed to the top of his rifle, Blackford soon spied the slender man who was his quarry.

"Quomuz! Damn you! Is it you?" Blackford swore, recalling vividly his review of the dossier in Aran's office.

As he sighted the man he believed to be Quomuz, Blackford tried to recall every detail of the photographs he'd seen during the briefings. Director Aran had shown him photographs of a man with only a moustache. The man in his gun sight was clean shaven.

"Wait. Wait. Wait until you're damned sure!"

Blackford admonished himself.

But as the solitary man turned his face toward the mountainside, a seemingly endless stream of other men approached him and then ran off to other tasks.

"He's giving the orders down there, it must be him."

Blackford took the measure of the man he now knew to be Quomuz, but swung his rifle around the camp in an effort to sight any other who might be the real terrorist leader.

"No. It's him. The way he carries himself, the way he gives orders, and the way his men react to him. Now, if only I can manage a clean shot...."

Blackford dug his elbows into the dirt and snuggled the shoulder stock hard under his chin. "Breathe, boy...breathe," Blackford steadied himself. "Now, if that lot of men will just stand clear, we can be done with this mess..."

Suddenly, Quomuz stepped into the clear, and Blackford steadied the rifle. He peered carefully thought the scope and centered the cross hairs on Quomuz's chest. All right you bastard, hold steady....."

Two deafening blasts and flashes of yellow light exploded in the center of Quomuz's compound, frightening the wits out of Blackford and Deng.

"What the bloody fucking hell?" Blackford swore openly, as Quomuz dove behind a truck in the distance.

A pair of Israeli drones soared overhead and

took aim, yet again, on Quomuz's camp, now filled with the screams of men and gunfire and the roar of engines.

Blackford glanced up to see the pair of *Heron* unmanned aerial vehicles.

Shocked, Blackford could barely collect his wits about him, as the drones launched a second volley into the terrorist camp.

Brilliant explosions of red and orange rocked the canyon as open stores of munitions began to ignite and drums of gasoline and diesel fuel ruptured and exploded. The explosive sound waves reverberated back and forth and back again into the canyon, shattering the eardrums of anyone within a thousand-meter radius.

Blackford looked quickly at Deng, who returned a look of stark confusion and fear as the Quomuz camp was enveloped in a choking black cloud of burning petroleum.

"That's not our mission, Deng. We've got to get the hell out of here, back to your men..."

But before he could rise and turn, Ja'afer al Hashim struck.

The man who had shared the small ravine with Blackford and Deng quickly pulled a handgun from beneath his robes, leveled the barrel at Blackford's skull, and fired. No sooner had Blackford dropped than did the traitor Ja'afer aim at Jonah Deng's back and fire twice into the tribesman.

A searing bolt of pain flashed down Blackford's spinal cord, dropping the young British officer to the hard ground on the footpath between two larger boulders. His breath rushed from his lungs as the light disappeared from his eyes. The traitor Ja'afer quickly returned his pistol to his waistband, and, reaching for his knife, screamed above the din, "Die you infidel pig! Die!"

Ja'afer grasped the wooden handle of his blade and spun Colin over onto his back. Colin only moaned slightly as the traitor jerked back his forehead and raised his knife upward. "Allahu Akbar!" al Hashim screamed. But before he could inflict the fatal wound to Colin's throat, a dozen nine-millimeter slugs riddled his torso with enough force to splay him backward nearly ten feet. His body lurched sideways as his head slammed into a rocky outcropping. Dark blood oozed from each of the blackened exit wounds and flowed into a small puddle.

Suddenly, Magda Reisner stepped forward, the barrel of her Uzi submachine gun still smoking. "La'azazel!" she muttered, and snapping in a fresh magazine, she ordered one of her three-man squad to attend to Blackford. A professional soldier, she could not afford an emotional reunion with Colin at this moment.

In the camp beyond, secondary bursts and explosions were louder than even Magda's team had anticipated. Streams of burning diesel and gasoline traced their way along the rocky gullies and ignited still more cases of carelessly stored ammunition.

A choking billow of oil smoke filled the canyon,

making visibility all but impossible. Yet Quomuz shouted frantically between the explosions to those of his men who had survived the initial rocket attacks. Each of Quomuz's fighters now ran for defensive cover, arms at the ready.

Reisner had to think fast. The medical member of her team was preoccupied with Blackford, but she could ill afford to spare him. Quomuz was the target and her specific instructions from Aran were to kill Quomuz above all other considerations, even personal ones.

"Leave him!" she yelled to her subordinate. "Get Quomuz!"

The man sprang to his feet and, grabbing his assault rifle, joined Reisner and another of their team. "Spread out, find and kill Quomuz! This may be our only chance. Now RUN!"

From high atop the ridgeline, Deng's lieutenant, a man named Samuel, had seen the explosive action below and now ordered his men down from the plateau into a position where they could supply covering fire. Deng's twelve remaining kinsmen spread themselves out and scurried down the rocky slope, drawing up to within two hundred meters, well within range of their AK-47 and M-16 weapons.

Deng's men neither anticipated nor recognized the strange Israeli commando uniforms, but quickly surmised that anyone who fought the hated Quomuz was an ally. "Kill only the Janjaweed and Quomuz!" Samuel ordered. "These others are our friends."

As quickly as Deng's tribesmen had taken position in the rocks above the fray, Quomuz's men took aim, found range and began to fire, setting the hillsides of the canyon ablaze with crossfire. Any moving thing in the burning camp was a target from the snipers secreted on opposite sides of the canyon walls.

Meanwhile, Colin Blackford laid face-down and semiconscious in the ravine where Magda Reisner had ordered him abandoned. His head throbbed and the left side of his face was a bloody mass of hair and bone. The terrorist's bullet had pierced the officer's skin and traced along his thick British skull. The shock of the blast had been horrific and it left Blackford badly wounded; but his brain was intact and his blood loss, though grotesque, was superficial. He would survive.

Magda turned and examined the scene before her. No more munitions were exploding, but fire, smoke, and confusion abounded. Bodies and parts of bodies seemed to litter the camp. Burning drums of gasoline and oil were strewn haphazardly and several trucks, set ablaze by the attack, still burned wildly.

As Reisner surveyed the destruction, looking for Quomuz, she saw that all the tents were either demolished or on fire. "Not likely in one of those," she reasoned. "Munitions and oil drums are all afire. I can't see a damned thing through all this!"

And then she spotted him through the billowing smoke. It was Quomuz, standing upright in the back of a hurtling service truck, as his driver dodged the debris field that had once been the camp's access road. "Bastard!" Magda swore silently as Quomuz drove out of range. "Too damned far! I must get closer for a shot!" She quickly darted her way among the boulders and burning trucks until she spotted the helicopter at the edge of the camp, still intact. "Of course! He's headed toward the helicopter!"

As the smoke parted, the major could see a ground crew was making the helicopter ready for flight. Wheel chocks and tie-down chains had been removed, and the rotors were being slowly cycled. If she were to kill Quomuz, Magda knew, she needed to move quickly.

As a *Heron* drone circled low overhead and his remaining forces exchanged murderous fire with Deng's kinsmen, the terrorist chieftain huddled behind the wreckage of a truck and quickly rethought his tactical situation. He correctly guessed that the roads would be monitored and denied to him and that he did not know the extent of his attacker's control of the air. If he could simply disappear into the confusion and then into the hillsides above, then make his way overland to Chad, he would have a chance to fight another day, Allah willing, of course.

Eyeing the *Gazelle* helicopter, Magda double-timed in the direction of the undamaged craft. Her M-16 was the finest assault rifle in the world, but it was intended for combat at close quarters, not long-distance precision shooting. She had to get closer. Crouching low behind a rock pile, momentarily, to catch her breath, she spotted an AK-47 not three meters from its now-dead owner. Snatching it as she resumed her run, Magda was pleased with her good luck. "At least I might get a shot from a safer distance," she thought, her mind racing in anticipation.

As she ran, Reisner charged the handle to jack a round into the chamber. She noticed that no round pushed forward into the breech, and realized that the weapon felt a bit light. So she detached the thirty-round box magazine and found it completely empty. "Damn it!" she screamed out loud, as she dropped the worthless weapon to the ground.

Obscured by smoke, Quomuz scrambled his way to the helicopter, which sat on a dirt pad atop a twenty-foot-high berm. He shouted quick instructions to his few remaining soldiers and rapidly assessed the situation. Few were still living who could hear him. Except for his men fighting in the hills above, anyone still alive in the camp was attempting to flee the scene. Of the few still standing, all had lost their hearing and sense of equilibrium due to the repeated concussion blasts, and most of the badly wounded would not survive the night.

Magda advanced within a hundred meters of the helicopter and saw its rotors begin to turn. She radioed to one of her lieutenants, some three hundred meters away, to circle behind the helicopter and find Quomuz. Quickly catching her breath, Magda spied Quomuz standing behind and protected by the helicopter.

But Quomuz was too frantic to notice the lone

female working her way through the ruins of his camp.

Quomuz was quickly analyzing his options. It appeared he had only two choices; make a run for it in the helicopter, or flee to the hills.

"Daoud!" Quomuz yelled to his willing lieutenant. "Get to my truck from the ravine. Quickly, ready it for a long journey. Wait there for me, I shall not be long." An obedient "Yes, my commander!" was all Daoud had time to reply.

Quomuz hurriedly called to another lieutenant, who stood guard with a fully-loaded assault rifle, "Tariq, get aboard my helicopter!" Quomuz ordered. "This day Allah has seen fit to save you to fight again."

"Yes, my leader!" Tariq blurted, jumping aboard the now flight-ready helicopter.

Meanwhile, Magda had drawn to within fifty meters of the whirling helicopter blades. Her heart rate quickened and beads of grimy sweat formed on her forehead. Her hands gripped the M-16, a weapon ineffective at this range.

Then she spotted it.

Not more than ten meters distant lay the mangled corpses of two dead fighters. Between them was a fully loaded rocket-propelled-grenade-launcher. Thinking fast and obscured by smoke, Magda ran forward to seize the weapon. Then in a blinding instant, an explosion from a nearby ammunition pallet sent 20-mm rounds exploding all around her with an irregular and dangerous rhythm.

Out of the corner of her eye, Magda saw one of her men fall from the blast. Undeterred, she decided to make a run for it. Bounding over the rock-strewn ground, she snatched the shoulder-fired weapon, as she rolled onto her right side behind a disabled Volvo truck. A quick once-over of the weapon told Magda that it was functional.

The resourceful officer knew that she would only have one opportunity to bring down the helicopter and kill Quomuz.

As the battle raged around him, Quomuz quickly boarded the helicopter and took a seat next to the exit. He barked instructions to the pilot to fly due west, over the protecting mountains, and toward the safety of the Chad border.

Having set the decoy in motion, Quomuz then blurted to his subordinate, Tariq, and the pilot, "I must stay behind and reorganize the defenders of the camp. Tariq, if I die, you must carry the fight against the infidels!" And with those words of mock nobility, Quomuz slipped out of the smoke-obscured helicopter and jumped to the ravine below. Then, running at full speed toward the loyal Daoud, Quomuz quickly mounted the waiting vehicle and sped, unnoticed, into the protective confines of a rocky cavern.

Her vision of the helicopter obscured by smoke, Reisner finalized her preparation of the RPG. Thus, she didn't notice Quomuz's quick departure from the far side of the helicopter. As the craft lifted from the ground, she took one final sighting. Believing the man next to the pilot to be Quomuz, Magda placed her finger on the launch button.

As the pilot pulled up on the collective lever with his left hand, he held the cyclic stick still with his right. The rotor blades slowly tilted their angle of attack as they bit into the dust and smoke-filled air. Her vision still obscured, Reisner waited for the craft to lift off and begin its flight. Suddenly, from above the smoke, she saw the craft. "Wait for a clean shot!" she demanded of herself. "Ten meters, twenty meters." She counted aloud. At approximately sixty meters, the pilot gently nudged the cyclic stick forward and the nose pitched slightly downward; the aircraft transitioned to forward flight.

"I'm in luck! He'll fly right over me!" Magda Reisner smiled in certain victory. "A clear shot at the exposed underbelly of the fuselage." As the whirling craft approached, she aimed for the main fuel tanks, which would assure an instant and fiery death for all aboard. She readjusted the weapon and waited for the precise moment.

Just a few more seconds!

Magda's finger hit the launch button just as the helicopter approached, nearly overhead.

A flash-second later, the sky erupted in an ominous and terrible explosion of light and heat. The *Gazelle* disintegrated into an orange and black fireball, killing all aboard. The wreckage fell to the earth, and scattered itself over a square kilometer area.

"Burn in Hell!" Reisner screamed out loud, as she dove to the ground, covering her head from the falling rain of debris.

Samuel's marksmen had the upper hand. The helicopter's explosion seemed to take the fight out of the few surviving Jihadists, who scrambled off high into the hills to escape the Dinka rifles.

As the broken remnants of the helicopter lay strewn and smoking, the remaining member of Reisner's team snapped three-dozen quick digital photographs to document Quomuz's death and the camp's destruction.

"Ready for pickup. You have the GPS coordinates on my beacon. No one survived the explosion, sir," Reisner confirmed to Chaim Aran via her satellite uplink telephone. "The camp has been sanctioned, but it's too hot for a full recon."

"Excellent work, major! We'll come back another day for the special weapons. Perhaps a good whacking by someone's air forces will close those caves for good! Now, get out of there quickly! No delay!" Aran ordered. And, folding the telephone shut, Magda made her way back to the ravine where her remaining teammate helped the stunned Blackford to his feet.

"God, I must look a bloody awful mess," Blackford complained slowly through the haze of a blinding headache, his knees unable to bear his full weight. "Did you get him?" he asked the woman, who was shouldering one of his arms.

"I can only presume so," she said, gesturing toward what remained of the now-destroyed Gazelle. "But there's no time for forensic proof. We've got to make a quick egress. No telling when his forces will regroup and retaliate."

Blackford smiled thinly in agreement. It would be some time before he could resume the fight.

A few minutes later Blackford, Reisner and her subordinate began the slow trek back up the mountainside and into the waiting arms of Samuel and the tribesmen. "The Lord has blessed us," Samuel said, smiling at the trio. "Our losses have been great, with the death of Jonah Deng, but we may have hurt our enemy far worse. The season may have changed for us, thanks to you."

As the small gaggle of tired warriors trudged up the ridge, and then back down to their waiting vehicles, Magda Reisner heard the unmistakable roar of two giant Royal Navy *Merlin* night-ops helicopters approaching from the south in the gathering darkness. "Right on cue!" she said, with a sense of relief.

Blackford raised his head to spot the inbound helicopters, and, swabbing away the dried blood from near his eyes, smiled thinly.

"Friends of yours, Major Blackford?" Reisner asked softly. "Here to give us a lift, I think."

Landing softly not fifty meters from Blackford, Reisner and their company, the helicopters' whirling blades beat the dust into a frenzy, momentarily blinding everyone on the ground. A petty officer leaned out of an open hatch and, smiling, yelled, "Oy! Someone call for a lift, then?"

Blackford looked to Samuel, the new leader of the small band of Dinka fighters. "Gather your men,

Samuel. I shan't leave you here…we can get you safely away."

"No, Major Blackford," the Dinka replied, his hand on the Englishman's shoulder. "We've our trucks to see to. You'll need some protection from the ground as you fly away. No way to know how many of Quomuz's men are still in the area. And, besides, there is more to be done here. After all, this is OUR fight."

"No my friend…this fight belongs to us all. I swear to you, I will see you again. You saved our lives, and I will never forget you."

"Then go with God's peace!" Samuel cried, leading his small troop of men back to their vehicles and homeward to their transient camp.

As the Dinka men departed, a large hatch opened on the lead Merlin, and the boots of Sir Harold Malcolm DeBrassure MacHugh jumped to the ground in a whirling cloud of dust.

Blackford was dumbstruck. He had not expected to see MacHugh again for a very long time, if ever.

"Don't just stand there bleeding, man. Get your team aboard and let's be gone from this God-forsaken place. We haven't time to linger, you know. We're here quite illegally, after all!"

Blackford managed a smile as he, Magda and her lieutenant climbed aboard and strapped themselves into the now rising craft.

MacHugh then reached out to Blackford with genuine affection. "I've received word from Credenhill! It seems that Brigadier Arthur Chelmsford-

Gray tells me that your services are required else-where straightaway!"

Blackford could only manage a weak smile. "The bastard," he smiled to himself, thinking back on all the events of the past three years.

"So no more lagging about on holiday as you've been doing at the Yard, eh?" MacHugh smiled through his deep Scottish brogue. "Oh, yes. There's more. That's why I came out to tell you my-self....Petra Voss. She's talked."

"What?" a genuinely surprised Blackford began to inquire, keen for any detail MacHugh could share. But before he could utter another sound, Magda Reisner placed her fingers over his lips to quiet the wounded officer.

"Plenty of time for that...but later," Reisner said gently into Blackford's ear as the Briton shut his eyes against the headache that now nearly con-sumed him.

A Royal Navy medic looked carefully at Black-ford's head wound, advising, "You'll need hospi-talization for at least a fortnight, Major. That cut on your head will need attending. But I shouldn't think you'll be seriously inconvenienced!"

"Same damned spot where I got cut in Afghani-stan!" Blackford said, wincing.

Magda Reisner reached to press a sterile bandage over Blackford's swollen wound, thankful that the man she had fallen in love with had not perished.

Although dazed and in pain, Blackford collected his thoughts as he looked out through the open hatch while the giant Merlin banked in a graceful climbing arc to the south.

"Bloody inhospitable place, this," Colin said quietly to Magda, looking back over the battlefield and the hard country beyond.

"Isn't it," Magda replied, tightening her grip on his left arm.

He leaned heavily against her, as she gently, but firmly said, "Colin, let's go home."

EPILOGUE

June
Vatican City

Monsignor Enrique Alvarez stood silently by the balustrade in the Tower of the Winds and gazed upon the hazy remnants of the afternoon. At his side, the American Secretary of Defense shared a moment of reflection with his old classmate from Harvard's Kennedy School of Government.

The Bourbon they sipped flowed smoothly as had their conversations throughout the day.

"I'm grateful you shared your confidence with me about the 'situation' involving the Sanchez boy, Eldon," the Monsignor said, softly breaking the silence. "On behalf of His Holiness, I sincerely apologize for our role, however inadvertent, that led to the terrorism in England. Our interest was purely to facilitate some smattering of decency and to ensure the boy received the last rites."

"Enrique, it was not your doing. You bear no responsibility at all and we remain grateful for your intercession. It was a horrible, horrible tragedy made more so by the terrorists' abuse of your good offices."

"Thank you, Mr. Secretary," the Papal emissary offered, sincerely.

"Let us make no further mention of it," Klein responded, changing the topic of their reflections. "I must say that I was moved by President Kiwibali's words today. He was eloquent, as usual. The poor man...."

"It saddens me deeply that Kenya must yet again brace for a prolonged drought." Alvarez sighed, recounting the dire meteorological forecasts of earlier in the day. "The rains due in the coming weeks will be insufficient to reverse the current drought, and millions suffer on the brink of starvation."

"Neither the World Food Program nor the UNESCO offered any real hope, beyond urging President Kiwibali to take stronger measures to prepare for the pending catastrophe," Klein said, shaking his head sadly.

"The Kenyans are still far short of the food stores needed to fill the stomachs of millions of people at risk," Klein admitted. "Of course, we will be ready to donate food and money and airlift as much as we can. But you know, Enrique, that our flight crews and the relief workers will face the wrath of the starving. They always do."

Slowly, thoughtfully, the Monsignor said, "It's futile, this war on hunger…"

"Perhaps…" Klein responded, letting his colleague's words sink in deeply. "It is a war that we cannot afford to fight, yet it is also a war we cannot afford to lose."

"I am sympathetic to your plight, Eldon. You Americans bear an enormous burden. You are the remaining strength, the power, the wealth in the world. It is, of course, you whom the hungry men will seek with their grievances. You know the plight of the untold multitudes in Africa, in Asia; even in South America, for whom a decent meal is only a dream...they live in squalor. The terrorism you fight, Eldon, grows in the bellies of hungry men, and the world continues to breed millions more of them every year. This incessant cycle of attack and counter-attack, of vengeance-upon-vengeance, must be broken."

Klein knew instinctively what Alvarez meant. "You speak truthfully, my friend. The likes of Hitler and bin Laden and Quomuz have known one unassailable truth forever….that an army stands at their ready command if the hungry men before them believe that dying today is a better fate than living until tomorrow. But we…."

The Puerto Rican priest softly interrupted his friend's thoughts. "It is not your burden alone, Eldon. Even if America were to beat all her swords into plowshares, you could still not feed a starving world, and His Holiness is not naïve enough to ask the people of my second home to freely open her gates to the wolf. America gives much, this I know...and yet, much is still demanded from her. To stop this insanity," Alvarez emphasized, "you must feed the hungry. You must clothe them. You must give them no reason to hate. That way, the terrorist is denied his army. Bread, my friend....bread is the antidote to terrorism!"

Klein took a long sip from the crystal glass.

"I have appreciated your intercession with the French and the Germans, Enrique. Your quiet diplomacy may yet yield results. But our friends in Paris and Berlin must dance on the knife's edge between their large Muslim populations and their secretly expressed desires to help hunt the terrorists."

"Ah, yes...there is yet too much vengeance in the blood for that. Even reasonable men of power still seek revenge because the people demand it. And when that retribution is wrought, the people bemoan the risk. "

The Secretary nodded thoughtfully as both men took another sip from their glasses. Klein paused for several moments before facing the Monsignor. "But we'll continue to do what we can, Enrique...That, I can promise you."

ABOUT JONATHAN BRUCE

"Jonathan Bruce" is the pen name of co-authors, John H. Schumacher and Bruce T. Smith.

John H. Schumacher is the son of a career Air Force master sergeant. John enlisted in the U.S. Navy in 1970 and was deployed on three different aircraft carriers. He served first as a rescue air crewman in Helicopter Combat Support Squadron Two (HC-2), and subsequently as an airborne radar counter-measurers special operator in Tactical Electronic Warfare Squadron Thirty-Three (VAQ-33). After leaving the Navy, John served as a professional firefighter in Aurora, Colorado, where he earned an associates' degree in fire science technology and a bachelor's degree in business administration. John earned his law degree in 1984 and then entered the Air Force JAG Corps in 1985, where he served on active duty for twelve years. He served in the United Kingdom and was present when USAF F-111 fighter/bombers flew from the U.K. to bomb Libya in April 1986. Subsequently, he spent three years at the Air Force Special Operations Command Headquarters at Hurlburt Field, Florida. While there, he provided counsel on the Geneva Conventions, international law and the law of war to Air Force special operations crews engaged in "black world" missions around the globe. He also deployed to Somalia, Kenya, Bosnia and Honduras. John retired from the Air Force Reserve in 2004 in the grade of Lieutenant Colonel. John is now a United States Administrative Law Judge in Washington, DC.

Bruce T. Smith is the son of a career Navy captain. During his career as an Air Force Judge Advocate in Europe, Bruce spent three years based at Royal Air Force bases in Mildenhall and Lakenheath, which were the U.K. bases from which American F-111 fighter/bombers flew to bomb Libya in April 1986. After earning his LL.M. degree in military law at the Army Judge Advocate General's School, Bruce spent three years on the faculty at the Air Force Judge Advocate General's School at Maxwell AFB, Alabama. Thereafter, he served as a staff judge advocate and military judge in criminal trials by courts-martial. While serving at HQ CENTAF/JA, he was also involved in several classified aspects of Operation SOUTHERN WATCH and Operation IRAQI FREEDOM. He has instructed in trial advocacy, military justice, and the Law of International Military Operations. Bruce is now a United States Administrative Law Judge, with an agency headquartered in Washington, DC.

Printed in the United States
100147LV00001B/1-6/A